## SISTERS IN CRIME

"*SISTERS IN CRIME* IS GREAT READING . . . YOU
CAN SAMPLE THE TERRIFIC NEWER WOMEN
CRIME WRITERS AND FIND OUT WHICH YOU
WANT TO PURSUE AT LENGTH—IF YOU'RE LIKE
ME, IT MAY BE ALL OF THEM!"

—Carol Brenner, Murder Ink

"*Critics have called the eighties the second Golden Age of American mysteries and women are a significant factor in this renais-
sance. No longer are women writers restricted to the cozy confines
of a quaint village or are female characters relegated to the ranks
of the spinster sleuth . . .*"

—editor Marilyn Wallace

The idea for this exciting new anthology came to Ms. Wallace
at a seminar in New York called "Sisters in Crime." And
although this book is not an official publication of the organization, it succeeds in capturing the innovative spirit of these
remarkable writers. A fresh, contemporary approach to mystery and suspense, *SISTERS IN CRIME* features characters
and plots as diverse, savvy, and intriguing as the writers themselves.

So settle back in your favorite armchair and prepare yourself
for a nerve-wracking evening of delicious mystery and suspense . . .

## SISTERS IN CRIME

*The Very Best in Modern Mystery—For the First Time in One
Volume!*

# SISTERS IN CRIME

edited by

**Marilyn Wallace**

**BERKLEY BOOKS, NEW YORK**

*Thanks to Sue Dunlap and Julie Smith for their enthusiasm when this anthology was conceived, to Marcia Muller and Bill Pronzini for sharing with me what they've learned about editing anthologies, to Barbara Michaels/Elizabeth Peters for helping to shepherd my idea to the right people—and, once again, to my husband Bruce for his loving support and to our sons Mark and Jeremy for their encouragement.*

SISTERS IN CRIME

A Berkley Book/published by arrangement with the editor

PRINTING HISTORY
Berkley edition/May 1989

ISBN: 0-425-11582-8

A BERKLEY BOOK ® TM 757,375
Berkley Books are published by The Berkley Publishing Group,
200 Madison Avenue, New York, N.Y. 10016.
The name "BERKLEY" and the "B" logo
are trademarks belonging to Berkley Publishing Corporation.

PRINTED IN THE UNITED STATES OF AMERICA

10  9  8  7  6  5  4  3  2  1

For Karen Bozdech—my sister, my friend.

# Contents

# Foreword

*Sisters in Crime*—a book about safecracking nuns? About a family in which the daughters are talented embezzlers? Actually, not bad ideas for a novel. But no—this is an anthology of short stories by American women who write mystery and suspense fiction; most of the stories were written especially for *Sisters in Crime* and appear here for the first time.

This anthology reflects some of the changes in culture and in literature that have shaped our lives and our work. As roles were redefined, beginning in the sixties, women (who already counted perseverance and resourcefulness among their talents) began to identify with other significant characteristics of the good detective: physical strength and agility; decisiveness; lack of encumbrances; independence. At the same time, the modern mystery moved inexorably away from the pure puzzle form to become, increasingly, a work of character. The puzzle element, of course, is still strong, but the sole criteria for evaluating today's mysteries are not how cleverly the author has devised a new means of murder or how artfully the identity of the culprit has been concealed. While these remain singularly delicious components, the contemporary mystery is judged by the same standards as is all good fiction. Are the characters complex, multidimensional, intriguing? Is the setting finely rendered and palpable? Is the plot engrossing? Is the voice convincing and consistent?

These, then, are truly tales for our time. They've been written by women who aren't afraid to take risks, women who thrive on the audacious act of transforming the chaos of the perceived world into a little bit of order. As writers, we use the magic and the music of language to tell a story whose primary goal is to entertain—in these pages, you'll find elegance and earthiness, compassion and contempt, sardonic commentary on roles and rules. Our methods differ; our intentions are diverse—*Sisters in Crime* is a celebration of that variety.

This collection was conceived several years ago, in the afterglow of my first Bouchercon, the annual movable (the convention is in a different city each year) feast of the mystery world. I met many of the contributors—in person and in print—for the first time during those hectic and stimulating four days, and the impressive range of styles and subjects of these extraordinary women stayed with me. The notion of bringing such talents together in a single book sprang up fully formed from that fertile ground.

There it was, a compelling idea that I couldn't ignore. Should such an anthology have a theme? Would it be more interesting if all the stories had a female protagonist? If they all dealt with female/male relationships? In the end, I decided that such limitations were artificial. The best writing, I have always believed, is infused with a passion to tell a specific story in a particular way. I was certain that the absence of restrictions would result in a terrific collection . . . and I've never regretted that decision.

The following May, at a seminar in New York called Sisters in Crime, some disturbing questions were raised. Was it really true that of the ninety-seven mysteries reviewed in 1987 by *The New York Times*, only seven were by women? (Yes, although by mid-1988 the proportion had improved to twenty-three percent.) Was this consistent with what was happening around the country? (Many major newspapers seem to do a bit better, but the final tallies aren't in yet.) What, in fact, is the percentage of women in the total of mystery writers? (According to current membership rolls of Mystery Writers of America, approximately forty percent are women.) Are women who write mysteries treated the same as their male colleagues? (No one's figured this one out yet, although indications are that gender isn't the critical factor.) If inequities exist, what can be done?

The discussions were important and provocative; by the end of the day an organization was born—and I had a fitting title for the anthology. *Sisters in Crime* (the book) is not an official publication of Sisters in Crime (the organization); some of the contributors are members of the group, while others are not. *Sisters in Crime* (the book) is simply a collection of short stories by American women who have earned a place on the roster of contemporary mystery writers. Happily, that list is large and still growing—even the next two volumes won't cover everyone.

The stories are arranged in reverse alphabetical order by author's name, my small revenge for being a *W*. In the individual introductions you'll see that many of the writers have been honored with awards. In case you're not familiar with them, Edgars are the Edgar Allan Poe awards, presented every May by Mystery Writers of

America; Anthonys are named after writer/critic Anthony Boucher and are presented every October at Bouchercon; Macavitys are awarded each summer by Mystery Readers of America; and Shamus awards are presented at Bouchercon by Private Eye Writers of America.

I'm grateful to all the contributors for making my job as editor such fun; the developing friendships are a personal bonus for me. My thunderbolt idea is still echoing happily in my life—I have no doubt that the next two volumes of *Sisters in Crime* will be an equally diabolical delight.

—Marilyn Wallace
June 1988
San Anselmo, California

*Teri White's 1982 debut,* Triangle, *won an Edgar for Best Paperback Original.* Bleeding Hearts *and* Tightrope *followed, both featuring Spaceman Kowalski and Blue Maguire, Los Angeles policemen whose prickly partnership works despite their disparate backgrounds and temperaments.* Max Trueblood and the Jersey Desperado *and* Fault Lines *continue to explore the contradictions, the pressures, and the alternative version of reality of people living on the periphery of society.*

*In "Role Model," two characters come together accidentally; both are irrevocably affected. Moral ambiguities are examined and difficult questions are raised as the distinctions between insider and outsider blur in this engrossing story.*

# ROLE MODEL

## by Teri White

THE McDONALD HIT in Brownsville went down just the way it was supposed to. No surprise there, of course. When Zach took on a job, everybody could be sure that things would run smoothly. McDonald never even suspected what was happening until it was much too late. Maybe he had time to say a quick prayer before crashing facedown into the pasta du jour, but that was all.

Because the assignment had gone so well, Zach was feeling really good as he headed back for California. The weather was great, nothing like winters had been when he was growing up in Ohio. His new little Italian car handled like a dream, and Zach Cassidy decided that he was a happy man.

He reached Los Angeles at dinnertime, ready to splurge on a great meal. A steak, he decided, pulling up in front of the Palm. It was as crowded as usual, but he was in no hurry. After the meal he even treated himself to a snifter of brandy. The good life; hell, he earned it. Now he was ready for the rest of the drive home to San Francisco.

Before leaving, though, he used the phone to call home and check for messages on his answering machine. There was only one message.

Zach leaned against the wall, listening. Not believing what he'd heard, he played the tape again.

The words didn't change.

But it was impossible. How the hell could anybody have pinned the McDonald hit on him, at least this fast? Unless, of course, the whole job had been a setup, which was always possible, considering the kind of slimebags he had to deal with in this business. Anyway, if the message was to be taken seriously, somebody's hired guns were now looking to waste him.

A woman trying to squeeze by gave him a dirty look. "Holding up the building?" she muttered.

Bitch, he thought absently.

Zach moved slowly out of her way. He was a big man, six-four almost, and right at the moment he weighed in at about twenty-five more pounds than he should have. Maybe thirty. Still thinking about the words on the tape, he paid for the dinner—the once-great meal that was suddenly a leaden lump in his stomach—and left the restaurant.

He sat in the car with the engine idling for several minutes, listening to the soft purr of all the expensive machinery under the hood, and considered the situation. Whatever the message might have meant, however seriously it ought to be taken, he realized that it probably would be a good idea to stay away from home for a while. The thought annoyed him because he liked his apartment, liked the quiet, solitary life he led there.

But he consoled himself with the thought that this involuntary exile wouldn't be for long. This trouble, whatever it was, would blow over soon.

So, he concluded, maybe it was time for a little vacation. He gassed up the car and headed for the mountains. Zach liked to think of himself as a man who could adapt. A man who could take a small setback like this one and make the most of it.

As he drove, he kept one eye on the rearview mirror. If there was a tail on him, it was a damned good one.

But then, it would be, wouldn't it?

The boy turned up the collar of his denim jacket and hunched his shoulders against the increasing blasts of wind. Jesus, it was cold. How come nobody ever told him that it got so fucking cold in California? Back in Omaha, all you ever heard about were blue skies and sunshine. Tanned people lying around on the beach. But he wasn't on the beach, and up here in the sticks it was cold. He sniffed the air. Hell, it even smelled like snow. Great. That was all he needed.

He could hear another car approaching from around the curve. Automatically the thumb went into the air again, and he put a friendly smile on his face. The last ten cars had gone right by, not even slowing down long enough to check him out. It was getting harder and harder to smile.

At first, it looked like this car would keep going too. But then the long black Caddy slowed and stopped about twenty-five feet beyond where he was standing. The driver tapped lightly on the horn. Jamie took a better grip of his duffel bag and ran toward the car. He opened the passenger door and leaned in.

The driver was a man. "Cold night to be walking," he said.

Jamie nodded. "Sure is. Where you headed?"

"You particular?"

After a moment, Jamie shook his head. "Not really," he said, sliding into the car. The leather was soft and warm against his chilled body. "Wherever you're going has got to beat the hell out of standing there."

The man laughed.

Jamie shook some of the dampness from his long brown hair. He didn't fasten the seat belt or lock the door. One of the first things you learned on the road was to always leave yourself an out. There were rules to this game, just like any other.

Something soft and classical-sounding was playing on the car radio. The driver looked about fifty and he was dressed in fancy clothes, like he'd just come from a party. Or maybe he was on his way to one. Whatever, he was in a good mood, whistling along with the music.

Maybe this ride would be one of those that worked out okay. Jamie hoped so, because he was cold and tired. All he wanted to do was ride along inside the warm car for a while. Rest a little.

No hassle.

Zach cursed the snow that had been falling for over an hour, making the driving increasingly difficult. The idea of a few days in the mountains didn't sound nearly as good by this time as it had last night when he'd left Los Angeles. Evening was coming on again, and he was getting hungry. As well as tired of fighting the road and the weather.

When he saw the lights ahead, he gave a sigh of relief. A diner, open, and next door, a motel. Nothing fancy, but just what he needed. Some hot food and coffee, a room in which to spend the night; it all sounded good.

The parking lot held two trucks, a state police car, and two other cars parked way over to one side, which probably meant they belonged to employees of the café. It wasn't a night that many people would be out traveling through the mountains. Zach parked next to the trucks. The thought of there being cops inside didn't bother him at all; nobody here knew who the hell he was. Anyway, the people he had to stay clear of weren't carrying badges, not by a long shot.

He zipped up his windbreaker and got out of the car, not forgetting to lock the door. Car rip-off artists were everywhere these days. His first stop was at the motel office to get a room. Although the place was empty, except for the drivers of a couple of out-of-state cars parked in front, he requested a room way in the back, telling the bored clerk that he needed lots of peace and quiet.

When the details of checking in were taken care of—with the name Blaine written down on the registration card—he carried his bag to the isolated room, stowed it in the closet, and headed over to the café.

Inside, it was warm and steamy, the air thick with the smell of too many greasy meals. There were only four customers—two cops, one a woman; and two truck drivers. They were all sitting around the curved counter, talking to a blond waitress and a fat black man leaning in from the kitchen.

Zach made a quick, practiced survey of the room, then walked over to a booth in the corner farthest from the door and sat down. The waitress finished laughing over something one of the truck drivers had said before bringing him a menu and a glass of water.

"Road getting bad out there?" she asked cheerfully, setting the glass down on the Formica tabletop.

Zach nodded and opened the menu.

"Glad I live only five minutes away. Coffee while you decide?"

"Yeah." He scanned the offerings quickly and decided on the meat loaf special. It probably wasn't all that special but it probably wouldn't kill him off, either. Once the order was in, he left the booth and walked through the doorway labeled REST ROOMS. At the end of the corridor there was a rear exit. For emergency use only. But a closer look showed him that the lock was a joke. Not that there was anything to worry about, of course, but a smart man stayed ready. Zach believed that he was a smart man.

Satisfied, he went into the can.

By the time he got back to his table, there was a salad waiting. The bottled orange-colored dressing was too sweet for his taste, but he ate it all anyway, and drank a cup of coffee.

Already he was starting to feel better. He leaned back against the padded seat and watched the truck drivers trying to score with the waitress and the lady cop.

Jamie sat by the side of the road, trying to ease the painful throbbing in his knee. Damn the bastard, he thought, wiping at the tears on his face. Did everybody in the world have to be such a creep? He clutched his duffel, glad not to have lost it during his rapid exit from the Caddy.

After a couple more minutes, his twisted knee felt better. Screw the jerk, he thought, getting to his feet. Just forget him. Jamie took a deep breath and started walking again. He kept changing the duffel from his left hand to his right, trying to keep one hand warm inside his deep jacket pockets.

Not much chance of getting another ride at this hour, especially with all the damned snow. The important thing was to keep moving so he didn't freeze.

It was almost fifteen minutes before he saw the blinking diner sign ahead. He gulped in cold air and tried to walk faster through the snow.

At last he got there, plunging in through the door and then leaning against it in relief. The heated air felt wonderful. He just stood there, enjoying it so much that it took him several moments even to notice the other people in the place.

Cops. Wonderful. That was just what he needed to make the night perfect. All the way from Nebraska he'd been hassled by cops. He needed food, but from painful experience he knew that it would be hard to negotiate a free meal with the storm troopers sitting there. It really seemed to bug the Fascists that he could be out on the road alone with no bread. Why couldn't they just concentrate on doing their job, which was supposed to be catching the bad guys, right?

The one cop, the broad, was looking at him. The usual hard-ass Fascist stare; they must learn it in the academy. Obviously she didn't think that somebody in a light jacket and soaking wet tennis shoes should be out walking around in the mountains on this kind of night.

Jamie shifted the duffel again and quickly looked around the room. There was one old guy sitting by himself in the back.

Jamie forced another smile onto his lips and headed back there. The big guy looked up from his meal in surprise as Jamie sat down across from him. Something kind of scary flickered through the pale blue eyes and Jamie almost got up again. But then the man relaxed.

"Hey, pal," Jamie said in a low, urgent voice.

"Do I know you?"

"Those pigs over there are gonna start hassling me. I'm hitching and I'm busted. Can I just sit here with you and warm up? Make like we're friends, okay? I don't want to get hauled off to juvie."

The man took another bite of his meat loaf, then set his fork down. "What are you running from?"

"Life," Jamie replied curtly. He was still leaning across the table. "So how about it, buddy?"

After a moment the man handed him a menu. "Better make it look good. Order some food."

"Like I said, I'm busted."

"Doesn't matter. Get whatever you want."

The waitress came over. Jamie ordered a double cheeseburger with bacon, some home fries, and coffee. Then, figuring what the hell, a piece of apple pie.

The man smiled faintly. "You're hungry."

"Yeah, well." Jamie rubbed his hands together.

"You have a name?"

"I hafta play fucking twenty questions to pay for the meal, do I?"

The man reached across the table and lightly slapped his face, more a tap than a slap. "Mind your manners, kiddo."

Jamie picked up his coffee, holding the mug with both hands. "Jamie."

"How old are you?"

"Sixteen," he said, adding a few months. "How old are you?" The smart-assed remark came out before he could help it. He half braced himself for another slap, probably one that would hurt this time.

Instead there was only another faint smile. "I'm forty."

One of the truck drivers left, letting a blast of cold air into the room.

"Pretty lousy weather for walking."

"Sure is," Jamie agreed.

"By the way," the man said, "I'm Zach."

Jamie nodded. He sat back with the coffee and eyed his dinner partner. Big guy, with faded blond-gray hair and those changeable eyes. Might as well set him straight right off the top. "Some asshole picked me up about twenty miles down the road. Figured because he was giving me a lift, that gave him the right to do what he wanted."

"You let him know different, I guess."

"Yeah." Jamie grinned. "He's probably still bent over from the pain. But maybe that was dumb. No night to be walking around."

Zach shook his head. "It wasn't dumb. You can't let the bastards of the world use you. And by the way, the dinner is free. No strings."

Jamie didn't say anything.

Zach finished his meat loaf. "Sixteen. That's a little young to be running away from life, isn't it?"

"I guess that depends on the life."

"You have a point."

His food arrived and Jamie began to eat enthusiastically. "Where you live, Zach?" he asked through a mouthful of cheeseburger.

There was a sight pause.

"San Francisco," Zach said finally.

"Nice place?" He dumped catsup on his potatoes.

"I like it."

Jamie talked his way through the meal. He told Zach about Omaha—about the beatings from his father, the indifference of his mother the drunk, about all of the mess he was leaving behind. He said much more than he had intended to tell a stranger.

Zach didn't say much; mostly he just listened. He didn't mind when Jamie ordered a second piece of pie. In fact, Zach ate a slice along with him, and they got another pot of coffee too.

Finally Jamie shut up.

Another blast of cold air invaded the café as the door opened again. Zach glanced up, and abruptly his face changed. The scary look came back into his eyes.

"What's the matter?" Jamie whispered.

Zach just shook his head.

Jamie turned to watch as the two newcomers took a booth on the other side of the room. One was a tall, thin black man and the other was bald, with the body of a weight lifter. Jamie watched them, then looked back at Zach.

Zach leaned toward him and spoke softly. "Listen up, kiddo. I'm going to the can. Soon as I get in there, you count to five hundred. Then create a distraction."

"Do what?"

"Create a distraction. Do something, anything, to get everybody looking at you, so they forget how long I've been in there." He took out his wallet and slid a fifty across the table. "Take this. Pay for the meal and the rest is yours."

"But, Zach—"

"I don't have time to argue with you, dammit. Just do like I say."

Jamie picked up the money and nodded.

"Take care of yourself, Jamie." Zach stood. In a normal voice, easily overheard by everyone in the room, he said, "Be right back." He headed for the john.

Jamie twisted the fifty between his fingers and counted slowly.

Zach carefully loaded both guns.

When the knock came only a few minutes later, he picked up one—the Magnum—and walked over to the door. He unlocked it with one hand and stepped back, raising the weapon.

"Yeah?" he said.

"It's me, Zach."

He lowered the gun. Should have known, he thought, those creeps weren't going to knock. "Go away, kid."

"Lemme in. It's a damned blizzard out here."

After a moment, Zach opened the door. A swirl of snow and cold came into the room, along with Jamie. The boy stamped his snow-covered shoes and blew on his reddened fingers. "I did like you told me," he announced.

Zach closed and locked the door again. "Fine. Except that I didn't tell you to come here."

"I followed your tracks. But they're almost gone by now."

"Wonderful. Go follow somebody else."

Instead, Jamie blinked, suddenly seeming to notice the gun for the first time. He dropped the duffel and crossed his arms in front of his chest. "This is some heavy shit, huh?"

"Smart boy."

"Those two guys are after you."

"Yes."

"Why?"

Instead of answering, Zach went into the bathroom. He opened a bottle of whiskey, poured a healthy slug into a plastic cup, and added some tap water. When he walked back into the other room, Jamie was sitting on the bed. Zach leaned against the desk, looking at him. "You don't want to get mixed up in this, Jamie."

"Hey, you helped me before."

"A damned meal isn't worth your life."

A suddenly old smile appeared briefly on the young man's face. "Guess that depends on the life."

"Don't be a jackass."

Jamie frowned then and played with the fringe on the bedspread. "We could leave now. Before they come."

Zach grunted. "Sure. Except that my car would get about three feet in this snow."

"So if I left, how far would I get on foot?" He sounded smug.

"Go sit in the coffee shop."

"Gonna close in half an hour."

Which gave Zach an idea of about how much time he had. "Take a goddamned room, then. Just get the hell away from me." He swallowed half the drink.

"Two against two is better odds."

Zach didn't know whether to laugh or rage at the boy's stupidity. "You're not an advantage to me. You're just one more problem."

"I helped in the coffee shop. Don't you even wanna know what I did?"

"Okay. What'd you do?"

Jamie smiled. "I knocked over the pie rack that was sitting by the cash register. There was whipped cream and stuff everywhere."

"That was great. Thanks. But your part of this is over now."

"I'm not scared, Zach, if that's what you're thinking. I've been hurt before."

Very patiently Zach said, "These guys are not going to beat your ass like your old man did. They're going to shoot you."

His wet tennis shoes were making a dark stain across the bedspread. "Why are they after you?"

"Because I killed a business acquaintance of theirs."

Jamie nodded solemnly, as if that made all the sense in the world to him.

"That's what I do, Jamie. Understand? People pay me to kill other people." As he lifted the cup again, he couldn't help smiling. "What goes around comes around."

"Zach?"

He drank. "Just go now, please." He set the empty cup down and reached for his wallet. "Here's some more money. Get a room. Tomorrow you can hitch a ride out of here." He tossed some bills down onto the bed.

Jamie picked up the money and counted it quickly. "This is three hundred dollars."

"Don't worry about it."

"And what about you? You're just gonna sit here and wait for them?"

Zach nodded. "I don't like to leave things hanging. Might as well end it here, one way or the other."

After another moment, Jamie stood and tucked the money into the watch pocket of his jeans. He picked up his duffel and walked to the door. There he stopped. "I think this really sucks," he said.

"I know you do. You're a good kid."

Jamie started to say something more; instead he unlocked the door and left.

Zach immediately locked the door again. He picked up the Magnum and went to sit on the bed.

It was cold in the alcove, even though he was sheltered a little from the biting wind. Jamie crouched in the shadows, watching the door of Zach's room. The howling of the wind was a steady roar.

Jamie didn't know why he was waiting there, or what he hoped to accomplish by staying. But something kept him from leaving.

It seemed much longer than it actually was before he saw one of the men from the café. The black guy appeared suddenly out of the darkness and snow, now carrying a short rifle under one arm.

Jamie didn't know if it was the cold or his own fear that was making him shake. He pressed closer to the wall, watching, waiting, although for what, he didn't know. Why didn't Zach do something?

The man stood in front of the door for a moment, then abruptly raised one booted foot and kicked. The flimsy wooden door crashed open and the man jumped through, already firing. Jamie could barely hear the shots above the roar of the storm, but he did see the black man's body flip backward and land in the snow.

Jamie started breathing again.

Fool. Did he think it was going to be simple to walk in on somebody like Zach? Fat chance. Dumb-ass deserved to die, just for being so stupid.

Jamie stood.

Zach came out of the room, stepping over the body without even looking down at it. He was wearing his coat and carrying a gun in each hand. Keeping his back against the building, he moved to the corner. Going left, he'd be heading for the parking lot; to the right there was only darkness and a sharp incline that ended in a gulley.

Jamie took a deep breath and quickly worked his way over to where Zach was, keeping himself pressed against the bricks as well. "You got the bastard," Jamie said.

"I almost got you, asshole," Zach replied, lowering his gun.

"The two of us can get the other guy, right?"

"We can't even see the other guy."

"So what's the plan?"

Zach looked at him, then shook his head. "The plan is to make it to the parking lot, hopefully without getting killed. In case you didn't notice, those creeps showed up in a four-wheel-drive monster. No trouble moving in that."

Jamie poked Zach's arm. "I can hot-wire."

"So can every other punk in this country. So can I, in fact." They both leaned around the corner. The café was closed now and the parking lot was empty, except for the Jeep Cherokee and Zach's car. "You stay here, Jamie."

"But—"

"This time do what I say."

Jamie knew, somehow, that he couldn't disobey again. "Okay, Zach," he said.

"When you see I've got it going, get your ass over there in a hurry."

"I can come with you?"

"Do I have a choice?" Zach held out the smaller of the two guns. "Take this. Just in case."

"I don't—"

Zach didn't wait to hear the objection.

Suddenly Jamie was alone. He shoved the gun to the bottom of his jacket pocket.

Zach ran as quickly as he could through the snow, half expecting a shot to end his trip at any moment. But he reached the cars safely. Before worrying about the Jeep, he knelt in the snow and quickly removed the plates from his own car. All the other identifying numbers were already gone.

That done, he used the butt of the gun to smash the window of the Jeep and reached inside to unlock the door. It had been a long time, but he actually managed to get the damned thing running in just two minutes. Probably only twice as long as it would have taken the smart-mouthed juvenile delinquent.

He waited, but there was no sign of Jamie.

After a moment, he risked a light tap on the horn.

Still nothing. Zach eased the brake off and drove slowly across the lot. What the hell?

Just as he was about to get out and go looking for him, the boy appeared. The bald man—whose name Zach suddenly remembered was Nolan—had an arm around Jamie's neck and a .45 pressed against his temple.

Zach sighed and killed the engine.

"Throw the gun out first," Nolan ordered.

It was a terrible thing to do to a fine piece of equipment, but Zach tossed the Magnum through the broken window. It landed in the snow. "Let the boy go," he said.

"Sure. Get out. And I want to see your hands all the time."

He opened the door and climbed down, both hands in the air. "See?" he said. "Now let him go."

"Okay." With a grin, Nolan shoved Jamie hard and the boy slid, off-balance, over the edge of the ravine. Jamie gave one sharp yell and disappeared into the darkness below.

Zach shook his head.

"Turn around and hug the car, Cassidy."

"We don't have to make a big production out of this, do we? Just do the job."

"Shut up and do like I said."

Zach did. Fools like this guy always had to play games. When he was on a job, he just made the damned hit, none of this screwing around.

"Who put the contract out on McDonald?"

Zach was staring at the ground. "Does it matter?"

"To some people it does."

Zach wondered if maybe he should just turn around and try something. The odds sucked, but what did he have to lose at this point? "Sorry," he said.

"You might as well tell me." Nolan sounded disgusted. "What difference will it make to you once you're dead?"

"Maybe none," Zach admitted. "But that's just the way I run my business."

"You're a dope, Cassidy."

"Probably."

Zach sensed the man getting ready to shoot and he readied himself for some kind of action. Now or never. But before thought could become movement, he heard the shot. Heard it, yes, but felt nothing. Puzzled, he jerked around in time to see Nolan fall forward.

Jamie was sprawled over the top of the incline, holding the gun Zach had given him with both hands. He was staring at the fallen man. "He dead?" he said hoarsely.

"He's dead," Zach replied. "Not a bad shot."

Jamie dropped the gun. "I think my leg is busted," he said. "And something in my side. It really hurts."

"Okay. I'll take care of it." He picked up both of his guns and put them into his pocket.

Then he turned his attention to Jamie. He tried to be careful lifting him, but the boy groaned in pain at the first movement. It was probably for the best that he'd passed out. Zach carried him back into the room.

He lowered Jamie onto the bed and covered him with the blanket. The boy's face was pale and damp with sweat, but his breathing seemed regular enough.

Zach quickly packed up his few belongings, including the bottle of whiskey. He resisted the temptation to take another drink, however. A smart man didn't fuzz up his mind just when he needed to be sharp. When the room was stripped of any sign that Zach Cassidy had ever been in there, he picked up the phone and dialed 911. It didn't take long to get some help on the way.

As he was going out the door, Zach paused for a brief moment to look at the boy on the bed. "Hang in there, Jamie," he said. "And look out for the bastards of the world."

This time he got the Jeep going much more quickly. He had only traveled a couple of miles down the road when he was passed by an ambulance and a cop car headed for the motel.

Jamie tried to move his leg into a more comfortable position. He was tired of the cast, tired of hospital food, and more than anything else, tired of dealing with the juvie creeps who kept hanging around. They were talking about sending him back to Omaha as soon as his ribs were healed.

Fat chance.

He would never go back. And if they somehow forced him to

return, he'd just run away again. But this time it would be better when he took off, because this time he had a plan.

As soon as he was sprung from this place, Jamie would be on his way to San Francisco.

Jamie picked up the television remote control and pointed it at the blank screen. "Ka-boom," he whispered. "Ka-boom."

There had been only a few vague stories in the paper about what had happened at the motel that night. Zach's name hadn't appeared anywhere, which meant he must've gotten away clean.

Which didn't surprise Jamie. Zach was smarter than the damned cops. Smarter than anybody.

The Nazis had tried to get Jamie to talk, to spill his guts about what had happened at the motel that night. But he just played dumb. Didn't tell the Fascists a damned thing. Zach would be really proud when he heard about how Jamie had stonewalled the pigs.

He frowned a little.

It might be hard to find Zach in San Francisco, but Jamie knew he could do it. The creep he'd killed had called Zach "Cassidy." Zach Cassidy. Somewhere in San Francisco. Wouldn't he be surprised when Jamie showed up on his doorstep? He'd probably also be a little mad at first, but that wouldn't last long.

Jamie grinned as he aimed the remote control at the patient sleeping across the room. Some old creep with a rotten kidney.

"Bang," Jamie said. "You're dead."

*Carolyn Wheat's Cass Jameson shares several qualities with her creator. Both are attorneys familiar with New York City's law-enforcement bodies—Carolyn has worked for the Legal Aid Society and currently ". . . gives legal advice to New York's Finest in the Police Department's Legal Bureau"—and both share an appreciation for the nuances of human behavior. Nominated for an Edgar for Best First Novel of 1983, Dead Man's Thoughts introduced Cass; it was followed by Where Nobody Dies.*

*In "Crime Scene," a rookie cop, involved with her first homicide, has a crucial moment of insight after meeting with a veteran detective. She learns a powerful lesson—and teaches the reader a thing or two.*

# CRIME SCENE

## by Carolyn Wheat

POLICE OFFICER TONI Ramirez stood in the doorway of the East Side apartment, one regulation brogue resting lightly on top of the other. Her stance was exactly the same as that of the barefoot child who had stood in the doorway of her Uncle Rafael's butcher shop in San Juan fifteen years earlier. Now, as then, she prayed not to be noticed, for to be noticed was to be shooed away. Now, as then, there was the rich smell of blood.

There were four cops in the room: Monelli on prints, Olivera on pix, Jacobs bagging evidence, and Gruschen drawing the floor plan. They each worked alone, yet the combined effect of busily moving hands and task-directed bodies was pure ritual. A High Mass, perhaps, or a bullfight.

The squat detective with the polyester hairpiece sprinkled fingerprint powder on the dark polished surface of the coffee table. "You shoulda seen it, Manny," he said, as though continuing rather than starting a conversation. "Broad was hacked up like gefilte fish."

"Like this one, you mean?" Detective Olivera gestured toward the

15

body, sprawled like a broken doll on the parquet floor. He held a camera in his hand, ready to photograph the corpse.

"Nah," Monelli replied. "Worse'n this, amigo. This here's just a little slice-and-dice. Somebody got one a them Vegematics for Christmas and hadda try it out." He opened his vinyl bag and took out the kind of big soft brush women use to put on blusher. Plying it with the delicacy of a makeup artist, he smoothed away the powder around each fingerprint. "The one I'm talkin' about needed a duplex coffin."

Toni bit her lips as a nervous giggle rose from her stomach. This was her first homicide, and so far she'd taken it like a cop. No tears, no hysterics, no tossed cookies. She'd hustled the shocked neighbors away, called the detectives, and secured the crime scene until their arrival.

She had always been curious. Her dark eyes opened wide and her mind overflowed with questions whenever something unusual crossed her path. In the new world of Nueva York, where her family had moved when she was eight, her saving grace had been her willingness to learn new ways, new words. Her curiosity led her at last to the Police Academy, where she graduated with honors.

Now she was learning the street. The body was just another lesson. And thanks to the crime-scene detectives, she was seeing first-hand the way real cops reacted to violent death—with humor that etched like acid, turning thin skin to thick scar tissue.

"Remember that stiff in the Four-fourth Precinct?" Manny Olivera directed his remarks at the fingerprint man, but Toni's female instinct told her that at the same time he was showing off for her. Of the four cops in the room, only he seemed to see her in the doorway. Only he exchanged glances with her, spoke as though she could hear. Now he looked at her with a distinct gleam in his eye, the look that told her he'd want her phone number before the day was over.

She smiled back. She liked his lean, swarthy face, his swaggery walk, his cynical smile. It would be fun to sit in a cop bar with a crime-scene detective and listen to war stories.

"Which one?" Monelli moved from the table to the doorknobs of the French doors in search of more prints. In the china closet, the gold rims of the dinner plates gleamed in the sunlight, while crystal goblets glittered like diamonds.

"You know, where the guy was cut up in quarters, like a steer or something. We only found one of the two lower halves, remember?"

"Yeah," Monelli replied, grunting as he knelt on one knee. He placed cellophane tape over the knob where he'd already dusted and brushed, lifting the prints with the precision of an eye doctor handling a contact lens. "Just another half-assed case, right, Manny?"

Toni's laugh exploded with a little snort. The jokes were terrible, but they helped in a way she couldn't explain. Helped to calm the jumping nerves and sweaty palms, the prickly feeling under her skin. Helped her look at the rusty black pools of dried blood caking the pink terry cloth robe.

"At least McCarthy ain't here," Monelli said. There was a sly smile on his face that told Toni he was baiting Olivera.

"Thank God for small favors," Olivera replied. He left the body, walking over to the pool of blood where the cleaver lay, obscene in its crusted blackness.

"I mean," Monelli went on, "most people, if they're gonna cry, they save it for weddings. They don't cry at crime scenes."

"Sentimental Irish bastard." Olivera snapped pictures as he talked, moving around the cleaver like a fashion photographer taking close-ups of Christie Brinkley. Unlike a model, the cleaver didn't tease the camera. It just lay flatly on the gleaming parquet floor, amid splatters of blood.

"McCarthy's still the best, Manny," Detective Arlene Jacobs murmured absently, as though she'd made the assertion many times before. She circled behind the body, walking toward the coffee table. "You shoot these?" she asked Olivera, waving a beautifully manicured hand at the teacup and saucer resting on the edge of the table. "I want to bag them."

Toni fixed her eyes on the coffee table, noting the way the patina gleamed in the sunlight. She focused on Detective Jacobs's long violet nails, on the delicate thinness of the bone-china cup and saucer. Anything to keep from seeing the bloody cleaver, the broken body at the other end of the room.

"Yeah, I got 'em, Arl," Olivera called over his shoulder. He knelt on one knee, leaning closer to the blood spatters around the cleaver. Toni's jaw clenched; she turned away.

Detective Jacobs took out a handkerchief, lifted the cup gingerly and placed it into a plastic evidence bag. She jotted her initials on the bag, just as Toni had learned to do at the Academy, then turned her attention to the saucer.

Toni was so engrossed in the synchronized activity of the crime-scene unit that she jumped when she realized there was someone behind her. She raised herself to her full five feet three and prepared herself for a dressing-down. She should have been back on patrol half an hour ago. Her job at the crime scene was over the minute the detectives arrived.

"At ease, Officer," a soft voice said. Toni edged her gaze to the left, noting a gray-blue tie with what appeared to be yellow spermatozoa imprinted on it. Raising her eyes, she saw a wrinkled white shirtfront, a shiny gray suit coat, a thick neck, and a face that could only belong to a cop. Toni remembered McCarthy from his lectures at the Academy, where he'd showed slides the police cadets labeled "New York's Goriest."

She interpreted his nod as an invitation to stay. He walked past her into the apartment, ignoring the technicians, stopping inches from the blood spatters on the shiny floor. He bent his head, in an attitude almost of prayer.

McCarthy was a shabby mountain of a man, at least six feet tall, with a shambling walk and cracked black shoes. Fifty-odd years of living, of eating and drinking and looking at corpses, were stamped on his ruddy face. Like a run-down boardinghouse in a decaying neighborhood, his sagging body looked as though it had outgrown his spirit some years before.

There was the distinct sound of sniffling. "Oh, Christ," Olivera said under his breath.

McCarthy reached his hand up and put his fingers to the bridge of his nose. If Toni hadn't heard the detectives' conversation, she never would have realized he was crying. The gesture would have passed for a tired man rubbing his eyes.

Detective Arlene Jacobs stepped over to where Olivera knelt. She stooped down and with deft fingers lifted the bloody meat cleaver off the floor, swiftly placing it into a plastic bag. She sealed the bag and wrote her initials on it for identification.

"Officer—ah, is it Rodriguez?" a diffident voice asked.

Toni started, then answered quickly, "Ramirez, sir." The face she turned toward McCarthy was the carefully controlled mask she'd learned at the Academy to present to superior officers.

"You found the poor girl, didn't you?"

"Yes, sir. I was on patrol when I was approached by the super of the building. He said the tenant in 5C hadn't picked up her mail and he was worried. He opened the door with a key, and I—" She broke off, swallowing hard.

Memory hit in pictures, quick, vivid images that churned her stomach and burned her eyes. The cheerful, heart-shaped welcome mat in front of 5C's door, the homemade wreath of straw twined with cornflowers and a lace-trimmed blue ribbon. The sun pouring in through sheer peach curtains, making golden squares on the parquet floor, where death lay waiting.

McCarthy's voice, softly insistent, seemed to come from far away. "Tell me, what did you feel when you saw her lying there?" He pointed to the contorted figure in the pink terry robe. Obscene splashes of red blotched the front, which opened to reveal a naked, mutilated young woman.

"Feel, sir?" Toni asked, her lips stiff. Feeling was not something for which you gained points in the Department. Was McCarthy trying to trick her, to show her up as a rookie?

"I—I tried not to feel anything, sir," she said, faltering. "I knew I had to contact my CO and the Crime Scene Unit, so I went to my radio and did that. And then I waited."

McCarthy nodded, sighing heavily. "You followed the Patrol Guide perfectly, Officer Ramirez," he said. "And it's true the Patrol Guide doesn't say anything about feelings. Or about tears," he added in a near whisper. The pink in his cheeks could have come from embarrassment or whiskey.

"How old are you?" he asked softly. "Not more than twenty-one, I'd guess. And how old do you think that poor child was?" When Toni didn't answer, he went on: "Her driver's license puts her at twenty-three. She's had two more years of life than you, Officer. Two more years of sunshine and chocolate-covered peanuts at the movies and lilacs in the spring and waking up between clean sheets in the morning. And now it's over. It's over forever, and it ended in agony. And so I ask you again, what did you feel when you saw her lying there in her own blood?"

Blood. Uncle Rafael's shop, with its dead Easter lambs. Lambs like the white woolly ones in her picture book, frolicking in green fields. Only these lambs hung from the hooks in the *carnicería*, their wool matted with rusty blood. She had cried for the dead lambs, their frolicking lives drained out of them.

The sob burst from her like a pressure cooker overflowing. Before she knew it, a strong arm enveloped her and guided her out of the apartment. She crossed the heart-shaped mat and leaned her forehead against the cool hallway wall. As she wept, McCarthy's meaty hand worked her shoulder; a handkerchief the size of the flag of Puerto Rico found its way into her hand.

"Let me tell you a story," the old cop began. "I was about your age. As new and green a rookie as ever stumbled over his regulation clodhoppers. I came upon my first dead body. A baby it was, about nine months old.''

Toni blew her nose, then looked at McCarthy. The blue eyes seemed to turn as cold and gray as a steel gun. "It was covered with blood," he said. "And there were welts and old yellowed bruises, and half the tiny head was dented in from the force of a blow. And I stood there, all nineteen years of me, and I cried. I tried not to let the others see, brushing the tears away so they wouldn't notice what a pansy-ass I was, but the tears wouldn't stop, no matter what I did."

McCarthy drew in a huge breath. Even now his red-rimmed eyes threatened to overflow. "And as I cried, the pictures started coming. I saw a hand reaching out toward that soft, smooth skin, ready to strike. I noticed the reek of whiskey and felt the terror that baby felt whenever that smell filled the house. I was wiping my nose on my sleeve when up comes my sergeant and bellows, 'What are you, bawlin'? McCarthy, we need *cops* here, not mollycoddles. We *know* who did it,' he goes on. 'All we have to do is find the kid's father and we can close this one out.'

"I turned as red as a brick wall," McCarthy went on, a sheepish smile on his face. "As soon as the tears stopped, so did the pictures. The baby was just a piece of meat, like a leg of lamb. Just a job.

"Then one of the detectives called me over. Roth, his name was. A real tough guy with a mug like a baseball mitt. Wore a fedora, like they all did in those days. Looked like he'd been *born* in the goddamn thing. I figured I was in for another lecture, so I went all stiff—just like you are now, Ramirez." McCarthy gave a throaty chuckle that ended in a cough. Toni relaxed her mouth into a wan smile.

" 'You know, kid,' Roth said to me, 'I never see a stiff without crying inside. It don't show, but I cry just the same. And you know something, kid,' he said, 'there ain't a homicide dick worth jack who don't do the same. You don't cry for the victim, you don't care enough to nail the bastard who killed him. So don't listen to your sergeant, kid. You go ahead and cry, and maybe someday we'll see you in Homicide.' "

Toni stood motionless, spellbound by the quiet, insistent voice and the mesmerizing blue eyes. She was close enough to see silver stubble on the old man's pink cheeks, and to smell the reek of tobacco that clung to him like perfume.

"Then Roth said to me, 'What happened here, kid?' I closed my eyes and saw pictures again. I felt the tears starting, but I didn't care anymore. I remembered the washed bottles in the dish rack and the vaporizer under the crib. I remembered the fresh diaper. I blurted it right out: 'Somebody loved him, and somebody else killed him.'

" 'Good,' Roth says. Like he already knows, and he's glad I know too. 'Go on.'

"I close my eyes again. Something about the diaper strikes me. It's clean and it's pinned nice, but it's all bunched up. It would take a strong hand to force pins through the knot of fabric. Then I think back to the ashtray next to the glass of whiskey. Half-smoked cigarettes with red lipstick stains on the filters.

" 'Holy shit!' I burst out. It's almost like a sob, maybe because I just buried my own mother in Greenwood Cemetery. 'It wasn't the father. It was the mother,' I tell Roth. 'The drunken bitch mother killed her own baby.' "

McCarthy shook his head slowly. He sighed. "I was right," he said. "It was the mother. We found her body in the air shaft. When she got sober and saw what she'd done, she took a dive. And that's why when I get to a crime scene, I let my experts roam all over, taking pictures and prints and picking up souvenirs, while I just look at the body and let myself feel everything I can. I refuse to wear the shell of cynicism the Department issues its officers along with the dress blues. Does this make sense to you?"

Toni nodded.

"My people in there," McCarthy went on, "are good cops. They do one hell of a job. But they don't use all the equipment they were born with. They use hands and eyes and brains, and most of the time that's good enough. But once in a while it helps to use the heart."

McCarthy put his arm around the rookie's shoulders. "Would you care to look at the body again?" he asked gently.

As if in a trance, Toni walked through the doors of apartment 5C. She was hyperconscious, aware of the smells of Jacobs's perfume and Gruschen's cigar underneath the smells of blood and excrement from the body. She willed herself to ignore irrelevancies, walking straight to the corpse on the polished floor. She stared a long time at the honey-colored hair with the dark roots just starting to show, at the coral-painted toenails, at the thin gold ankle bracelet. This time she didn't turn away from the blood-soaked pink terry cloth robe.

As she looked down at the dead woman, Toni felt herself becoming the girl in the pink robe. She was wiping her makeup off, getting ready for bed. Under her bare feet the wooden floor was cold, yet she hated slippers. She moved toward the kitchen, to make her nightly cup of herbal tea.

Teacup in hand, she walked toward the comfortable green-and-peach chair in the living room and set the tea on the coffee table. She turned on the television, taking a videotape from the library of tapes in the wood-grain rack. Settling herself in the flowered chair, she tucked her legs underneath her and pulled her robe a little tighter.

A wave of loneliness hit Toni. How many nights had the dead girl sat in her cozy chair, wearing her fuzzy pink robe? How many nights had she spent alone, with only the TV for company? Toni's eyes traveled toward the large color TV on its wheeled stand. A tape lay on top of the VCR. It appeared to have been played halfway through.

Things nagged at Toni. A tiny silver object on top of the TV console. She looked more closely—a loose nut. On the lower shelf beside the VCR sat a tiny jeweler's screwdriver.

She closed her eyes and became again the girl. She was watching her video, tea cooling in the thin cup. The picture on the screen stopped. She reached for the remote-control box, then hunted for the instruction book. Finally she went to the phone.

Toni took a ragged breath, bringing herself back to the reality of now, of the girl dead on the floor. She looked at the VCR. Its digital clock read 12:00, yet Toni knew it had to be at least 3:30. She stared at the green numbers, her ears hearing sounds that came from the past.

A knock at the blue-wreathed door. The padding sounds of the girl's bare feet as she crossed the parquet floor. The scraping of locks as she undid her elaborate security system to let in her always helpful super. Laughter and joking, an offer of tea. Warmth and gratitude in the girl's voice, turning to fear and terror as she realized the kind of payment he expected.

"Oh, God," Toni murmured, closing her eyes. She felt faint. "Don't. Please don't." A shudder ran through her, shaking her slight body with a violence she didn't expect. "I just wanted the VCR fixed," she whispered.

Toni closed her mind, shutting out the rest. She felt McCarthy's warm, steady hand on her shoulder, heard him say, "Tell Homicide to check out the super."

She opened her eyes and looked down at the slight, still figure on the floor. "We'll get him, *chica*," she promised softly.

*Marilyn Wallace introduced Oakland homicide detectives Jay Gold-
stein and Carlos Cruz in* A Case of Loyalties, *which shared a Macavity Award for Best First Novel of 1986. The philosopher/cop and
his family-oriented partner came to the aid of the first woman to make
a serious bid for the presidency in* Primary Target.

*"The Sentence" (the first minimalist mystery?) is a departure into
satire. It explores the consequences of obsession and serves as a warning
about the effectiveness of poetic justice.*

# THE SENTENCE

## by Marilyn Wallace

### Spring

"YOU BEEN UP to the city? Hain't seen you since you
brought in that Harvester with the throwed rod. Tommy
up to the garage says you ain't the kind to let machinery
go and there was plenty of oil, valves worked just fine he says. So
what you think done it?" Henry shifts the large brown-paper-
wrapped parcel in his left arm and shuffles his feet on the post office
porch. Thin light slants through the bare branches of a maple and
splinters to the ground in bright shards.

Gregory knocks one booted foot against the bottom step, then
bangs the other. Chunks of mud fly from the grooves of his neoprene
soles. "I haven't been to the city. I've been working."

"Which kind of working?"

"Writing," Gregory says. "A new project. It's the most important
thing I've ever done."

Henry nods and rubs his chin stubble against the shoulder of his
jacket. His eyes narrow, falling into place among the lines that years

23

of plowing, cutting, raking, and baling have laid down. "If you can spare the time, maybe you best think on what you're going to do about the west field over by Hotalen's barn."

"You still want to lease that field, Henry? Go ahead and work it this year. I don't understand how you do so much."

"Being sheriff don't take hardly any time. Drunks and speeders is about all around here. It's the farm—hell, I get more trouble from my old John Deere than from any law violators. Most of the time, anyhow."

"I guess I'm one of those people who can only do one thing at a time," Gregory says. His smile is filled with admiration for Henry's versatility.

"Whoa. Hold on there." Henry's voice stops him. "How about setting a price? Good way to make trouble, my ma used to say, is to think you know what t'other person's thinking. Now, I'd want to put that field in corn but it might be that you was wanting it in alfalfa. And what're we gonna do about keeping the fences?" The bottoms of Henry's green pants flap against his ankles as a puff of wind scurries around the corner and up onto the porch.

"Plant what you want, Henry. You talk to Maggie about a price— she's taking over the business end of things so that I can just write. Figure you'll keep the fences. Come by on Thursday after evening milking and we'll sign an agreement."

Henry's eyebrows lift, moving his scalp and raising the small knitted cap on the back of his head. "Okay," he says. "Say a hello to Maggie for me."


Gregory loves the desk in his study, nut-colored and unmarred except for a single stain left by a coffee cup eight years ago. He had gone right out to Miller's Hardware and bought a terra-cotta tile, glued four round felt lozenges to the bottom, and then set it over the stain. When he is writing, something is always on the tile—a coffee cup, a lemonade glass, a tumbler of water.

He taps the pencils into a more orderly arrangement and shifts the sheet of yellow paper so that it rests square to the corners of the desk. His lips move slowly as he reads.

*Tarpaper tight, the drumskin waits to release its throbbing, thrumming, boasting beat into the thickened air.*

Since Gregory has decided that a sentence is a word sculpture, he checks each one for balance, space, movement, weight. This one is shapely, with a pleasing off-center symmetry: word pairs at each end and a change of pattern in the middle. But it lacks substance, he concludes as he slips the paper into a folder labeled THE SENTENCE, marks an *X* on the cover sheet beside #54, and slides the folder back into the file drawer.

He drops a stray paper clip into the hammered brass dish and closes his eyes. His breathing slows as he rummages through a mental catalog. Justice. Courage. Honor. Courage . . .

A crash from the kitchen is followed by Maggie's muffled cursing. A door slams and a straw broom scrapes across the floor. He rubs his eyes and waits. The noise stops but Maggie's throaty singing takes its place. She must be cooking. For fifteen years, Maggie has sung whenever she's preparing something complicated. It had begun with her first try at Armenian rice and chicken livers, progressed through her exotic chutney, mustard, and vinegar phase, and revitalized during a round of gnocchi.

What is she doing and why can't she be quiet? He will try to shut it out. This is too important. He twists his legs around the chair, untwists them, tries rhythmic breathing. Engine noises sputter in the distance.

Gregory sighs and rolls his chair to the window. He squints through the glare. A green dot, Henry's John Deere, chugs along the rise of the west field. Is it May already?

## Summer

Maggie dips her hand into the pan, comes up with a chunk of lamb, brown from sitting overnight in the marinade, and runs it through with the skewer, slides it up to the cherry tomato, and lays the whole thing on a platter. She is only humming. This is easy cooking. This is what she likes about summertime, its effortlessness, its liquid passing from one moment to the next. Except for damned Gregory, who has been locked inside himself for the past two months. So she has devised a plan she hopes will work. She doesn't know what else to do.

Richard is bearded and solemn, his brown eyes warm with wisdom; he perches on the stool and slices peaches on the cutting board until Maggie shows him how to work over the blue crockery bowl to catch all the juice. He has come from the city at Maggie's invitation, for a barbecue, and to see if he can rescue his childhood friend Gregory, or at least look things over and give Maggie something to hold on to. "This won't work, you know," he says. He tosses another peach pit, red and yellow strings clinging to the dark convolutions, into the bag on the floor. "Just a friendly visit from old friend Richard. Uh uh. He smells a setup, I know he does."

Maggie reaches for a tomato with fingers flecked with rosemary. "No. He doesn't. He's hardly even aware that you're here." Her graying hair, lately cut with spiky bangs that make her want to get three new holes for earrings in her ears, is not long enough for her to hide behind. She recognizes that she has arranged for Richard's visit at least as much for her own comfort as for the help he might be with Gregory. "He's always loved being off with you, trekking in the woods. You know, man to man," Maggie says. Richard's grin is the first smile she's seen in this kitchen in a long time.

"I'll ask him to come for a walk after dinner. Maybe if I'm alone with him . . ." He grips Maggie's shoulders and kisses her cheek.

Maggie holds herself away, not letting herself feel his hands or his lips. "Please try. If this doesn't work . . ." She examines the cherry tomato between her fingers and without realizing that she's going to do it, squeezes hard. The juice and a shower of pale seeds plop onto the butcher block.

"Tell me, Mag, has it affected your sexual relationship too?"

Maggie stares out at the garden. Stooped beside the knee-high bush beans, Gregory is still peering at the ground. "Richard, he only comes out of his study to use the bathroom or to refill his water glass. Literally. This is the first time in weeks that he's even been outside." She jabs a curl of bell pepper onto a skewer. "I can't take it much longer. He says he's got to write the perfect sentence and that he can't stop for anything."

Richard looks out the window and one corner of his mouth turns down. What does his expression mean? Maggie isn't certain but at least he believes her.


Gregory knows that the longer he stares at the soil, the more life he'll see. He stirs the newly-hoed path between the rows with his fingers. A fat earthworm, gray-brown and bulging, humps over a ball of dirt and disappears. A round black bug with delicate legs hurries toward the lettuce. Seven ants march by, bearing booty.

Let it beat down on me, he thinks, and feed me like the sun feeds this garden into fullness. Let it nourish the perfect sentence that grows inside me, this word-embryo.

A cabbage moth flutters to a stop on the tip of a brussels sprout stalk. He thinks: I might pin its wings, pale green like underripe honeydew flesh, and write the sentence and then watch it fly away. He smiles. It is happening; his censor is learning to sit patiently while the images gather.

"Beans are looking fine but you best put some garlic spray on the crucifers or the moths'll turn them cabbages into French stockings." Henry pulls the cap from his head, wipes his forehead with the back of his wrist, then replaces the cap, giving the peak a final tug to set it straight.

Gregory stands up; his knees snap into place.

"Maggie said you was out here. I seen that you have a guest—I'll be on my way in a minute. Just wanted to bring by this month's rent."

Gregory thanks Henry for the check, then follows his gaze through the waves of heat that rise from the pond at the far end of the knoll. "You're up to second haying already?"

Henry bobs his head, a sign that the work is going well. "If the rain holds off another three days, we'll have it all safe away. Oh, Maggie asked me to tell you to bring in some of them little tomatoes for the shish kee bop."

Gregory tingles.

Shish kebab. Stuck.

Skewered.

Spitted.

The words come from such wonderful, unexpected places. Who would have thought that Henry would be a source?

"How's the work?" Henry asks. "Maggie says you been at it like a dog at its fleas."

"I'm really close, Henry. But it's not quite there yet. It's like when the hay is ready. Can't cut it too soon and yet you have to get it in before the rain." Gregory squints up at the sun. "Old wisdom but true."

"Yep," Henry says, wiping a trickle of sweat from his neck with a damp handkerchief, "gotta keep at it, when the time's right. My ma, she used to say, 'Henry,' she'd tell me, 'the days are short and the night's a mere nothing.'" He stuffs the handkerchief back into his pocket. "Wellsir, I gotta get back."

"I'll walk you to the truck." Gregory steps along the dirt, flattening a path of heel and toe marks into the soil as he moves to the gate. Has he trod on any bugs? Are they squashed?

Tremulous?

Timorous?

Pellucid?

Glutinous?

Moribund?

"You okay?" Henry's voice calls him back.

"Fine, Henry. I was just thinking about the bugs. Being in this garden makes me remember how important it is to experience everything." Gregory swings the gate shut behind himself.

"Everything?"

"Theoretically," Gregory says. "Pleasure. Pain. Triumph. Fear. Theoretically, everything." They walk in the silent heat. "For a writer, anyway," Gregory adds. He has come to the knowledge that, within the syntactical constraints of formal language, the sentence must contain images that synthesize the sensory, pre-rational nature of experience.

The little O that Henry makes with his mouth flattens the wrinkles that mark where his cheeks begin. "Attitude like that could get an ordinary man in trouble. Good thing you're a writer."

They have reached the end of the path. A small bird lights on the sill of his study window. Gregory feels as if he's been away from his desk far too long. "Thanks for stopping by," he says, "and good luck with the haying."

"Don't need luck. Just a few more dry days." Henry hauls himself into the cab of his blue pickup and waves as Gregory continues up the flagstones to the back door.

"Damn, there's another one!" Maggie yells, swinging a towel at a fly that follows Gregory into the kitchen. "Sorry," she says, reaching for a piece of onion with her glistening fingers, "I didn't mean you. Those wily bastards just lay in wait for the door to be opened." She turns to Richard, whose eyes seem to be measuring the scene, then looks at Gregory. "Did you get the tomatoes? I need about six more. Didn't Henry tell you?"

"Just a minute," Gregory calls. He sprints down the hall into his study and slams the door shut with his foot. Still standing, he grabs a pencil and yellow pad and writes.

*Stick me with golden pins and let my juices form a river which will flood the stars and wash them from the burntcork sky into an iron pot where I shall steam until they are pink and serve them with dark salty sauce.*

Nice, he thinks. A kaleidoscope. An evocation. A Jungian archetype shimmering in a Joycean epiphany. But a bit contrived. He writes a number, 959, on the page and slips the sheet onto the pile in the bushel basket. So much more is possible, he thinks. Fill me; pour from me.

But it becomes an effort to keep his eyes open. Sweet heaviness descends and he lets his head fall forward slowly. In a dream, when I am an open channel, it will issue from me, he vows as the sweat rolls down his sternum toward his navel.

## Autumn

"You're making too much of this, Mag." Gregory smiles at his wife's worried eyes. The sun is tired and warms only the surface of his skin as they step among the dry vines to retrieve the last pumpkin.

"Can't you see what's happening, for God's sake? You wake me up every night with your mumbling, grinding your teeth and thrashing around. You don't talk to anyone, won't go anywhere, don't care about anything except your damn sentence."

Maggie stops walking. Gregory looks at her red plaid jacket; it echoes the color of the sycamore leaves behind her. The hills stand sharp against the slate sky. Patterns are everywhere—repeating, complementing, ordering the chaos. And it can all be captured in words—the right words.

"Don't stare at me like that!" Maggie's voice breaks across the sound of the wind sifting through a pile of leaves. "You don't hear me at all, do you? You haven't heard a word I've said for months."

A word. Which word? Gregory wonders. Have I missed the word I need?

Maggie pulls her left hand out of her jacket pocket and touches his cheek. The warmth of her fingers startles him. "I miss you. Seven months, Gregory. Do you realize that we haven't made love for seven months?" She laughs then, a sound of indelicacy and derision. Gregory turns away. "This problem won't just disappear," she says softly. "You have to come back to reality, Gregory. Come back to life."

Life.

Anima.

Animus.

Animate.

Animal.

An' 'e 'ad a 'eavy 'eart.

Like a student of Zen who suddenly understands a koan given to him years ago, Gregory knows now that the sentence will come when the moment is right, like a gift from the universe. He feels the words. They tumble over him. Tumble. He pulls a stub of pencil and a scrap of paper from his jacket. Maggie whirls around, jams her fists against her thighs, and marches toward the house. Gregory writes quickly.

*The town tumbled down the hillside, falling from east, west, and north to a flatter place where the houses could stand upright and the streets had room to spill forward, moving insistently to the south.*

"I just need a little more time." He shouts after her and shakes his head as Maggie gets smaller and smaller until finally she is small enough to fit into the tiny door of the little house at the end of the narrow path.


Richard stands like he's posing for an L. L. Bean ad, one foot on the porch, one in the doorway. His watch catches the brightness of the sun along its thin gold rim, spins it off onto the window. He sways; his breath smells like brandy and lemons. "Fine friend, that's all I can say," he mutters as he leans on the rifle.

"I told you. I haven't opened my mail in—I don't know, a very long time." Gregory is tired of explaining and annoyed at Maggie for bringing Richard here from the train station and then leaving. She'll be gone for a week, visiting friends in the city, so he will have to deal with this interruption on his own. "I didn't know you were coming. I wouldn't have agreed to a visit if I'd known. My work takes all my time." The bite of the air hurts his eyes.

"Come on, Greg. I promised Al that I'd come home with a five-point buck, but I can't do it alone. I need you with me. Let's go get us a big one, Greg boy." Richard's nose is red and he pulls his head in close to the collar of the orange hunting jacket.

"I've got to get back to work, Richard. I'm sorry. Maggie shouldn't have made this arrangement without asking me. Of all people, I'd hoped you'd understand."

"Sometimes, Gregory, I think I do. Sometimes I even envy you." Richard blinks slowly; the smell of brandy drifts out from his hiccup.

"Thank you," Gregory says. On impulse, he reaches for the white scarf that has been hanging from the peg beside the door since last March. "Here. Wrap this around your neck and tuck the edges into your jacket."

Edges.

Language has edges, boundaries, demarcations that keep things clear. Why hasn't he recognized this concept before? Perhaps when he understands where the edges belong, he'll have the principle of the thing and that will be a start.

"Come with me, Greg. It'll be like when we were young. The smells . . . the pine needles crushed under your feet, the leaves and the goddamn intense drama of it. Waddaya say?"

Maybe, Gregory thinks as his hand curls around his pencil, he should go with Richard. Just for a little while. Just to get him to keep quiet.

"Okay. But only for an hour. If you want to stay out longer, that's up to you."

"Terrific." Richard grins and steps backward, juggles the rifle, then steadies himself. "That'sh great," he slurs.

Gregory is already buttoning his coat and thinking about edges.

## Winter

Gregory shivers and pulls up the collar of his old Navy peacoat. He'll get out the heating pad, unless Maggie took it with her. He certainly doesn't have time to call the oil company for a delivery, and besides, what would he pay them with? Maggie has gone off with the bankbooks.

It had only taken half a day to master writing with the pencil in his gloved hand; he could push past these obstacles. In early December his way had become illuminated. The beacon was Reduction. The word gleamed, tantalizing him, taunting him with its obviousness. It had been there all along; he had somehow missed the seduction of the simple, the reduced, the less. Maggie had actually done him a favor by taking most of the furniture when she left. It had given him the word—Reduction.

Where to begin today? He taps his chest. From deep beneath the blue wool jacket and the checked flannel shirt, between his skin and the long-sleeved thermal undershirt, he hears the reassuring crumple of the paper. The mathematics is so easy—assign positive weight to the negative elements of a sentence and then reduce the total value to zero. After working so diligently on the equation, it has committed itself to his memory without conscious effort:

Nonspecific nouns and verbs  =   + 4
Excessive use of modifiers  =   + 3
Passive voice  =   + 2
Non Anglo-Saxon words  =   + 1

The last still gives him some trouble; excluding words based on their country of origin, he thinks, is undemocratic, elitist, not ideals he wants to perpetuate. But if he is to achieve purity, he has to be firm.

He carries the paper over to the window. A sound, sharp and loud as a gunshot, pierces him and he looks up in time to see a branch snap neatly under its burden of snow. The snow blankets everything, producing a stillness that is comforting, its whiteness a vast, potential page. As he reads, blasts of steam blow from his mouth.

So much to remove here! He trembles with excitement, teeth chattering. A beam of sun hits the paper and Gregory rearranges himself so that he is standing directly in its warmth. First, the non-specifics. He strikes through *man*, *creature*, *quiet*. Now to take out the modifiers. Good-bye, *merciful*. See you around, *benevolent*. Ta ta, *natural* and *orderly*. Pleasure warms him and he grins.

A movement outside catches his eye. A blue pickup truck is making its way up the driveway. Gregory is annoyed. Why now, when he is so close? Go away, he wills.

When he notices the plow blade on the nose of the truck, Gregory sighs with relief. Maggie probably hired someone before she left, to come and clear the drive after big snows. Or maybe he has made the arrangement himself. He can't remember. But the truck stops and the driver gets out, then pulls a bulky green plastic bag from the cab. Soon, a rapping on the door breaks the silence.

Gregory waits. He sits down and drags the chair in closer to the comfort of his desk. Surely if no one answers, whoever it is will go away. The pounding grows louder, more insistent.

"You in there, Gregory? It's me, Henry," the voice from outside calls.

Gregory picks up the paper again and goes on crossing out words. Footsteps crunch on the snow and he waits for the sound of the engine. Nothing. He looks out the window. Henry's eyes and nose look back at him.

"You musta been working real hard not to hear me. I been banging away at the door," Henry shouts through the glass. He shades his eyes with a gloved hand as he peers through the window. "You okay in there?"

Gregory laughs. "I'm wonderful, Henry. I've really got it this time."

Henry nods. "Brought your mail. Jeannie down to the post office said you hain't been in for a spell, so I brought it by. Come around and open the door." Henry's face is gone from the window.

Gregory clutches the paper and thinks. If he lets Henry in, the work will be interrupted. He'll lose the rhythm of it. If he ignores him, will Henry go away?

The knocking on the front door rings through the house.

Sighing, Gregory sets the paper on his desk and hurries to the entryway. His woolly fingers slip against the door lock. He tries again and it turns. The door opens and Henry stares up at him.

"As cold in here as it is outside."

Gregory knows about the cold. He turns and walks briskly to his study, Henry's steps sounding behind him.

"Here's your mail," Henry says, and hands him a thick bundle held together by a fat, cracking rubber band. "You still working on that same project?" he asks as he reaches for the yellow paper on the desk.

Gregory feels prickles of pain along his arm, as if his skin were pulled too tight against his muscles, as if each hair were anchored to a nerve. "Please don't touch my papers," he says as evenly as he can. Henry doesn't move, except for his eyes which start at the top of the page and read every word; Gregory can see where he is just by the position of his eyes. When Henry sets the paper down, Gregory grabs it up.

Henry bends and opens the plastic bag. "Found this rifle in the woods. You recognize it?" He pulls it out until Gregory can see the nick just over the brass screw in the stock.

"That's mine."

The rifle thumps against the plastic with a soft *whoosh* as Henry drops it in. Then he reaches deeper into the large green bag and pulls out another bag, smaller, transparent, with a ball of white inside. "And this?" he asks.

Gregory stares at it, looks at the desk. It takes all his strength not to grab up pencil and paper and run into the bathroom and lock the door. "What's that?"

Henry is quiet; two red circles have appeared on his cheeks and are spreading out toward his earflaps. He lifts a corner of the white ball and pulls. It is not completely white, Gregory sees. Two large rust-colored stains sit in the center of the scarf, like blobs in a child's painting. Little spatters of the same color drift toward the edges.

"It might be mine but mine wasn't stained."

Henry lays both plastic bags on the floor. Gregory decides that Henry will understand that he has things to do.

"I must get to work. Please go now, Henry." He tries a smile to soften the harshness and realizes that it wasn't harsh; it was simple, reduced, the fewest words possible to deliver the message.

"Can't do that, Gregory. You see, some kids found a body in the woods. Your friend, it was. That fellow who was talking to Maggie in the kitchen when I brought the rent by this summer. Sure does look like he was shot with your rifle."

Gregory searches the speck of a memory. Richard, interrupting his work to ask him to go hunting. Richard's one-sided grin when he'd agreed to go along for an hour. Richard, stumbling as they made their way to the stand of shagbark hickory trees. His own expansive relief when he was finally settled at his desk again. He recalls Maggie returning from her visit to the city but he can't fix on Richard coming back. And then, it seemed like the next day although it could have been a week or even a month, he remembers Maggie leaving with the furniture.

"I'm sorry I got to do this," Henry says, "but you're gonna have to come in with me."

Gregory thinks he should do something but he can't imagine what it should be.

"You really worked on it—experiencing everything, didn't you?" Henry asks.

What in the world is Henry talking about? He is working on the same thing he's been working on for nearly a year now.

"And this writing." Henry taps the paper. "I think you figured out a way to use your experience, the one in the woods with your friend, and that's what you're writing about, isn't it, Gregory?"

Now Gregory remembers: he is nearly finished. He has to get back to it. "Just a minute, Henry. I don't mean to be rude but there's something I have to do right now." He reaches for the pencil.

~~There was quiet~~ and the man ~~stood~~ beside the ~~animal~~ and consigned the ~~creature~~ to a ~~merciful,~~ yes, a ~~benevolent, natural,~~ and ~~orderly~~ demise.

He has already marked all the nonspecifics, the excessive modifiers, the passive voice. He crosses out the non-Anglo-Saxon words with precise strokes. Closer. It's so much closer. His stomach rumbles and the taste of the sausage he'd eaten earlier rises to his throat. It had been gray with age, the last thing in the freezer. Block it out, he tells himself. Block out the sounds that Henry is making, too. Keep focused.

And now he knows, with no need to look again, that he is finished. He slashes the articles, the conjunctions, the prepositions, and is thrilled at what remains.

*yes*

A halo hovers around the word.

*yes*

Henry looks down at him. "I guess you didn't reckon on how it would turn out. Well, we got to go. You done?"

"Yes," Gregory answers reverently. "The perfect sentence."

*Julie Smith, a former reporter for the New Orleans* Times–Picayune *and the San Francisco* Chronicle, *is wickedly inventive as she gets her thoroughly contemporary characters out of the sticky situations they've managed to get themselves into. Julie's wit and charm infuse the adventures of clever, attractive attorney Rebecca Schwartz (*Death Turns a Trick, The Sourdough Wars, *and* Tourist Trap*) and enliven the foibles of Paul MacDonald (*True-life Adventure *and* Huckleberry Fiend*), an aspiring mystery writer who accepts freelance sleuthing jobs to keep his cat in canned mackerel.*

*In "Blood Types," the irreverent Rebecca discovers just how risky a potion the milk of human kindness can be.*

# BLOOD TYPES

## by Julie Smith

"REFRESH MY RECOLLECTION, counselor. Are holographic wills legal in California?"

Though we'd hardly spoken in seven years or more, I recognized the voice on the phone as easily if I'd heard it yesterday. I'd lived with its owner once. "Gary Wilder. Aren't you feeling well?"

"I feel fine. Settle a bet, okay?"

"Unless you slept through more classes than I thought, you know perfectly well they're legal."

"They used to be. It's been a long time, you know? How are you, Rebecca?"

"Great. And you're a daddy, I hear. How's Stephanie?"

"Fine."

"And the wee one?"

"Little Laurie-bear. The best thing that ever happened to me."

"You sound happy."

"Laurie's my life."

I was sorry to hear it. That was a lot of responsibility for a ten-month-old.

"So about the will," Gary continued. "Have the rules changed since we were at Boalt?"

"A bit. Remember how it could be invalidated by anything pre-printed on it? Like in that case where there was a date stamped on the paper the woman used, and the whole thing was thrown out?"

"Yeah. I remember someone asked whether you could use your own letterhead."

"That was you, Gary."

"Probably. And you couldn't, it seems to me."

"But you probably could now. Now only the 'materially relevant' part has to be handwritten. And you don't have to date it."

"No? That seems odd."

"Well, you would if there were a previous dated will. Otherwise just write it out, sign it, and it's legal."

Something about the call, maybe just the melancholy of hearing a voice from the past, put me in a gray and restless mood. It was mid-December and pouring outside—perfect weather for doleful ruminations on a man I hardly knew anymore. I couldn't help worrying that if Laurie was Gary's whole life, that didn't speak well for his marriage. Shouldn't Stephanie at least have gotten a small mention? But she hadn't, and the Gary I knew could easily have fallen out of love with her. He was one of life's stationary drifters—staying in the same place but drifting from one mild interest to another, none of them very consuming and none very durable. I hoped it would be different with Laurie; it wouldn't be easy to watch your dad wimp out on you.

But I sensed it was already happening. I suspected that phone call meant little Laurie, who was his life, was making him feel tied down and he was sending out feelers to former and future lady friends.

The weather made me think of a line from a poem Gary used to quote:

> *Il pleure dans mon coeur*
> *Comme il pleut sur la ville.*

He was the sort to quote Paul Verlaine. He read everything, retained everything, and didn't do much. He had never finished law school, had sold insurance for a while and was now dabbling in real estate, I'd heard, though I didn't know what that meant, exactly. Probably trying to figure out a way to speculate with Stephanie's money, which, out of affection for Gary, I thanked heaven she had.

If you can't make up your mind what to do with your life, you should at least marry well and waffle in comfort.

Gary died that night. Reading about it in the morning *Chronicle*, I shivered, thinking the phone call was one of those grisly coincidences. But the will came the next day.

The *Chronicle* story said Gary and Stephanie were both killed instantly when their car went over a cliff on a twisty road in a blinding rainstorm. The rains were hellish that year. It was the third day of a five-day flood.

Madeline Bell, a witness to the accident, said Gary had swerved to avoid hitting her Mercedes as she came around a curve. The car had exploded and burned as Bell watched it roll off a hill near San Anselmo, where Stephanie and Gary lived.

Even in that moment of shock I think I felt more grief for Laurie than I did for Gary, who had half lived his life at best. Only a day before, when I'd talked to Gary, Laurie had had it made—her mama was rich and her daddy good-looking. Now she was an orphan.

I wondered where Gary and Stephanie were going in such an awful storm. To a party, probably, or home from one. It was the height of the holiday season.

I knew Gary's mother, of course. Would she already be at the Wilder house, for Hanukkah, perhaps? If not, she'd be coming soon; I'd call in a day or two.

In the meantime I called Rob Burns, who had long since replaced Gary in my affections, and asked to see him that night. I hadn't thought twice of Gary in the past five years, but something was gone from my life and I needed comfort. It would be good to sleep with Rob by my side and the sound of rain on the roof—life-affirming, as we say in California. I'd read somewhere that Mark Twain, when he built his mansion in Hartford, installed a section of tin roof so as to get the best rain sounds. I could understand the impulse.

It was still pouring by mid-morning the next day, and my throat was feeling slightly scratchy, the way it does when a cold's coming on. I was rummaging for vitamin C when Kruzick brought the mail in—Alan Kruzick, incredibly inept but inextricably installed secretary for the law firm of Nicholson and Schwartz, of which I was a protesting partner. The other partner, Chris Nicholson, liked his smart-ass style, my sister Mickey was his girlfriend, and my mother had simply laid down the law—hire him and keep him.

"Any checks?" I asked.

"Nope. Nothing interesting but a letter from a dead man."

"What?"

He held up an envelope with Gary Wilder's name and address in the upper left corner. "Maybe he wants you to channel him."

The tears that popped into my eyes quelled even Kruzick.

The will was in Gary's own handwriting, signed, written on plain paper, and dated December 17, the day of Gary's death. It said: "This is my last will and testament, superseding all others. I leave everything I own to my daughter, Laurie Wilder. If my wife and I die before her 21st birthday, I appoint my brother, Michael Wilder, as her legal guardian. I also appoint my brother as executor of this will."

My stomach clutched as I realized that Gary had known when we talked that he and Stephanie were in danger. He'd managed to seem his usual happy-go-lucky self, using the trick he had of hiding his feelings that had made him hard to live with.

But if he knew he was going to be killed, why hadn't he given the murderer's identity? Perhaps he had, I realized. I was a lawyer, so I'd gotten the will. Someone else might have gotten a letter about what was happening. I wondered if my old boyfriend had gotten involved with the dope trade. After all, he lived in Marin County, which had the highest population of coke dealers outside the greater Miami area.

I phoned Gary's brother at his home in Seattle but was told he'd gone to San Anselmo. I had a client coming in five minutes, but after that, nothing pressing. And so, by two o'clock I was on the Golden Gate Bridge, enjoying a rare moment of foggy overcast, the rain having relented for a while.

It was odd about Gary's choosing Michael for Laurie's guardian. When I'd known him well he'd had nothing but contempt for his brother. Michael was a stockbroker and a go-getter; Gary was a mooner-about, a romantic, and a rebel. He considered his brother boring, stuffy, a bit crass, and utterly worthless. On the other hand, he adored his sister, Jeri, a free-spirited dental hygienist married to a good-natured sometime carpenter.

Was Michael married? Yes, I thought. At least he had been. Maybe fatherhood had changed Gary's opinions on what was important—Michael's money and stability might have looked good to him when he thought of sending Laurie to college.

I pulled up in front of the Wilder-Cooper house, a modest redwood one that had probably cost nearly half a million. Such were real-estate values in Marin County—and such was Stephanie's bank account.

At home were Michael Wilder—wearing a suit—and Stephanie's parents, Mary and Jack Cooper. Mary was a big woman, comfortable and talkative; Jack was skinny and withdrawn. He stared into space, almost sad, but mostly just faraway, and I got the feeling watching TV was his great passion in life, though perhaps he drank as well. The idea, it appeared, was simply to leave the room without anyone noticing, the means of transportation being entirely insignificant.

It was a bit awkward, my being the ex-girlfriend and showing up unexpectedly. Michael didn't seem to know how to introduce me, and I could take a hint. It was no time to ask to see him privately.

"I'd hoped to see your mother," I said.

"She's at the hospital," said Mary. "We're taking turns now that—" She started to cry.

"The hospital!"

"You don't know about Laurie?"

"She was in the accident?"

"No. She's been very ill for the last two months."

"Near death," said Mary. "What that child has been through shouldn't happen to an animal. Tiny little face just contorts itself like a poor little monkey's. Screams and screams and screams; and *rivers* flow out of her little bottom. *Rivers*, Miss Schwartz!"

Her shoulders hunched and began to shake. Michael looked helpless. Mechanically Jack put an arm around her.

"What's wrong?" I asked Michael.

He shrugged. "They don't know. Can't diagnose it."

"Now, Mary," said Jack. "She's better. The doctor said so last night."

"What hospital is she in?"

"Marin General."

I said to Michael: "I think I'll pop by and see your mother— would you mind pointing me in the right direction? I've got a map in the car."

When we arrived at the curb, I said, "I can find the hospital. I wanted to give you something."

I handed him the will. "This came in today's mail. It'll be up to you as executor to petition the court for probate." As he read, a look of utter incredulity came over his face. "But . . . I'm divorced. I can't take care of a baby."

"Gary didn't ask in advance if you'd be willing?"

"Yes, but . . . I didn't think he was going to die!" His voice got higher as reality caught up with him. "He called the day of the accident. But I thought he was just depressed. You know how people get around the holidays."

"What did he say exactly?"

"He said he had this weird feeling, that's all—like something bad might happen to him. And would I take care of Laurie if anything did."

"He didn't say he was scared? In any kind of trouble?"

"No—just feeling weird."

"Michael, he wasn't dealing, was he?"

"Are you kidding? I'd be the last to know." He looked at the ground a minute. "I guess he could have been."

Ellen Wilder was cooing to Laurie when I got to the hospital. "Ohhhh, she's much better now. She just needed her grandma's touch, that's all it was."

She spoke to the baby in the third person, unaware I was there until I announced myself, whereupon she almost dropped the precious angel-wangel and dislodged her IV. We had a tearful reunion, Gary's mother and I. We both missed Gary, and we both felt for poor Laurie.

Ellen adored the baby more than breath, to listen to her, and not only that, she possessed the healing power of a witch. She had spent the night Gary and Stephanie were killed with Laurie, and all day the next day, never even going home for a shower. And gradually the fever had broken, metaphorically speaking. With Grandma's loving attention, the baby's debilitating diarrhea had begun to ease off, and little Laurie had seemed to come back to life.

"Look, Rebecca." She tiptoed to the sleeping baby. "See those cheeks? Roses in them. She's getting her pretty color back, widdle Waurie is, yes, her is." She seemed not to realize she'd lapsed into baby talk.

She came back and sat down beside me. "Stephanie stayed with her nearly around the clock, you know. She was the best mother anyone ever—" Ellen teared up for a second and glanced around the room, embarrassed.

"Look. She left her clothes here. I'll have to remember to take them home. The *best* mother . . . she and Gary were invited to a party that night. It was a horrible, rainy, rainy night, but poor Stephanie hadn't been anywhere but the hospital in weeks—"

"How long had you been here?"

"Oh, just a few days. I came for Hanukkah—and to help out if I

could. I knew Stephanie had to get out, so I offered to stay with
Laurie. I was just dying to have some time with the widdle fweet
fing, anyhow—" This last was spoken more or less in Laurie's direction. Ellen seemed to have developed a habit of talking to the child
while carrying on other conversations.

"What happened was Gary had quite a few drinks before he
brought me over. Oh, God, I never should have let him drive! We
nearly had a wreck on the way over—you know how stormy it was.
I kept telling him he was too drunk to drive, and he said I wanted
it that way, just like I always wanted him to have strep throat when
he was a kid. He said he felt fine then and he felt fine now."

I was getting lost. "You *wanted* him to have strep throat?"

She shrugged. "I don't know what he meant. He was just drunk,
that's all. Oh, God, my poor baby!" She sniffed, fumbled in her
purse, and blew her nose into a tissue.

"Did he seem okay that day—except for being drunk?"

"Fine. Why?"

"He called me that afternoon—about his will. And he called Michael to say he—well, I guess to say he had a premonition about his
death."

"His will? He called you about a will?"

"Yes."

"But he and Stephanie had already made their wills. Danny Goldstein drew them up." That made sense, as Gary had dated his ho-
lograph. Danny had been at Boalt with Gary and me. I wondered
briefly if it hurt Ellen to be reminded that all Gary's classmates had
gone on to become lawyers just like their parents would have wanted.

A fresh-faced nurse popped in and took a look at Laurie. "How's
our girl?"

"Like a different baby."

The nurse smiled. "She sure is. We were really worried for a while
there." But the smile faded almost instantly. "It's so sad. I never saw
a more devoted mother. Laurie never needed us at all—Stephanie
was her nurse. One of the best I ever saw."

"I didn't know Stephanie was a nurse." The last I'd heard she was
working part-time for a caterer, trying to make up her mind whether
to go to chef's school. Stephanie had a strong personality, but she
wasn't much more career-minded than Gary was. Motherhood, everyone seemed to think, had been her true calling.

"She didn't have any training—she was just good with infants.
You should have seen the way she'd sit and rock that child for hours,

Laurie having diarrhea so bad she hardly had any skin on her little butt, crying her little heart out. She must have been in agony like you and I couldn't imagine. But finally Stephanie would get her to sleep. Nobody else could."

"Nobody else could breast-feed her," I said, thinking surely I'd hit on the source of Stephanie's amazing talent.

"Stephanie couldn't, either. Didn't have enough milk." The nurse shrugged. "Anyone can give a bottle. It wasn't that."

When she left, I said, "I'd better go. Can I do anything for you?"

Ellen thought a minute. "You know what you could do? Will you be going by Gary's again?"

"I'd be glad to."

"You could take some of Stephanie's clothes and things. They're going to let Laurie out in a day or two and there's so much stuff here." She looked exasperated.

Glad to help, I gathered up clothes and began to fold them. Ellen found a canvas carryall of Stephanie's to pack them in. Zipping it open, I saw a bit of white powder in the bottom, and my stomach flopped over. I couldn't get the notion of drugs out of my mind. Gary had had a "premonition" of death, the kind you might get if you burned someone and they threatened you—and now I was looking at white powder.

I found some plastic bags in a drawer that had probably once been used to transport diapers or formula, and lined the bottom of the carryall with them, to keep the powder from sticking to Stephanie's clothes.

But instead of going to Gary's, I dropped in at my parents' house in San Rafael. It was about four o'clock and I had some phoning to do before five.

"Darling!" said Mom. "Isn't it awful about poor Gary Wilder?"

Mom had always liked Gary. She had a soft spot for ne'er-do-wells, as I knew only too well. She was the main reason Kruzick was currently ruining my life. The person for whom she hadn't a minute was the one I preferred most—the blue-eyed and dashing Mr. Rob Burns, star reporter for the San Francisco *Chronicle*.

Using the phone in my dad's study, Rob was the very person I rang up. His business was asking questions that were none of his business, and I had a few for him to ask.

Quickly explaining the will, the odd phone call to Michael, and the white powder, I had him hooked. He smelled the same rat I smelled, and more important, he smelled a story.

While he made his calls I phoned Danny Goldstein. "Becky baby."

"Don't call me that."

"Terrible about Gary, isn't it? Makes you *think*, man."

"Terrible about Stephanie too."

"I don't know. She pussy-whipped him."

"She was better than Melissa."

Danny laughed unkindly, brayed you could even say. Everyone knew Gary had left me for Melissa, who was twenty-two and a cutesy-wootsy doll-baby who couldn't be trusted to go to the store for a six-pack. Naturally everyone thought *I* had Gary pussy-whipped when the truth was, he wouldn't brush his teeth without asking my advice about it. He was a man desperate for a woman to run his life, and I was relieved to be rid of the job.

But still, Melissa had hurt my pride. I thought Gary's choosing her meant he'd grown up and no longer needed me. It was a short-lived maturity, however—within two years Stephanie had appeared on the scene. I might not see it exactly the way Danny did, but I had to admit that if he'd had any balls, she was the one to bust them.

"I hear motherhood mellowed her," I said.

"Yeah, she was born for it. Always worrying was the kid too hot, too cold, too hungry—one of those poo-poo moms."

"Huh?"

"You know. Does the kid want to go poo-poo? Did the kid already go poo-poo? Does it go poo-poo enough? Does it go poo-poo too much? Is it going poo-poo *right now*? She could discuss color and consistency through a whole dinner party, salmon mousse to kiwi tart."

I laughed. Who didn't know the type? "Say, listen, Danny," I said. "Did you know Laurie's been in the hospital?"

"Yeah. Marina, my wife, went to see Stephanie—tried to get her to go out and get some air while she took care of the baby, but Stephanie wouldn't budge."

"I hear you drew up Gary's and Stephanie's wills."

"Yeah. God, I never thought—poor little Laurie. They asked Gary's sister to be her guardian—he hated his brother and Stephanie was an only child."

"Guess what? Gary made another will just before he died, naming the brother as Laurie's guardian."

"I don't believe it."

"Believe it. I'll send you a copy."

"There's going to be a hell of a court fight."

I wasn't so sure about that. The court, of course, wouldn't be bound by either parent's nomination. Since Stephanie's will nominated Jeri as guardian, she and Michael might choose to fight it out, but given Michael's apparent hesitation to take Laurie, I wasn't sure there'd be any argument at all.

"Danny," I said, "you were seeing a lot of him, right?"

"Yeah. We played racquetball."

"Was he dealing coke? Or something else?"

"Gary? No way. You can't be a dealer and be as broke as he was."

The phone rang almost the minute I hung up. Rob had finished a round of calls to what he called "his law-enforcement sources." He'd learned that Gary's brakes hadn't been tampered with, handily blowing my murder theory.

Or seemingly blowing it. Something was still very wrong, and I wasn't giving up till I knew what the powder was. Mom asked me to dinner, but I headed back to the city—Rob had said he could get someone to run an analysis that night.

It was raining again by the time I'd dropped the stuff off, refused Rob's dinner invitation (that was two) and gone home to solitude and split pea soup that I make up in advance and keep in the freezer for nights like this. It was the second night after Gary's death; the first night I'd needed to reassure myself I was still alive. Now I needed to mourn. I didn't plan anything fancy like sackcloth and ashes, just a quiet night home with a book, free to let my mind wander and my eyes fill up from time to time.

But first I had a message from Michael Wilder. He wanted to talk. He felt awful calling me like this, but there was no one in his family he felt he could talk to. Couldn't we meet for coffee or something?

Sure we could—at my house. Not even for Gary's brother was I going out in the rain again.

After the soup I showered and changed into jeans. Michael arrived in wool slacks and a sport coat—not even in repose, apparently, did he drop the stuffy act. Maybe life with Laurie would loosen him up. I asked if he'd thought any more about being her guardian.

It flustered him. "Not really," he said, and didn't meet my eyes.

"I found out the original wills named Jeri as guardian. If Stephanie didn't make a last-minute one, too, hers will still be in effect. Meaning Jeri could fight you if you decide you want Laurie."

"I can't even imagine being a father," he said. "But Gary must have had a good reason—" he broke off. "Poor little kid. A week ago everyone thought *she* was the one who was going to die."

"What's wrong with her—besides diarrhea?" I realized I hadn't had the nerve to ask either of the grandmothers because I knew exactly what would happen—I'd get details that would give *me* symptoms, and two hours later, maybe three or four, I'd be backing toward the door, nodding, with a glazed look on my face, watching matriarchal jaws continue to work.

But Michael only grimaced. "That's all I know about—just life-threatening diarrhea."

*"Life-threatening?"*

"Without an IV, a dehydrated baby can die in fifteen minutes. Just ask my mother." He shrugged. "Anyway, the doctors talked about electrolyte abnormalities, whatever they may be, and did every test in the book. But the only thing they found was what they called 'high serum sodium levels.' " He shrugged again, as if to shake something off. "Don't ask—especially don't ask my mom or Stephanie's."

We both laughed. I realized Michael had good reasons for finding sudden parenthood a bit on the daunting side.

I got us some wine and when I came back, he'd turned deadly serious. "Rebecca, something weird happened today. Look what I found." He held out a paper signed by Gary and headed "Beneficiary Designation."

"Know what that is?"

I shook my head.

"I used to be in insurance—as did my little brother. It's the form you use to change your life insurance beneficiary."

The form was dated December 16, the day before Gary's death. Michael had been named beneficiary and Laurie contingent beneficiary. Michael said, "Pretty weird, huh?"

I nodded.

"I also found both Gary's and Stephanie's policies—each for half a million dollars and each naming the other as beneficiary, with Laurie as contingent. For some reason, Gary went to see his insurance agent the day before he died and changed his. What do you make of it?"

I didn't at all like what I made of it. "It goes with the will," I said. "He named you as Laurie's guardian, so he must have wanted to make sure you could afford to take care of her."

"I could afford it. For Christ's sake!"

"He must have wanted to compensate you." I stopped for a minute. "It might be his way of saying thanks."

"You're avoiding the subject, aren't you?"

I was. "You mean it would have made more sense to leave the money to Laurie directly."

"Yes. Unless he'd provided for her some other way."

"Stephanie had money."

"I don't think Gary knew how much, though."

I took a sip of wine and thought about it, or rather thought about ways to talk about it, because it was beginning to look very ugly. "You're saying you think," I said carefully, "that he knew she was going to inherit the half million from Stephanie's policy. Because she was going to die and he was the beneficiary, and he was going to die and his new will left his own property to Laurie."

Michael was blunt: "It looks like murder-suicide, doesn't it?"

I said, "Yeah," unable to say any more.

Michael took me over ground I'd already mentally covered: "He decided to do it in a hurry, probably because it was raining so hard—an accident in the rain would be much more plausible. He made the arrangements. Then he called me and muttered about a premonition, to give himself some sort of feeble motive for suddenly getting his affairs in order; he may have said the same thing to other people as well. Finally he pretended to be drunk, made a big show of almost having an accident on the way to the hospital, picked up Stephanie, and drove her over a cliff."

Still putting things together, I mumbled, "You couldn't really be sure you'd die going over just any cliff. You'd have to pick the right cliff, wouldn't you?" And then I said, "I wonder if the insurance company will figure it out."

"Oh, who cares! He probably expected they would but wanted to make the gesture. And he knew I didn't need the money. That's not the point. The point is why?" He stood up and ran his fingers through his hair, working off excess energy. "Why kill himself, Rebecca? And why take Stephanie with him?"

"I don't know," I said. But I hadn't a doubt that that was what he'd done. There was another why—why make Michael Laurie's guardian? Why not his sister as originally planned?

The next day was Saturday, and I would have dozed happily into mid-morning if Rob hadn't phoned at eight. "You know the sinister white powder?"

"Uh-huh."

"Baking soda."

"That's all?"

"That's it. No heroin, no cocaine, not even any baby talc. Baking soda. Period."

I thanked him and turned over, but the next couple of hours were full of vaguely disquieting dreams. I woke upset, feeling oddly tainted, as if I'd collaborated in Gary's crimes. It wasn't till I was in the shower—performing my purification ritual, if you believe in such things—that things came together in my conscious mind. The part of me that dreamed had probably known all along.

I called a doctor friend to find out if what I suspected made medical sense. It did. To a baby Laurie's age, baking soda would be a deadly poison. Simply add it to the formula and the excess sodium would cause her to develop severe, dehydrating diarrhea; it might ultimately lead to death. But she would be sick only as long as someone continued to doctor her formula. The poisoning was not cumulative; as soon as it stopped, she would begin to recover, and in only a few days she would be dramatically better.

In other words, he described Laurie's illness to a $T$. And Stephanie, the world's greatest mother, who was there around the clock, must have fed her—at any rate, would have had all the opportunity in the world to doctor her formula.

It didn't make sense. Well, part of it did. The part I could figure out was this: Gary saw Stephanie put baking soda in the formula, already knew about the high sodium reports, put two and two together, may or not have confronted her . . . no, definitely didn't confront her. Gary never confronted anyone.

He simply came to the conclusion that his wife was poisoning their child and decided to kill her, taking his own aimless life as well. That would account for the hurry—to stop the poisoning without having to confront Stephanie. If he accused her, he might be able to stop her, but things would instantly get far too messy for Gary-the-conflict-avoider. Worse, the thing could easily become a criminal case, and if Stephanie was convicted, Laurie would have to grow up knowing her mother had deliberately poisoned her. If she were acquitted, Laurie might always be in danger. I could follow his benighted reasoning perfectly.

But I couldn't, for all the garlic in Gilroy, imagine why Stephanie would want to kill Laurie. By all accounts, she was the most loving of mothers, would probably even have laid down her own life for her child's. I called a shrink friend, Elaine Alvarez.

"Of course she loved the child," Elaine explained. "Why shouldn't she? Laurie perfectly answered her needs." And then she told me some things that made me forget I'd been planning to consume a large breakfast in a few minutes. On the excuse of finally remembering to take Stephanie's clothes, I drove to Gary's house.

The family was planning a memorial service in a day or two for the dead couple; Jeri had just arrived at her dead brother's house; friends had dropped by to comfort the bereaved; yet there was almost a festive atmosphere in the house. Laurie had come home that morning.

Michael and I took a walk. "Bullshit!" he said. "Dog crap! No one could have taken better care of that baby than Stephanie. Christ, she martyred herself. She stayed up night after night—"

"Listen to yourself. Everything you're saying confirms what Elaine told me. The thing even has a name. It's called Munchausen Syndrome by Proxy. The original syndrome, plain old Munchausen, is when you hurt or mutilate yourself to get attention.

" 'By proxy' means you do it to your nearest and dearest. People say, 'Oh, that poor woman. God, what she's been through. Look how brave she is! Why, no one in the world could be a better mother.' And Mom gets off on it. There are recorded cases of it, Michael, at least one involving a mother and baby."

He was pale. "I think I'm going to throw up."

"Let's sit down a minute."

In fact, stuffy, uptight Michael ended up lying down in the dirt on the side of the road, nice flannel slacks and all, taking breaths till his color returned. And then, slowly, we walked back to the house.

Jeri was holding Laurie, her mother standing over her, Mary Cooper sitting close on the couch. "Oh, look what a baby-waby. What a darling girly-wirl. Do you feel the least bit hot? Laurie-baurie, you're not running a fever, are you?"

The kid had just gotten the thumbs-up from a hospital, and she was wrapped in half a dozen blankets. I doubted she was running a fever.

Ellen leaned over to feel the baby's face. "Ohhh, I think she might be. Give her to Grandma. Grandma knows how to fix babies, doesn't she, Laurie girl? Come to Grandma and Grandma will sponge you with alcohol, Grandma will."

She looked like a hawk coming in for a landing, ready to snare its prey and fly up again, but Mary was quicker still. Almost before you saw it happening, she had the baby away from Ellen and in her own lap. "What you need is some nice juice, don't you, Laurie-bear? And then Meemaw's going to rock you and rock you . . . oh, my goodness, you're burning up." Her voice was on the edge of panic. "Listen, Jeri, this baby's wheezing! We've got to get her breathing damp air. . . ."

She wasn't wheezing, she was gulping, probably in amazement. I felt my own jaw drop and, looking away, unwittingly caught the eye of Mary's husband, who hadn't wanted me to see the anguish there. Quickly he dropped a curtain of blandness. Beside me, I heard Michael whisper, "My God!"

I knew we were seeing something extreme. They were all excited to have Laurie home, and they were competing with each other, letting out what looked like their scariest sides if you knew what we did. But a Stephanie didn't come along every day. Laurie was in no further danger, I was sure of it. Still, I understood why Gary had had the sudden change of heart about her guardianship.

I turned to Michael. "Are you going to try to get her?"

He plucked at his sweater sleeve, staring at his wrist as if it had a treasure map on it. "I haven't decided."

An image from my fitful morning dreams came back to me: a giant in a forest, taller than all the trees and built like a mountain; a female giant with belly and breasts like boulders, dressed in white robes and carrying, draped across her outstretched arms, a dead man, head dangling on its flaccid neck.

In a few days Michael called. When he got home to Seattle, a letter had been waiting for him—a note, rather, from Gary, postmarked the day of his death. It didn't apologize, it didn't explain— it didn't even say, "Dear Michael." It was simply a quote from *Hamlet* typed on a piece of paper, not handwritten, Michael thought, because it could be construed as a confession and there was the insurance to think about.

This was the quote:

> Diseases desperate grown
> By desperate appliance are relieved,
> Or not at all.

I didn't ask Michael again whether he intended to take Laurie. At the moment, I was too furious with one passive male to trust myself to speak civilly with another. Instead, I simmered inwardly, thinking how like Gary it was to confess to murder with a quote from Shakespeare. Thinking that, as he typed it, he probably imagined grandly that nothing in his life would become him like the leaving of it. The schmuck.

*Poker-playing Shelley Singer's Jake Samson series includes* Free Draw, Full House, Spit in the Ocean, Samson's Deal, *and* Suicide King. *Jake, an apolitical anarchist, and Rosie Vicente, a self-employed carpenter who is his tenant and friend, work together in Oakland as unlicensed private investigators. The series, Shelley says ". . . is about Northern California, the mix of cultures and lifestyles, the land, the ocean, the cities. Jake looks at it all with wry humor and love."*

*In "A Terrible Thing," Shelley introduces Barrett Lake, a new private eye who needs every bit of her formidable perseverance, perspicacity, and personable charm to rise above the threats that someone hopes will scare her away.*

# A TERRIBLE THING

## by Shelley Singer

WHEN I WAS a little girl, I was a bookworm-tomboy who wanted to grow up to be an explorer, a knight errant, Robin Hood, a pirate. I was very unhappy when I found out that I couldn't be any of those people because, first of all, I was a girl, and second, those job descriptions were pretty much a thing of the past.

I settled for a degree in history and a career of teaching other children about the dead people I had wanted to be. Until the morning of my thirty-sixth birthday, when I woke up thinking I'd rather be dead, too, if that's all there was.

I got on my horse, so to speak, and went looking for a new career. Much to my amazement I found one. I'd been working at it for two months when Howard Barron called with a problem—something about a lost will and the retirement condo Howard managed.

"I called you because you're the only private eye that I know, Barrett," he said. Always a great flatterer, Howard.

"I'm not exactly a private investigator yet, Howard, but my boss is. Why don't I set up an appointment and the three of us can sit down and talk?"

"When?"

"Well, he's not here. He took one of those bus excursions to Tahoe. He won't be back until Tuesday—"

"No. Now. I want you to start work on it right away."

Howard, I recalled, had never been much good at delayed gratification.

I took his number and told him I'd call him right back. The truth was, I had never handled a case on my own and I needed help.

Luckily but not surprisingly, since it was only 10:30 and he would have been up very late the night before, my boss, Frank "Tito" Broz, had not yet left his motel room. He grunted hello and made me hold the line. Then he dropped the phone on the floor.

What I couldn't hear, I could imagine. Tito, in pajamas, hauling his ice-cube-shaped body out of bed, scratching his butt, stumbling across the room. A toilet flushng. Then he stumbled back and picked the phone off the carpeting.

He cleared his throat. "Okay."

I told him what I knew, which wasn't very much.

"Good," he said. "Handle it yourself. I got big plans for the weekend."

"Right," I retorted. "You're working on the Tahoe mystery—why you can't break even at the poker tables."

"Keep in touch, though, okay?" He hung up before I could tell him I was afraid I couldn't do it alone.

I tried not to feel panicky. I'd worked with Tito on cases. I was smart. I could take care of myself. If only it hadn't been Howard. A stranger would have been better. Howard and I had dated. I didn't like him. He was so sure of himself, and he had no reason to be.

Howard suggested we meet for lunch at a restaurant in Berkeley, not far from my office. A Thai restaurant where we had often gone when we were seeing each other.

"Nostalgia?" I asked as we sat down.

"You have a big ego, Barrett." He ran his fingers fetchingly through his yellow hair and looked distraught.

"Thank you, Howard." The waiter came. I ordered squid sautéed in garlic and oyster sauce, very hot. Howard made a face and ordered something mild with beef. I forget what.

"So," I began, "the will?" I took out my notebook and pen.

He nodded. "Yes. One of our people at the condo died, a couple of weeks ago. A man named George Lustig. I know he left a will. I know it because I saw it. Twice. Once, when he showed it to me. Once in his sock-and-underwear drawer when I was going through his dresser to put together clothing for the funeral. But two hours later—I forgot the socks and had to go back—it was gone."

"And why do you care?"

Lunch arrived. Howard's eyes skimmed over my plate. He closed them for a moment.

"I can't believe you eat that stuff."

"And why do you care?" I repeated.

"I care," he said, "because Upper Valley Spa was a beneficiary. He left a big bundle for an addition—exercise room, hot tub, swimming pool. So he'd be remembered, he said. It would have been great for the old folks, and my management company was pretty happy too."

"And you saw this provision?"

He nodded.

"Did you read the rest of the will?"

"He pointed out that paragraph and I read it."

"What about when you were going through his drawers?"

"I just scanned it to see if the provision was still there."

"And?"

"It was." He hesitated. "And I noticed he left a small amount of money to his girlfriend and nothing to his nephew."

"Girlfriend?" I scribbled some notes.

"She lives at Upper Valley too. She's in her seventies. Nice old thing."

Patronizing young jerk, I thought.

"And it just disappeared?"

He nodded again.

"Any signs of a break-in?"

He shook his head.

"So what happens without a will? Where's the money go?"

"As far as I know, the nephew is the only relative."

I finished the last of my squid. Howard, as usual, had vacuumed up his food in ten minutes.

"How did the man die?"

"Heart attack. Went to the hospital. Died the next day."

I thought for a moment. No signs of a break-in.

"Who had keys to his apartment?"

"I have keys to all the apartments. I don't know who he would have given keys to."

"The nephew? The woman friend?"

"I guess."

Well, I had something to start with. If I took it all step by step, did my legwork, used my head . . . the case might even turn out to be more interesting than it looked at first glance, more exciting. Even so, I didn't think I needed to bother stopping back at the office, on the way, for the gun Tito had insisted I buy.

Howard pulled his car around the back of the condo building and I followed in my aging RX-7, parking next to him.

"You can't leave your car there," he informed me when I slid out of the driver's seat. "That space belongs to someone. Find a spot on the street. I'll meet you around front." Just then a man came out the back door, greeted Howard, and glanced at me. I heard him say something about "checking to see everything was cleared out" as I put the car in gear.

I parked on a quiet side street and walked in through the gate in the six-foot redwood fencing, past a fountain with water splashing and dribbling down a metal sculpture. Howard was waiting at the door.

"That guy who talked to me out back?"

I nodded.

"That was the nephew."

"Lustig's nephew? Why in the name of—" I stopped. Howard was a client. This was a professional relationship. "It would have been good for me to meet him."

Howard shook his head. "I didn't want him to know I hired a detective."

"He's going to find out, Howard." I kept my tone even and polite.

We took the elevator to Lustig's apartment, on the third and top floor. It was open; there were drop cloths everywhere, a ladder in the middle of the living room, paint buckets and roller pans, rollers and brushes, and nothing else.

"Not much here to look at," I said.

"I had to get it ready for the next person, didn't I?"

Followed by Howard, I checked out the two bedrooms, the bath, the tiny kitchen. Empty. Not so much as a piece of junk mail, a comb, a can of tomato soup. Empty and swept clean. I pulled out the kitchen drawers. Nothing jammed down behind.

"When exactly was it you saw the will last?"

"The day before the funeral. May third, in the morning."

"When you were getting his clothes together, right?"

He nodded.

"Why you? Why were you doing that?"

"The nephew was out of town. A friend of the old guy, Charney his name is, he asked me if I'd take care of it. But I forgot socks. Had to go back again that afternoon. The will was gone."

I wrote it all down in my notebook. Logistics. Very important.

I searched for a while longer, checking out ceiling light fixtures, the toilet tank. I didn't expect anything and I didn't find anything. As Tito liked to say, "Just routine."

"Who cleaned the place out? And when?"

"The nephew asked us—management—to clear it out and put everything in storage until he could get to it. That was, oh, two or three days after the funeral. Something like that."

Long after the will was already gone, I thought.

"I'll need a list of his friends, where to reach his nephew."

Howard had that information, he said, in his office, so we trotted down the service stairs to the first floor, where he very carefully wrote it all out for me.

First on the list was Evelyn Miner, Lustig's love. I used Howard's desk phone to call her apartment. No answer. Next was Lustig's best friend and down-the-hall neighbor, Wallace Charney. He was at home and said he'd be delighted to talk to me.

I took the elevator up to the third floor in company with a woman in her seventies who moved with the help of a walker and who seemed to be escorting a woman in her nineties who walked all right but seemed confused. The younger woman smiled at me, a beautiful sunny smile that said she enjoyed seeing my relative youth. I decided she was a saint.

Charney was a short, round old man with almost no hair, just a few gray wisps over his ears and around the back. He bowed me into his apartment, two doors from Lustig's, sat me down on a French Provincial couch, and offered me coffee, or "perhaps a little wine?"

I declined.

"A real lady detective," he said, shaking his head. "My wife would have loved that. So, what do you want to know?"

"Were you aware that your friend George Lustig left a will?"

He sat down in a wing chair facing me across the coffee table. "No. No, he never mentioned it to me. But why would he? A man doesn't like to talk about such things. You make it, you stick it somewhere safe, you forget about it."

"Did you know he had a nephew?"

"Oh, sure, that I knew. His name is Andrew. A professional bowler. Lives in Concord."

I tried not to react to that information, but I must have failed. Charney smiled. "That's right, a bowler. An odd family, in some ways. I'm not surprised George's will got lost. Did he keep it under the mattress?"

"Close enough," I said. "You were Mr. Lustig's best friend?"

He nodded.

"But you asked Howard to pick out the clothes for the funeral. Why not you?"

"I was making funeral arrangements. Besides, to tell you the truth, the idea of pawing through his things made me feel bad."

"What about some of his other family? No children? No wife tucked away somewhere?"

"No one. He was a widower, like me. And there were never any children. Andrew was the only relative I ever heard him mention."

"What kind of terms was he on with his uncle?"

"You mean, did George like him? Well, what can I say? Sometimes family is family, sometimes it's just family."

"He didn't like him."

Charney shrugged, hesitated, and admitted it. "Not too much."

"So if he wrote a will, he might have left him out of it?"

Again, the shrug. "George could do that, sure." And had, and hadn't been careful with the will.

I had one more topic to broach with the gentle Mr. Charney. If he didn't like his friend's sweetheart, would he admit it?

"Mr. Lustig had a special friend, I hear. A woman."

He smiled broadly, happily. "Oh, yes. Evelyn. A wonderful woman. Wonderful. I spent many a pleasant evening with George and Evelyn." He shook his head. "Such a terrible thing." It took me a second to catch up and realize he was now talking about George's death and Evelyn's loss. And his.

"So he and Evelyn got along, were happy together?"

"Like a couple of kids sometimes. I remember once she surprised him with a five-course meal, not for anything, not a birthday, he just walked in and there it was. Like a couple of kids. He even bought her flowers sometimes. Everyone should have such a romance."

I thanked him and left wondering—Was he happy for his friend?

Was he wistful? Was he jealous? How wonderful did he think Evelyn was?

I took the stairs down to two and knocked on Evelyn Miner's door. No answer. Down to Howard's office, to use his phone to call Andrew Lustig's number. No answer. Howard said he needed to make a call. I walked to his window and looked out. A thorny pyracantha, trimmed to humility, pressed against the fence. Howard was talking to a plumber, arguing about a bill. For a bathtub. After a lot of whining, he hung up. I picked up the phone again and dialed Evelyn's number. She was home. She would see me right away. But she had only a few minutes—she had just gotten home from the store and she was due at her card club. A busy lady.

Evelyn Miner was plump, with sparkling young blue eyes behind bifocals. She was wearing platform sandals, a blue polyester pantsuit, and a white blouse with a big bow at the front. Her gray hair was puffed up a couple of inches on top. She moved quickly, with a slight limp, on short legs, leading me to the dinette set that filled the part of the L-shaped living room next to the small kitchen. A bag of groceries sat on the kitchen counter, half unpacked, items waiting to be put away. A box of soda crackers. A frozen dinner. Soup. Frozen orange juice. Tissues. But she didn't return instantly to her work. Instead, she went to a table in the living room, picked up a framed photo, and brought it to me.

"This is George, may he rest in peace. When a bunch of us took a bus to Reno." Just like Tito, I thought, only older and in a group.

I looked at the picture. There was Evelyn, festive in a red pantsuit, standing with an actorish man in a tan leisure suit. He had long gray hair, brushed back and up from his temples, an aquiline nose, thick gray eyebrows, and a bushy mustache. He was tall and thin, and held his arm around the short, tubular woman. They were standing at the entrance to a casino.

"He was a very handsome man," I said, meaning it.

She sighed and smiled. "So, tell me, Ms. Lake. What exactly is it you're looking for here? What do you want to know?"

She had gone to the kitchen, and was opening cupboards, opening and closing the refrigerator, putting away her groceries.

"I'm looking for his will."

"Ah. Who says there's a will?"

"Howard Barron. He says he saw it."

She folded the paper bag and placed it carefully under the sink, grunting a little and holding her right hip when she straightened up again.

"Don't ever get old." She limped out of the kitchen.

"I'd like to, I think."

She smiled ruefully and sat down. "Don't be so sure." She looked at my left hand. "Not married?" I shook my head. "Lake. What kind of a name is that, English?" She scrutinized my features. Although my hair is light brown, my olive skin, dark eyes, and long nose confuse the issue.

"It was du Lac about a hundred years ago. Anglicized then. I'm actually Ojibway, Norwegian, and French. I was named Barrett for a lake in Minnesota."

"That must be fun," she said firmly.

"Yes. Did Mr. Lustig ever mention a will to you?"

"He mentioned it. He said he was leaving me something. I never took it seriously. A man says things to a woman, you know."

"I know. Did he say what he was leaving you?"

"Some money, maybe. I'll tell you something, dear, it's no joke these days, on a fixed income. It's just terrible." She looked angry for a moment. Then, abruptly, "You've always been a lady detective?"

"No. I used to teach history. In high school. For thirteen years."

"A magic number." She looked at her watch, a tiny thing with a gold expansion band. "I should offer you something. You look like you don't eat enough. But I have to go soon."

"That's all right. Did you know George's nephew, Andrew?"

She shrugged. "I met him."

"Did you get any feeling for what kind of man he might be?"

"Just a man. Not too smart, not too dumb."

"I hear he and George didn't get along too well."

"You know how it is."

I waited. She realized I wanted to hear more.

"George thought he was kind of a . . . a little bit of a bum. That's all."

"Why?" It was clear she felt uncomfortable with this subject, but I persisted.

"Because he didn't have a real job, George said. Because he ran around to bowling tournaments."

"Isn't that how he made money?"

"I don't know. How should I know? Do I do his taxes? Listen, darling, I got to get going or they'll start the game without me."

I let her escort me to the door.

I went back down to Howard's office. He was dialing the phone and informed me that there was another one in the game room, just down the hall. I went looking, wondering if Howard really wanted me to solve the case.

I found the game room—it had its name on the door—and, inside, three men playing pool. Well, two playing, one kibitzing. They greeted me with friendly stares. I nodded and smiled; they nodded and smiled. Five ball in the side pocket, nice leave, seven in the corner, lousy leave. The telephone—a pay phone—was hanging on the wall over a green plastic-upholstered chair. I dialed Andrew Lustig's number again.

A woman answered, curious and chatty. She said he'd been in and out, had left again awhile ago, but she thought he wouldn't be gone long and could she take a message. I told her I'd call back in an hour.

I sat there for a few minutes, going over my skimpy notes, listening to the crack of ball on ball, the crowing and groaning of the elderly players. I glanced up once; one of them was strutting past me. He winked. I winked back.

I was getting nervous again, wishing I had Tito's experienced help. Oh, it seemed reasonable to work on the assumption that the nephew had done it, since he benefited from the loss of the will, but where was the proof? And how did I solve the problem the missing will presented for my client? I made myself think about Howard. Howard, I was sure, never doubted himself. Never questioned, never agonized, never felt the gnawing of the worm of self-doubt. I crushed my own worm, mercilessly, brutally, beneath the massive ego Howard thought I had.

Politely declining an invitation to play the winner, I said good-bye to the gentlemen and headed for my car. I would go back to the office and think about things while I tried to reach Andrew Lustig.

I was delayed.

The driver's side window of my RX-7 was smashed out, pieces of it lying all over the street. Carefully I looked inside. My beautiful car. There were splotches of red paint on every surface—on the insides of the windows, on the dashboard, on the doors. I opened the door. On the passenger seat was a single intact paint pellet, the kind used in those war games—they call them "survival" games, but who's kidding who?—that a lot of people seem to think are fun. I went to one on a first and last date once. All the trees on the five-acre private war zone were spotted with paint. I got killed five times that day. Those pellets hurt like hell. I was supposed to feel like a soldier, but what I felt like was pellet fodder. Quarry. I hated it. And that was how I felt now.

Red paint. And a note taped to my steering wheel that said, "Next time real blood." I didn't feel nervous anymore. Adrenaline had lifted me above petty tension. I was scared and I was angry. With nowhere else to put that energy at the moment, it was probably fortunate I had a physical chore to do. I went back to Howard's office and asked for a bucket, soap, and rags. Howard insisted on knowing why, so I told him. He didn't offer to help. I had a nasty thought. Howard getting even because I dumped him. Howard busily preparing a fake will for me to find. I dismissed the thought. He wasn't lovable, but I didn't think he'd bother committing a crime.

An hour's labor cleaned the car up enough to drive. It would take more than a quick wash to restore it, but car repairs were going to have to wait for a more convenient day.

Whoever did this, I hoped, was going to pay for the repairs with his fillings.

When I got to the office, the answering-machine light was on. I crossed the room and flicked the play button.

"Hiya, Barrett. What's up? How's the case of the purloined will going? Hah!" That smug bark of a laugh meant Tito was happy. "I won a hundred bucks at the hold-'em table. Here's my hotel number if you need anything." I didn't even write it down. I didn't need anything, and if I did I wouldn't call him. I would handle the case myself.

I sat down at my desk. I unlocked the middle drawer and pulled out the gun Tito had insisted I buy. The .38 I'd taken to the shooting range every day for weeks and had never taken anywhere else. I slid it out of its case and stuck it into the waistband of my pants, in back, under my jacket. Heavy and clumsy. Felt like it would pull my pants down. And it poked my back. I realized I didn't have the faintest idea of where to carry a gun. I rarely carry a purse. Tito carried his in his waistband or in a shoulder holster. I didn't have a holster. I stuck the gun in my jacket pocket. That worked okay.

I tried the nephew's number again. He wasn't home yet. I told his wife or whoever she was to have him call me at the office number.

Half an hour later Andrew Lustig called. He had a slow, sullen voice. I wanted to talk to him? What for? Oh, yeah? A will? A detective, huh? Sure, I could come out to Concord, he didn't care, but make it right now so I wouldn't interrupt their dinner.

The rush-hour traffic was just getting started, and a lot of commuters from San Francisco head home to Contra Costa county in late afternoon, but I managed to make it to Concord in forty-five minutes. Lustig's house, a tiny, pale green stucco fifties box, was on a narrow street lined with other boxes of the same generation and of slightly varying shapes and sizes, some stucco, some with aluminum siding. I rang the bell.

A woman answered the door. She was pretty the way cheerleaders are pretty: bouncy hair, bouncy walk, bouncy everything. But not overdone. Just bouncy enough. She should have had some gray in her hair, because she was close to forty, but she didn't and her hair looked tinted. There were a few wrinkles that I guessed got creamed every night. She looked like she should be growing rounder with age but had managed to keep her figure by fighting herself every inch of the way. She had blue eyes and white teeth and a smile that wasn't real, and even while she chirped at me her eyes looked sad and bewildered.

"Ms. Lake?"

I nodded.

"My husband is expecting you. He'll be out in a minute." She led me into a small, dull living room with beige carpeting and pastel furniture and cheap ornate lamps. A three-tiered table in the corner held half a dozen bowling trophies. I could smell dinner in the kitchen. Pot roast?

We both sat down, waiting. I glanced toward the trophies.

"Your husband is quite an athlete, isn't he?"

She smiled uncertainly.

"I hear he's a real expert in those—what are they called—survival games too. I've always wanted to try that."

"Oh, well, he hasn't been to one in a year or so. But I'm sure he can tell you all about it." Bingo, I thought.

He came into the room. The same wiry, middle-sized man I'd seen at the back entrance of Upper Valley earlier that afternoon. Thinning hair and suspicious eyes. Good-looking in a sleazy way. He sat on the couch beside me. He looked at his wife.

"You don't have to bother with this, honey."

"Oh, that's all right, Andy. Everything's under control in the kitchen." I thought she knew what message she was supposed to be getting, but was pretending she didn't.

He shrugged and smiled, but he didn't look happy. "What can I do for you, Ms. Lake?"

"You can tell me where you were at around three this afternoon."

He looked me straight in the eye. "Around three? Let's see. Running an errand. Got some gas in the car."

"Where?"

"I don't remember." I glanced at his wife. She was listening tensely.

Lustig went on the offensive. "So, Miss Detective, you say you're looking for some will my uncle wrote. Where'd you get the idea there was a will? I sure never heard about one." He said it blandly, the way liars do.

His wife lurched to her feet. "Would you like some coffee?" I shook my head. She escaped anyway. She'd lost her courage.

"That your RX-7 out at the curb?" He was smiling slightly. I didn't answer. "Looks like something bad happened to it. I'm surprised you'd drive it in that condition. I'm surprised you came out to see me."

I pressed my elbow against the gun in my pocket. "What made you think I'd get scared?"

First he glanced at my breasts, then he gazed at me as though he had no idea what I was talking about. I gazed back, trying to look a whole lot cooler than I felt.

"I hear you were out of town when your uncle died."

He shrugged, tsk-ed. "You know, I feel really bad about that. I'm just glad I was able to fly back in time for his funeral. See, the thing was, he died during a big tournament I was in down in Palm Springs. I don't know what I would have done without that friend of his, that Charney? He helped my wife make all the arrangements."

"So you flew in for the funeral—the day before, I suppose?"

"No. Same day." He grinned at me.

"You flew in the morning of the funeral?" He couldn't have. I didn't want it to be true.

"Yeah." He grinned again. "I'll show you the ticket if you want. In fact, I can show you something else." He strolled over to the three-tiered table and picked up a tiny trophy, about six inches high. He handed it to me. He had won fourth place in the tournament, on May 3, the day before the funeral. The day the will had been stolen.

"This was presented that night. The third. At the awards dinner."

"I'd like to see your airline ticket."

He shrugged, left the room, came back with the ticket.

"Where were you staying down there?"

He gave me the name of a motel.

"Where was the award ceremony?"

"Same place." Still grinning.

"One more thing, Mr. Lustig."

"I hope it's just one more. Dinner's ready."

"You do this for a living, isn't that so?"

He looked defensive. "Yes, I do."

"What do you make when you come in fourth?"

I'd finally made him stop smiling. "I don't think that's any of your business."

I thanked him insincerely for his help and drove back to Berkeley.

There were a couple of messages on the office machine for Tito. I made notes of the names and numbers. He'd get back to them when he lost his hundred and came home. Then I made some calls of my own. After a couple of hours I had an intact alibi for Andrew Lustig. He had definitely been in Palm Springs on the day the will had disappeared. He had bowled all that day—and every day—in the tournament, and he had been at the awards dinner.

I decided on one more foray into Upper Valley.

Wallace Charney ushered me into his apartment politely, offering me a glass of wine. This time I accepted. The adrenaline rush was long gone. I was feeling tired, in need of another boost.

"George gave me this," he said, picking up a bottle of Manischewitz and pouring. "We'll drink in his honor."

I did my best. The heavy, sweet wine stuck a bit going down, but I thought it might unstick my mind.

"Howard tells me you had some trouble today? Your car?" I said yes, that was so. "Terrible. Such a world. Who would do such a thing?"

"Probably the man who stole the will," I said.

"A shame." He sighed.

"Wallace, do you think George would have given his nephew Andrew a key to his place for any reason?"

"Oh, I don't think so. No."

"Did you have a key?"

"Why, yes, I have one here somewhere. Do you want it?"

"No. Tell me this. Did Andrew's wife ever go in George's apartment during the time you were making funeral arrangements?"

"As far as I know, she never even came over here. We talked on the phone. Why are you asking?"

I didn't answer him. I wasn't hearing anything I wanted to hear. "Did Evelyn have a key?"

"Oh, I wouldn't know about that." He was blushing. If he did know, he would never tell. Not the gentlemanly thing to do.

"The night she surprised him with dinner—remember, you told me about that? You said he 'walked in'—you meant into his own apartment, didn't you? Right here, on this floor? Didn't he walk into his own apartment and find dinner ready?"

"What can I say?"

"You said Andrew asked you to help. Did his wife call you, or did he call you from Palm Springs?"

"He did."

I thanked him and took the elevator down to Howard's office. Locked and dark. I went to the game room. One old man wearing bottle-bottom-thick glasses was playing pool. An equally old woman sat near the pool table, watching. Two other men were playing checkers. The chair under the phone was free. Once more I dialed the number of the Palm Springs motel. This time I identified myself as Mrs. Andrew Lustig. A matter of tax records, I said. The phone charges on the motel bill. There were, I thought, several calls made to two numbers at the same exchange. I had one of the numbers— I gave him Wallace Charney's—but the other one, well, my husband had spilled coffee on it, so I needed to be sure.

Obligingly the clerk found what I was looking for. There had, indeed, been calls to another number at the same exchange. He read the number for me. Three calls, he said. One long call on the evening of May 2. Two shorter ones on May 3.

Evelyn was at home, watching television.

She clutched my arm very tightly. "Are you all right? I heard what happened to your car. I'm so sorry."

"I'm fine."

"Good. Good." She wasn't looking at me. "What can I say? Terrible."

"It's okay, Evelyn. But why don't you tell me how Andrew convinced you to steal the will for him." She limped over to an easy chair, sat down heavily, looked at the TV screen, turned down the sound. "I know he called you from Palm Springs," I persisted, "the night before you took it. I suppose he offered you money?"

She pulled a wadded tissue out of her overblouse pocket and blew her nose.

"I'm sorry about your car. He was here earlier today, talking to me so nice, telling me it was all going to be wonderful, I should just hang on. So when you came to see me, I thought I should call him, let him know about you. I feel so bad." She wiped her eyes.

I was feeling pretty bad, too, but I was also feeling like one great detective.

"How did he convince you to steal the will?"

"He said he'd give me twenty thousand more than George left me. Just for walking in, taking the will, and throwing it away. What could I say? Was it such a terrible thing to do, letting the nephew get the money? And I can't live these days. To buy food, clothing— A woman has to provide for herself." She began to cry harder.

I walked over and put my arm around her. "It's all right, Evelyn." It wasn't all right. Not a bit. "So you destroyed the will?"

"No. I kept it."

"You kept it? Really?"

"Of course! What do you think? I wanted something to remember him by. Also, how could I know that Andrew was going to give me the money just because he said so? Maybe I'd still need the will. And let me tell you, when I found out he broke your car—well, I'm glad I didn't trust him. A son of a bitch who'd do such a thing."

"That was very good planning."

"Here. I'll get it for you." She had stopped crying. She got up and went into the bedroom. I heard a drawer open and close. She brought the will back and handed it to me.

"Will I have to go to jail, Barrett?"

I doubted that, but even so, she could be in for some real problems. I was pretty sure Howard would press charges. I didn't know what to say. I couldn't let Andrew Lustig get away with it, the will, the smug grin—my car! I had done a great job. Damn. I'd been so clever. Damn. Evelyn was watching my face, watching me wage war with myself. Arrows. Battering rams. Boiling oil over the parapets. I was cooked. The war ended. I would tell Tito; that would help.

"For finding the will in your apartment? Where George left it? I don't see why, Evelyn."

*Sandra Scoppettone has been nominated for an Edgar for her young adult novel,* Playing Murder. *An astute observer of the urban scene and of the currents that lie beneath the surface of human interactions, she has written three crime novels for adults:* Some Unknown Person, Such Nice People, *and* Innocent Bystanders. *Her incisive renderings of people and the passions that move them have earned her an Edgar nomination for Best First Novel for a mystery she wrote using a pseudonym; she has written two other novels under the same name.*

*"He Loved Her So Much" could well be a story from today's headlines; tension mounts as subtle but inevitable changes, little by little, affect a relationship and move events toward their shattering conclusion.*

# HE LOVED HER SO MUCH

## by Sandra Scoppettone

WHEN KAREN BRADLEY said yes to Jeff Hark's invitation, he couldn't believe it. The first semester at the university he hadn't even been able to look her way as she passed him on campus, and it was deep into the second semester before he'd screwed up enough courage to sit across from her in the library.

Karen was blond and wore her hair loose and wavy. She had eyes the color of his favorite faded work shirt, and her mouth made him think about mangos and kiwi fruit. But he was sure she was out of his reach, unattainable. And then she smiled at him.

Karen Bradley never noticed Jeff Hark before the day he sat across from her in the library. She thought he was cute and particularly liked the way his dusky hair slooped down over his forehead and covered one of his brown eyes. She smiled at him and he smiled back, not trying to act cool or anything, and she liked that. Most guys tried to be so cool, they just seemed sappy to her. The book he had in front of him was on anthropology. She was reading about Henry James.

"Hi," he said softly.

"Hi."

"Henry James, huh?"

"Yeah." She said it as noncommittally as possible because, for all she knew, this guy loved James. Or maybe hated him. "You're into anthropology?"

"Yeah."

She couldn't tell if he liked it or not, so she nodded.

They looked at each other and Karen felt nervous. She didn't know who he was or what crowd he hung around with. Not that it made much difference. Unlike her parents, she didn't judge people by those kinds of standards. And the truth was, she felt surprisingly attracted to him. There were lots of guys she went out with, but none of them was very important or meaningful to her.

They told each other their names, and when he asked her if she'd like to go to dinner and a movie on Friday night, she said yes. She would break the date she already had.

The first date was nearly a total disaster. Jeff couldn't believe he was actually out with Karen. It was almost more unreal to be with her than to have her in his thoughts. He was clumsy and kept bumping into her as they walked through the campus to the bus stop. And he wasn't good at making small talk. But she was, thank Christ. Even so, he found himself giving her monosyllabic answers, worried he'd say the wrong thing, something that might turn her off.

At dinner he couldn't eat. That appeared to bother her. She kept asking him why he wasn't eating, and the only answer he could come up with was that he felt a bit sick. And that turned out to be the dumbest thing he could've said, because she suggested they call it a night. Fearful of losing her, he forced himself to eat half of his pasta. Karen ate the rest and he marveled at her appetite as she was so slim. It also made him wonder about her feelings for him. How could she eat if she dug him the way he dug her?

Although he hated them, after dinner he suggested a French film thinking it was the kind of movie she'd like. But she said she despised foreign films. He felt like an asshole.

Then Karen said, "We could see the new Spielberg movie."

He hated Spielberg's films but agreed enthusiastically.

"How about going for a drink," he asked when they came out of the theater.

"Neat," she said.

"The Hobbit?" he asked.

She wrinkled her nose in distaste. "I go there a lot. How about Danzinger's?"

Danzinger's was a little more exclusive than the Hobbit, and Jeff prayed he had enough money. Also, he couldn't help wondering if she'd nixed the Hobbit because she didn't want to be seen with him.

By the time they got to the bar, he was feeling like shit.

By the time they got to the bar Karen was feeling like shit. She was sure he didn't like her. It had been dumb to say no to the French film. Ditto the Hobbit. But if they'd gone there, everybody she knew would have joined them, and she wanted to be alone with Jeff, get to know him.

Danzinger's was fairly crowded but they got a table for two in the back. Even though Jeff was the shiest guy she'd ever gone out with, the evening turned around when they both ordered Coors beers at the same time. It was then that she discovered how much they had in common.

When he took her back to her apartment, he didn't even try to kiss her good night. At first she felt lousy about it, believing he didn't like her at all, but when he called the next day, asking to see her that night, she realized his behavior had been a compliment. Jeff was the only guy she'd ever known who didn't try to hit on her on the first date.

They saw each other every night for a week before they slept together. It wasn't that Jeff didn't want to before that, but he was scared. In the past, with the two other women he'd been with, sex hadn't gone well. And Karen meant so much to him that he wanted it to be perfect. When they finally got to it, it wasn't awful but it wasn't good.

"Don't worry about it," Karen said. "We have to get to know each other."

She calmed him down, made him feel better, but later he wondered just how many guys she'd been with before. How did she know it was not so hot because they had to get to know each other? Thinking about her with other guys made him angry, and for a moment, he imagined himself twisting her arm, forcing her to tell him who they were. Then the fantasy vanished as quickly as it had appeared.

Karen had been right. Sex did get better. And better. For the first time Jeff felt manly. And adored. He couldn't believe that someone like Karen really cared for him. Even though he knew it bugged her, he asked her a lot if she really loved him. She said she did. Still, it was hard to believe, and even harder to believe things were going so great. Then at Easter she took him home to meet her parents and as they pulled up in front of the big Colonial house, he started to feel like shit.

Karen knew it wasn't going to be easy. Jeff wasn't exactly her father's idea of the perfect boy for her to date. And her mother wasn't going to be overjoyed either. But, hell, it was her life, and she thought it was time they met him. She knew Jeff was going to be very important in her life.

Her parents were polite to Jeff, as Karen knew they would be. Then, while Jeff was taking a walk, her father called her into his study and started grilling her about Jeff.

Finally Karen said, "Look, Dad, he's very shy. It takes a while to get to know him and see how neat he is."

Larry Bradley, who was a large and imposing man with a perennial tan, said, "He's not right for you, Karen."

"Why not? How can you say that when you don't even know Jeff?"

"I know him," he insisted.

"What's that supposed to mean?"

"It means he's a hustler. I know his type. I've seen hundreds of Jeff Harks in my life, believe me. He knows a good thing when he sees one."

"For your information, Dad, Jeff didn't know a damn thing about me when we met. Like if you're talking about money, Jeff couldn't care less about money. He's going to school on a full scholarship, you know."

"Why?"

"Because he's so smart."

"And because his family doesn't have a pot to piss in, right?" Karen felt furious. "So what? Is that a crime?"

"No. But if he comes from a poor family, believe me, Karen, money means plenty to him."

"I think your attitude is disgusting," Karen said.

"Maybe so. But I don't like what I see. I know I can't control you; you're grown and living away from home. Still, I'm telling you that this bozo isn't for you. He gives me the creeps."

Karen was taking psychology as a minor and was sure that her father was feeling threatened because he could see that Jeff meant more to her than any other guy she'd ever brought home. She thought about telling him this but knew he wouldn't understand. Instead she said, "I love Jeff."

Larry closed his eyes for a second, as if he'd been punched. "There's nothing I can do about that, but please don't ever bring him here again."

"I can't believe this," she said. "I can't believe what you're saying to me."

Her father said nothing, just looked at her with his cold blue eyes. Karen slammed out of the study.

Jeff didn't know how to tell Karen that he never wanted to go to her parents' house again, but it didn't come up before the semester ended.

He thought he would die being away from her for three months. There was no way he was going to her place, and definitely no way he was inviting her to his home. His parents were divorced and his mother lived with a man Jeff hated.

Anyway, Jeff had to work in a gas station all summer, so he tried to content himself with letters and occasional phone calls. But they didn't help, and often made things worse. Most of the calls ended with one or the other of them hanging up, furious. He accused her of seeing other guys. She swore she wasn't, but he found it hard to believe. After these fights she always called him back, and for a while he was soothed. Then the doubts would creep back, and he'd make another call to her, starting the whole thing over again.

When school began in the fall, he saw right away that he'd been stupid. She loved him more than she ever had.

As the months flew by, Karen felt closer to Jeff than she'd ever felt to another person. Her parents' attitude toward him hadn't changed, so she didn't go home for Thanksgiving and only stayed home for three days over the Christmas holiday, choosing to come back to school to be with Jeff, who hadn't bothered to go home at all.

In January he moved into her apartment. Karen continued paying because, although Jeff worked two jobs, he couldn't afford to contribute. He said he felt lousy about the arrangement, but she assured him it was fine. Secretly Karen enjoyed the idea of her father unknowingly supporting Jeff.

When she told Jeff she was going home for the Easter holiday, he became livid. He accused her of wanting to see some other guy, calling her horrendous names. And he slapped her.

On the plane ride home she reviewed what had happened. Of course, he'd been remorseful and had begged her forgiveness, promising never to hit her again. Still, something nagged at her. But when she got home and saw her father's stern face, her mother's long-suffering one, and they grilled her again about Jeff, she buried her doubts about him and extolled his good points, refusing to give him up. And when her father threatened to cut her off, she retaliated with a threat of her own: She'd marry Jeff if they didn't stop harassing her.

The second summer apart was much harder for Jeff than the first one. Karen was touring Europe with her best friend. The letters were fewer and took longer to arrive, and the rare phone calls were even more unsatisfying than they'd been the year before. This time, if they fought and he hung up on her, she didn't call back.

When they returned for their junior year, Jeff was convinced Karen had met someone else, and nothing she said could reassure him. It wasn't until the beginning of November that he felt good about things again. But when she said she was going home for Thanksgiving, he had a fit.

"You didn't go last year. What the hell's this about?"

"My father's insisting, Jeff. I mean, he *is* paying my bills, you know. Sometimes I have to do what he says."

"Like a whore," he accused, and saw the hurt in her eyes. Still, he couldn't stop, and continued badgering her even while he felt she was slipping away from him. And then he started again on the summer before, insisting she'd had an affair.

Finally she broke down and admitted that she had met someone, that they'd gone out a few times, but nothing had happened because she loved Jeff and wasn't about to cheat on him. He slapped her twice, knocking her to the ground.

Of course he'd apologized as they stood at the airport, waiting for the plane that would take her home for Thanksgiving. She said it would be all right, but he knew it would never be the same. How would he ever believe her now? He should break off with her. She was untrustworthy, just as he'd always thought. But he loved her so much. They would have to have some serious discussions when she got back.

Between Thanksgiving and Christmas, Karen tried many times to tell Jeff it was over. But she couldn't go through with it, because if she even hinted that something was wrong, he'd either become so angry she felt frightened or he'd cry, touching her in a way that made her feel he'd die without her. Still, she was anxious to go home again for the holidays, anxious to get away from him.

During Christmas vacation they had their usual, awful phone calls, and finally Karen decided that, cowardly as it was, she would tell him on the phone.

"Jeff, I need to tell you something," she said the day before New Year's Eve.

"I don't see why you can't come back so we can be together tomorrow night," he said, not hearing her.

She tried again. "I want to tell you something, Jeff. It's over."

"What is?"

"Us."

There was a long silence.

"Did you hear me, Jeff?"

"Who is he? Is it the guy you met last summer?"

"There's nobody," she answered truthfully.

"Then why?"

"Because I just can't take it anymore. Your possessiveness and jealousy."

"Don't give me that shit, Karen. I know there's someone else."

"No," she said simply. "It's you."

"You said you loved me," he yelled into the phone.

Holding the receiver away from her ear, she was glad she wasn't in the same room with him.

Again she said, "I did love you, but I don't anymore."

He swore at her, and when he stopped, she told him that she would expect him to move out of the apartment by the time she returned to school.

For the rest of the vacation he phoned three or four times a day until Karen had her father answer. He made it clear that if Jeff called again, he would have the police intervene.

Jeff didn't call again, but Karen knew there was no way he wouldn't confront her when she got back. Still, she was shocked when she returned to the apartment to find that he was waiting for her and hadn't moved out any of his belongings.

"What the hell is this, Jeff? I told you to move."

"I'm not going anywhere until you tell me the truth," he said, and walked toward her, his hands in fists at his sides.

Karen felt incredibly frightened and turned to leave. He caught her by the sleeve of her jacket.

He'd never been so angry. He pulled her around so that his back was to the door, blocking her exit. Everything inside him was shaking. Jeff couldn't believe this bitch was really going to dump him. He hadn't taken her seriously when she'd told him to move out. And then when her father threatened him, he figured that Karen was forced to say things she didn't mean. Now he knew for sure that she was seeing someone else.

"Who is he?" he asked once more.

"Oh, Christ, don't start that shit again," she said.

"Tell me who he is, Karen."

"There's nobody, Jeff. I just don't want to be with you anymore. I told you, I don't love you."

He heard the words, and suddenly he believed them. It was over. They'd been together eighteen months, meant everything to each other, and now, just like that, she didn't love him. The room turned many colors, as if he were on acid. A rage came up from his toes, filling his gut, bursting through the top of his head.

And then he saw her, eyes bulging, face a shade of blue. His hands were around her throat, his thumbs pressed deep into her pink flesh. She was limp. Gently he laid her down on the floor.

Standing over her, looking down, he couldn't believe that she was dead. But it wasn't his fault. Still, how was he going to describe what had transpired? Who could comprehend what he'd done? If only she hadn't smiled at him that day in the library. She was all he'd ever had and she'd wanted to leave him. So maybe when he told them, maybe when he explained that he loved her so much he had to kill her, maybe they'd understand, after all.

*Gillian Roberts introduced Amanda Pepper in* Caught Dead in Philadelphia, *which won an Anthony for Best First Mystery of 1987, and
followed up with* Philly Stakes. *Amanda teaches at a small private
high school and has an on-again, off-again relationship with C. K.
Mackenzie, a Philadelphia policeman. Gillian Roberts is a psue-
donym for Judith Greber, whose* Easy Answers, Silent Partners, *and*
Medocino *reflect her concern for how ordinary people deal with in-
timacy, the challenges of life, and contradictions.*

*In "Hog Heaven," an aging Romeo can hardly believe his luck
when a beautiful woman approaches him. As Gillian explains it: "I
heard about the event that resulted in "Hog Heaven" twenty-five years
ago—and it's still a pleasure to fantasize revenge, after all these years."*

# HOG HEAVEN

## by Gillian Roberts

HARRY TOWERS WALKED out of his office building and blinked
in the late-afternoon light. The sea of homebound bodies
divided around him as he deliberated how, and with whom,
to fill the hours ahead.

The redheaded receptionist had other plans. Lucy, his usual
standby, had run off to Vegas with a greeting-card salesman. Char-
lene was back with her husband, at least for tonight. Might as well
check out Duffy's.

He stood a little straighter, smoothed his hair over his bald spot,
and sucked in his stomach. Duffy's was a giant corral into which the
whole herd of thirty-plus panic-stricken single women stampeded at
nightfall. Duffy's Desperates, he called them. Not prime stock, but
all the same, the roundup saved time.

He walked briskly. Everything would be fine. He didn't need that
stupid redheaded receptionist.

"Harry? Harry Towers?"

The sidewalks were still crowded, but Harry spotted the owner of the melodic voice so easily, it was as if nobody but the two of them were on the streets.

He had seen her a few times before, recently, right around this time of day. She was the blonde, voluptuous kind you had to notice. A glossy sort of woman, somebody you see in magazines or on TV. Not all that young, not a baby, but not a bimbo. And definitely not a Duffy's Desperate.

She repeated his name and continued moving resolutely toward him. He tried not to gape.

"You *are* Harry Towers, aren't you?" A small, worried frown marred her perfect face.

He smiled and nodded, straightening up to his full height. He was a tall man, but her turquoise eyes were on a level with his.

"I thought so!" Her face relaxed into a wide smile. "Remember me?" Her voice was so creamy, he wanted to lick it.

"I . . . well—" In his forty-five years, he had never before laid eyes on this woman, except for the sidewalk glimpses this week. Harry did not pay a whole lot of the remembering kind of attention to most women, but this was not most women. This one you'd remember even if you had Alzheimer's.

She was using the old don't-I-know-you-from-somewhere? line, and it amused him. She'd even gone to the trouble to find out his name. Flattering, to say the least.

"Does the name Leigh Endicott sound familiar?" she prompted.

"Oh!" he said emphatically, nodding, playing the game. "Leigh . . . Endicott. Sure . . . now I—well, it must be—"

"Years," she said with one of those woeful smiles women give when they talk about time. "Even though it seems like yesterday." She shook her head, as if to clear away the time in between. "I've thought about you so often, wondered what became of you." She put her hand on his sleeve, tenderly.

If only the redhead hadn't left the building before him—if only she could see him now!

"I always hoped I'd find you again someday," she purred.

She was overdoing it. Should he tell her to skip the old-friend business? They didn't need a make-believe history. He decided to keep quiet, not rock the boat, follow her lead. "Why don't we find someplace comfortable?" he said. "To, uh, reminisce?"

She glanced at her watch, then shrugged and smiled at him, nodding.

"There's a place around the corner," he said. "Duffy's." The Desperates would shrivel up and turn to dust when they saw this one. Then they'd know, all those self-important spritzer drinkers, that Harry Towers still had it. All of it.

They started walking, her arm linked through his. Suddenly she stopped short. "I just had a wonderful idea. I have a dear little farmhouse in the country. Very peaceful and private. Would you mind skipping the bar? I'm sure it's too noisy and crowded for a really good . . . talk. My car's over there. I can drive you back later— if you feel like leaving."

What a woman! Right to the point! He hated the preliminaries, the song-and-dance routine, anyway. He followed her to the parking lot, grinning.

*I am in hog heaven*, he thought. *Hog heaven*.

The ride was a timeless blur. Harry was awash, drowning in the mixed perfumes of the car's leather, the spring evening, the woman beside him, and the anticipation of the hours ahead. When Leigh spoke, her voice, rich and sensuous, floated around him. He had to force himself to listen to the words instead of letting them tickle his pores and ruffle his hair.

"Almost there, Harry," she was saying. "Don't you love this area? Open country. Free. Natural. I love the farmhouses, the space . . ."

Almost there. Free. Natural. Wonderful words.

Leigh, eyes still on the road, voice talking about the wonders of the countryside, placed a manicured hand on his thigh.

God? he said silently, needing the Deity for the first time in years. God, let this really be happening.

After dinner she sent Harry into the living room. "Make yourself comfortable," she insisted, "while I clean up. I'll bring in coffee." No number about sharing the work. He couldn't believe his luck.

The tape stopped, and he picked out a mellow one. Make-out music, they called it a century or two ago when he was young. Why did that seem so funny? He stifled a giggle. He turned the volume to a soft, inviting level, then settled into the rich velvet sofa. He felt a little weird. Almost like a teenager again, that racing high, that thrumming excitement.

What a woman! He couldn't believe his luck. He stretched and enjoyed the memory of the meal. Her own recipe, her own invention. Spicy, delicious, exotic. Like Leigh herself, like the charged talk that had hovered around the table, like the possibilities of a long night in the remote countryside.

"Here you are," she announced, carrying a tray with a coffeepot, creamer, sugar bowl, and cups. She bent close and his giddy light-headedness, the speeding double-time rush of blood through his veins, intensified.

She poured the coffee, then stepped back and spread her arms as if to embrace the room. "Do you like my place?" she asked. "The people at work think I'm crazy to be this isolated, this far from everything. But I love my privacy. Or maybe I like animals better than people." She laughed. "Present company excluded, of course."

Bubbles of excitement popped in Harry's veins. "Have a seat," he suggested, patting the sofa next to him. He wiggled his lips. They felt thick, a little foreign and tingly. Stupid to have eaten so much. And all that wine, too. Now he was bloated, sluggish.

Leigh, on the other hand, seemed wired. "This is a working farm," she said. "Cows, pigs, horses. There's a caretaker, of course." She stopped her pacing. "But don't worry—he won't bother us. He's all the way on the other side of the property, and anyway, he's away for the night."

"Leigh—" he began. He sounded whiny and stopped himself. But all the same, why couldn't they start enjoying this nice private place before her stupid roosters crowed? He was reminded of his teens, of dates with nervous girls chattering furiously to keep his attention— and hands—off their bodies. It had annoyed him even then. He decided to see if actions would speak louder than words, and smacked at the sofa's velvet.

It worked. She finally sat down. But just out of easy reach.

He considered strategy. He felt planted in the soft cushions. He took a moment to evaluate the pros and cons of uprooting himself.

"Do you know which is the most intelligent barnyard animal?" she asked.

Who cared? Frankly, even a brainless chicken was beginning to seem brighter than this woman. Didn't she remember why they were here?

She refilled his coffee cup. He sipped at it while he tried to figure a way to change the subject.

"Pigs," she said. "It's almost a curse on them, being that smart. They know when they're going to slaughter. They scream and fight and try to prevent their own destruction."

Harry finished the coffee. There was no subtle way to stop her, so he'd be direct. "I don't care about pigs," he said emphatically. "I care about you. Come closer."

"I'm fond of pigs." She stayed in place. "Don't you care about what I care about? About who I am?"

"Of course! I didn't mean to . . ." Damn. She was one of those. He hadn't expected it, from the way she'd come on to him, but she was one more of them who needed to discuss their innermost feelings first, get to know the man, make things serious and important.

"Let's take things slowly," she said. "I've waited years and years to be with you again."

"Ah, c'mon," he said. "We're adults. Don't pretend anymore. I like you, you like me. Tha's enough. Don't need games."

She refilled his cup, then held it out to him.

He stared at her hands, confused.

"Games can be fun, Harry," she murmured. "And so can the prizes at the end." She put his cup in his hands.

It required a great deal of effort to bring it to his lips.

"You still haven't answered the first question, you know," she said with a small smile.

He shook his head. He had no idea what she was talking about. "I really don't like games," he said. The whole idea made him tired.

"Yes you do." Her voice was a croon, a lullaby. "Sure you do. I know that about you. You just like the game to be yours, the old familiar one. But this one is new. This is mine, and it's called 'Do You Remember Me?' "

She was all smiles and burbles, but he felt suddenly chilled.

"Oh, you look puzzled," she said. "I'll give you a clue." She stood up. "*Campus.*" She clicked musically, sounding like a game-show timer.

"College?" he asked, frowning. "State?"

"Good!" She waited. "Any more? Who am I, Harry Towers? You have fifteen seconds." She began her manic clicking noise again.

"You were there?" His voice sounded remote and dislocated, as if it weren't coming out of his own throat.

She nodded pertly. "A freshman when you were a junior. Think." He was afraid she would begin her timer again, but instead she asked him if he wanted brandy.

He shook his head. "Feel a little . . ." He clutched the arm of the sofa for support.

She nodded. "So, how are we doing with those clues?"

"I . . ." He said her name silently, hoping it would connect with something, but all it did was bang from side to side in his brain. Leeleeleelee . . . a sharp bell tolling painfully.

"Ahhh," she said, "so you really don't remember me. How about that."

He couldn't think of what he should say. She was all snap-and-crackle confusion, and he was fuzzy lint. "Sorry," he whispered. Actually, he decided, she wasn't worth it. Too much time and effort. As soon as he felt a little better, he wanted out.

"Harry," she whispered. "Your mouth is open. You're drooling."

He tried to close it.

"I guess it would be hard to remember one girl out of that crowd of them you had." She smiled down at him, and he felt the tension ease.

There had been so many girls sticking to him as if he were made of Velcro. Such a good time. While it lasted. He wondered where his old letter sweater was, whether it still fit him, then remembered he was supposed to be trying to remember Leigh. But the girls were one big blur of sweet-smelling hair, firm breasts, lips, assorted parts.

She sat down so close to him that her perfume increased his dizziness. "Poor baby," she crooned. "You're woozy. Rest your head in my lap."

She stroked his thinning hair as if she loved every strand. Beneath her hand, his head swirled and popped, as the dinner wine and spices fermented. Maybe she wasn't such a bitch. He couldn't get a fix on her. Maybe it was good she liked the sound of her own voice too much. He needed time. She'd been at State with him. He rummaged again through his memories of all those girls, those legs and arms and shiny hair. Which one had been Leigh? He couldn't remember any of them. Female faces had a way of blurring away by the next morning, let alone after decades.

"Innasorority?" he said in a soft hiss.

She shook her head. "I was so shy. A loner. Until Harry Towers invited me to his fraternity party and everything was magically changed."

Which party? No way to separate out all those drunken, sweaty, wonderful nights. God, but those guys were fun. So many laughs. Best years of his life.

"Except that I never saw you again," Leigh said.

"Musta been outa my mind," he gasped chivalrously. Maybe it would appease her.

She chuckled very softly. "Wish you hadn't been. You can't imagine what a difference it would have made to me if you'd asked me out again."

So he hadn't been the most steady guy. That's how he was, who he was. But he'd never been a fool, so why hadn't he seen as much of this one as possible? Had something happened? Damn, but the memory slate was clean. Not even a chalk smear on it. He tried to sit up, to face her, to say something, but he only made it halfway.

Abruptly, she stood. He flopped down onto the cushions, then grabbed the back of the sofa and tried to pull into a sitting position.

She was going into the bedroom. Maybe talking time was over, just like that. Maybe they weren't going to have to deal with ancient history and guessing games, after all. He staggered to his feet.

"No. Stay," she called out. "I need something."

Safe sex, he realized. Sure. Okay. His legs wobbled and he couldn't stop swaying. He sank back into the sofa.

She returned and handed him a ragged-edged snapshot.

"Whadoss . . ." He gave up the effort of asking what this had to do with anything.

"It's part of the game," she said. "The last clue."

He focused his eyes with difficulty. When he had managed the feat, he regretted the effort. The girl in the photograph had a moon-shaped face with dark hair pulled back severely so that her ears stuck out like flaps. Sunlight bounced off her glasses, emphasizing the shadows cast by her enormous nose, her chubby cheeks, and her collection of chins. For no reason Harry could think of, she was smiling, revealing teeth that gaped like pickets on a wobbly fence. A real loser. A dog. A pig. Harry let the picture drop onto the coffee table.

"Too bad," she said. "We're out of time. Ladies and gentlemen, our contestant has forfeited the game. But don't turn off that set— we've got a few surprises left! It's not over till it's over!" She loomed above him, a giantess. Then she pushed the picture back in front of him. "Harry Towers, meet Leigh Endicott," she said.

"Wha?" He had an overwhelming sense of wrongness. His mouth was painfully dry. He reached toward the coffee, but his fingers weren't working properly. He sat, arms hanging loose, staring at the old black-and-white snapshot on the table.

"How could you not recognize me?" Her voice was sweet and coquettish. "The only changes have been from time—oh, and a few superficial adjustments, like a diet, a nose bob, contact lenses, ear pinning, chin enlarging, straightening and capping the teeth and bleaching the hair. Nothing compared to what's possible nowadays. But that was a long time ago."

A whoosh came out of the hollowness inside Harry. He'd taken her—that photo girl—to a party. He felt chilly, then hot. Something wanted to be remembered. Something hovered just above his head, ready to fall.

"I left school to earn the money for the changes," she said. "Took me four years, same as my degree would have." She walked toward the window. "Only thing is, at the end I was still the same girl inside, but who cares about that, right?"

He put up his hand like a traffic cop, to stop her words from falling onto his skull. He was cold again, afraid, needed to explain and defend himself, as if he were on trial, but when he opened his mouth, he gagged. When was it? Why? Did he really remember certain times . . . ? Why did Duffy's Desperates suddenly stampede into his mind in a great cloud of dust?

"Your party," she said. "My first date on campus. My first date, actually. I had such a good time. Every little girl knows the story of Cinderella—why shouldn't it happen to all of us? And Prince Charming had nothing on you, Harry. But when I left the room to powder my oversized nose, I overheard two of your darling fraternity brothers. Very drunk and very happy fraternity brothers. They were laughing so much, I could barely make out the joke, except that they kept repeating one particular word. This is the last question in the game, Harry. Do you know the word?"

His heart was going to explode. Party—ugly girl. Laughing. It all connected, turned fiery and molten. Pig. Pig party. Had forgotten all about them. Probably didn't have them anymore. Defunct, part of the world of the dinosaurs, but back then . . .

"Weren't supposed to know . . ." he said. "Just a . . . prank. Fun. No harm meant."

She loomed over him, stony and enormous. A warrior woman.

"F'give," he begged. "Boys will be . . ." What? What will boys be? What did he mean? Now or then—what? His mind was falling apart, great chunks slopping like mud into heaps. His hands were damp and cold. He tried to smile, although his mouth had become enormous, like a clown's, and rubbery.

"Stop groveling," she said. "There's no point. Or do you still think we're here because I *yearn* for you?" She laughed harshly but with real amusement.

He was freezing. His hands trembled uncontrollably, even while they lay in place.

She waved her arms at her imaginary audience, somewhere outside the windows. "The game is over, folks. Over," she said. Then she turned back to Harry. "You thought you caught a dream tonight, didn't you?" she said. "Maybe I'd make up for everybody else's indifference, would see past the sad slick of failure you wear like skin, past your dead-end job, your saggy gut, your stupid life, your smell of loneliness. You wanted me to find the real you—the special person inside, didn't you?"

Her voice was low and cool, only distantly interested in him, as if he were a specimen. He wished she would scream, maybe blot out the deafening sound of his own pulse.

"I understand it all, Harry," she said, "because that's what I wanted, what I believed, too, the night you asked me to your party. And get this: Neither of us—not me years ago, not you tonight—understood one damn thing that was going on."

His head ached as if she'd physically beaten him.

"I found out accidentally," she said. "You're going to find out very deliberately. That's the only difference." She walked away. "Pig party," she said. "Where all you perfect, self-important fraternity jackasses could observe and be amused by a freak show of imperfect but oblivious females. How sidesplitting of us to think we were actual dates, actual lovable, desirable humans! What fun it must have been to wink and poke each other in the ribs, award the man who'd found the absolute worst, laugh through the night about us. It's quite an experience, Harry, finding out you're a laughing matter. Changes a person forever."

He had to get the hell out of here, but his limbs were boneless, he couldn't stand.

"Of course, it was also a learning experience," she said. "A chance to grow. For years now I've wanted you to share it, have the same chance, but I don't belong to a fraternity, and besides, I'd like to think there aren't any more pig parties. So I had to find a way to return the favor personally." She came very close, kneeled in front of him.

A wave of nausea engulfed him. He swallowed hard and struggled to get to his feet.

"You're not going anywhere!" she snapped, pushing him back in place with one hand. "Do you really think it's the wine, or a few peppers making you feel so rotten? Aren't you worried?"

His burning eyes opened wide. "Poison?" he gasped.

She smiled. "It's a possibility, isn't it? I've had years to prepare for tonight. But why be concerned? This is a party, Harry. Your very own pig party. In fact, my dear, you *are* the party—the pig's party."

He nearly wept from the sawtooth edge of screams slicing the edges of his mind.

"The pigs behind the house, remember? Poor babies, they can't enjoy the miracles of cosmetic surgery. They're stuck as pigs forever, so surely they're entitled to a little piggy treat now and then. You'll give them such pleasure!"

"Hhhhh?"

"How?" Her voice traveled from a great distance and echoed through him, down to his fingertips.

"They eat almost anything, of course. But you—you'll be the best dish they ever had. Of course, we won't let them have all of you, will we? Nobody's ever had that. We'll do it bit by bit. Start with gourmet tidbits. The, uh, choice cuts, shall we say? The sought-after, prized, yummy parts."

Tears dribbled from his eyes.

"You know what they call pig food? Slops, Harry. How appropriare."

He heard dreadful, guttural sounds.

"Be still," she said. "And your nose is running. How disgusting."

He was small and lost and terrified, poisoned and paralyzed on a velvet sofa, about to be butchered, to have pigs eat his—pigs swallow his—

He summoned all of his strength, determined to get free. But his knees buckled and he dropped to the floor. "Please," he said between sobs, "was so long ago . . ."

"Not long enough," she said. "I realized that two weeks ago, when I saw you downtown. My jolt of pain wasn't old or faded. Some things are forever. You killed a part of me that night. However plain or fat or shy I was, I had an innocent pride and dignity, and you took it away. You turned me into a pig."

He howled at the top of his lungs.

"Hush. Nobody can hear," she reminded him. "Nobody knows you're here. For that matter, nobody knows *I'm* here. This isn't my house—it's a friend's, and he's away. So is the caretaker." She walked around him. "And for the record, my married name isn't Leigh Endicott. Anyway, we're both going to simply disappear from here.

But you'll do it bit by bit." She paused in an exaggerated pose of thought. "Or should we say bite by bite?" she asked with a grin.

He crawled, crying. An inch. No more.

"Why struggle so?" she said. "You are, quite literally, dead meat. On the other hand, you're about to be reborn, to give of yourself at last, to become whole—swine, inside and out."

The door was impossibly far away. He sprawled, numb and exhausted, gasping as the dark closed in. He could feel himself begin to die at the edges. His fingers were already gone, and his feet.

Through static and splutters and whirs in his brain, he heard her move around, run water, open cabinets.

"All clean now," she said. "Not a trace." She leaned down and pulled up one of his eyelids. "Tsk, tsk," she said. "Look what's become of the big bad wolf."

He dissolved into a shapeless, quivering stain on the floor. All his mind could see was a pig, heavy and bloated, pushing its hideous, hairy snout into its trough, into the slops, grunting with pleasure as it ate . . . him.

Glass broke, a door slammed, but all Harry heard was a fat sow's squeal of pleasure as it chewed and smacked and swallowed . . . him.

He felt a hand on his shoulder. He gasped, ran his own hands over his body once, then twice. Everything was there. He was intact and whole! He burst into tears.

"Damn drunk. Probably a junkie," a voice said. "Breaks in to use the place as a toilet. Jesus." Harry was pulled to his feet by men with badges. Police.

"Listen, I—" he began. His head hurt.

"You have the right to remain silent," the taller man began. He droned through his memorized piece. Harry couldn't believe it. They searched him and looked disappointed when they found nothing. "Passed out before you could take anything," the tall man said.

"But I wasn't—" They weren't interested. He told them about Leigh. They ignored him. He found out that an anonymous caller—female—had alerted the police to a prowler on the farm. He told them they had it all wrong, that it was her, Leigh Somebody who'd picked him up, taken him here, drugged him, smashed the window so it'd look like he'd broken in, and called them, setting him up. He explained it to them, to the lawyer they appointed, to the psychiatrist, to the technician who analyzed the drugs in his bloodstream—

street drugs they were, nothing fancy or traceable, damn the woman. He explained it to the judge. Nobody listened or believed or cared.

He stopped explaining. He endured the small jail until they released him. He paid for the broken window and the soiled rug. Paid the fine for trespassing, for breaking and entering. Paid through the nose for a taxi back to the city and his apartment.

In his mailbox, the only personal mail was a heart-shaped card with a picture of two enormous pigs nuzzling each other. He burned it.

From that day on, Harry Towers's stoop became more pronounced. He no longer combed his hair over his bald spot or sucked in his stomach. He stayed home nights, watching television alone.

And he never ate bacon or pork chops or ham steaks, for they, along with many other former delights, tasted like ashes in his mouth.

*Nancy Pickard's Jenny Cain is smart, funny, brave, and equal measures of shrewd and impulsive—qualities that have endeared her to legions of mystery fans.* Say No to Murder *won an Anthony for Best Original Paperback of 1985;* No Body *was nominated for an Anthony for Best Novel of 1986; and* Marriage Is Murder *was nominated for an Anthony and won a Macavity for Best Novel of 1987. In* Dead Crazy, *Nancy—and Jenny—continue to deal with ". . . themes of social responsibility, family life, and the role of humor, love, and courage in everyday life . . ." with the keen sense of what truly moves people that we've come to expect of them.*

*"Afraid All the Time" (not a Jenny Cain story) embodies the uniqueness of the American prairie and the emotions it evokes. Open space figures strongly in this story and becomes one of the significant threads woven into the shocking conclusion.*

# AFRAID ALL THE TIME

## by Nancy Pickard

"RIBBON A DARKNESS over me . . ."

Mel Brown, known variously as Pell Mell and Animel, sang the line from the song over and over behind his windshield as he flew from Missouri into Kansas on his old black Harley-Davidson motorcycle.

Already he loved Kansas, because the highway that stretched ahead of him was like a long, flat, dark ribbon unfurled just for him.

"Ribbon a darkness over me . . ."

He flew full throttle into the late-afternoon glare, feeling as if he were soaring gloriously drunk and blind on a skyway to the sun. The clouds in the far distance looked as if they'd rain on him that night, but he didn't worry about it. He'd heard there were plenty of empty farm and ranch houses in Kansas where a man could break in to spend the night. He'd heard it was like having your choice of free motels, Kansas was.

"Ribbon a darkness over me . . ."

\* \* \*

Three hundred miles to the southwest, Jane Baum suddenly stopped what she was doing. The fear had hit her again. It was always like that, striking out of nowhere, like a fist against her heart. She dropped her clothes basket from rigid fingers and stood as if paralyzed between the two clotheslines in her yard. There was a wet sheet to her right, another to her left. For once the wind had died down, so the sheets hung as still and silent as walls. She felt enclosed in a narrow, white, sterile room of cloth, and she never wanted to leave it.

Outside of it was danger.

On either side of the sheets lay the endless prairie where she felt like a tiny mouse exposed to every hawk in the sky.

It took all of her willpower not to scream.

She hugged her own shoulders to comfort herself. It didn't help. Within a few moments she was crying, and then shaking with a palsy of terror.

She hadn't known she'd be so afraid.

Eight months ago, before she had moved to this small farm she'd inherited, she'd had romantic notions about it, even about such simple things as hanging clothes on a line. It would feel so good, she had imagined, they would smell so sweet. Instead, everything had seemed strange and threatening to her from the start, and it was getting worse. Now she didn't even feel protected by the house. She was beginning to feel as if it were fear instead of electricity that lighted her lamps, filled her tub, lined her cupboards and covered her bed—fear that she breathed instead of air.

She hated the prairie and everything on it.

The city had never frightened her, not like this. She knew the city, she understood it, she knew how to avoid its dangers and its troubles. In the city there were buildings everywhere, and now she knew why—it was to blot out the true and terrible openness of the earth on which all of the inhabitants were so horribly exposed to danger.

The wind picked up again. It snapped the wet sheets against her body. Janie bolted from her shelter. Like a mouse with a hawk circling overhead, she ran as if she were being chased. She ran out of her yard and then down the highway, racing frantically, breathlessly, for the only other shelter she knew.

When she reached Cissy Johnson's house, she pulled open the side door and flung herself inside without knocking.

*"Cissy?"*

\* \* \*

"I'm afraid all the time."

"I know, Janie."

Cissy Johnson stood at her kitchen sink peeling potatoes for supper while she listened to Jane Baum's familiar litany of fear. By now Cissy knew it by heart. Janie was afraid of: being alone in the house she had inherited from her aunt; the dark; the crack of every twig in the night; the storm cellar; the horses that might step on her, the cows that might trample her, the chickens that might peck her, the cats that might bite her and have rabies, the coyotes that might attack her; the truckers who drove by her house, especially the flirtatious ones who blasted their horns when they saw her in the yard; tornadoes, blizzards, electrical storms; having to drive so far just to get simple groceries and supplies.

At first Cissy had been sympathetic, offering daily doses of coffee and friendship. But it was getting harder all the time to remain patient with somebody who just burst in without knocking and who complained all the time about imaginary problems and who—

"You've lived here all your life," Jane said, as if the woman at the sink had not previously been alert to that fact. She sat in a kitchen chair, huddled into herself like a child being punished. Her voice was low, as if she were talking more to herself than to Cissy. "You're used to it, that's why it doesn't scare you."

"Um," Cissy murmured, as if agreeing. But out of her neighbor's sight, she dug viciously at the eye of a potato. She rooted it out—leaving behind a white, moist, open wound in the vegetable—and flicked the dead black skin into the sink where the water running from the faucet washed it down the garbage disposal. She thought how she'd like to pour Janie's fears down the sink and similarly grind them up and flush them away. She held the potato to her nose and sniffed, inhaling the crisp, raw smell.

Then, as if having gained strength from that private moment, she glanced back over her shoulder at her visitor. Cissy was ashamed of the fact that the mere sight of Jane Baum now repelled her. It was a crime, really, how she'd let herself go. She wished Jane would comb her hair, pull her shoulders back, paint a little coloring onto her pale face, and wear something else besides that ugly denim jumper that came nearly to her heels. Cissy's husband, Bob, called Janie "Cissy's pup," and he called that jumper the "pup tent." He was right, Cissy thought, the woman did look like an insecure, spotty adolescent, and not at all like a grown woman of thirty-five-plus years. And darn it, Janie did follow Cissy around like a neurotic nuisance of a puppy.

"Is Bob coming back tonight?" Jane asked.

*Now she's even invading my mind*, Cissy thought. She whacked resentfully at the potato, peeling off more meat than skin. "Tomorrow." Her shoulders tensed.

"Then can I sleep over here tonight?"

"No." Cissy surprised herself with the shortness of her reply. She could practically feel Janie radiating hurt, and so she tried to make up for it by softening her tone. "I'm sorry, Janie, but I've got too much book work to do, and it's hard to concentrate with people in the house. I've even told the girls they can take their sleeping bags to the barn tonight to give me some peace." The girls were her daughters, Tessie, thirteen, and Mandy, eleven. "They want to spend the night out there 'cause we've got that new little blind calf we're nursing. His mother won't have anything to do with him, poor little thing. Tessie has named him Flopper, because he tries to stand up but he just flops back down. So the girls are bottle-feeding him, and they want to sleep near . . ."

"Oh." It was heavy with reproach.

Cissy stepped away from the sink to turn her oven on to 350°. Her own internal temperature was rising too. God forbid she should talk about her life! God forbid they should ever talk about anything but Janie and all the damned things she was scared of! She could write a book about it: *How Jane Baum Made a Big Mistake by Leaving Kansas City and How Everything About the Country Just Scared Her to Death*.

"Aren't you afraid of anything, Cissy?"

The implied admiration came with a bit of a whine to it—*anything*—like a curve on a fastball.

"Yes." Cissy drew out the word reluctantly.

"You *are*? What?"

Cissy turned around at the sink and laughed self-consciously.

"It's so silly . . . I'm even afraid to mention it."

"Tell me! I'll feel better if I know you're afraid of things, too."

*There!* Cissy thought. *Even my fears come down to how they affect you!*

"All right." She sighed. "Well, I'm afraid of something happening to Bobby, a wreck on the highway or something, or to one of the girls, or my folks, things like that. I mean, like leukemia or a heart attack or something I can't control. I'm always afraid there won't be enough money and we might have to sell this place. We're so happy here. I guess I'm afraid that might change." She paused, dismayed by the sudden realization that she had not been as happy since Jane Baum moved in down the road. For a moment, she stared accusingly at her neighbor. "I guess that's what I'm afraid of." Then Cissy added deliberately, "But I don't think about it all the time."

"I think about mine all the time," Jane whispered.

"I know."

"I hate it here!"

"You could move back."

Janie stared reproachfully. "You know I can't afford that!"

Cissy closed her eyes momentarily. The idea of having to listen to *this* for who knew how many years . . .

"I love coming over here," Janie said wistfully, as if reading Cissy's mind again. "It always makes me feel so much better. This is the only place I feel safe anymore. I just hate going home to the big old house all by myself."

*I will not invite you to supper*, Cissy thought.

Janie sighed.

Cissy gazed out the big square window behind Janie. It was October, her favorite month, when the grass turned as red as the curly hair on a Hereford's back and the sky turned a steel gray like the highway that ran between their houses. It was as if the whole world blended into itself—the grass into the cattle, the roads into the sky, and she into all of it. There was an electricity in the air, as if something more important than winter were about to happen, as if all the world were one and about to burst apart into something brand-new. Cissy loved the prairie, and it hurt her feelings a little that Janie didn't. How could anyone live in the middle of so much beauty, she puzzled, and be frightened of it?

"We'll never get a better chance." Tess ticked off the rationale for the adventure by holding up the fingers of her right hand, one at a time, an inch from her sister's scared face. "Dad's gone. We're in the barn. Mom'll be asleep. It's a new moon." She ran out of fingers on that hand and lifted her left thumb. "And the dogs know us."

"They'll find out!" Mandy wailed.

"*Who'll* find out?"

"Mom and Daddy will!"

"They won't! Who's gonna tell 'em? The gas-station owner? You think we left a trail of toilet paper he's going to follow from his station to here? And he's gonna call the sheriff and say lock up those Johnson girls, boys, they stole my toilet paper!"

"Yes!"

Together they turned to gaze—one of them with pride and cunning, the other with pride and trepidation—at the small hill of hay that was piled, for no apparent reason, in the shadows of a far corner of the barn. Underneath that pile lay their collection of six rolls of toilet paper—a new one filched from their own linen closet, and five partly used ones (stolen one trip at a time and hidden in their school jackets) from the ladies' bathroom at the gas station in town. Tess's plan was for the two of them to "t.p." their neighbor's house that night, after dark. Tess had lovely visions of how it would look—all ghostly and spooky, with streamers of white hanging down from the tree limbs and waving eerily in the breeze.

"They do it all the time in Kansas City, jerk," Tess proclaimed. "And I'll bet they don't make any big deal crybaby deal out of it." She wanted to be the first one in her class to do it, and she wasn't about to let her little sister chicken out on her. This plan would, Tess was sure, make her famous in at least a four-county area. No grown-up would ever figure out who had done it, but all the kids would know, even if she had to tell them.

"Mom'll kill us!"

"Nobody'll know!"

"It's gonna rain!"

"It's not gonna rain."

"We shouldn't leave Flopper!"

Now they looked, together, at the baby bull calf in one of the stalls. It stared blindly in the direction of their voices, tried to rise, but was too frail to do it.

"Don't be a dope. We leave him all the time."

Mandy sighed.

Tess, who recognized the sound of surrender when she heard it, smiled magnanimously at her sister.

"You can throw the first roll," she offered.

In a truck stop in Emporia, Mel Brown slopped up his supper gravy with the last third of a cloverleaf roll. He had a table by a window. As he ate, he stared with pleasure at his bike outside. If he moved his head just so, the rays from the setting sun flashed off the handlebars. He thought about how the leather seat and grips would feel soft and warm and supple, the way a woman in leather felt, when he got back on. At the thought he got a warm feeling in his crotch, too, and he smiled.

God, he loved living like this.

When he was hungry, he ate. When he was tired, he slept. When he was horny, he found a woman. When he was thirsty, he stopped at a bar.

Right now Mel felt like not paying the entire $5.46 for this lousy chicken-fried steak dinner and coffee. He pulled four dollar bills out of his wallet and a couple of quarters out of his right front pocket and set it all out on the table, with the money sticking out from under the check.

Mel got up and walked past the waitress.

"It's on the table," he told her.

"No cherry pie?" she asked him.

It sounded like a proposition, so he grinned as he said, "Nah." *If you weren't so ugly,* he thought, *I just might stay for dessert.*

"Come again," she said.

You wish, he thought.

If they called him back, he'd say he couldn't read her handwriting. Her fault. No wonder she didn't get a tip. Smiling, he lifted a toothpick off the cashier's counter and used it to salute the man behind the cash register.

"Thanks," the man said.

"You bet."

Outside, Mel stood in the parking lot and stretched, shoving his arms high in the air, letting anybody who was watching get a good look at him. Nothin' to hide. Eat your heart out, baby. Then he strolled over to his bike and kicked the stand up with his heel. He poked around his mouth with the toothpick, spat out a sliver of meat, then flipped the toothpick onto the ground. He climbed back on his bike, letting out a breath of satisfaction when his butt hit the warm leather seat.

Mel accelerated slowly, savoring the surge of power building between his legs.

Jane Baum was in bed by 10:30 that night, exhausted once again by her own fear. Lying there in her late aunt's double bed, she obsessed on the mistake she had made in moving to this dreadful, empty place in the middle of nowhere. She had expected to feel nervous for a while, as any other city dweller might who moved to the country. But she hadn't counted on being actually phobic about it—of being possessed by a fear so strong that it seemed to inhabit every cell of her body until at night, every night, she felt she could die from it. She hadn't known—how could she have known?—she would be one of those people who is terrified by the vastness of the prairie. She had visited the farm only a few times as a child, and from those visits she had remembered only warm and fuzzy things like caterpillars and chicks. She had only dimly remembered how antlike a human being feels on the prairie.

Her aunt's house had been broken into twice during the period between her aunt's death and her own occupancy. That fact cemented her fantasies in a foundation of terrifying reality. When Cissy said, "It's your imagination," Janie retorted, "But it happened twice before! Twice!" She wasn't making it up! There *were* strange, brutal men—that's how she imagined them, they were never caught by the police—who broke in and took whatever they wanted—cans in the cupboard, the radio in the kitchen. It could happen again, Janie thought obsessively as she lay in the bed; it could happen over and over. *To me, to me, to me.*

On the prairie, the darkness seemed absolute to her. There were millions of stars but no streetlights. Coyotes howled, or cattle bawled. Occasionally the big night-riding semis whirred by out front. Their tire and engine sounds seemed to come out of nowhere, build to an intolerable whine and then disappear in an uncanny way. She pictured the drivers as big, rough, intense men hopped up on amphetamines; she worried that one night she would hear truck tires turning into her gravel drive, that an engine would switch off, that a truck door would quietly open and then close, that careful footsteps would slur across her gravel.

Her fear had grown so huge, so bad, that she was even frightened of it. It was like a monstrous balloon that inflated every time she breathed. Every night the fear got worse. The balloon got bigger. It nearly filled the bedroom now.

The upstairs bedroom where she lay was hot because she had the windows pulled down and latched, and the curtains drawn. She could have cooled it with a fan on the dressing table, but she was afraid the fan's noise might cover the sound of whatever might break into the first floor and climb the stairs to attack her. She lay with a sheet and a blanket pulled up over her arms and shoulders, to just under her chin. She was sweating, as if her fear-frozen body were melting, but it felt warm and almost comfortable to her. She always wore pajamas and thin wool socks to bed because she felt safer when she was completely dressed. She especially felt more secure in pajama pants, which no dirty hand could shove up onto her belly as it could a nightgown.

Lying in bed like a quadriplegic, unmoving, eyes open, Janie reviewed her precautions. Every door was locked, every window was permanently shut and locked, so that she didn't have to check them every night; all the curtains were drawn; the porch lights were off; and her car was locked in the barn so no trucker would think she was home.

Lately she had taken to sleeping with her aunt's loaded pistol on the pillow beside her head.

Cissy crawled into bed just before midnight, tired from hours of accounting. She had been out to the barn to check on her giggling girls and the blind calf. She had talked to her husband when he called from Oklahoma City. Now she was thinking about how she would try to start easing Janie Baum out of their lives.

"I'm sorry, Janie, but I'm awfully busy today. I don't think you ought to come over . . ."

Oh, but there would be that meek, martyred little voice, just like a baby mouse needing somebody to mother it. How would she deny that need? She was already feeling guilty about refusing Janie's request to sleep over.

"Well, I will. I just will do it, that's all. If I could say no to the FHA girls when they were selling fruitcakes, I can start saying no more often to Janie Baum. Anyway, she's never going to get over her fears if I indulge them."

Bob had said as much when she'd complained to him longdistance. "Cissy, you're not helping her," he'd said. "You're just letting her get worse." And then he'd said something new that had disturbed her. "Anyway, I don't like the girls being around her so much. She's getting too weird, Cissy."

She thought of her daughters—of fearless Tess and dear little Mandy—and of how *safe* and *nice* it was for children in the country. . . .

"Besides," Bob had said, "she's *got* to do more of her own chores. We need Tess and Mandy to help out around our place more; we can't be having them always running off to mow her grass and plant her flowers and feed her cows and water her horse and get her eggs, just because she's scared to stick her silly hand under a damned hen. . . ."

Counting the chores put Cissy to sleep.

"Tess!" Mandy hissed desperately. "Wait!"

The older girl slowed, to give Mandy time to catch up to her, and then to touch Tess for reassurance. They paused for a moment to catch their breath and to crouch in the shadow of Jane Baum's porch. Tess carried three rolls of toilet paper in a makeshift pouch she'd formed in the belly of her black sweatshirt. ("We gotta wear black, remember!") and Mandy was similarly equipped. Tess decided that now was the right moment to drop her bomb.

"I've been thinking," she whispered.

Mandy was struck cold to her heart by that familiar and dreaded phrase. She moaned quietly. "What?"

"It might rain."

"I told you!"

"So I think we better do it inside."

*"Inside?"*

"Shh! It'll scare her to death, it'll be great! Nobody else'll ever have the guts to do anything as neat as this! We'll do the kitchen, and if we have time, maybe the dining room."

"Ohhh, noooo."

"*She* thinks she's got all the doors and windows locked, but she doesn't!" Tess giggled. She had it all figured out that when Jane Baum came downstairs in the morning, she'd take one look, scream, faint, and then, when she woke up, call everybody in town. The fact that Jane might also call the sheriff had occurred to her, but since Tess didn't have any faith in the ability of adults to figure out anything important, she wasn't worried about getting caught. "When I took in her eggs, I unlocked the downstairs bathroom window! Come on! This'll be great!"

The ribbon of darkness ahead of Mel Brown was no longer straight. It was now bunched into long, steep hills. He hadn't expected hills. Nobody had told him there was any part of Kansas that wasn't flat. So he wasn't making as good time, and he couldn't run full-bore. But then, he wasn't in a hurry, except for the hell of it. And this was more interesting, more dangerous, and he liked the thrill of that. He started edging closer to the centerline every time he roared up a hill, playing a game of highway roulette in which he was the winner as long as whatever coming from the other direction had its head-lights on.

When that got boring, he turned his own headlights off.

Now he roared past cars and trucks like a dark demon.

Mel laughed every time, thinking how surprised they must be, and how frightened. They'd think, *Crazy fool, I could have hit him*. . . .

He supposed he wasn't afraid of anything, except maybe going back to prison, and he didn't think they'd send him down on a speeding ticket. Besides, if Kansas was like most states, it was long on roads and short on highway patrolmen. . . .

Roaring downhill was even more fun, because of the way his stomach dropped out. He felt like a kid, yelling "Fuuuuck," all the way down the other side. What a goddamned roller coaster of a state this was turning out to be.

The rain still looked miles away.

Mel felt as if he could ride all night. Except that his eyes were gritty, the first sign that he'd better start looking for a likely place to spend the night. He wasn't one to sleep under the stars, not if he could find a ceiling.

Tess directed her sister to stack the rolls of toilet paper underneath the bathroom window on the first floor of Jane Baum's house. The six rolls, all white, stacked three in a row, two high, gave Tess the little bit of height and leverage she needed to push up the glass with her palms. She stuck her fingers under the bottom edge and labori-ously attempted to raise the window. It was stiff in its coats of paint.

"Damn," she exclaimed, and let her arms slump. Beneath her feet, the toilet paper was getting squashed.

She tried again, and this time she showed her strength from lifting calves and tossing hay. With a crack of paint and a thump of wood on wood, the window slid all the way up.

"Shhh!" Mandy held her fists in front of her face and knocked her knuckles against each other in excitement and agitation. Her ears picked up the sound of a roaring engine on the highway, and she was immediately sure it was the sheriff, coming to arrest her and Tess. She tugged frantically at the calf of her sister's right leg.

Tess jerked her leg out of Mandy's grasp and disappeared through the open window.

The crack of the window and the thunder of the approaching motorcycle confused themselves in Jane's sleeping consciousness, so that when she awoke from dreams full of anxiety—her eyes flying open, the rest of her body frozen—she imagined in a confused, hallucinatory kind of way that somebody was both coming to get her and already there in the house.

Jane then did as she had trained herself to do. She had practiced over and over every night, so that her actions would be instinctive. She turned her face to the pistol on the other pillow and placed her thumb on the trigger.

Her fear—of rape, of torture, of kidnapping, of agony, of death—was a balloon, and she floated horribly in the center of it. There were thumps and other sounds downstairs, and they joined her in the balloon. There was an engine roaring, and then suddenly it was silent, and a slurring of wheels in her gravel drive, and these sounds joined her in her balloon. When she couldn't bear it any longer, she popped the balloon by shooting herself in the forehead.

In the driveway, Mel Brown heard the gun go off.

He slung his leg back onto his motorcycle and roared back out onto the highway. So the place had looked empty. So he'd been wrong. So he'd find someplace else. But holy shit. Get the fuck outta here.

Inside the house, in the bathroom, Tess also heard the shot and, being a ranch child, recognized it instantly for what it was, although she wasn't exactly sure where it had come from. Cussing and sobbing, she clambered over the sink and back out the window, falling onto her head and shoulders on the rolls of toilet paper.

"It's the sheriff!" Mandy was hysterical. "He's shooting at us!"

Tess grabbed her little sister by a wrist and pulled her away from the house. They were both crying and stumbling. They ran in the drainage ditch all the way home and flung themselves into the barn.

Mandy ran to lie beside the little blind bull calf. She lay her head on Flopper's side. When he didn't respond, she jerked to her feet. She glared at her sister.

"He's dead!'

"Shut up!"

Cissy Johnson had awakened, too, although she hadn't known why. Something, some noise, had stirred her. And now she sat up in bed, breathing hard, frightened for no good reason she could fathom. If Bob had been home, she'd have sent him out to the barn to check on the girls. But why? The girls were all right, they must be, this was just the result of a bad dream. But she didn't remember having any such dream.

Cissy got out of bed and ran to the window.

No, it wasn't a storm, the rain hadn't come.

A motorcycle!

That's what she'd heard, that's what had awakened her!

Quickly, with nervous fingers, Cissy put on a robe and tennis shoes. Darn you, Janie Baum, she thought, your fears are contagious, that's what they are. The thought popped into her head: If you don't have fears, they can't come true.

Cissy raced out to the barn.

*Elizabeth Peters, alter ego of Barbara Michaels, has given the mystery world twenty-one books. Her doctorate in Egyptology and her strong interests in history and archaeology provide the background for three of mystery's most distinctive characters: Jacqueline Kirby (The Seventh Sinner, Die for Love) is a librarian who also happens to write bodice rippers; Vicky Bliss (Borrower of the Night, Silhouette in Scarlet, Trojan Gold) is an art historian who is ". . . six feet tall, blonde, stacked, brilliant"; and Amelia Peabody Emerson (The Mummy Case, Lion in the Valley, Deeds of the Disturber) is a Victorian feminist and archaeologist.*

*In "The Locked Tomb Mystery," an Egyptian variation on a classic mystery form takes a new turn. A time and place thousands of years and thousands of miles away come to life—a testament to the Peters skills of scholarship and seamless writing.*

# THE LOCKED TOMB MYSTERY

## by Elizabeth Peters

SENEBTISI'S FUNERAL WAS the talk of southern Thebes. Of course, it could not compare with the burials of Great Ones and Pharaohs, whose Houses of Eternity were furnished with gold and fine linen and precious gems, but ours was not a quarter where nobles lived; our people were craftsmen and small merchants, able to afford a chamber-tomb and a coffin and a few spells to ward off the perils of the Western Road—no more than that. We had never seen anything like the burial of the old woman who had been our neighbor for so many years.

The night after the funeral, the customers of Nehi's tavern could talk of nothing else. I remember that evening well. For one thing, I had just won my first appointment as a temple scribe. I was looking forward to boasting a little, and perhaps paying for a round of beer, if my friends displayed proper appreciation of my good fortune. Three of the others were already at the tavern when I arrived, my linen shawl wrapped tight around me. The weather was cold even for winter, with a cruel, dry wind driving sand into every crevice of the body.

"Close the door quickly," said Senu, the carpenter. "What weather! I wonder if the Western journey will be like this—cold enough to freeze a man's bones."

This prompted a ribald comment from Rennefer, the weaver, concerning the effects of freezing on certain of Senebtisi's vital organs. "Not that anyone would notice the difference," he added. "There was never any warmth in the old hag. What sort of mother would take all her possessions to the next world and leave her only son penniless?"

"Is it true, then?" I asked, signaling Nehi to fetch the beer jar. "I have heard stories—"

"All true," said the potter, Baenre. "It is a pity you could not attend the burial, Wadjsen; it was magnificent!"

"You went?" I inquired. "That was good of you, since she ordered none of her funerary equipment from you."

Baenre is a scanty little man with thin hair and sharp bones. It is said that he is a domestic tyrant, and that his wife cowers when he comes roaring home from the tavern, but when he is with us, his voice is almost a whisper. "My rough kitchenware would not be good enough to hold the wine and fine oil she took to the tomb. Wadjsen, you should have seen the boxes and jars and baskets— dozens of them. They say she had a gold mask, like the ones worn by great nobles, and that all her ornaments were of solid gold."

"It is true," said Rennefer. "I know a man who knows one of the servants of Bakenmut, the goldsmith who made the ornaments."

"How is her son taking it?" I asked. I knew Minmose slightly; a shy, serious man, he followed his father's trade of stone carving. His mother had lived with him all his life, greedily scooping up his profits, though she had money of her own, inherited from her parents.

"Why, as you would expect," said Senu, shrugging. "Have you ever heard him speak harshly to anyone, much less his mother? She was an old she-goat who treated him like a boy who has not cut off the side lock; but with him it was always 'Yes, honored mother,' and 'As you say, honored mother.' She would not even allow him to take a wife."

"How will he live?"

"Oh, he has the shop and the business, such as it is. He is a hard worker; he will survive."

In the following months I heard occasional news of Minmose. Gossip said he must be doing well, for he had taken to spending his leisure time at a local house of prostitution—a pleasure he never had dared enjoy while his mother lived. Nefertiry, the loveliest and most expensive of the girls, was the object of his desire, and Rennefer remarked that the maiden must have a kind heart, for she could command higher prices than Minmose was able to pay. However, as time passed, I forgot Minmose and Senebtisi, and her rich burial. It was not until almost a year later that the matter was recalled to my attention.

The rumors began in the marketplace, at the end of the time of inundation, when the floodwater lay on the fields and the farmers were idle. They enjoy this time, but the police of the city do not; for idleness leads to crime, and one of the most popular crimes is tomb robbing. This goes on all the time in a small way, but when the Pharaoh is strong and stern, and the laws are strictly enforced, it is a very risky trade. A man stands to lose more than a hand or an ear if he is caught. He also risks damnation after he has entered his own tomb; but some men simply do not have proper respect for the gods.

The king, Nebmaatre (may he live forever!), was then in his prime, so there had been no tomb robbing for some time—or at least none had been detected. But, the rumors said, three men of west Thebes had been caught trying to sell ornaments such as are buried with the dead. The rumors turned out to be correct, for once. The men were questioned on the soles of their feet and confessed to the robbing of several tombs.

Naturally all those who had kin buried on the west bank—which included most of us—were alarmed by this news, and half the nervous matrons in our neighborhood went rushing across the river to make sure the family tombs were safe. I was not surprised to hear that that dutiful son Minmose had also felt obliged to make sure his mother had not been disturbed.

However, I was surprised at the news that greeted me when I paid my next visit to Nehi's tavern. The moment I entered, the others began to talk at once, each eager to be the first to tell the shocking facts.

"Robbed?" I repeated when I had sorted out the babble of voices. "Do you speak truly?"

"I do not know why you should doubt it," said Rennefer. "The richness of her burial was the talk of the city, was it not? Just what the tomb robbers like! They made a clean sweep of all the gold, and ripped the poor old hag's mummy to shreds."

At that point we were joined by another of the habitués, Merusir. He is a pompous, fat man who considers himself superior to the rest of us because he is Fifth Prophet of Amon. We put up with his patronizing ways because sometimes he knows court gossip. On that particular evening it was apparent that he was bursting with excitement. He listened with a supercilious sneer while we told him the sensational news. "I know, I know," he drawled. "I heard it much earlier—and with it, the other news which is known only to those in the confidence of the Palace."

He paused, ostensibly to empty his cup. Of course, we reacted as he had hoped we would, begging him to share the secret. Finally he condescended to inform us.

"Why, the amazing thing is not the robbery itself, but how it was done. The tomb entrance was untouched, the seals of the necropolis were unbroken. The tomb itself is entirely rock-cut, and there was not the slightest break in the walls or floor or ceiling. Yet when Minmose entered the burial chamber, he found the coffin open, the mummy mutilated, and the gold ornaments gone."

We stared at him, openmouthed.

"It is a most remarkable story," I said.

"Call me a liar if you like," said Merusir, who knows the language of polite insult as well as I do. "There was a witness—two, if you count Minmose himself. The sem-priest Wennefer was with him."

This silenced the critics. Wennefer was known to us all. There was not a man in southern Thebes with a higher reputation. Even Senebtisi had been fond of him, and she was not fond of many people. He had officiated at her funeral.

Pleased at the effect of his announcement, Merusir went on in his most pompous manner. "The king himself has taken an interest in the matter. He has called on Amenhotep Sa Hapu to investigate."

"Amenhotep?" I exclaimed. "But I know him well."

"You do?" Merusir's plump cheeks sagged like bladders punctured by a sharp knife.

Now, at that time Amenhotep's name was not in the mouth of everyone, though he had taken the first steps on that astonishing career that was to make him the intimate friend of Pharaoh. When I first met him, he had been a poor, insignificant priest at a local shrine. I had been sent to fetch him to the house where my master lay dead of a stab wound, presumably murdered. Amenhotep's fame had begun with that matter, for he had discovered the truth and saved an innocent man from execution. Since then he had handled several other cases, with equal success.

My exclamation had taken the wind out of Merusir's sails. He had hoped to impress us by telling us something we did not know. Instead it was I who enlightened the others about Amenhotep's triumphs. But when I finished, Rennefer shook his head.

"If this wise man is all you say, Wadjsen, it will be like inviting a lion to rid the house of mice. He will find there is a simple explanation. No doubt the thieves entered the burial chamber from above or from one side, tunneling through the rock. Minmose and Wennefer were too shocked to observe the hole in the wall, that is all."

We argued the matter for some time, growing more and more heated as the level of the beer in the jar dropped. It was a foolish argument, for none of us knew the facts; and to argue without knowledge is like trying to weave without thread.

This truth did not occur to me until the cool night breeze had cleared my head, when I was halfway home. I decided to pay Amenhotep a visit. The next time I went to the tavern, I would be the one to tell the latest news, and Merusir would be nothing!

Most of the honest householders had retired, but there were lamps burning in the street of the prostitutes, and in a few taverns. There was a light, as well, in one window of the house where Amenhotep lodged. Like the owl he resembled, with his beaky nose and large, close-set eyes, he preferred to work at night.

The window was on the ground floor, so I knocked on the wooden shutter, which of course was closed to keep out night demons. After a few moments the shutter opened, and the familiar nose appeared. I spoke my name, and Amenhotep went to open the door.

"Wadjsen! It has been a long time," he exclaimed. "Should I ask what brings you here, or shall I display my talents as a seer and tell you?"

"I suppose it requires no great talent," I replied. "The matter of Senebtisi's tomb is already the talk of the district."

"So I had assumed." He gestured me to sit down and hospitably indicated the wine jar that stood in the corner. I shook my head.

"I have already taken too much beer, at the tavern. I am sorry to disturb you so late—"

"I am always happy to see you, Wadjsen." His big dark eyes reflected the light of the lamp, so that they seemed to hold stars in their depths. "I have missed my assistant, who helped me to the truth in my first inquiry."

"I was of little help to you then," I said with a smile. "And in this case I am even more ignorant. The thing is a great mystery, known only to the gods."

"No, no!" He clapped his hands together, as was his habit when annoyed with the stupidity of his hearer. "There is no mystery. I know who robbed the tomb of Senebtisi. The only difficulty is to prove how it was done."

At Amenhotep's suggestion I spent the night at his house so that I could accompany him when he set out next morning to find the proof he needed. I required little urging, for I was afire with curiosity. Though I pressed him, he would say no more, merely remarking piously, " 'A man may fall to ruin because of his tongue; if a passing remark is hasty and it is repeated, thou wilt make enemies.' "

I could hardly dispute the wisdom of this adage, but the gleam in Amenhotep's bulging black eyes made me suspect he took a malicious pleasure in my bewilderment.

After our morning bread and beer we went to the temple of Khonsu, where the sem-priest Wennefer worked in the records office. He was copying accounts from pottery ostraca onto a papyrus that was stretched across his lap. All scribes develop bowed shoulders from bending over their writing; Wennefer was folded almost double, his face scant inches from the surface of the papyrus. When Amenhotep cleared his throat, the old man started, smearing the ink. He waved our apologies aside and cleaned the papyrus with a wad of lint.

"No harm was meant, no harm is done," he said in his breathy, chirping voice. "I have heard of you, Amenhotep Sa Hapu; it is an honor to meet you."

"I, too, have looked forward to meeting you, Wennefer. Alas that the occasion should be such a sad one."

Wennefer's smile faded. "Ah, the matter of Senebtisi's tomb. What a tragedy! At least the poor woman can now have a proper reburial. If Minmose had not insisted on opening the tomb, her *ba* would have gone hungry and thirsty through eternity."

"Then the tomb entrance really was sealed and undisturbed?" I asked skeptically.

"I examined it myself," Wennefer said. "Minmose had asked me to meet him after the day's work, and we arrived at the tomb as the sun was setting; but the light was still good. I conducted the funeral service for Senebtisi, you know. I had seen the doorway blocked and mortared and with my own hands had helped to press the seals of the necropolis onto the wet plaster. All was as I had left it that day a year ago."

"Yet Minmose insisted on opening the tomb?" Amenhotep asked.

"Why, we agreed it should be done," the old man said mildly. "As you know, robbers sometimes tunnel in from above or from one side, leaving the entrance undisturbed. Minmose had brought tools. He did most of the work himself, for these old hands of mine are better with a pen than a chisel. When the doorway was clear, Minmose lit a lamp and we entered. We were crossing the hall beyond the entrance corridor when Minmose let out a shriek. 'My mother, my mother,' he cried—oh, it was pitiful to hear! Then I saw it too. The thing—the thing on the floor. . . ."

"You speak of the mummy, I presume," said Amenhotep. "The thieves had dragged it from the coffin out into the hall?"

"Where they despoiled it," Wennefer whispered. "The august body was ripped open from throat to groin, through the shroud and the wrappings and the flesh."

"Curious," Amenhotep muttered, as if to himself. "Tell me, Wennefer, what is the plan of the tomb?"

Wennefer rubbed his brush on the ink cake and began to draw on the back surface of one of the ostraca.

"It is a fine tomb, Amenhotep, entirely rock-cut. Beyond the entrance is a flight of stairs and a short corridor, thus leading to a hall broader than it is long, with two pillars. Beyond that, another short corridor; then the burial chamber. The august mummy lay here." And he inked in a neat circle at the beginning of the second corridor.

"Ha," said Amenhotep, studying the plan. "Yes, yes, I see. Go on, Wennefer. What did you do next?"

"I did nothing," the old man said simply. "Minmose's hand shook so violently that he dropped the lamp. Darkness closed in. I felt the presence of the demons who had defiled the dead. My tongue clove to the roof of my mouth and—"

"Dreadful," Amenhotep said. "But you were not far from the tomb entrance; you could find your way out?"

"Yes, yes, it was only a dozen paces; and by Amon, my friend, the sunset light has never appeared so sweet! I went at once to fetch the necropolis guards. When we returned to the tomb, Minmose had rekindled his lamp—"

"I thought you said the lamp was broken."

"Dropped, but fortunately not broken. Minmose had opened one of the jars of oil—Senebtisi had many such in the tomb, all of the finest quality—and had refilled the lamp. He had replaced the mummy in its coffin and was kneeling by it praying. Never was there so pious a son!"

"So then, I suppose, the guards searched for the tomb."

"We all searched," Wennefer said. "The tomb chamber was in a dreadful state; boxes and baskets had been broken open and the contents strewn about. Every object of precious metal had been stolen, including the amulets on the body."

"What about the oil, the linen, and the other valuables?" Amenhotep asked.

"The oil and the wine were in large jars, impossible to move easily. About the other things I cannot say; everything was in such confusion—and I do not know what was there to begin with. Even Minmose was not certain; his mother had filled and sealed most of the boxes herself. But I know what was taken from the mummy, for I saw the golden amulets and ornaments placed on it when it was wrapped by the embalmers. I do not like to speak evil of anyone, but you know, Amenhotep, that the embalmers . . ."

"Yes," Amenhotep agreed with a sour face. "I myself watched the wrapping of my father; there is no other way to make certain the ornaments will go on the mummy instead of into the coffers of the embalmers. Minmose did not perform this service for his mother?"

"Of course he did. He asked me to share in the watch, and I was glad to agree. He is the most pious—"

"So I have heard," said Amenhotep. "Tell me again, Wennefer, of the condition of the mummy. You examined it?"

"It was my duty. Oh, Amenhotep, it was a sad sight! The shroud was still tied firmly around the body; the thieves had cut straight through it and through the bandages beneath, baring the body. The arm bones were broken, so roughly had the thieves dragged the heavy gold bracelets from them."

"And the mask?" I asked. "It was said that she had a mask of solid gold."

"It, too, was missing."

"Horrible," Amenhotep said. "Wennefer, we have kept you from your work long enough. Only one more question. How do you think the thieves entered the tomb?"

The old man's eyes fell. "Through me," he whispered.

I gave Amenhotep a startled look. He shook his head warningly.

"It was not your fault," he said, touching Wennefer's bowed shoulder.

"It was. I did my best, but I must have omitted some vital part of the ritual. How else could demons enter the tomb?"

"Oh, I see." Amenhotep stroked his chin. "Demons."

"It could have been nothing else. The seals on the door were intact, the mortar untouched. There was no break of the smallest size in the stone of the walls or ceiling or floor."

"But—" I began.

"And there is this. When the doorway was clear and the light entered, the dust lay undisturbed on the floor. The only marks on it were the strokes of the broom with which Minmose, according to custom, had swept the floor as he left the tomb after the funeral service."

"Amon preserve us," I exclaimed, feeling a chill run through me.

Amenhotep's eyes moved from Wennefer to me, then back to Wennefer. "That is conclusive," he murmured.

"Yes," Wennefer said with a groan. "And I am to blame—I, a priest who failed at his task."

"No," said Amenhotep. "You did not fail. Be of good cheer, my friend. There is another explanation."

Wennefer shook his head despondently. "Minmose said the same, but he was only being kind. Poor man! He was so overcome, he could scarcely walk. The guards had to take him by the arms to lead him from the tomb. I carried his tools. It was the least—"

"The tools," Amenhotep interrupted. "They were in a bag or a sack?"

"Why, no. He had only a chisel and a mallet. I carried them in my hand as he had done."

Amenhotep thanked him again, and we took our leave. As we crossed the courtyard I waited for him to speak, but he remained silent; and after a while I could contain myself no longer.

"Do you still believe you know who robbed the tomb?"

"Yes, yes, it is obvious."

"And it was not demons?"

Amenhotep blinked at me like an owl blinded by sunlight.

"Demons are a last resort."

He had the smug look of a man who thinks he has said something clever; but his remark smacked of heresy to me, and I looked at him doubtfully.

"Come, come," he snapped. "Senebtisi was a selfish, greedy old woman, and if there is justice in the next world, as our faith decrees, her path through the Underworld will not be easy. But why would diabolical powers play tricks with her mummy when they could torment her spirit? Demons have no need of gold."

"Well, but—"

"Your wits used not to be so dull. What do you think happened?"

"If it was not demons—"

"It was not."

"Then someone must have broken in."

"Very clever," said Amenhotep, grinning.

"I mean that there must be an opening, in the walls or the floor, that Wennefer failed to see."

"Wennefer, perhaps. The necropolis guards, no. The chambers of the tomb were cut out of solid rock. It would be impossible to disguise a break in such a surface, even if tomb robbers took the trouble to fill it in—which they never have been known to do."

"Then the thieves entered through the doorway and closed it again. A dishonest craftsman could make a copy of the necropolis seal. . . ."

"Good." Amenhotep clapped me on the shoulder. "Now you are beginning to think. It is an ingenious idea, but it is wrong. Tomb robbers work in haste, for fear of the necropolis guards. They would not linger to replace stones and mortar and seals."

"Then I do not know how it was done."

"Ah, Wadjsen, you are dense! There is only one person who could have robbed the tomb."

"I thought of that," I said stiffly, hurt by his raillery. "Minmose was the last to leave the tomb and the first to reenter it. He had good reason to desire the gold his mother should have left to him. But, Amenhotep, he could not have robbed the mummy on either occasion; there was not time. You know the funeral ritual as well as I. When the priests and mourners leave the tomb, they leave together. If Minmose had lingered in the burial chamber, even for a few minutes, his delay would have been noted and remarked upon."

"That is quite true," said Amenhotep.

"Also," I went on, "the gold was heavy as well as bulky. Minmose could not have carried it away without someone noticing."

"Again you speak truly."

"Then unless Wennefer the priest is conspiring with Minmose—"

"That good, simple man? I am surprised at you, Wadjsen. Wennefer is as honest as the Lady of Truth herself."

"Demons—"

Amenhotep interrupted with the hoarse hooting sound that passed for a laugh with him. "Stop babbling of demons. There is one man besides myself who knows how Senebtisi's tomb was violated. Let us go and see him."

He quickened his pace, his sandals slapping in the dust. I followed, trying to think. His taunts were like weights that pulled my mind to its farthest limits. I began to get an inkling of truth, but I could not make sense of it. I said nothing, not even when we turned into the lane south of the temple that led to the house of Minmose.

There was no servant at the door. Minmose himself answered our summons. I greeted him and introduced Amenhotep.

Minmose lifted his hands in surprise. "You honor my house, Amenhotep. Enter and be seated."

Amenhotep shook his head. "I will not stay, Minmose. I came only to tell you who desecrated your mother's tomb."

"What?" Minmose gaped at him. "Already you know? But how? It is a great mystery, beyond—"

"You did it, Minmose."

Minmose turned a shade paler. But that was not out of the way; even the innocent might blanch at such an accusation.

"You are mad," he said. "Forgive me, you are my guest, but—"

"There is no other possible explanation," Amenhotep said. "You stole the gold when you entered the tomb two days ago."

"But, Amenhotep," I exclaimed. "Wennefer was with him, and Wennefer saw the mummy already robbed when—"

"Wennefer did not see the mummy," Amenhotep said. "The tomb was dark; the only light was that of a small lamp, which Minmose promptly dropped. Wennefer has poor sight. Did you not observe how he bent over his writing? He caught only a glimpse of a white shape, the size of a wrapped mummy, before the light went out. When next Wennefer saw the mummy, it was in the coffin, and his view of it then colored his confused memory of the first supposed sighting of it. Few people are good observers. They see what they expect to see."

"Then what did he see?" I demanded. Minmose might not have been there. Amenhotep avoided looking at him.

"A piece of linen in the rough shape of a human form, arranged on the floor by the last person who left the tomb. It would have taken him only a moment to do this before he snatched up the broom and swept himself out."

"So the tomb was sealed and closed," I exclaimed. "For almost a year he waited—"

"Until the next outbreak of tomb robbing. Minmose could assume this would happen sooner or later; it always does. He thought he was being clever by asking Wennefer to accompany him—a witness of irreproachable character who could testify that the tomb entrance was untouched. In fact, he was too careful to avoid being compromised; that would have made me doubt him, even if the logic of the facts had not pointed directly at him. Asking that same virtuous man to share his supervision of the mummy wrapping, lest he be suspected of connivance with the embalmers; feigning weakness so that the necropolis guards would have to support him, and thus be in a position to swear he could not have concealed the gold on his person. Only a guilty man would be so anxious to appear innocent. Yet there was reason for his precautions. Sometime in the near future, when that loving son Minmose discovers a store of gold hidden in the house, overlooked by his mother—the old do forget sometimes—then, since men have evil minds, it might be necessary for Minmose to prove beyond a shadow of a doubt that he could not have laid hands on his mother's burial equipment."

Minmose remained dumb, his eyes fixed on the ground. It was I who responded as he should have, questioning and objecting.

"But how did he remove the gold? The guards and Wennefer searched the tomb, so it was not hidden there, and there was not time for him to bury it outside."

"No, but there was ample time for him to do what had to be done in the burial chamber after Wennefer had tottered off to fetch the guards. He overturned boxes and baskets, opened the coffin, ripped through the mummy wrappings with his chisel, and took the gold. It would not take long, especially for one who knew exactly where each ornament had been placed."

Minmose's haggard face was as good as an admission of guilt. He did not look up or speak, even when Amenhotep put a hand on his shoulder.

"I pity you, Minmose," Amenhotep said gravely. "After years of devotion and self-denial, to see yourself deprived of your inheritance . . . And there was Nefertiry. You had been visiting her in secret, even before your mother died, had you not? Oh, Minmose, you should have remembered the words of the sage: 'Do not go in to a woman who is a stranger; it is a great crime, worthy of death.' She has brought you to your death, Minmose. You knew she would turn from you if your mother left you nothing."

Minmose's face was gray. "Will you denounce me, then? They will beat me to make me confess."

"Any man will confess when he is beaten," said Amenhotep, with a curl of his lip. "No, Minmose, I will not denounce you. The court of the vizier demands facts, not theories, and you have covered your tracks very neatly. But you will not escape justice. Nefertiry will consume your gold as the desert sands drink water, and then she will cast you off; and all the while Anubis, the Guide of the Dead, and Osiris, the Divine Judge, will be waiting for you. They will eat your heart, Minmose, and your spirit will hunger and thirst through all eternity. I think your punishment has already begun. Do you dream, Minmose? Did you see your mother's face last night, wrinkled and withered, her sunken eyes accusing you, as it looked when you tore the gold mask from it?"

A long shudder ran through Minmose's body. Even his hair seemed to shiver and rise. Amenhotep gestured to me. We went away, leaving Minmose staring after us with a face like death.

After we had gone a short distance, I said, "There is one more thing to tell, Amenhotep."

"There is much to tell." Amenhotep sighed deeply. "Of a good man turned evil; of two women who, in their different ways, drove him to crime; of the narrow line that separates the virtuous man from the sinner. . . ."

"I do not speak of that. I do not wish to think of that. It makes me feel strange. . . . The gold, Amenhotep—how did Minmose bear away the gold from his mother's burial?"

"He put it in the oil jar," said Amenhotep. "The one he opened to get fresh fuel for his lamp. Who would wonder if, in his agitation, he spilled a quantity of oil on the floor? He has certainly removed it by now. He has had ample opportunity, running back and forth with objects to be repaired or replaced."

"And the piece of linen he had put down to look like the mummy?"

"As you well know," Amenhotep replied, "the amount of linen used to wrap a mummy is prodigious. He could have crumpled that piece and thrown it in among the torn wrappings. But I think he did something else. It was a cool evening, in winter, and Minmose would have worn a linen mantle. He took the cloth out in the same way he had brought it in. Who would notice an extra fold of linen over a man's shoulders?

"I knew immediately that Minmose must be the guilty party, because he was the only one who had the opportunity, but I did not see how he had managed it until Wennefer showed me where the supposed mummy lay. There was no reason for a thief to drag it so far from the coffin and the burial chamber—but Minmose could not afford to have Wennefer catch even a glimpse of that room, which was then undisturbed. I realized then that what the old man had seen was not the mummy at all, but a substitute."

"Then Minmose will go unpunished."

"I said he would be punished. I spoke truly." Again Amenhotep sighed.

"You will not denounce him to Pharaoh?"

"I will tell my lord the truth. But he will not choose to act. There will be no need."

He said no more. But six weeks later Minmose's body was found floating in the river. He had taken to drinking heavily, and people said he drowned by accident. But I knew it was otherwise. Anubis and Osiris had eaten his heart, just as Amenhotep had said.

———

*Author's note*: Amenhotep Sa Hapu was a real person who lived during the fourteenth century B.C. Later generations worshiped him as a sage and scholar; he seems like a logical candidate for the role of ancient Egyptian detective.

*Sara Paretsky, named by* MS *magazine as one of the Women of the Year in 1987, is the creator of V. I. Warshawski who, like Sara, ". . . is interested in singing and has the misfortune to be a fan of the Chicago Cubs." V. I. is a hard-boiled Chicago-based private investigator with a penchant for silk blouses. She hates pretension and isn't intimidated by longshoremen, mobsters, and corporate criminals in* Indemnity Only, Deadlock *(which won a Friends of American Writers Award),* Killing Orders, Bitter Medicine, *and* Blood Shot.

*In "The Case of the Pietro Andromache," which first appeared in* Alfred Hitchcock's Mystery Magazine, *V. I.'s friend, physician Lotty Herschel, finds herself in trouble; it's up to V. I. to prove to others what she already believes in her heart.*

# The Case of the Pietro Andromache

## by Sara Paretsky

"**Y**OU ONLY AGREED to hire him because of his art collection. Of that I'm sure." Lotty Herschel bent down to adjust her stockings. "And don't waggle your eyebrows like that—it makes you look like an adolescent Groucho Marx."

Max Loewenthal obediently smoothed his eyebrows, but said, "It's your legs, Lotty; they remind me of my youth. You know, going into the Underground to wait out the air raids, looking at the ladies as they came down the escalators. The updraft always made their skirts billow."

"You're making this up, Max. I was in those Underground stations, too, and as I remember the ladies were always bundled in coats and children."

Max moved from the doorway to put an arm around Lotty. "That's what keeps us together, *Lottchen:* I am a romantic and you are severely logical. And you know we didn't hire Caudwell because of his collection. Although I admit I am eager to see it. The board wants Beth Israel to develop a transplant program. It's the only way we're going to become competitive—"

113

"Don't deliver your publicity lecture to me," Lotty snapped. Her thick brows contracted to a solid black line across her forehead. "As far as I am concerned he is a cretin with the hands of a Caliban and the personality of Attila."

Lotty's intense commitment to medicine left no room for the mundane consideration of money. But as the hospital's executive director, Max was on the spot with the trustees to see that Beth Israel ran at a profit. Or at least a smaller loss than they'd achieved in recent years. They'd brought Caudwell in part to attract more paying patients—and to help screen out some of the indigent who made up twelve percent of Beth Israel's patient load. Max wondered how long the hospital could afford to support personalities as divergent as Lotty and Caudwell in their radically differing approaches to medicine.

He dropped his arm and smiled quizzically at her. "Why do you hate him so much, Lotty?"

"*I* am the person who has to justify the patients I admit to this—this troglodyte. Do you realize he tried to keep Mrs. Mendes from the operating room when he learned she had AIDS? He wasn't even being asked to sully his hands with her blood and he didn't want me performing surgery on her."

Lotty drew back from Max and pointed an accusing finger at him. "You may tell the board that if he keeps questioning my judgment they will find themselves looking for a new perinatologist. I am serious about this. You listen this afternoon, Max, you hear whether or not he calls me 'our little baby doctor.' I am fifty-eight years old, I am a Fellow of the Royal College of Surgeons besides having enough credentials in this country to support a whole hospital, and to him I am a 'little baby doctor.' "

Max sat on the daybed and pulled Lotty down next to him. "No, no, *Lottchen*: don't fight. Listen to me. Why haven't you told me any of this before?"

"Don't be an idiot, Max: you are the director of the hospital. I cannot use our special relationship to deal with problems I have with the staff. I said my piece when Caudwell came for his final interview. A number of the other physicians were not happy with his attitude. If you remember, we asked the board to bring him in as a cardiac surgeon first and promote him to chief of staff after a year if everyone was satisfied with his performance."

"We talked about doing it that way," Max admitted. "But he wouldn't take the appointment except as chief of staff. That was the only way we could offer him the kind of money he could get at one of the university hospitals or Humana. And, Lotty, even if you don't like his personality you must agree that he is a first-class surgeon."

"I agree to nothing." Red lights danced in her black eyes. "If he patronizes me, a fellow physician, how do you imagine he treats his patients? You cannot practice medicine if—"

"Now it's my turn to ask to be spared a lecture," Max interrupted gently. "But if you feel so strongly about him, maybe you shouldn't go to his party this afternoon."

"And admit that he can beat me? Never."

"Very well then." Max got up and placed a heavily-brocaded wool shawl over Lotty's shoulders. "But you must promise me to behave. This is a social function we are going to, remember, not a gladiator contest. Caudwell is trying to repay some hospitality this afternoon, not to belittle you."

"I don't need lessons in conduct from you: Herschels were attending the emperors of Austria while the Loewenthals were operating vegetable stalls on the Ring," Lotty said haughtily.

Max laughed and kissed her hand. "Then remember these regal Herschels and act like them, *Eure Hoheit*."

## II

Caudwell had bought an apartment sight unseen when he moved to Chicago. A divorced man whose children are in college only has to consult with his own taste in these matters. He asked the Beth Israel board to recommend a realtor, sent his requirements to them— twenties construction, near Lake Michigan, good security, modern plumbing—and dropped seven hundred and fifty thousand for an eight-room condo facing the lake at Scott Street.

Since Beth Israel paid handsomely for the privilege of retaining Dr. Charlotte Herschel as their perinatologist, nothing required her to live in a five room walkup on the fringes of Uptown, so it was a bit unfair of her to mutter "Parvenu" to Max when they walked into the lobby.

Max relinquished Lotty gratefully when they got off the elevator. Being her lover was like trying to be companion to a Bengal tiger: you never knew when she'd take a lethal swipe at you. Still, if Caudwell were insulting her—and her judgment—maybe he needed to talk to the surgeon, explain how important Lotty was for the reputation of Beth Israel.

Caudwell's two children were making the obligatory Christmas visit. They were a boy and a girl, Deborah and Steve, within a year of the same age, both tall, both blond and poised, with a hearty sophistication born of a childhood spent on expensive ski slopes. Max wasn't very big, and as one took his coat and the other performed brisk introductions, he felt himself shrinking, losing in self-assurance. He accepted a glass of special *cuvee* from one of them—was it the boy or the girl, he wondered in confusion—and fled into the melee.

He landed next to one of Beth Israel's trustees, a woman in her sixties wearing a grey textured mini-dress whose black stripes were constructed of feathers. She commented brightly on Caudwell's art collection, but Max sensed an undercurrent of hostility: wealthy trustees don't like the idea that they can't out-buy the staff.

While he was frowning and nodding at appropriate intervals, it dawned on Max that Caudwell did know how much the hospital needed Lotty. Heart surgeons do not have the world's smallest egos: when you ask them to name the world's three leading practitioners, they never can remember the names of the other two. Lotty was at the top of her field, and she, too, was used to having things her way. Since her confrontational style was reminiscent more of the Battle of the Bulge than the Imperial Court of Vienna, he didn't blame Caudwell for trying to force her out of the hospital.

Max moved away from Martha Gildersleeve to admire some of the paintings and figurines she'd be discussing. A collector himself of Chinese porcelains, Max raised his eyebrows and mouthed a soundless whistle at the pieces on display. A small Watteau and a Charles Demuth watercolor were worth as much as Beth Israel paid Caudwell in a year. No wonder Mrs. Gildersleeve had been so annoyed.

"Impressive, isn't it."

Max turned to see Arthur Gioia looming over him. Max was shorter than most of the Beth Israel staff, shorter than everyone but Lotty. But Gioia, a tall muscular immunologist, loomed over everyone. He had gone to the University of Arkansas on a football scholarship and had even spent a season playing tackle for Houston before starting medical school. It had been twenty years since he last lifted weights, but his neck still looked like a redwood stump.

Gioia had led the opposition to Caudwell's appointment. Max had suspected at the time that it was due more to a medicine man's not wanting a surgeon as his nominal boss than from any other cause, but after Lotty's outburst he wasn't so sure. He was debating whether to ask the doctor how he felt about Caudwell now that he'd worked with him for six months when their host surged over to him and shook his hand.

"Sorry I didn't see you when you came in, Loewenthal. You like the Watteau? It's one of my favorite pieces. Although a collector shouldn't play favorites any more than a father should, eh, sweetheart?" The last remark was addressed to the daughter, Deborah, who had come up behind Caudwell and slipped an arm around him.

Caudwell looked more like a Victorian seadog than a surgeon. He had a round red face under a shock of yellow-white hair, a hearty Santa Claus laugh, and a bluff, direct manner. Despite Lotty's vituperations, he was immensely popular with his patients. In the short time he'd been at the hospital, referrals to cardiac surgery had increased fifteen percent.

His daughter squeezed his shoulder playfully. "I know you don't play favorites with us, Dad, but you're lying to Mr. Loewenthal about your collection; come on, you know you are."

She turned to Max. "He has a piece he's so proud of he doesn't like to show it to people—he doesn't want them to see he's got vulnerable spots. But it's Christmas, Dad, relax, let people see how you feel for a change."

Max looked curiously at the surgeon, but Caudwell seemed pleased with his daughter's familiarity. The son came up and added his own jocular cajoling.

"This really is Dad's pride and joy. He stole it from Uncle Griffen when Grandfather died and kept Mother from getting her mitts on it when they split up."

Caudwell did bark out a mild reproof at that. "You'll be giving my colleagues the wrong impression of me, Steve. I didn't steal it from Grif. Told him he could have the rest of the estate if he'd leave me the Watteau and the Pietro."

"Of course he could've bought ten estates with what those two would fetch," Steve muttered to his sister over Max's head.

Deborah relinquished her father's arm to lean over Max and whisper back, "Mom, too."

Max moved away from the alarming pair to say to Caudwell, "A Pietro? You mean Pietro d'Alessandro? You have a model, or an actual sculpture?"

Caudwell gave his staccato admiral's laugh. "The real McCoy, Loewenthal. The real McCoy. An alabaster."

"An alabaster?" Max raised his eyebrows. "Surely not. I thought Pietro worked only in bronze and marble."

"Yes, yes," chuckled Caudwell, rubbing his hands together. "Everyone thinks so, but there were a few alabasters in private collections. I've had this one authenticated by experts. Come take a look at it—it'll knock your breath away. You come, too, Gioia," he barked at the immunologist. "You're Italian, you'll like to see what your ancestors were up to."

"A Pietro alabaster?" Lotty's clipped tones made Max start—he hadn't noticed her joining the little group. "I would very much like to see this piece."

"Then come along, Dr. Herschel, come along." Caudwell led them to a small hallway, exchanging genial greetings with his guests as he passed, pointing out a John William Hill miniature they might not have seen, picking up a few other people who for various reasons wanted to see his prize.

"By the way, Gioia, I was in New York last week, you know. Met an old friend of yours from Arkansas. Paul Nierman."

"Nierman?" Gioia seemed to be at a loss. "I'm afraid I don't remember him."

"Well, he remembered you pretty well. Sent you all kinds of messages—you'll have to stop by my office on Monday and get the full strength."

Caudwell opened a door on the right side of the hall and let them into his study. It was an octagonal room carved out of the corner of the building. Windows on two sides looked out on Lake Michigan. Caudwell drew salmon drapes as he talked about the room, why he'd chosen it for his study even though the view kept his mind from his work.

Lotty ignored him and walked over to a small pedestal which stood alone against the paneling on one of the far walls. Max followed her and gazed respectfully at the statue. He had seldom seen so fine a piece outside a museum. About a foot high, it depicted a woman in classical draperies hovering in anguish over the dead body of a soldier lying at her feet. The grief in her beautiful face was so poignant that it reminded you of every sorrow you had ever faced.

"Who is it meant to be?" Max asked curiously.

"Andromache," Lotty said in a strangled voice. "Andromache mourning Hector."

Max stared at Lotty, astonished equally by her emotion and her knowledge of the figure—Lotty was totally uninterested in sculpture.

Caudwell couldn't restrain the smug smile of a collector with a true coup. "Beautiful, isn't it? How do you know the subject?"

"I should know it." Lotty's voice was husky with emotion. "My grandmother had such a Pietro. An alabaster given her great-grandfather by the Emperor Joseph the Second himself for his help in consolidating imperial ties with Poland."

She swept the statue from its stand, ignoring a gasp from Max, and turned it over. "You can see the traces of the imperial stamp here still. And the chip on Hector's foot which made the Hapsburg wish to give the statue away to begin with. How came you to have this piece? Where did you find it?"

The small group that had joined Caudwell stood silent by the entrance, shocked at Lotty's outburst. Gioia looked more horrified than any of them, but he found Lotty overwhelming at the best of times—an elephant confronted by a hostile mouse.

"I think you're allowing your emotions to carry you away, doctor." Caudwell kept his tone light, making Lotty seem more gauche by contrast. "I inherited this piece from my father, who bought it—legitimately—in Europe. Perhaps from your—grandmother, was it? But I suspect you are confused about something you may have seen in a museum as a child."

Deborah gave a high-pitched laugh and called loudly to her brother, "Dad may have stolen it from Uncle Grif, but it looks like Grand-father snatched it to begin with anyway."

"Be quiet, Deborah," Caudwell barked sternly.

His daughter paid no attention to him. She laughed again and joined her brother to look at the imperial seal on the bottom of the statue.

Lotty brushed them aside. "*I* am confused about the seal of Joseph the Second?" she hissed at Caudwell. "Or about this chip on Hec-tor's foot? You can see the line where some Philistine filled in the missing piece. Some person who thought his touch would add value to Pietro's work. Was that you, *doctor*? Or your father?"

"Lotty." Max was at her side, gently prising the statue from her shaking hands to restore it to its pedestal. "Lotty, this is not the place or the manner to discuss such things."

Angry tears sparked in her black eyes. "Are you doubting my word?"

Max shook his head. "I'm not doubting you. But I'm also not

supporting you. I'm asking you not to talk about this matter in this way at this gathering."

"But, Max: either this man or his father is a thief!"

Caudwell strolled up to Lotty and pinched her chin. "You're working too hard, Dr. Herschel. You have too many things on your mind these days. I think the board would like to see you take a leave of absence for a few weeks, go someplace warm, get yourself relaxed. When you're this tense, you're no good to your patients. What do you say, Loewenthal?"

Max didn't say any of the things he wanted to—that Lotty was insufferable and Caudwell intolerable. He believed Lotty, believed that the piece had been her grandmother's. She knew too much about it, for one thing. And for another, a lot of artworks belonging to European Jews were now in museums or private collections around the world. It was only the most godawful coincidence that the Pietro had ended up with Caudwell's father.

But how dare she raise the matter in the way most likely to alienate everyone present? He couldn't possibly support her in such a situation. And at the same time, Caudwell's pinching her chin in that condescending way made him wish he were not chained to a courtesy that would have kept him from knocking the surgeon out even if he'd been ten years younger and ten inches taller.

"I don't think this is the place or the time to discuss such matters," he reiterated as calmly as he could. "Why don't we all cool down and get back together on Monday, eh?"

Lotty gasped involuntarily, then swept from the room without a backward glance.

Max refused to follow her. He was too angry with her to want to see her again that afternoon. When he got ready to leave the party an hour or so later, after a long conversation with Caudwell that taxed his sophisticated urbanity to the utmost, he heard with relief that Lotty was long gone. The tale of her outburst had of course spread through the gathering at something faster than the speed of sound; he wasn't up to defending her to Martha Gildersleeve who demanded an explanation of him in the elevator going down.

He went home for a solitary evening in his house in Evanston. Normally such time brought him pleasure, listening to music in his study, lying on the couch with his shoes off, reading history, letting the sounds of the lake wash over him.

Tonight, though, he could get no relief. Fury with Lotty merged into images of horror, the memories of his own disintegrated family, his search through Europe for his mother. He had never found anyone who was quite certain what became of her, although several people told him definitely of his father's suicide. And stamped over these wisps in his brain was the disturbing picture of Caudwell's children, their blond heads leaning backward at identical angles as they gleefully chanted, "Grandpa was a thief, Grandpa was a thief," while Caudwell edged his visitors out of the study.

By morning he would somehow have to reconstruct himself enough to face Lotty, to respond to the inevitable flood of calls from outraged trustees. He'd have to figure out a way of soothing Caudwell's vanity, bruised more by his children's behavior than anything Lotty had said. And find a way to keep both important doctors at Beth Israel.

Max rubbed his grey hair. Every week this job brought him less joy and more pain. Maybe it was time to step down, to let the board bring in a young MBA who would turn Beth Israel's finances around. Lotty would resign then, and it would be an end to the tension between her and Caudwell.

Max fell asleep on the couch. He awoke around five muttering, "By morning, by morning." His joints were stiff from cold, his eyes sticky with tears he'd shed unknowingly in his sleep.

But in the morning things changed. When Max got to his office he found the place buzzing, not with news of Lotty's outburst but word that Caudwell had missed his early morning surgery. Work came almost completely to a halt at noon when his children phoned to say they'd found the surgeon strangled in his own study and the Pietro Andromache missing. And on Tuesday, the police arrested Dr. Charlotte Herschel for Lewis Caudwell's murder.

### III

Lotty would not speak to anyone. She was out on two hundred fifty thousand dollars' bail, the money raised by Max, but she had gone directly to her apartment on Sheffield after two nights in County Jail without stopping to thank him. She would not talk to reporters, she remained silent during all conversations with the police, and she emphatically refused to speak to the private investigator who had been her close friend for many years.

Max, too, stayed behind an impregnable shield of silence. While

Lotty went on indefinite leave, turning her practice over to a series of colleagues, Max continued to go to the hospital every day. But he, too, would not speak to reporters: he wouldn't even say, "No comment." He talked to the police only after they threatened to lock him up as a material witness, and then every word had to be pried from him as if his mouth were stone and speech Excalibur. For three days V. I. Warshawski left messages which he refused to return.

On Friday, when no word came from the detective, when no reporter popped up from a nearby urinal in the men's room to try to trick him into speaking, when no more calls came from the state's attorney, Max felt a measure of relaxation as he drove home. As soon as the trial was over he would resign, retire to London. If he could only keep going until then, everything would be—not all right, but bearable.

He used the remote release for the garage door and eased his car into the small space. As he got out he realized bitterly he'd been too optimistic in thinking he'd be left in peace. He hadn't seen the woman sitting on the stoop leading from the garage to the kitchen when he drove in, only as she uncoiled herself at his approach.

"I'm glad you're home—I was beginning to freeze out here."

"How did you get into the garage, Victoria?"

The detective grinned in a way he usually found engaging. Now it seemed merely predatory. "Trade secret, Max. I know you don't want to see me, but I need to talk to you."

He unlocked the door into the kitchen. "Why not just let yourself into the house if you were cold? If your scruples permit you into the garage, why not into the house?"

She bit her lip in momentary discomfort but said lightly, "I couldn't manage my picklocks with my fingers this cold."

The detective followed him into the house. Another tall monster; five foot eight, athletic, light on her feet behind him. Maybe American mothers put growth hormones or steroids in their children's cornflakes. He'd have to ask Lotty. His mind winced at the thought.

"I've talked to the police, of course," the light alto continued behind him steadily, oblivious to his studied rudeness as he poured himself a cognac, took his shoes off, found his waiting slippers, and padded down the hall to the front door for his mail.

"I understand why they arrested Lotty—Caudwell had been doped with a whole bunch of Xanax and then strangled while he was sleeping it off. And, of course, she was back at the building Sunday night. She won't say why, but one of the tenants I.D.'d her as the woman who showed up around ten at the service entrance when he was walking his dog. She won't say if she talked to Caudwell, if he let her in, if he was still alive."

Max tried to ignore her clear voice. When that proved impossible he tried to read a journal which had come in the mail.

"And those kids, they're marvelous, aren't they? Like something out of the *Fabulous Furry Freak Brothers*. They won't talk to me but they gave a long interview to Murray Ryerson over at the *Star*.

"After Caudwell's guests left, they went to a flick at the Chestnut Street Station, had a pizza afterwards, then took themselves dancing on Division Street. So they strolled in around two in the morning—confirmed by the doorman—saw the light on in the old man's study. But they were feeling no pain and he kind of overreacted—their term—if they were buzzed, so they didn't stop in to say good-night. It was only when they got up around noon and went in that they found him."

V. I. had followed Max from the front hallway to the door of his study as she spoke. He stood there irresolutely, not wanting his private place desecrated with her insistent, air-hammer speech, and finally went on down the hall to a little-used living room. He sat stiffly on one of the brocade armchairs and looked at her remotely when she perched on the edge of its companion.

"The weak piece in the police story is the statue," V. I. continued.

She eyed the Persian rug doubtfully and unzipped her boots, sticking them on the bricks in front of the fireplace.

"Everyone who was at the party agrees that Lotty was beside herself. By now the story has spread so far that people who weren't even in the apartment when she looked at the statue swear they heard her threaten to kill him. But if that's the case, what happened to the statue?"

Max gave a slight shrug to indicate total lack of interest in the topic.

V. I. ploughed on doggedly. "Now some people think she might have given it to a friend or a relation to keep for her until her name is cleared at the trial. And these people think it would be either her Uncle Stefan here in Chicago, her brother Hugo in Montreal, or you. So the Mounties searched Hugo's place and are keeping an eye on his mail. And the Chicago cops are doing the same for Stefan. And I presume someone got a warrant and went through here, right?"

Max said nothing, but he felt his heart beating faster. Police in his house, searching his things? But wouldn't they have to get his permission to enter? Or would they? Victoria would know, but he couldn't bring himself to ask. She waited for a few minutes, but when he still wouldn't speak, she plunged on. He could see it was becoming an effort for her to talk, but he wouldn't help her.

"But I don't agree with those people. Because I know that Lotty is innocent. And that's why I'm here. Not like a bird of prey, as you think, using your misery for carrion. But to get you to help me. Lotty won't speak to me, and if she's that miserable I won't force her to. But surely, Max, you won't sit idly by and let her be railroaded for something she never did."

Max looked away from her. He was surprised to find himself holding the brandy snifter and set it carefully on a table beside him.

"Max!" Her voice was shot with astonishment. "I don't believe this. You actually think she killed Caudwell."

Max flushed a little, but she'd finally stung him into a response. "And you are God who sees all and knows she didn't?"

"I see more than you do," V. I. snapped. "I haven't known Lotty as long as you have, but I know when she's telling the truth."

"So you are God." Max bowed in heavy irony. "You see beyond the facts to the innermost souls of men and women."

He expected another outburst from the young woman, but she gazed at him steadily without speaking. It was a look sympathetic enough that Max felt embarrassed by his sarcasm and burst out with what was on his mind.

"What else am I to think? She hasn't said anything, but there's no doubt that she returned to his apartment Sunday night."

It was V. I.'s turn for sarcasm. "With a little vial of Xanax that she somehow induced him to swallow? And then strangled him for good measure? Come on, Max, you know Lotty: honesty follows her around like a cloud. If she'd killed Caudwell, she'd say something like, 'Yes, I bashed the little vermin's brains in.' Instead she's not speaking at all."

Suddenly the detective's eyes widened with incredulity. "Of course. She thinks you killed Caudwell. You're doing the only thing you can to protect her—standing mute. And she's doing the same thing. What an admirable pair of archaic knights."

"No!" Max said sharply. "It's not possible. How could she think such a thing? She carried on so wildly that it was embarrassing to be near her. I didn't want to see her or talk to her. That's why I've felt so terrible. If only I hadn't been so obstinate, if only I'd called her Sunday night. How could she think I would kill someone on her behalf when I was so angry with her?"

"Why else isn't she saying anything to anyone?" Warshawski demanded.

"Shame, maybe," Max offered. "You didn't see her on Sunday. I did. That is why I think she killed him, not because some man let her into the building."

His brown eyes screwed shut at the memory. "I have seen Lotty in the grip of anger many times, more than is pleasant to remember, really. But never, never have I seen her in this kind of—uncontrolled rage. You could not talk to her. It was impossible."

The detective didn't respond to that. Instead she said, "Tell me about the statue. I heard a couple of garbled versions from people who were at the party, but I haven't found anyone yet who was in the study when Caudwell showed it to you. Was it really her grandmother's, do you think? And how did Caudwell come to have it if it was?"

Max nodded mournfully. "Oh, yes. It was really her family's, I'm convinced of that. She could not have known in advance about the details, the flaw in the foot, the imperial seal on the bottom. As to how Caudwell got it, I did a little looking into that myself yesterday. His father was with the Army of Occupation in Germany after the war. A surgeon attached to Patton's staff. Men in such positions had endless opportunities to acquire artworks after the war."

V. I. shook her head questioningly.

"You must know something of this, Victoria. Well, maybe not. You know the Nazis helped themselves liberally to artwork belonging to Jews everywhere they occupied Europe. And not just Jews—they plundered Eastern Europe on a grand scale. The best guess is that they stole sixteen million pieces—statues, paintings, altarpieces, tapestries, rare books. The list is beyond reckoning, really."

The detective gave a little gasp. "Sixteen million! You're joking."

"Not a joke, Victoria. I wish it were so, but it is not. The U.S. Army of Occupation took charge of as many works of art as they found in the occupied territories. In theory, they were to find the rightful owners and try to restore them. But in practice few pieces were ever traced, and many of them ended up on the black market.

"You only had to say that such-and-such a piece was worth less than five thousand dollars and you were allowed to buy it. For an officer on Patton's staff, the opportunities for fabulous acquisitions would have been endless. Caudwell said he had the statue authenti-

cated, but of course he never bothered to establish its provenance.
Anyway, how could he?'' Max finished bitterly. "Lotty's family had
a deed of gift from the Emperor, but that would have disappeared
long since with the dispersal of their possessions.''

"And you really think Lotty would have killed a man just to get
this statue back? She couldn't have expected to keep it. Not if she'd
killed someone to get it, I mean.''

"You are so practical, Victoria. You are too analytical, sometimes,
to understand why people do what they do. That was not just a
statue. True, it is a priceless artwork, but you know Lotty, you know
she places no value on such possessions. No, it meant her family to
her, her past, her history, everything that the war destroyed forever
for her. You must not imagine that because she never discusses such
matters that they do not weigh on her.''

V. I. flushed at Max's accusation. "You should be glad I'm analytical. It convinces me that Lotty is innocent. And whether you
believe it or not I'm going to prove it.''

Max lifted his shoulders slightly in a manner wholly European.
"We each support Lotty according to our lights. I saw that she met
her bail, and I will see that she gets expert counsel. I am not convinced that she needs you making her innermost secrets public.''

V. I.'s grey eyes turned dark with a sudden flash of temper. "You're
dead wrong about Lotty. I'm sure the memory of the war is a pain
that can never be cured, but Lotty lives in the present, she works in
hope for the future. The past does not obsess and consume her as,
perhaps, it does you.''

Max said nothing. His wide mouth turned in on itself in a narrow
line. The detective laid a contrite hand on his arm.

"I'm sorry, Max. That was below the belt.''

He forced the ghost of a smile to his mouth.

"Perhaps it's true. Perhaps it's why I love these ancient things so
much. I wish I could believe you about Lotty. Ask me what you
want to know. If you promise to leave as soon as I've answered and
not to bother me again, I'll answer your questions.''

## IV

Max put in a dutiful appearance at the Michigan Avenue Presbyte-
rian Church Monday afternoon for Lewis Caudwell's funeral. The
surgeon's former wife came, flanked by her children and her hus-

band's brother Griffen. Even after three decades in America Max found himself puzzled sometimes by the natives' behavior: since she and Caudwell were divorced, why had his ex-wife draped herself in black? She was even wearing a veiled hat reminiscent of Queen Victoria.

The children behaved in a moderately subdued fashion, but the girl was wearing a white dress shot with black lightning forks which looked as though it belonged at a disco or a resort. Maybe it was her only dress or her only dress with black in it, Max thought, trying hard to look charitably at the blonde Amazon—after all, she had been suddenly and horribly orphaned.

Even though she was a stranger both in the city and the church, Deborah had hired one of the church parlors and managed to find someone to cater coffee and light snacks. Max joined the rest of the congregation there after the service.

He felt absurd as he offered condolences to the divorced widow: did she really miss the dead man so much? She accepted his conventional words with graceful melancholy and leaned slightly against her son and daughter. They hovered near her with what struck Max as a stagey solicitude. Seen next to her daughter, Mrs. Caudwell looked so frail and undernourished that she seemed like a ghost. Or maybe it was just that her children had a hearty vitality that even a funeral couldn't quench.

Caudwell's brother Griffen stayed as close to the widow as the children would permit. The man was totally unlike the hearty seadog surgeon. Max thought if he'd met the brothers standing side by side he would never have guessed their relationship. He was tall, like his niece and nephew, but without their robustness. Caudwell had had a thick mop of yellow-white hair; Griffen's domed head was covered by thin wisps of grey. He seemed weak and nervous, and lacked Caudwell's outgoing *bonhomie*; no wonder the surgeon had found it easy to decide the disposition of their father's estate in his favor. Max wondered what Griffen had gotten in return.

Mrs. Caudwell's vague, disoriented conversation indicated that she was heavily sedated. That, too, seemed strange. A man she hadn't lived with for four years and she was so upset at his death that she could only manage the funeral on drugs? Or maybe it was the shame of coming as the divorced woman, not a true widow? But then why come at all?

To his annoyance, Max found himself wishing he could ask Victoria about it. She would have some cynical explanation—Caudwell's death meant the end of the widow's alimony and she knew she wasn't remembered in the will. Or she was having an affair with Griffen and was afraid she would betray herself without tranquilizers. Although it was hard to imagine the uncertain Griffen as the object of a strong passion.

Since he had told Victoria he didn't want to see her again when she left on Friday, it was ridiculous of him to wonder what she was doing, whether she was really uncovering evidence that would clear Lotty. Ever since she had gone he had felt a little flicker of hope in the bottom of his stomach. He kept trying to drown it, but it wouldn't quite go away.

Lotty, of course, had not come to the funeral, but most of the rest of the Beth Israel staff was there, along with the trustees. Arthur Gioia, his giant body filling the small parlor to the bursting point, tried finding a tactful balance between honesty and courtesy with the bereaved family; he made heavy going of it.

A sable-clad Martha Gildersleeve appeared under Gioia's elbow, rather like a furry football he might have tucked away. She made bright, unseemly remarks to the bereaved family about the disposal of Caudwell's artworks.

"Of course, the famous statue is gone now. What a pity. You could have endowed a chair in his honor with the proceeds from that piece alone." She gave a high, meaningless laugh.

Max sneaked a glance at his watch, wondering how long he had to stay before leaving would be rude. His sixth sense, the perfect courtesy that governed his movements, had deserted him, leaving him subject to the gaucheries of ordinary mortals. He never peeked at his watch at functions, and at any prior funeral he would have deftly pried Martha Gildersleeve from her victim. Instead he stood helplessly by while she tortured Mrs. Caudwell and other bystanders alike.

He glanced at his watch again. Only two minutes had passed since his last look. No wonder people kept their eyes on their watches at dull meetings: they couldn't believe the clock could move so slowly.

He inched stealthily toward the door, exchanging empty remarks with the staff members and trustees he passed. Nothing negative was said about Lotty to his face, but the comments cut off at his approach added to his misery.

He was almost at the exit when two newcomers appeared. Most of the group looked at them with indifferent curiosity, but Max suddenly felt an absurd stir of elation. Victoria, looking sane and modern in a navy suit, stood in the doorway, eyebrows raised, scanning the room. At her elbow was a police sergeant Max had met with her a few times. The man was in charge of Caudwell's death, too: it was that unpleasant association that kept the name momentarily from his mind.

V. I. finally spotted Max near the door and gave him a discreet sign. He went to her at once.

"I think we may have the goods," she murmured. "Can you get everyone to go? We just want the family, Mrs. Gildersleeve, and Gioia."

"*You* may have the goods," the police sergeant growled. "I'm here unofficially and reluctantly."

"But you're here." Warshawski grinned, and Max wondered how he ever could have found the look predatory. His own spirits rose enormously at her smile. "You know in your heart of hearts that arresting Lotty was just plain dumb. And now I'm going to make you look real smart. In public, too."

Max felt his suave sophistication return with the rush of elation that an ailing diva must have when she finds her voice again. A touch here, a word there, and the guests disappeared like the hosts of Sennacherib. Meanwhile he solicitously escorted first Martha Gildersleeve, then Mrs. Caudwell to adjacent armchairs, got the brother to fetch coffee for Mrs. Gildersleeve, the daughter and son to look after the widow.

With Gioia he could be a bit more ruthless, telling him to wait because the police had something important to ask him. When the last guest had melted away, the immunologist stood nervously at the window rattling his change over and over in his pockets. The jingling suddenly was the only sound in the room. Gioia reddened and clasped his hands behind his back.

Victoria came into the room beaming like a governess with a delightful treat in store for her charges. She introduced herself to the Caudwells.

"You know Sergeant McGonnigal, I'm sure, after this last week. I'm a private investigator. Since I don't have any legal standing, you're not required to answer any questions I have. So I'm not going to ask you any questions. I'm just going to treat you to a travelogue. I wish I had slides, but you'll have to imagine the visuals while the audio track moves along."

"A private investigator!" Steve's mouth formed an exaggerated "O"; his eyes widened in amazement. "Just like Bogie."

He was speaking, as usual, to his sister. She gave her high-pitched laugh and said, "We'll win first prize in the 'How I Spent My Winter Vacation' contests. Our daddy was murdered. Zowie. Then his most valuable possession was snatched. Powie. But he'd already stolen it from the Jewish doctor who killed him. Yowie! And then a P.I. to wrap it all up. Yowie! Zowie! Powie!"

"Deborah, please," Mrs. Caudwell sighed. "I know you're excited, sweetie, but not right now, okay?"

"Your children keep you young, don't they, ma'am?" Victoria said. "How can you ever feel old when your kids stay seven all their lives?"

"Oo, ow, she bites, Debbie, watch out, she bites!" Steve cried.

McGonnigal made an involuntary movement, as though restraining himself from smacking the younger man. "Ms. Warshawski is right: you are under no obligation to answer any of her questions. But you're bright people, all of you: you know I wouldn't be here if the police didn't take her ideas very seriously. So let's have a little quiet and listen to what she's got on her mind."

Victoria seated herself in an armchair near Mrs. Caudwell's. McGonnigal moved to the door and leaned against the jamb. Deborah and Steve whispered and poked each other until one or both of them shrieked. They then made their faces prim and sat with their hands folded on their laps, looking like bright-eyed choirboys.

Griffen hovered near Mrs. Caudwell. "You know you don't have to say anything, Vivian. In fact, I think you should return to your hotel and lie down. The stress of the funeral—then these strangers—"

Mrs. Caudwell's lips curled bravely below the bottom of her veil. "It's all right, Grif; if I managed to survive everything else, one more thing isn't going to do me in."

"Great." Victoria accepted a cup of coffee from Max. "Let me just sketch events for you as I saw them last week. Like everyone else in Chicago, I read about Dr. Caudwell's murder and saw it on television. Since I know a number of people attached to Beth Israel, I may have paid more attention to it than the average viewer, but I didn't get personally involved until Dr. Herschel's arrest on Tuesday."

She swallowed some coffee and set the cup on the table next to her with a small snap. "I have known Dr. Herschel for close to twenty years. It is inconceivable that she would commit such a murder, as those who know her well should have realized at once. I don't fault the police, but others should have known better: she is hot-tempered. I'm not saying killing is beyond her—I don't think it's beyond any of us. She might have taken the statue and smashed Dr. Caudwell's head in the heat of rage. But it beggars belief to think she went home, brooded over her injustices, packed a dose of prescription tranquilizer, and headed back to the Gold Coast with murder in mind."

Max felt his cheeks turn hot at her words. He started to interject a protest but bit it back.

"Dr. Herschel refused to make a statement all week, but this afternoon, when I got back from my travels, she finally agreed to talk to me. Sergeant McGonnigal was with me. She doesn't deny that she returned to Dr. Caudwell's apartment at ten that night—she went back to apologize for her outburst and to try to plead with him to return the statue. He didn't answer when the doorman called up, and on impulse she went around to the back of the building, got in through the service entrance, and waited for some time outside the apartment door. When he neither answered the doorbell nor returned home himself, she finally went away around eleven o'clock. The children, of course, were having a night on the town."

"*She* says," Gioia interjected.

"Agreed." V. I. smiled. "I make no bones about being a partisan: I accept her version. The more so because the only reason she didn't give it a week ago was that she herself was protecting an old friend. She thought perhaps this friend had bestirred himself on her behalf and killed Caudwell to avenge deadly insults against her. It was only when I persuaded her that these suspicions were as unmerited as—well, as accusations against herself—that she agreed to talk."

Max bit his lip and busied himself with getting more coffee for the three women. Victoria waited for him to finish before continuing.

"When I finally got a detailed account of what took place at Caudwell's party, I heard about three people with an axe to grind. One always has to ask, what axe and how big a grindstone? That's what I've spent the weekend finding out. You might as well know that I've been to Little Rock and to Havelock, North Carolina."

Gioia began jingling the coins in his pockets again. Mrs. Caudwell said softly, "Grif, I am feeling a little faint. Perhaps—"

"Home you go, Mom," Steve cried out with alacrity.

"In a few minutes, Mrs. Caudwell," the sergeant said from the doorway. "Get her feet up, Warshawski."

For a moment Max was afraid that Steve or Deborah was going to attack Victoria, but McGonnigal moved over to the widow's chair and the children sat down again. Little drops of sweat dotted Griffen's balding head; Gioia's face had a greenish sheen, foliage on top of his redwood neck.

"The thing that leapt out at me," Victoria continued calmly, as though there had been no interruption, "was Caudwell's remark to Dr. Gioia. The doctor was clearly upset, but people were so focused on Lotty and the statue that they didn't pay any attention to that.

"So I went to Little Rock, Arkansas, on Saturday and found the Paul Nierman whose name Caudwell had mentioned to Gioia. Nierman lived in the same fraternity with Gioia when they were undergraduates together twenty-five years ago. And he took Dr. Gioia's anatomy and physiology exams his junior year when Gioia was in danger of academic probation, so he could stay on the football team.

"Well, that seemed unpleasant, perhaps disgraceful. But there's no question that Gioia did all his own work in medical school, passed his boards, and so on. So I didn't think the board would demand a resignation for this youthful indiscretion. The question was whether Gioia thought they would, and if he would have killed to prevent Caudwell making it public."

She paused, and the immunologist blurted out, "No. No. But Caudwell—Caudwell knew I'd opposed his appointment. He and I—our approaches to medicine were very opposite. And as soon as he said Nierman's name to me, I knew he'd found out and that he'd torment me with it forever. I—I went back to his place Sunday night to have it out with him. I was more determined than Dr. Herschel and got into his unit through the kitchen entrance; he hadn't locked that.

"I went to his study, but he was already dead. I couldn't believe it. It absolutely terrified me. I could see he'd been strangled and—well, it's no secret that I'm strong enough to have done it. I wasn't thinking straight. I just got clean away from there—I think I've been running ever since."

"You!" McGonnigal shouted. "How come we haven't heard about this before?"

"Because you insisted on focusing on Dr. Herschel," V. I. said nastily. "I knew he'd been there because the doorman told me. He would have told you if you'd asked."

"This is terrible," Mrs. Gildersleeve interjected. "I am going to talk to the board tomorrow and demand the resignations of Dr. Gioia and Dr. Herschel."

"Do," Victoria agreed cordially. "Tell them the reason you got to stay for this was because Murray Ryerson at the *Herald-Star* was doing a little checking for me here in Chicago. He found out that part of the reason you were so jealous of Caudwell's collection is that you're living terribly in debt. I won't humiliate you in public by telling people what your money has gone to, but you've had to sell your husband's art collection and you have a third mortgage on your house. A valuable statue with no documented history would have taken care of everything."

Martha Gildersleeve shrank inside her sable. "You don't know anything about this."

"Well, Murray talked to Pablo and Eduardo. . . . Yes, I won't say anything else. So anyway, Murray checked whether either Gioia or Mrs. Gildersleeve had the statue. They didn't, so—"

"You've been in my house?" Mrs. Gildersleeve shrieked.

V. I. shook her head. "Not me. Murray Ryerson." She looked apologetically at the sergeant. "I knew you'd never get a warrant for me, since you'd made an arrest. And you'd never have got it in time, anyway."

She looked at her coffee cup, saw it was empty and put it down again. Max took it from the table and filled it for her a third time. His fingertips were itching with nervous irritation; some of the coffee landed on his trouser leg.

"I talked to Murray Saturday night from Little Rock. When he came up empty here, I headed for North Carolina. To Havelock, where Griffen and Lewis Caudwell grew up and where Mrs. Caudwell still lives. And I saw the house where Griffen lives, and talked to the doctor who treats Mrs. Caudwell, and—"

"You really are a pooper snooper, aren't you," Steve said.

"Pooper snooper, pooper snooper," Deborah chanted. "Don't get enough thrills of your own so you have to live on other people's shit."

"Yeah, the neighbors talked to me about you two." Victoria looked at them with contemptuous indulgence. "You've been a two-person wolfpack terrifying most of the people around you since you were three. But the folks in Havelock admired how you always stuck up for your mother. You thought your father got her addicted to tranquilizers and then left her high and dry. So you brought her newest version with you and were all set—you just needed to decide when to give it to him. Dr. Herschel's outburst over the statue played right into your hands. You figured your father had stolen it from your uncle to begin with—why not send it back to him and let Dr. Herschel take the rap?"

"It wasn't like that," Steve said, red spots burning in his cheeks.

"What was it like, son?" McGonnigal had moved next to him.

"Don't talk to them—they're tricking you," Deborah shrieked. "The pooper snooper and her gopher gooper."

"She—Mommy used to love us before Daddy made her take all this shit. Then she went away. We just wanted him to see what it was like. We started putting Xanax in his coffee and stuff; we wanted to see if he'd fuck up during surgery, let his life get ruined. But then he was sleeping there in the study after his stupid-ass party, and we thought we'd just let him sleep through his morning surgery. Sleep forever, you know, it was so easy, we used his own Harvard necktie. I was so fucking sick of hearing 'Early to bed, early to rise' from him. And we sent the statue to Uncle Grif. I suppose the pooper snooper found it there. He can sell it and Mother can be all right again."

"Grandpa stole it from Jews and Daddy stole it from Grif, so we thought it worked out perfectly if we stole it from Daddy," Deborah cried. She leaned her blond head next to her brother's and shrieked with laughter.

## V

Max watched the line of Lotty's legs change as she stood on tiptoe to reach a brandy snifter. Short, muscular from years of racing at top speed from one point to the next, maybe they weren't as svelte as the long legs of modern American girls, but he preferred them. He waited until her feet were securely planted before making his announcement.

"The board is bringing in Justin Hardwick for a final interview for chief of staff."

"Max!" She whirled, the Bengal fire sparkling in her eyes. "I know this Hardwick and he is another like Caudwell, looking for cost-cutting and no poverty patients. I won't have it."

"We've got you and Gioia and a dozen others bringing in so many non-paying patients that we're not going to survive another five years at the present rate. I figure it's a balancing act. We need someone who can see that the hospital survives so that you and Art can practice medicine the way you want to. And when he knows what happened to his predecessor, he'll be very careful not to stir up our resident tigress."

"Max!" She was hurt and astonished at the same time. "Oh. You're joking, I see. It's not very funny to me, you know."

"My dear, we've got to learn to laugh about it: it's the only way we'll ever be able to forgive ourselves for our terrible misjudgments." He stepped over to put an arm around her. "Now where is this remarkable surprise you promised to show me?"

She shot him a look of pure mischief, Lotty on a dare as he first remembered meeting her at eighteen. His hold on her tightened and he followed her to her bedroom. In a glass case in the corner, complete with a humidity-control system, stood the Pietro Andromache.

Max looked at the beautiful, anguished face. I understand your sorrows, she seemed to say to him. I understand your grief for your mother, your family, your history, but it's all right to let go of them, to live in the present and hope for the future. It's not a betrayal.

Tears pricked his eyelids, but he demanded, "How did you get this? I was told the police had it under lock and key until lawyers decided on the disposition of Caudwell's estate."

"Victoria," Lotty said shortly. "I told her the problem and she got it for me. On the condition that I not ask how she did it. And Max, you know—*damned* well that it was not Caudwell's to dispose of."

It was Lotty's. Of course it was. Max wondered briefly how Joseph the Second had come by it to begin with. For that matter, what had Lotty's great-great-grandfather done to earn it from the emperor? Max looked into Lotty's tiger eyes and kept such reflections to himself. Instead he inspected Hector's foot where the filler had been carefully scraped away to reveal the old chip.

*With the introduction of Sharon McCone in* Edwin of the Iron Shoes *in 1977, Marcia Muller opened the floodgates for the modern woman detective. Her three series characters, McCone (*Eye of the Storm, There's Nothing to be Afraid of), *Elena Oliverez (*Legend of the Slain Soldiers, The Tree of Death), *and Joanna Stark (*Cavalier in White, There Hangs the Knife) *are all contemporary women who haven't given up their feelings or their femininity to compete in the male-dominated world; instead they've brought additional talents to bear in the pursuit of truth and justice.*

*"All the Lonely People"—where did they all come from? More to the point in this story: Is one of them using a local business to turn a not-quite legal profit? Sharon McCone, with typical humor and sharp wit, puts herself on the roster of a dating service to solve a crime.*

# ALL THE LONELY PEOPLE

## by Marcia Muller

"NAME, SHARON MCCONE. Occupation . . . I can't put private investigator. What should I be?" I glanced over my shoulder at Hank Zahn, my boss at All Souls Legal Cooperative. He stood behind me, his eyes bemused behind thick horn-rimmed glasses.

"I've heard you tell people you're a researcher when you don't want to be bothered with stupid questions like 'What's a nice girl like you . . .' "

"*Legal* researcher." I wrote it on the form. "Now—'About the person you are seeking.' Age—does not matter. Smoker—does not matter. Occupation—does not matter. I sound excessively eager for a date, don't I?"

Hank didn't answer. He was staring at the form. "The things they ask. Sexual preference." He pointed at the item. "Hetero, bi, lesbian, gay. There's no place for 'does not matter.' "

As he spoke, he grinned wickedly. I glared at him. "You're enjoying this!"

"Of course I am. I never thought I'd see the day you'd fill out an application for a dating service."

I sighed and drummed my fingertips on the desk. Hank is my best male friend, as well as my boss. I love him like a brother—sometimes. But he harbors an overactive interest in my love life and delights in teasing me about it. I would be hearing about the dating service for years to come. I asked, "What should I say I want the guy's cultural interests to be? I can't put 'does not matter' for everything."

"I don't think burglars *have* cultural interests."

"Come on, Hank. Help me with this!"

"Oh, put film. Everyone's gone to a movie."

"Film." I checked the box.

The form was quite simple, yet it provided a great deal of information about the applicant. The standard questions about address, income level, whether the individual shared a home or lived alone, and hours free for dating were enough in themselves to allow an astute burglar to weed out prospects—and pick times to break in when they were not likely to be on the premises.

And that apparently was what had happened at the big singles apartment complex down near the San Francisco–Daly City line, owned by Hank's client, Dick Morris. There had been three burglaries over the past three months, beginning not long after the place had been leafleted by All the Best People Introduction Service. Each of the people whose apartments had been hit were women who had filled out the application forms; they had had from two to ten dates with men with whom the service had put them in touch. The burglaries had taken place when one renter was at work, another away for the weekend, and the third out with a date whom she had also met through Best People.

Coincidence, the police had told the renters and Dick Morris. After all, none of the women had reported having dates with the same man. And there were many other common denominators among them besides their use of the service. They lived in the same complex. They all knew one another. Two belonged to the same health club. They shopped at the same supermarket, shared auto mechanics, hairstylists, dry cleaners, and two of them went to the same psychiatrist.

Coincidence, the police insisted. But two other San Francisco area members of Best People had also been burglarized—one of them male—and so they checked the service out carefully.

What they found was absolutely no evidence of collusion in the burglaries. It was no fly-by-night operation. It had been in business ten years—a long time for that type of outfit. Its board of directors included a doctor, a psychologist, a rabbi, a minister, and a well-known author of somewhat weird but popular novels. It was respectable—as such things go.

But Best People was still the strongest link among the burglary victims. And Dick Morris was a good landlord who genuinely cared about his tenants. So he put on a couple of security guards, and when the police couldn't run down the perpetrator(s) and backburnered the case, he came to All Souls for legal advice.

It might seem unusual for the owner of a glitzy singles complex to come to a legal services plan that charges its clients on a sliding-fee scale, but Dick Morris was cash-poor. Everything he'd saved during his long years as a journeyman plumber had gone into the complex, and it was barely turning a profit as yet. Wouldn't be turning any profit at all if the burglaries continued and some of his tenants got scared and moved out.

Hank could have given Dick the typical attorney's spiel about leaving things in the hands of the police and continuing to pay the guards out of his dwindling cash reserves, but Hank is far from typical. Instead he referred Dick to me. I'm All Souls' staff investigator, and assignments like this one—where there's a challenge—are what I live for.

They are, that is, unless I have to apply for membership in a dating service, plus set up my own home as a target for a burglar. Once I started "dating," I would remove anything of value to All Souls, plus Dick would station one of his security guards at my house during the hours I was away from there, but it was still a potentially risky and nervous-making proposition.

Now Hank loomed over me, still grinning. I could tell how much he was going to enjoy watching me suffer through an improbable, humiliating, *asinine* experience. I smiled back—sweetly.

" 'Your sexual preference.' Hetero." I checked the box firmly. "Except for inflating my income figure, so I'll look like I have a lot of good stuff to steal, I'm filling this out truthfully," I said. "Who knows—I might meet someone wonderful."

When I looked back up at Hank, my evil smile matched his earlier one. He, on the other hand, looked as if he'd swallowed something the wrong way.

* * *

My first "date" was a chubby little man named Jerry Hale. Jerry was *very* into the singles scene. We met at a bar in San Francisco's affluent Marina district, and while we talked, he kept swiveling around in his chair and leering at every woman who walked by. Most of them ignored him, but a few glared; I wanted to hang a big sign around my neck saying, "I'm not really with him, it's only business." While I tried to find out about his experiences with All the Best People Introduction Service, plus impress him with all the easily fenceable items I had at home, he tried to educate me on the joys of being single.

"I used to be into the bar scene pretty heavily," he told me. "Did all right too. But then I started to worry about herpes and AIDS— I'll let you see the results of my most recent test if you want—and my drinking was getting out of hand. Besides, it was expensive. Then I went the other way—a health club. Did all right there too. But goddamn, it's *tiring.* So then I joined a bunch of church groups— you meet a lot of horny women there. But churches encourage matrimony, and I'm not into that."

"So you applied to All the Best People. How long have you—?"

"Not right away. First I thought about joining AA, even went to a meeting. Lots of good-looking women are recovering alcoholics, you know. But I like to drink too much to make the sacrifice. Dear Abby's always saying you should enroll in courses, so I signed up for a couple at U.C. Extension. Screenwriting and photography."

My mouth was stiff from smiling politely, and I had just about written Jerry off as a possible suspect—he was too busy to burglarize anyone. I took a sip of wine and looked at my watch.

Jerry didn't notice the gesture. "The screenwriting class was terrible—the instructor actually wanted you to write stuff. And photography—how can you see women in the darkroom, let alone make any moves when you smell like chemicals?"

I had no answer for that. Maybe my own efforts at photography accounted for my not having a lover at the moment. . . .

"Finally I found All the Best People," Jerry went on. "Now I really do all right. And it's opened up a whole new world of dating to me—eighties-style. I've answered ads in the paper, placed my own ad too. You've always got to ask that they send a photo, though, so you can screen out the dogs. There's Weekenders, they plan trips. When I don't want to go out of the house, I use the Intro Line— that's a phone club you can join, where you call in for three bucks and either talk to one person or on a party line. There's a video exchange where you can make tapes and trade them with people so you'll know you're compatible before you set up a meeting. I do all right."

He paused expectantly, as if he thought I was going to ask how I could get in on all these good eighties-style deals.

"Jerry," I said, "have you read any good books lately?"

"Have I . . . *what*?"

"What do you do when you're not dating?"

"I work. I told you, I'm in sales—"

"Do you ever spend time alone?"

"Doing what?"

"Oh, just being alone. Puttering around the house or working at hobbies. Just thinking."

"Are you crazy? What kind of a computer glitch are you, anyway?" He stood, all five-foot-three of him quivering indignantly. "Believe me, I'm going to complain to Best People about setting me up with you. They described you as 'vivacious,' but you've hardly said a word all evening!"

Morton Stone was a nice man, a sad man. He insisted on buying me dinner at his favorite Chinese restaurant. He spent the evening asking me questions about myself and my job as a legal researcher; while he listened, his fingers played nervously with the silverware. Later, over a brandy in a nearby bar, he told me how his wife had died the summer before, of cancer. He told me about his promise to her that he would get on with his life, find someone new, and be happy. This was the first date he'd arranged through All the Best People; he'd never done anything like that in his life. He'd only tried them because he wasn't good at meeting people. He had a good job, but it wasn't enough. He had money to travel, but it was no fun without someone to share the experience with. He would have liked to have children, but he and his wife had put it off until they'd be financially secure, and then they'd found out about the cancer. . . .

I felt guilty as hell about deceiving him, and for taking his time, money, and hope. But by the end of the evening I'd remembered a woman friend who was just getting over a disastrous love affair. A nice, sad woman who wasn't good at meeting people; who had a good job, loved to travel, and longed for children. . . .

Bob Gillespie was a sailing instructor on a voyage of self-discovery. He kept prefacing his remarks with statements such as, "You know,

I had a great insight into myself last week." That was nice; I was happy for him. But I would rather have gotten to know his surface persona before probing into his psyche. Like the two previous men, Bob didn't fit any of the recognizable profiles of the professional burglar, nor had he had any great insight into how All the Best People worked.

Ted Horowitz was a recovering alcoholic, which was admirable. Unfortunately he was also the confessional type. He began every anecdote with the admission that it had happened "back when I was drinking." He even felt compelled to describe how he used to throw up on his ex-wife. His only complaint about Best People—this with a stern look at my wineglass—was that they kept referring him to women who drank.

Jim Rogers was an adman who wore safari clothes and was into guns. I refrained from telling him that I own two .38 Specials and am a highly qualified marksman, for fear it would incite him to passion. For a little while I considered him seriously for the role of burglar, but when I probed the subject by mentioning a friend having recently been ripped off, Jim became enraged and said the burglar ought to be hunted down and shot.

"I'm going about this all wrong," I said to Hank.

It was ten in the morning, and we were drinking coffee at the big round table in All Souls' kitchen. The night before I'd spent hours on the phone with an effervescent insurance underwriter who was going on a whale-watching trip with Weekenders, the group that god-awful Jerry Hale had mentioned. He'd concluded our conversation by saying he'd be sure to note in his pocket organizer to call me the day after he returned. Then I'd been unable to sleep and had sat up hours longer, drinking too much and listening for burglars and brooding about loneliness.

I wasn't involved with anyone at the time—nor did I particularly want to be. I'd just emerged from a long-term relationship and was reordering my life and getting used to doing things alone again. I was fortunate in that my job and my little house—which I'm constantly remodeling—filled most of the empty hours. But I could still understand what Morton and Bob and Ted and Jim and even that dreadful Jerry were suffering from.

It was the little things that got to me. Like the times I went to the supermarket and everything I felt like having for dinner was packaged for two or more, and I couldn't think of anyone I wanted to have over to share it with. Or the times I'd be driving around a curve in the road and come upon a spectacular view, but have no one in the passenger seat to point it out to. And then there were the cold sheets on the other side of the wide bed on a foggy San Francisco night.

But I got through it, because I reminded myself that it wasn't going to be that way forever. And when I couldn't convince myself of that, I thought about how it was better to be totally alone than alone *with* someone. That's how *I* got through the cold, foggy nights. But I was discovering there was a whole segment of the population that availed itself of dating services and telephone conversation clubs and video exchanges. Since I'd started using Best People, I'd been inundated by mail solicitations and found that the array of services available to singles was astonishing.

Now I told Hank, "I simply can't stand another evening making polite chitchat in a bar. If I listen to another ex-wife story, I'll scream. I don't want to know what these guys' parents did to them at age ten that made the whole rest of their lives a mess. And besides, having that security guard on my house is costing Dick Morris a bundle that he can ill afford."

Helpfully Hank said, "So change your approach."

"Thanks for your great suggestion." I got up and went out to the desk that belongs to Ted Smalley, our secretary, and dug out a phone directory. All the Best People wasn't listed. My file on the case was on the kitchen table. I went back there—Hank had retreated to his office—and checked the introductory letter they'd sent me; it showed nothing but a post-office box. The zip code told me it was the main post office at Seventh and Mission streets.

I went back and borrowed Ted's phone book again, then looked up the post office's number. I called it, got the mail-sorting supervisor, and identified myself as Sharon from Federal Express. "We've got a package here for All the Best People Introduction Service," I said, and read off the box number. "That's all I've got—no contact phone, no street address."

"Assholes," she said wearily. "Why do they send them to a P.O. box when they know you can't deliver to one? For that matter, why do you accept them when they're addressed like that?"

"Damned if I know. I only work here."

"I can't give out the street address, but I'll supply the contact phone." She went away, came back, and read it off to me.

"Thanks." I depressed the disconnect button and redialed.

A female voice answered with only the phone number. I went into my Federal Express routine. The woman gave me the address without hesitation, in the 200 block of Gough Street near the Civic Center. After I hung up I made one more call: to a friend on the *Chronicle*. J. D. Smith was in the city room and agreed to leave a few extra business cards with the security guard in the newspaper building's lobby.

All the Best People's offices took up the entire second floor of a renovated Victorian. I couldn't imagine why they needed so much space, but they seemed to be doing a landslide business, because phones in the offices on either side of the long corridor were ringing madly. I assumed it was because the summer vacation season was approaching and San Francisco singles were getting anxious about finding someone to make travel plans with.

The receptionist was more or less what I expected to find in the office of that sort of business: petite, blond, sleekly groomed, and expensively dressed, with an elegant manner. She took J. D.'s card down the hallway to see if their director was available to talk with me about the article I was writing on the singles scene. I paced around the tiny waiting room, which didn't even have chairs. When the young woman came back, she said Dave Lester would be happy to see me and led me to an office at the rear.

The office was plush, considering the attention that had been given to decor in the rest of the suite. It had a leather couch and chairs, a wet bar, and an immense mahogany desk. There wasn't so much as a scrap of paper or a file folder to suggest anything resembling work was done there. I couldn't see Dave Lester, because he had swiveled his high-backed chair around toward the window and was apparently contemplating the wall of the building next door. The receptionist backed out the door and closed it. I cleared my throat, and the chair turned toward me.

The man in the chair was god-awful Jerry Hale.

Our faces must have been mirror images of shock. I said, "What are *you* doing here?"

He said, "You're not J. D. Smith. You're Sharon McCone!" Then he frowned down at the business card he held. "Or is Sharon McCone really J. D. Smith?"

I collected my scattered wits and said, "Which are you—Dave Lester or Jerry Hale?"

He merely stared at me, his expression wavering between annoyance and amusement.

I added, "I'm a reporter doing a feature article on the singles scene."

"So Marie said. How did you get this address? We don't publish it because we don't want all sorts of crazies wandering in. This is an exclusive service; we screen our applicants carefully."

They certainly hadn't screened me; otherwise they'd have uncovered numerous deceptions. I said, "Oh, we newspaper people have our sources."

"Well, you certainly misrepresented yourself to us."

"And you misrepresented yourself to *me*!"

He shrugged. "It's part of the screening process, for our clients' protection. We realize most applicants would shy away from a formal interview situation, so we have the first date take the place of that."

"You yourself go out with *all* the women who apply?"

"A fair amount, using a different name every time, of course, in case any of them know each other and compare notes." At my astonished look he added, "What can I say? I like women. But naturally I have help. And Marie"—he motioned at the closed door—"and one of the secretaries check out the guys."

No wonder Jerry had no time to read. "Then none of the things you told me were true? About being into the bar scene and the church groups and the health club?"

"Sure they were. My previous experiences were what led me to buy Best People from its former owners. They hadn't studied the market, didn't know how to make a go of it in the eighties."

"Well, you're certainly a good spokesman for your own product. But how come you kept referring me to other clients? We didn't exactly part on amiable terms."

"Oh, that was just a ruse to get out of there. I had another date. I'd seen enough to know you weren't my type. But I decided you were still acceptable; we get a lot of men looking for your kind."

The "acceptable" rankled. "What exactly *is* my kind?"

"Well, I'd call you . . . introspective. Bookish? No, not exactly. A little offbeat? Maybe intense? No. It's peculiar . . . you're peculiar—"

"Stop right there!"

Jerry—who would always be god-awful Jerry and never Dave Lester to me—stood up and came around the desk. I straightened my posture. From my five-foot-six vantage point I could see the beginnings of a bald spot under his artfully styled hair. When he realized where I was looking, his mouth tightened. I took a perverse delight in his discomfort.

"I'll have to ask you to leave now," he said stiffly.

"But don't you want Best People featured in a piece on singles?"

"I do not. I can't condone the tactics of a reporter who misrepresents herself."

"Are you sure that's the reason you don't want to talk with me?"

"Of course. What else—"

"Is there something about Best People that you'd rather not see publicized?"

Jerry flushed. When he spoke, it was in a flat, deceptively calm manner. "Get out of here," he said, "or I'll call your editor."

Since I didn't want to get J. D. in trouble with the *Chron*, I went.

Back at my office at All Souls, I curled up in my ratty armchair—my favorite place to think. I considered my visit to All the Best People; I considered what was wrong with the setup there. Then I got out my list of burglary victims and called each of them. All three gave me similar answers to my questions. Next I checked the phone directory and called my friend Tracy in the billing office at Pacific Bell.

"I need an address for a company that's only listed by number in the directory," I told her.

"Billing address, or location where the phone's installed?"

"Both, if they're different."

She tapped away on her computer keyboard. "Billing and location are the same: two-eleven Gough. Need anything else?"

"That's it. Thanks—I owe you a drink."

In spite of my earlier determination to depart the singles scene, I spent the next few nights on the phone, this time assuming the name of Patsy Newhouse, my younger sister. I talked to various singles about my new VCR; I described the sapphire pendant my former boyfriend had given me and how I planned to have it reset to erase old memories. I babbled excitedly about the trip to Las Vegas I was taking in a few days with Weekenders, and promised to make notes in my pocket organizer to call people as soon as I got back. I mentioned—in seductive tones—how I loved to walk barefoot over my genuine Persian rugs. I praised the merits of my new microwave oven. I described how I'd gotten into collecting costly jade carvings. By the time the Weekenders trip was due to depart for Vegas, I was constantly sucking on throat lozenges and wondering how long my voice would hold out.

Saturday night found me sitting in my kitchen sharing ham sandwiches and coffee by candlelight with Dick Morris's security guard, Bert Jankowski. The only reason we'd chanced the candles was that we'd taped the shades securely over the windows. There was something about eating in total darkness that put us both off.

Bert was a pleasant-looking man of about my age, with sandy hair and a bristly mustache and a friendly, open face. We'd spent a lot of time together—Friday night, all day today—and I'd pretty much heard his life story. We had a lot in common: He was from Oceanside, not far from where I'd grown up in San Diego; like me, he had a degree in the social sciences and hadn't been able to get a job in his field. Unlike me, he'd been working for the security service so long that he was making a decent wage, and he liked it. It gave him more time, he said, to read and to fish. I'd told him my life story, too: about my somewhat peculiar family, about my blighted romances, even about the man I'd once had to shoot. By Saturday night I sensed both of us were getting bored with examining our pasts, but the present situation was even more stultifying.

I said, "Something has *got* to happen soon."

Bert helped himself to another sandwich. "Not necessarily. Got any more of those pickles?"

"No, we're out."

"Shit. I don't suppose if this goes on that there's any possibility of cooking breakfast tomorrow? Sundays I always fix bacon."

In spite of having just wolfed down some ham, my mouth began to water. "No," I said wistfully. "Cooking smells, you know. This house is supposed to be vacant for the weekend."

"So far no one's come near it, and nobody seems to be casing it. Maybe you're wrong about the burglaries."

"Maybe . . . no, I don't think so. Listen: Andie Wyatt went to Hawaii; she came back to a cleaned-out apartment. Janie Roos was in Carmel with a lover; she lost everything fenceable. Kim New was in Vegas, where I'm supposed to be—"

"But maybe you're wrong about the way the burglar knows—"

There was a noise toward the rear of the house, past the current construction zone on the back porch. I held up my hand for Bert to stop talking and blew out the candles.

I sensed Bert tensing. He reached for his gun at the same time I did.

The noise came louder—the sound of an implement probing the back-porch lock. It was one of those useless toy locks that had been there when I'd bought the cottage; I'd left the dead bolt unlocked since Friday.

Rattling sounds. A snap. The squeak of the door as it moved inward.

I touched Bert's arm. He moved over into the recess by the pantry, next to the light switch. I slipped up next to the door to the porch. The outer door shut, and footsteps came toward the kitchen, then stopped.

A thin beam of light showed under the inner door between the kitchen and the porch—the burglar's flashlight. I smiled, imagining his surprise at the sawhorses and wood scraps and exposed wiring that make up my own personal urban-renewal project.

The footsteps moved toward the kitchen door again. I took the safety off the .38.

The door swung toward me. A half-circle of light from the flash illuminated the blue linoleum. It swept back and forth, then up and around the room. The figure holding the flash seemed satisfied that the room was empty; it stepped inside and walked toward the hall.

Bert snapped on the overhead light.

I stepped forward, gun extended, and said, "All right, Jerry. Hands above your head and turn around—slowly."

The flash clattered to the floor. The figure—dressed all in black— did as I said.

But it wasn't Jerry.

It was Morton Stone—the nice, sad man I'd had the dinner date with. He looked as astonished as I felt.

I thought of the evening I'd spent with him, and my anger rose. All that sincere talk about how lonely he was and how much he missed his dead wife. And now he turned out to be a common crook!

"You son of a bitch!" I said. "And I was going to fix you up with one of my friends!"

He didn't say anything. His eyes were fixed nervously on my gun.

Another noise on the back porch. Morton opened his mouth, but I silenced him by raising the .38.

Footsteps clattered across the porch, and a second figure in black came through the door. "Morton, what's wrong? Why'd you turn the lights on?" a woman's voice demanded.

It was Marie, the receptionist from All the Best People. Now I knew how she could afford her expensive clothes.

"So I was right about *how* they knew when to burglarize people, but wrong about *who* was doing it," I told Hank. We were sitting at the bar in the Remedy Lounge, his favorite Mission Street watering hole.

"I'm still confused. The Intro Line is part of All the Best People?"

"It's owned by Jerry Hale, and the phone equipment is located in the same offices. But as Jerry—Dave Lester, whichever incarnation you prefer—told me later, he doesn't want the connection publicized because the Intro Line is kind of sleazy, and Best People's supposed to be high-toned. Anyway, I figured it out because I noticed there were an awful lot of phones ringing at their offices, considering their number isn't published. Later I confirmed it with the phone company and started using the line myself to set the burglar up."

"So this Jerry wasn't involved at all?"

"No. He's the genuine article—a born-again single who decided to put his knowledge to turning a profit."

Hank shuddered and took a sip of Scotch.

"The burglary scheme," I went on, "was all Marie Stone's idea. She had access to the addresses of the people who joined the Intro Line club, and she listened in on the phone conversations and scouted out good prospects. Then, when she was sure their homes would be vacant for a period of time, her brother, Morton Stone, pulled the jobs while she kept watch outside."

"How come you had a date with Marie's brother? Was he looking you over as a burglary prospect?"

"No. They didn't use All the Best People for that. It's Jerry's pride and joy; he's too involved in the day-to-day workings and might have realized something was wrong. But the Intro Line is just a profit-making arm of the business to him—he probably uses it to subsidize his dating. He'd virtually turned the operation of it over to Marie. But he did allow Marie to send out mail solicitations for it to Best People clients, as well as mentioning it to the women he 'screened,' and that's how the burglary victims heard of it."

"But it still seems too great a coincidence that you ended up going out with this Morton."

I smiled. "It wasn't a coincidence at all. Morton also works for Best People, helping Jerry screen the female clients. When I had my date with Jerry, he found me . . . well, he said I was peculiar."

Hank grinned and started to say something, but I glared.

"Anyway, he sent Mort out with me to render a second opinion."

"Ye gods, you were almost rejected by a dating service."

"What really pisses me off is Morton's grieving-widower story. I really fell for the whole tasteless thing. Jerry told me Morton gets a lot of women with it—they just can't resist a man in pain."

"But not McCone." Hank drained his glass and gestured at mine. "You want another?"

I looked at my watch. "Actually, I've got to be going."

"How come? It's early yet."

"Well, uh . . . I have a date."

He raised his eyebrows. "I thought you were through with the singles scene. Which one is it tonight—the gun nut?"

I got off the bar stool and drew myself up in a dignified manner. "It's someone I met on my own. They always tell you that you meet the most compatible people when you're just doing what you like to do and not specifically looking."

"So where'd you meet this guy?"

"On a stakeout."

Hank waited. His eyes fairly bulged with curiosity.

I decided not to tantalize him any longer. I said, "It's Bert Jankowski, Dick Morris's security guard."

*Barbara Michaels, who received an Anthony Grandmaster award in 1987, writes the suspense and supernatural tales of the persona that is also Elizabeth Peters. As Michaels, she has written twenty-two books, including* The Master of Blacktower, Be Buried in the Rain, Shattered Silk, *and* Search the Shadows. *The last two have appeared on best-seller lists across the country. A Barbara Michaels story evokes delicious chills, compelling readers to keep turning pages, no matter how late the hour, until they reach the (ingenious) end.*

*In "The Runaway," two young sisters, naive in the ways of the world, run away from home. Weary and frightened, they find shelter in an abandoned house and are aided by a young boy whose mission they only later come to understand.*

# THE RUNAWAY

## by Barbara Michaels

THE YOUNGER GIRL was fifteen. She told people she was sixteen when they asked, but usually they didn't even bother. They just looked at her narrow shoulders and flat chest and skinny legs, and shook their heads. Mary knew they probably thought she was about twelve or thirteen. Nobody would hire a kid that age, and she couldn't show any proof she was older. The problem was that she wasn't old enough.

Some of the men would have hired Angie. She was almost seventeen and she was pretty. "Angie is the pretty one," their mother always said. Angie's best feature was her hair, long and smooth and shiny as yellow silk. *Flat* and *skinny* were words nobody would apply to Angie. The cloth of her tight jeans was straining at every seam. That was where the men looked—at the seat of Angie's jeans and the lush curves that pushed out the front of her shirt. Angie couldn't understand why Mary wouldn't let her take jobs from the men who looked at her that way.

Though she was the younger of the two, Mary had always been the one who looked after Angie, instead of the other way around.

Angie was . . . sensitive. Angie didn't understand some things. And when she was scared or unhappy, she stuck out her lip and made whimpering noises, like a homesick puppy.

She was whimpering now. Mary didn't blame her. She was scared, too, but she couldn't let Angie see that she was. One of them had to be tough.

It was so dark! Nights in town were never like this. There were always streetlights, lighted windows, cars passing by. They hadn't seen a car for a long time, not since they'd turned off the highway onto the narrow country road. The last house had been at least a mile back.

To make matters worse, there was a storm coming on. Heavy clouds obscured moon and stars. So far the rain had held off, but lightning and thunder were getting closer, louder. The wind made queer rustling noises in the bushes along the road. There were other noises that couldn't have been made by the wind, but Mary didn't mention them. Angie was upset enough already. She couldn't go much farther; she was scared to death of lightning. They had to find shelter soon.

As Mary looked anxiously around her, she tripped and fell. Gravel stung her palms, and something sharp, a stone or a piece of broken glass, ripped into her knee. She bit her lip and managed not to cry out.

Angie was the one who yelled. "Mary, what's the matter? Get up, get up, I can't—"

"I tripped, that's all." Mary staggered to her feet and reached for Angie's hand. "Shut up, Angie. Someone will hear you."

"I don't care if they do. I don't like this. We should have gone to that house back there."

"And have them call the cops?" Mary forced herself to limp forward. Angie hung back, dragging at Mary's arm, and Mary lost her temper. "Damn it, Angie, this whole thing was your idea. You want to give up?"

"No, I won't go back. You know what he'll do. You promised! You said you'd take care of everything—"

"I've done all right so far, haven't I?" Mary demanded, stung by the note of criticism in her sister's voice.

"It was fun at first. But I told you we shouldn't've gone down this road."

"We wouldn't have had to if you hadn't come on to that sleazy

character in the pizza place," Mary said. "He was following us—
you, I mean."

"He was kind of cute," Angie said.

Mary was about to reply when a bolt of lightning split the sky
and thunder rolled over them. Angie screamed.

"It's okay," Mary said, trying to steady her voice. "But we'd
better walk faster. I don't want to be caught in the rain any more
than you do. This damned road has to end up someplace."

Angie was genuinely terrified by lightning. She stumbled on, sobbing noisily, clutching Mary's hand till it ached.

Her distress softened Mary, as it always did. She got mad at
Angie sometimes, but it was impossible to stay mad at her, she was
so damned helpless. Giggling and grinning at that guy in the pizza
place . . . Angie didn't know any better. She trusted everybody,
even men whose eyes held that cold hunger when they looked at
her. But she had a stubborn streak. When she had threatened to
run away from home, Mary knew she meant it, and the thought
of Angie out on her own, with no one to look after her, was too
awful. She had had no choice but to go along. She wasn't all that
crazy about what was happening at home, either.

Two hundred dollars—the savings of several years of baby-sitting—
had seemed like a lot of money. But the bus fares had taken a big
chunk; Mary wouldn't hitchhike, although Angie wanted to. And
food cost a lot more than she had expected. Angie ate such a lot.
As soon as they got jobs, everything would be all right, but so far
they hadn't had any luck. Either people turned them down cold or
the men looked at Angie in that hungry way.

And now, thanks to Angie's dumb stunt, they were lost on a dark
country road with a storm about to cut loose. Mary wondered what
time it was. It had been almost ten when they left the pizza place.
It must be the middle of the night now. Her knee burned, and Angie
kept dragging at her hand. She felt as if she weighed a ton.

Another flash of lightning won a squeal from Angie. Mary stopped.
"There's a house over there. I saw it in the lightning. Come on,
Angie."

But when they reached the gate, Angie's mulish streak surfaced.
"The people who live here will ask questions," she whined. "I told
you, Mary, I won't go back. You'll have to think of a story to tell
them. Something smart."

"I won't have to be smart," Mary said wearily. "The house is empty, Angie. There're no lights, and everything is kind of falling down. Look."

Another flash of lightning proved her correct. The house was a farmhouse, of a type common in that part of the country—two stories high, with a steep-peaked roof. Children or tramps had broken most of the windows. The few remaining panes of glass reflected the livid flashes like blind white eyes.

Angie didn't like the look of the place, and said so in no uncertain terms. The first drops of rain spattering in the dust alongside the road ended her hesitation. Hands over her head, she ran with Mary. Before they reached the crumbling porch steps, the drops had thickened into a downpour.

Mary fell for the second time on the broken steps. She squatted on the porch, rocking back and forth in silent pain. Finally she got up, with Angie's help, and limped toward the door. It hung drunkenly on one hinge. It was so light, so rotted by time and weather, that they were able to push it back far enough to enter.

Angie took her comb from her purse. She started to run it through her damp hair. Soothed by the familiar gesture and by shelter, however poor, she spoke calmly.

"It smells funny."

"I guess it's been abandoned for a long time," Mary said, squinting into the darkness.

The house shuddered with every thunderclap. Rain trickled in through holes in the ceiling. Mary started as a chunk of wet plaster thudded to the floor. Anyhow, it was better than being outdoors.

The room was long and narrow. It was empty of furniture, but the floor was covered with debris. There was a fireplace on one wall.

"I'm hungry," Angie said.

"We've got those hamburgers. But I meant to save them for breakfast."

"We'll find a restaurant tomorrow. Let's eat now. But the hamburgers will be cold."

"I can't do anything about that," Mary said irritably.

"We could build a fire."

Mary looked at Angie in surprise. She came up with an idea so rarely that people tended to forget she could.

"Hey, yeah. There's lots of wood on the floor, and you have your lighter."

They cleared an area next to the fireplace and piled the scraps onto the hearth. Angie lit the heap. At first a lot of smoke billowed back into the room, making them cough, but finally the fire blazed up. The light was almost as welcome as the warmth, although it showed nothing but desolation—peeling wallpaper, rotted floorboards, and an ankle-deep layer of debris. Most of the latter burned nicely.

"It's funny," Mary said after dumping another load of scraps onto the fire.

"What is?" Angie was on her second hamburger. She was forced to eat it cold, after all, since her attempt to spit the first one on a stick had broken it apart.

"A lot of this wood looks like pieces of furniture," Mary said. "Like everything in the house has kind of fallen apart."

"I don't see what's so funny about that."

"Well, people don't leave their furniture when they move, do they? There's a table leg here, and enough pieces to make up a dozen chairs."

"Lucky for us," Angie said comfortably. "We can keep the fire going a long time."

"It's old wood," Mary said. "Dry. It burns fast."

It did burn fast, and it gave off a lot of heat. The part of the room near the fireplace was almost too warm. But a chill ran up Mary's back when she spoke those words. Dry . . . old . . . The syllables seemed to echo for a long time.

Angie finished her second hamburger and ate a candy bar. She wanted another, but Mary wouldn't let her have it. That was their emergency supply. If the rain continued, they might have to depend on it for longer than she had expected.

Angie accepted the decree without too much grumbling. She combed her hair again. The silky strands shone in the firelight; she spread them out across her hands, ran her fingers through the shimmering web.

"Where are we going to sleep?" she asked, stretching like a cat in the warmth.

"Where else? Right here."

"Maybe there are beds upstairs."

"If the stairs are as rotten as everything else, I wouldn't trust them. Besides," she added craftily, as Angie started to object, "you wouldn't want to sleep on any old mattresses. Mice."

"Ugh," Angie said.

After finishing her hamburger, Mary stretched out her leg and rolled up her jeans. It was no wonder her knee hurt. Angie exclaimed sympathetically. "You've got a million splinters in there."

"Yeah." Mary pulled out a couple of the longer ones. She hated things sticking into her. Mother always said she was an absolute baby about shots. Pulling out the splinters made her skin crawl. But it had to be done, and the dirt ought to be washed off. She didn't want to risk infection.

"Oh, damn," she muttered.

"Want me to pull them out?" Angie asked cheerfully. "I don't mind."

"That's not why I said *damn*. All that rain outside and we don't have any way to catch the water."

"I'm thirsty," Angie said promptly.

"Me too. And I'd like to wash my knee. Think of something."

"Who, me? You're the thinker in this family. 'Mary, she's the smart one,' " Angie mimicked their mother's voice.

"What about the cartons the hamburgers were in?"

"I threw them in the fire."

Mary said "Damn" again. "Go look in the kitchen, Angie. If the people who lived here left their furniture, maybe they left dishes too."

"I'm not going in there alone," Angie said. "There are probably rats and everything."

Mary glowered at her sister with sudden dislike. Angie looked so *fat*, sprawled out on the floor. Her thighs filled her jeans like sausage stuffing. It seemed as if she could do something for somebody once in a while, instead of expecting to be waited on all the time.

There was no use arguing about it. Stiffly Mary got to her feet. She found a splintered chair leg and lit one end of it. It sputtered and smoked, but gave enough light to let her see where she was going. Angie trailed along. She said she was afraid to be alone, and in a way Mary didn't blame her.

The kitchen wasn't hard to find; there were only four rooms downstairs. It was in a state of ruin that made the living room look tidy by comparison. Part of the ceiling had fallen, half burying the massive bulk of an old cookstove. There was no refrigerator, unless a heap of rusty metal and rotting wood had once served that function. An icebox, Mary thought—the kind that had big chunks of real ice, instead of electricity, to keep things cold.

In the debris along the wall, where shelves had collapsed, spilling their contents onto the floor, she found one unbroken cup and a dish with a chip out of the edge. They were black with grime, but the rain would wash them out.

When they reached the porch, she threw the burning stick onto the soggy grass and licked her singed fingers. The storm was passing, but it was still raining heavily. Mary washed the dishes as well as she could, and let them fill with rainwater.

It felt rather cozy to stretch out in front of the fire again. Mary began working on her knee. She got the biggest splinters out, but some of the smaller ones, deeply imbedded, were hard to get hold of, even with Angie's eyebrow tweezers. Mary was concentrating, her eyes blurred with tears; Angie was half asleep. Neither of them heard the boy coming. He was simply there, as if he had materialized out of thin air.

When Mary saw him, she let out a yelp of surprise. Angie woke up. Mary expected she'd scream, too; but when she saw Angie's mouth curve in a smile, she realized that Angie wasn't afraid of anything young and male. That was part of her trouble.

Anyhow, this boy didn't look frightening. As her pounding heart slowed, Mary saw that he was as startled as she was. He was tall and thin; his ragged clothes hung in limp folds, as if he had lost a lot of weight, or as if they had originally belonged to somebody bigger. His shaggy hair was shoulder-length; his feet were bare. He had raised his arms in front of his face, as if to shield it.

"It's okay," Mary said. "I guess you came in to get out of the rain, like us, didn't you? Come over to the fire."

The boy obeyed. His bare feet, stepping lightly, made no sound on the dusty floor. His eyes were fixed on Mary. They were dark eyes—she saw that as he came closer, out of the shadows; saw that his face, exposed when he lowered his protecting arms, was long and thin, with cheekbones that stood out sharply under the sunken pits of the eye sockets. His mouth was a clown's mouth, too long for the framework of his hollow cheeks, curving down at the corners.

He stopped a little distance from Mary; his eyes narrowed as he continued to study her. Then, as if some silent message had passed from her to him, he smiled.

Mary caught her breath. That was why his face had looked wrong. The wide lips were generously cut, designed for laughter. When his mouth curved up, all his other features fell into their proper places and proportions. But he was awfully thin. . . .

"My name's Rob," he said. His voice was soft, with a queer little hesitation.

"I'm Mary. This is Angie."

But Angie, disconcerted by a boy who looked at Mary instead of at her, had turned her back.

"Hello," Rob said gravely.

"Sit down if you want to."

"Thank you." Rob sat, crossing his legs. The soles of his feet were covered by a thick, hardened layer of skin. He must have gone barefoot for months, maybe years, Mary thought.

"You hurt yourself," he said, looking at Mary's knee.

"I fell down." Mary laughed self-consciously. "I'm the clumsy one, always falling over my own feet."

Rob did not laugh. "I bet it hurts. Why don't you pull out them splinters?"

"I'm chicken," Mary admitted. "I got out as many as I could, but . . ."

He took the tweezers from her hand. It was the lightest, gentlest movement; she scarcely felt the touch of the metal tips as he plucked out the splinters.

"I think that's most of 'em," he said finally. "You better wash it off now. You got some cloth or something?"

"I guess I could tear up a shirt."

But her pack yielded nothing that would serve. The clothes were all knits, except for an extra pair of jeans. Rob exclaimed with admiration over the T-shirts.

"Say, that's pretty. 'Specially that one with the birds and flowers. You don't wanna spoil that. Maybe I can find some old thing around here."

With the same light, almost furtive movements, he slipped out of the room.

"Boy," Angie said. "Boy, you really are a hypocrite, you know that?"

Mary started. Crazy as it might sound, she had almost forgotten about Angie.

"What do you mean?"

"Always lecturing *me* about picking up men," Angie said. "You practically fell all over him."

"You're just mad because he didn't look at you," Mary said.

"Ha!" Angie registered amused contempt. "I wouldn't want him to look at me. He's weird. Ugly. He talks funny—"

"That's the way they talk around here," Mary said coldly. "You're so ignorant, you think everybody but you talks funny. He's nice. I like him."

"Mary." Angie reached out her hand. Her face had lost its healthy color. Even in the firelight she looked pale. "Mary, he really is weird. There's something funny about him."

"Funny, weird—is that all you can say? You shut up, do you hear me? I don't want you hurting his feelings."

The warning was delivered just in time. Rob was back, carrying something. He held it out to Mary. It was an old calico shirt, faded so badly that the original print was almost gone.

"It's clean," he said anxiously. "I washed it myself. It's too small for me, anyways. You go on, tear it up."

Mary would have objected, but it was obvious that the garment was far too small for Rob. It must have been bought for him when he was thirteen or fourteen, before he had shot up to his present height.

"You been carrying this around with you?" she asked as she began to tear the cloth. "I wouldn't have bothered packing anything this old."

"No, it was upstairs," Rob said calmly.

Angie made a small sound, deep in her throat. Mary stared, a strip of cloth dangling from her fingers.

"Upstairs? You mean, you—"

"I useta live here," Rob said. "I was away for a long time, but I come back. They—they was all gone when I come. Musta moved away. . . ." His forehead wrinkled; for a moment the dark eyes went blank, like those of a sleepwalker. Then he smiled. "Sure is nice to have company. It's been lonesome."

That radiant smile dispelled Mary's uneasiness. She started dabbing at her knee.

"We ran away too," she said. "But we aren't going back."

"How come you run away?" Rob asked.

"Well, see, our father died . . ." Mary began.

She paused, waiting for the sympathetic comment that should have followed. She was a little taken aback when Rob nodded and said, "Mine too."

"Really?"

"He was killed in the war."

"Vietnam? Ours died of a heart attack." Mary realized it sounded kind of flat. A heart attack wasn't nearly as romantic or tragic as death in battle. She went on, "Then mother got married again. We have a stepfather."

"Me too."

"You're kidding."

"I guess they ain't that scarce," Rob said. "Stepfathers, I mean."

He smiled tentatively, to indicate he wasn't making fun of her, just joking. Mary's suspicions dissolved. He was right, stepfathers weren't uncommon.

"He was Pa's friend, in the war," Rob explained. "He brung Pa's things home, after it was over. Then he just . . . stayed. Ma had to have a man around. Woman can't run a farm by herself. I was too small to help." He paused, scraping at a frayed spot on his faded pants. Then he asked, "Was he mean to you? Your stepfather?"

"George? He was nice at first," Mary said darkly. "To lull our suspicions. Lately he's been on our backs all the time. Discipline, discipline, that's all we heard. Last week was the last straw. He said Angie should be sent away to school. Some awful boarding school where they make you get up at seven o'clock and have room checks and study hall every night, and no dates unless the boy has a certified letter from the President of the United States. . . ."

Rob was listening sympathetically, his flexible mouth reflecting her indignation; but somehow the description of the horrors of boarding school lacked drama, even to Mary. She added, with genuine distress, "We've always been together. You'd think that would make them happy, that we like each other. Most sisters fight all the time. We never . . . Well, we don't fight much. But George said we weren't good for each other. He said Angie depended on me too much, and I wasn't making friends of my own because I was always with her. . . ." Rob was looking bewildered. Mary gave it up. "You wouldn't understand," she said. "I guess girls have different problems from boys. What was the matter with your stepfather?"

"He useta lick me a lot. But it wasn't that so much, it was—"

Angie giggled.

"Lick you?" she repeated.

"Shut up," Mary snapped.

"You shouldn't talk mean to your little sister," Rob said reproachfully.

It was Mary's turn to laugh.

"She's not my little sister, she's my big sister. But she doesn't understand a lot of things. You mean, your stepfather actually hit you? You didn't have to put up with that. There are laws."

"Laws?"

"To protect kids from being beaten," Mary said impatiently. "Even back here in the boonies you must have heard of them. If he really hurt you—"

"Oh, he useta lay it on pretty good," Rob said matter-of-factly. And then, before Mary had any inkling of what he meant to do, he swung around and flipped up his shirt.

For a moment there was no sound in the room except the drip of rain and the crackle of the flames. Then Angie let out a gasp of hysterical laughter.

They were old scars, long healed; but it was obvious that the ridged patterns were not the product of a single beating but of systematic, long-range abuse. The play of firelight and shadow on Rob's back made them look even worse than they were.

Rob let his shirt fall, and turned. At the sight of Mary's face his mouth dropped miserably.

"Say, I didn't mean to make you feel bad. It don't hurt, honest. I'd almost forgot about it till you started talking about—"

"Forgot *that*?"

"Well, it's my head," Rob said apologetically. "It got hurt. . . . I don't remember so good since then. Seems like I forget a lot of things."

"Did your stepfather hit you on the head too?"

"He didn't much care where he hit me," Rob said with a touch of wry humor. "He was usually likkered up when he done it."

"Let me see," Mary said.

"Not if it makes you feel bad."

"It won't make me feel bad." Mary could not have explained why she felt the need to see for herself. Her reasons had nothing in common with the ghoulish interest that had drawn Angie closer.

"Okay," Rob said obediently. He bowed his head and parted his untidy brown hair. The raised scar stood up like a ridge of splintered bone.

Mary knew she mustn't upset him by any further expressions of distress, but as he sat patiently awaiting her comment, his head bowed and his long, dirty fingers passive in his tumbled hair, her eyes filled with tears. She put out her hand.

Suddenly Rob was on his feet, some distance away. His eyes were narrowed, and his thin chest rose and fell with his agitated breathing.

"Don't touch me," he whispered. "You mustn't touch me."

"I didn't mean any harm," Mary said. Two tears spilled over

and left muddy tracks through the grime on her cheeks. "I only wanted—"

"I know." The boy's taut body relaxed. "I thank you. But you mustn't . . ."

Slowly, step by step, he began to back away.

Mary rose to her knees, ignoring the pain.

"Don't go away!"

"I'll come right back." He smiled at her but continued to retreat. He faded into the shadows in the open doorway.

As soon as he was gone, Angie flung herself at her sister, her fingers clawing at Mary's arm.

"Let's get out of here, Mary. Hurry. Quick, before he comes back—"

"Are you crazy?" Mary tried to free her arm, but Angie hung on.

"I'm not crazy, he is! Can't you see he's some kind of psycho? The way he talks . . . All that about forgetting things, and those awful scars . . . He's a homicidal maniac, like on TV. He'll kill us—"

"No," Mary said. "No, he wouldn't hurt anybody."

"How do you know?"

"I know. Look, Angie, you stop that kind of talk. You haven't got any sense about people. Some of the guys you used to go out with—"

"Oh, so that's it," Angie said. "You think you've got yourself a boyfriend. First time anybody looks at you . . . That shows he's crazy." She tossed her head so that the long, shining locks flared out. "Just don't try anything. Even if you think I'm asleep, you can't get away with any funny business."

Mary stared at her sister. As the meaning of Angie's speech penetrated, she felt a deep flush warm her face.

"You're disgusting, Angie, you know that?"

Angie began to cry. "That's an awful thing to say," she sobbed. "I'm scared, and hungry, and cold, and all you can say—" The rest of the words were lost in gulping sobs.

"All right, all right," Mary said. "Stop bawling. We can't leave here; it's still raining, and it's pitch-dark, and I don't know where we are. I'll sit up all night and protect you from that fierce, dangerous boy. Go to sleep and stop worrying."

It took the last of the hamburgers to stop Angie's moans. When she had eaten it, she curled up by the fire, and after an interval her sobs smoothed out into soft snores. Mary didn't feel sleepy. She looked at her sister's huddled form and felt as if she were looking at a stranger.

It wasn't the first time Angie had made cracks about her not having boyfriends or dates, but never before had she expressed her malice so openly. And to suggest that Rob would . . . Mary felt her face get hot again, this time with anger. Nobody but a stupid fool could think of Rob that way. He was too pathetic. All he wanted was kindness and companionship, and some response to the gentleness that had miraculously survived the terrible treatment he had received.

He had been gone a long time. Maybe he had gone for good. The idea left Mary feeling a little sick. Had their unthinking cruelty driven him out into the rain and darkness, away from even the poor refuge he had found? But when she looked at the doorway, he was there, watching her.

"I thought you weren't coming back," she said.

"I said I would." Rob came forward, stepping softly. He jerked his head toward Angie. "She asleep?"

"Yes."

"I tried to find some blankets, or something to keep you warm. I guess everything around here is just too old or too dirty. I'm sorry."

"It's warm enough, with the fire." Mary tossed another handful of wood on it. The flames leapt. "But thanks for trying. Where do you sleep?"

"Upstairs. But I don't sleep much." Rob sat down a little distance from her. "If you want to go to sleep, I'll sort of keep an eye on things."

"What's there to watch out for?"

"Well, there's rats," Rob said calmly. "They wouldn't hurt you, but I know girls is scared of rats."

"Ugh." Mary shivered. "I hate them."

"They ain't so bad. They only bite people when they're scared or hungry. Right smart animals, rats are. I had one for a pet oncet."

"Really? I knew a boy who had a pet rat. It was a white one."

"Mine was brown. I called him Horatius, after that fella in the poem."

Mary didn't know what poem he was talking about, and she didn't want to admit her ignorance, so she changed the subject.

"What are you going to do, Rob? You can't stay here."

"I have to."

"No, you don't. You could—you could come with us."

"With you?"

"Yes." Mary felt herself blushing again. She lowered her eyes, cursing Angie; if Angie hadn't put ideas into her head, she wouldn't be embarrassed. Tracing patterns in the dust of the floor with her forefinger, she went on rapidly, "We're going to get jobs. You could work too. We could have an apartment—maybe even a little house. . . ."

"I sure would like to," Rob said. "I'd like to be with you. I never knew a girl like you before. I didn't know you, did I? Seems as if I did somehow. I forget so much. . . ."

Mary looked up sharply. Her cheeks were still flaming; as her eyes met Rob's she forgot to be self-conscious. He was speaking the simple, literal truth, as he felt it.

"No," she said, just as simply. "I never met you. But it's funny, I feel that way too. As if we had known each other someplace . . . sometime. . . ."

For a long, suspended moment, they looked at each other, not speaking, because there was no need to speak. Then Rob's mobile, expressive face lengthened. He bowed his head.

"No," he muttered. "I can't do it. I been telling you lies. Not lies, exactly, but not the truth, neither. I—I didn't run away from here. I was took from here. It was some other place I run away from, some place a long, long ways from here."

Mary felt as if a giant hand had clamped over her ribs, squeezing the breath out of her lungs. She stared at Rob's drooping head. His long, curved lashes cast delicate shadows across his bony cheeks.

So Angie had been right—for once.

Rob's stumbling, reluctant confession was like the missing piece in a jigsaw puzzle. The pattern was clear now. But then, it had been pretty obvious all along. Angie had seen it, and she herself would have recognized it if she had not refused to do so.

Rob was . . . different. Not crazy, not any of those ugly words Angie had used. He was sick; and no wonder, after what had been done to him. The place he had run away from was probably an institution, a kind of hospital. Some of those places were pretty bad; she had seen stories about them on TV. He must have been in—that place—for years, long enough for the house to fall into ruin after his family had moved away, abandoning him. But he had returned, like a sick animal, to the only place he knew, and his hurt mind couldn't understand what had happened.

Rob's head sank lower, till she could see only a mop of tumbled brown hair. In a sudden, final flash of insight Mary knew that Angie had been wrong, after all—Angie and those others who had locked Rob up. Rob's mind had been damaged, like his bruised body, but its essential quality had not been changed. He was still gentle, considerate of others, oddly innocent. He wouldn't hurt anybody; he was too vulnerable himself.

She wanted to touch him, to reassure him. But she remembered his reaction the first time she had reached out.

"It's okay," she said softly. "I understand. It's all right."

Rob looked up.

"No," he said. He spoke with difficulty. There were long pauses between phrases as he went on. "I guess it ain't all right. It's all wrong. I don't suppose I can explain it. I don't understand so good myself. But I understand better than I did. Having somebody to talk to—somebody like you, who listens, and don't yell or get mad. . . . All I know is, I can't come with you. I gotta go back there. It's no good running away from things."

He saw her face change and was quick to reassure her. "Say, now, I didn't mean you. You were right to run away when they treated you so bad. Guess you wouldn't do anything wrong, you're too smart. But I'm kind of mixed up. Seems like I'm always doing the wrong thing; seems like running away was another wrong thing. It wasn't a bad place, you know. They wanted to help me. If I go back and let them do what it was they wanted . . . Maybe later you and I could . . . You aren't mad, are you? Mary?"

It was the first time he had said her name. Mary couldn't speak, but she shook her head and managed to shape a watery smile. Rob smiled back at her.

"You look awful tired," he said, with a new note of gentle authority in his voice. "You lay down and get some sleep. I'll keep watch."

Suddenly she was tired—tired and strangely cold, as if she had worked hard through a long day and night of winter. She gathered up all the loose scraps that lay within reach, and heaped them on the fire. As it blazed up, she stretched out with her back to its warmth. She wanted to watch Rob; she was afraid he might try to sneak away while she slept. She was too tired to argue, but she hadn't given up. In the morning, when she wasn't so sleepy, she would try again to convince him.

Maybe he needed help, but the place he had run away from

couldn't be the right place. George would find a place. George was a lawyer; he knew about things like that. George would help.

She was too drowsy to realize that she had reached a decision until after it was irrevocably fixed in her mind. Yes, she would go home—crawl back in disgrace. It wouldn't be pleasant. She'd be grounded for weeks; probably she would have to have boring sessions with a dumb psychologist or counselor. Mother would cry, and Angie . . . Angie would have to take care of herself. Anything, so long as Rob got the help he needed. Anything, so she didn't lose him.

He was still there. Her eyes closed and her breathing slowed. The last thing she saw before exhaustion claimed her was the play of firelight on Rob's thin, thoughtful face.

She awoke to a nightmare—a swirling, smoky blackness shot with tongues of flame; air she couldn't breathe; and a hoarse, wordless shouting. The voice was unrecognizable; it might even have been her own. She knew she must be dreaming, because she couldn't move. It was a relief when the blackness overcame the fiery light and swallowed her.

She came fully awake much later, with hard hands shaking her and a face close to hers.

"Rob," she croaked, but it wasn't Rob; the face was that of a man she had never seen before—brown and weather-wrinkled, with parallel scarlike lines framing his thin-lipped mouth.

"This one's all right," he said. His voice sounded angry. "What about the other one?"

If there was an answer, Mary didn't hear it. Feeling dizzy and slightly sick to her stomach, she closed her eyes. When she opened them again, the man was gone. She raised herself on one elbow and looked around.

She was lying in the long, wet grass in front of the house. Her clothes were soaked, and she was shivering in a sharp breeze—a dawn breeze. The sky was streaked with light beyond the chimneys of the house. The house was burning.

There was a horrifying beauty about the way it burned. Long veils of fire rose like creatures trying to break free of earth. Rosy flame spouted from the empty windows and wreathed crimson blossoms around the chimneys. Then the roof fell in with a giant gush of flame and sparks, and her dazed senses came fully to life.

"Angie." She gasped and staggered to her feet.

Before she had time to panic, she saw her sister, flat on the grass a few feet away. A man was bending over her. As Mary stumbled toward them, the man looked up. He was not the man she had seen before; he was older. A stubble of white beard frosted his jaws, and when he spoke, she saw that his teeth were brown, with gaps in their rows.

"Friend o' yours?"

"My sister."

"She'll do," the old man said cheerfully. "Swallowed some smoke, but I reckon she'll be all right."

Then Mary remembered.

"Rob. Rob! Where—"

She spun around. The old man straightened, one hand clutching the small of his back.

"Was there somebody else with you, girl?"

"Yes. Rob. Didn't you find him? Oh, please . . ."

The old man's silence was answer enough.

Mary ran toward the incandescent bed of coals that had once been a house. The daylight had strengthened; against the dawn, the blackened chimney stood up like a gaunt sentinel. She heard the old man shout but did not stop running till someone grabbed her. She had forgotten the other man. When she tried to struggle, he slapped her hard. The older man came up, panting.

"Don't hit her, Frank."

"Too bad her folks didn't tan her hide a long time ago," Frank said angrily. "Damned spoiled brats. Wouldn't a been no fire if they hadn't set it. Lucky they didn't kill themselves."

"Frank, she says there was another youngster with them. A boy."

The hands that held Mary did not relax their grip, but when Frank spoke again, his voice had lost its hard edge.

"Didn't find anybody else. If he was in there . . ."

The three stared silently at the fiery grave of the house. Then the old man said gently, "Maybe he got out, child. Maybe he drug you out. Frank saw the smoke when he went to feed the stock, but we didn't get here till the place was blazing. Found you gals outside on the grass. Reckon your friend ran and hid when he saw us. Sure, that's what must of happened."

The words should have consoled Mary, because they made sense. She knew she hadn't dragged Angie out of the house; she couldn't even remember walking out herself. Strangely, she felt no emotion, neither horror nor loss of hope. She looked at the old man through the lank locks of hair that hung over her face, and his eyes shifted away.

"Better take 'em home, Frank. You wanna go fetch the car?"

"Why can't they walk?" Frank demanded.

"Other one's still snoring," the old man said with a faint grin. "You kin carry her if you want; she's too fat for me to hoist."

"All right," Frank said grudgingly. "Damned spoiled runaway brats, burning down a house. . . ."

"Maybe it's just as well," the old man said. The eyes of the two men met in a long, meaningful glance. Then Frank shrugged and set off across the lawn. When Mary looked in that direction, she saw chimneys beyond the trees. They had been close to shelter and human help. . . . Not that they would have sought it out.

The old man bent stiffly over Angie's recumbent form.

"She's all right," he said. "Sleeping it off."

"I'm sorry," Mary said. "About the house. It was raining so hard, I never thought it could catch fire."

"Don't suppose you thought at all," the old man said sarcastically. "Inside of the place was bone-dry and rotten."

"Why did you say that—about it being just as well the house was burned?"

The old man shrugged and looked away.

"Been falling for years. No good to anybody."

"Why wasn't it any good to anybody? Why did the people who owned it let it fall apart? Who lived there? What—what happened to them?"

"Full of questions, ain't you?" The old man grinned, but the glance he gave her from under his shaggy white brows was oblique and sly. Suddenly, though she could not have explained why, she had to know the answers to the questions she had asked.

"Why?" she demanded, her voice loud and shrill. "What was wrong with the house?"

The old man licked his lips. He glanced over his shoulder at the blackened ruins.

"Folks said it was haunted," he mumbled. "I seen lights there myself. Mighta been tramps, but . . ."

"Haunted," Mary repeated. She shivered. The early-morning air was cold, and she was wet to the bone.

As if the word had been a plug in his mind that held back speech, the old man became garrulous. After all, it was a good story and she was a fresh audience.

"There was a murder there one time. Years ago, it was. The widow moved away afterward, took the other kids with her. Place changed hands a couple of times; but nobody could live in that house for long. State took it over for taxes finally. Couldn't even rent it, people knew the story—"

He broke off, eyeing her uneasily. Mary had stopped listening. Now she repeated the phrase that had twisted into her mind like a knife.

"Other kids," she said in a strangled voice. "She took the other . . . Who was it who was killed?"

"The father," the old man said reluctantly. "Stepfather, he was, really. Say, you look kind of peaked. Maybe I better not—"

"Who killed him?"

"Here's Frank with the car," the old man said, looking relieved. "Come on."

The car had stopped by the tumbledown fence. Frank got out, holding a blanket.

"Mother says bring 'em right to the house," he said, looking at Angie. "Think you can take her feet, Granddad, if I—"

"Who was it?" Mary begged. "Who killed him?"

Frank gave the old man a disapproving look.

"You been telling her that story? Shame on you, Granddad. That's what's wrong with kids today, they hear too many stories about killing and stuff." He turned on Mary. "Just you forget all that. You oughta be thinking about this gal here—and your folks, bet they're worried sick about you. Get in the car."

Angie was coming out of her stupor, but she was always a good sleeper. Once in the car, she snuggled into the blanket, muttered something, and closed her eyes.

The two men stood staring at the remains of the house.

"So it's gone," the old man said. "Yep. Just as well. They say fire's a cleaning thing. If ever a place needed cleaning, that one did. And if ever a man deserved killing . . ."

"You never even knew him," Frank said.

"I heard Pop talk about him. Drunken brute he was, used to beat that poor woman to a pulp, and the kids . . . Nowadays they'd say the boy wasn't in his right mind. Not responsible."

"That's the trouble with nowadays. Nobody's ever responsible."

"Maybe so. But when you keep beating on a kid, stands to reason his brain isn't gonna be right. And seeing his ma knocked around . . . Pop said it was a cruel thing, the way she turned on the boy.

Wouldn't see him or say anything in his defense, even at the trial. And the way he died . . . Suicide, it was supposed to be, but the guard at the county jail was one of the Weavers, and the Weavers has always had a mean streak. . . ."

Frank shook himself like a dog coming out of the water.

"What're we standing around talking for?" he demanded grumpily. "It's over and done with, years ago, and I'm late with the chores, thanks to these fool girls. Get in the car, Granddad."

The old man obeyed, giving Mary a strange sidelong look. She had a feeling that he had remembered the name of the boy who had died in prison so many years before. He wouldn't say anything, though. He knew, as she did, how the reasonable, everyday world would react to such a story.

A story decades old, older than Granddad himself. How many years had it been since a certain man returned from a war—not Vietnam, she should have realized the dates were wrong. Maybe the horrors of that war had turned him into a drunkard and a sadist. She would never know. All she knew was that Rob had been a victim, not a killer. Just once, after years of abuse and misery, he had struck back. He hadn't meant to kill, only to defend himself and the others. She knew that as certainly as if she had been present when it happened.

As the car started forward, Mary pressed her face against the window for a last look. The sun was up and the damp grass glowed like a field of emeralds. From the dying embers trails of pale smoke rose and broke in the breeze.

When the ashes were cold, weeds and wildflowers would rise to cover the ruins. Animals would burrow and raise their young. But Rob would not come again. He had gone back, as she was going, but to a much more distant place. In her mind a voice said softly, "Maybe later. You and I . . ."

*Lia Matera's Willa Jansson is an acerbic lawyer bent on fighting ". . . the cannibalism of left-wing politics, rampaging careerism, and the conflict of personal versus professional ethics" while cracking wise about everything. Introduced as a law student in* Where Lawyers Fear to Tread, *which was nominated for an Anthony for Best Paperback Original of 1987, Willa goes from disillusioned left-wing lawyer in* A Radical Departure *to a bank lawyer (to the horror of her activist parents) in* Hidden Agenda. The Smart Money *features Laura Di Palma, an ambitious attorney who's a good bet to come out a winner.*

*In "Counsel for the Defense," Lia (an attorney herself who says it's more fun to satirize lawyers than to be one) shows just how far a lawyer will go to see that justice is done.*

# COUNSEL FOR THE DEFENSE

## by Lia Matera

"I'M YOUR LAWYER," I reminded him, in much the same tone I'd used in the not so distant past to say, "I'm your wife."

Jack Krauder glowered at the acrylic partition separating us from a yawning jailer. "Howard Frost is my lawyer."

"And Howard Frost is my associate—my *junior* associate! You hired a law firm, Jack, not a person!"

"I asked for Howard."

"He's in court. I'm not." And I'm a better lawyer, anyway. "Through the miracle of modern science"—I fiddled with a small tape recorder—"Howie can hear everything you tell me. *If* you make up your mind to tell me what happened!"

"You don't believe me." His voice was carefully uninflected; a contractor's trick he'd perfected on angry homeowners and stubborn zoning boards.

"You lived with Mary Sutter for how long? Six months?" Seven months and nine days, to be exact. "You must know *something*! More than what's in here!" I tapped the police report. "Remember how I used to complain about my clients lying by omission? Ransilov, remember him? Leaving me open to that surprise about . . . Jack?" I slid a sympathetic hand across the gouged metal table that separated us. "Don't booby-trap your own defense!"

Jack released the arm of his chair, dropping his hand onto the table like a piece of meat. He frowned at his chafed red knuckles, apparently unable to will the hand to touch mine. Two years of connubial hell will do that to a relationship.

"Okay, Jack, let's try this: Mary tries to kill you and kill herself, but something goes wrong. You don't drink your coffee and she drinks hers. She dies and you don't."

His hand formed a fist. "No!"

"What's the alternative? Someone hated Mary—or you—enough to kill you both. Someone close enough to know where you keep your coffee."

He looked at the dirty salmon walls, at the mesh-caged fluorescent lights, at the chipped expanse of metal table—at everything in the room except me. His dimpled jaw was tense enough to use as an anvil.

"That's it, isn't it? And you know who did it, don't you? Don't you, Jack?"

He pounded the table once, meeting my eye. "Don't try to bully me, Janet!"

"I just want the truth!"

There it was, the bare bones of the quarrel that had blown our marriage out of the water.

"Okay, Jack. Your bail hearing is tomorrow afternoon. I'll make the arrangements—"

"No!" he exploded.

"What do you mean, 'no'? It could be six, eight months until your trial! You can't stay here!"

"Goddammit—I can if I want to! I'll discuss it with Howard."

"Jack! I know you don't want to go back to— Look, you can stay at my place!"

"No!"

"Or a hotel! Anyplace is better than the county—"

He stood abruptly, turning his back on me. "Leave me alone, Janet!"

As the sheriff's deputy led him out of the room, Jack glanced back at me. My ex-husband looked worried.

Jack's kitchen table, his counter, his back door were still dusty with fingerprint powder. Traces of chalk defaced the hardwood floor.

Judging by the outline, Mary Sutter had died in a heap. Strychnine. The coroner said she'd convulsed violently enough to break two bones.

Howard Frost sighed deeply, polishing his camera lens. I'm a better photographer than Howie, but I didn't offer to take the pictures. Not this time.

"Lived here yourself once, did you?" Howie's English-accented voice was bland, as usual. A handicap in court.

"All this crap"—I indicated the cozy Americana, the maple table, the enamel-topped hutch, the rocker in the corner—"I picked it out."

"Mmm." He put the camera to his eye, twisting the focus, leaning closer to the graphite-dusted table. A cross-hatching of clean squares indicated where police tape had lifted prints.

I turned to the hutch. The drawers had already been rummaged. Old contracting bids, wholesalers' receipts for Sheetrock, receipts for Mary's art supplies, unmailed Publishers Clearing House envelopes, one of them addressed to me. "I wonder if the cops know this thing has a false bottom." I cleared the jumbled papers to one side, feeling for the catch.

Behind me Howie mused, "Poisoning coffee right in the canister!" A tinge of outrage; the most I'd ever heard in that well-modulated voice. "Bloody reckless! Suppose they'd had company?"

"Jack's lucky! I've never met a bigger caffeine addict! What are the odds of him being late for work and having to skip his morning cup—" The false bottom came loose. "Jesus, Howie! Look at this!"

I held up a photograph. It showed a young woman lying splay-legged beside a swimming pool, her hair wet and her eyes lost behind big sunglasses. At first glance the woman appeared to be Mary Sutter, but Mary's hair had been waist-length; in the photo the damp straggles barely reached her shoulders. Also, Mary had been gaunt and proud of her wrinkly, sun-baked hide. The woman in the photo had a plumper, more youthful figure.

There were two men with her, one lying down, one squatting. Both of them rippled with beautiful muscles. Young, Latino, dark hair and eyes; possibly brothers. All three wore suggestive smiles and nothing else. They might have been sunbathing; or they might have been doing something more interesting.

Howie stepped up behind me. "Strange the police missed it."

I let the false bottom fall back into place. "Just like in the movies.

Only I wonder . . ." I considered the photo. "A younger Mary Sutter? Wouldn't it be great if someone was blackmailing her? Talk about injecting reasonable doubt into the prosecution's case!"

"Dunno. Pretty tame stuff, this. And no reason Jacko should keep quiet about somebody blackmailing Mary. Not anymore."

I turned to face him. His baby-smooth skin was unusually pale as he regarded the photo.

"Jacko" had recently joined Howie's soccer team. It had been something of a trial, these last months, hearing my coworker praise Jack's "trapping." (Howie was *my* associate, *my* friend. Bad enough Jack got the house and the furniture.)

"I wasn't married to Jack Krauder two years too many without knowing when he's holding back. There's more to this—" I put the picture down on the powdered enamel. "I have a bad feeling about this picture, Howie. Like I'm standing over a trapdoor."

"Janet? I really would be happy to talk to him. Tonight? Or before my trial tomorrow?"

"I'll take care of it!" How many times did I have to explain? "If we want information, we're going to have to shake it out of him! Jack needs management—not friendship."

I'd never liked Carole Bissett, not from the moment she'd moved next door to me and Jack. An aerobics instructor, just my luck. Jack's luck, rather. Fortune always surrounded him with beautiful women. (I had been the exception.) I couldn't prove it, but I suspected Jack had been sleeping with Carole through most of the last year of our marriage. She was one of the reasons I'd let him keep the house; I loathed the sight of Carole's shiny spandex.

She dabbed her glowing cheeks with a terry wristband and pulled two bottles of Evian water out of her refrigerator. "Poor Jackie! I wish I could help him!"

I took one of the bottles, wishing it had about three fingers of whiskey in it. "Maybe you can. Did you notice anything unusual next door, odd comings and goings, people you wouldn't expect to see?"

Carole wrinkled her darling little nose. "Well, you know artists. Lots of Mary's friends were kind of weird." Then, remorsefully, "I shouldn't talk bad about her!"

"Any drugs?"

A tolerant smile. "Nothing hard, but sure. Mary smoked a little and did a few lines. Jackie doesn't—you know him!"

"Where did Mary get it?"

She hesitated. "I don't want to get anyone in trouble."

"Jack's in a lot of trouble." Carole's brain was certainly her least used muscle. "Was it those two good-looking Chicano guys—what were their names?"

"Jaime and Andy?" Her face contorted with the effort of thinking. Come on, I urged silently; no pain, no gain. "Maybe."

"Know where I can find them?"

"Try Stacy. They came over with her most of the time."

"Stacy?"

"Mary's kid sister."

Once again I stared at Jack across the metal table. Square of face, green eyes, black hair spilling over his forehead like Superman's: so damned handsome. Too bad about the divorce. Look where it had gotten him. Look where it had gotten me, for that matter.

"I know about Stacy now, Jack."

His expression grew wary. "What about her?"

"Nice try—*Jackie*. But I've been to see her." Been to see her, and been turned away at the door by a harried woman in a nurse's slacksuit. Apparently Stacy Sutter was taking her sister's death hard. Maybe she had good reason.

"I thought I'd better follow up on the snapshot I found in your hutch drawer. Under the false bottom."

"What snapshot?"

"The little orgy by your pool; naked kids and some unclassic coke."

His lips compressed to a white line; his eyes narrowed to glinting slits.

"Want to know what the picture says to me? One of two things: Either you and Mary were paying blackmailers to keep the negative private—and no one would want a picture like that made public, not even someone like Stacy Sutter."

Jack's nostrils began to flare; he was getting angrier.

"Or, second possibility: pornographic thrills for you. Nude girl young enough to be your daughter."

He was almost angry enough now.

"Then there's the drug angle. Stacy's addicted to cocaine. The two men in the picture are pushers."

I thought I had him, but he choked back what he meant to say.

"Look, Jack, you can protect Stacy Sutter if you want to. Maybe it doesn't matter to you that she killed Mary and tried to kill you! But I wonder what you did to make her so angry? Or was sleeping with both sisters enough?''

He stood, his chair toppling over backward. His face mottled; his hands shook.

The jailer immediately ran in, pinning him in a choke hold.

"You haven't changed a bit!" Jack hissed at me.

I paced around the office in my stocking feet. Howie lay on my couch, eyes closed.

"Here's my theory," I said. "Jack's sleeping with Stacy Sutter. She gets morbid about cheating with her sister's boyfriend and tries to kill both of them. Jack feels responsible and decides to keep his mouth shut for Stacy's sake."

"Bit of a stretch. Hard to imagine Jacko—or anybody—being so chivalrous."

"Not chivalrous—conventional! Conventional enough to feel like he's got it coming for sleeping with both—"

"You never seemed to find him too, um, 'conventional' when you were married to him."

Tactful Howie. "If you mean *faithful*, no. I'd never accuse him of that. But he's definitely a home-and-family kind of man; marrying me when we thought I was— Buying that house for us. There's a big difference between sleeping with a neighbor, which is a traditionally macho kind of thing to do"—I made a conscious effort to eliminate bitterness from my voice—"and sleeping with your lover's baby sister. And, Howie, you should have seen his reaction when I asked him about it. The veins in his neck practically exploded!"

"No doubt!" Howie rubbed his knuckles over a clean-shaven cheek. "But where does it leave us? Assuming Jack won't admit it and the baby sister won't, either?"

"Jaime and Andy."

"Beg your pardon?"

"The two men in the picture with Stacy Sutter. They supplied Mary with drugs. They were obviously in Stacy's pants, and maybe in her confidence too. Odds are they knew about Stacy and Jack." I crossed to my desk. "The trouble is, drug dealers are damned lousy witnesses."

"Easily impeached," Howie agreed.

"Vindictive too." Last time we'd subpoenaed a coke dealer, he'd put our client in the hospital.

"You don't suppose . . . ?" There was an uncharacteristic hesitancy in Howie's voice. "You're thinking Jacko'd rot in jail to protect a woman. Have you wondered if he might be guilty?"

I slipped my pumps on. "Can you imagine a more acrimonious divorce than ours, Howie? If Jack didn't kill *me*"—I shrugged—"he doesn't have it in him."

Howie blinked up at me. "Funny he'd want *you* to represent him."

"Well, he does!" Too defensive. I looked away. Outside my window, a billboard advertised KATY'S KOFFEE KUP, KOUNTRY BREAKFAST AND MMMM MMMM KOFFEE.

Let Howard learn the truth from Jack, later. By then I'd have Jack out, maybe have things resolved.

"See, Howie"—I laughed nervously—"when we were married, I used to toot my own horn all the time; tell Jack I was the best criminal lawyer in the state. Just to impress him; you know how it is."

"Mmm." I heard a whisper of amusement; Howie knew I believed it. "And the, um, history doesn't . . . *disturb* him?"

"Oh hell! Of course it disturbs him!" I began checking the contents of my briefcase. "He's guarded with me. Prickly. Probably thinks I still resent him leaving me for Mary." I bit my lip, rearranging my papers. "And maybe I do, a little!" I let the briefcase lid slam down. "But Jack can't do any better than me, and at some level he knows it!" Why else would he ask for my junior associate? They were friends, sure; but my name came first on the letterhead. "What I'm really afraid of—" I rubbed my breastbone; it was hot in the room, hard to breathe. "He doesn't want to post bail, Howie! He won't even discuss it."

Howard sat up, brows puckering. "Feeling too battered to care what happens to him? Life without Mary . . . ?"

Mary! I stuffed my fists into my pockets. "I wonder if he—? You don't suppose he *wants* to stay inside?" Refusing to discuss his defense; sticking to a bare outline of events. "Howie, he couldn't *want* to stay in jail, could he?"

Howie tilted his head, considering.

"Or—! What if he *expects* us to screw up?" Hiring an inexperienced kid to represent him—his ex-wife's employee. Maybe it wasn't a vote of confidence. Maybe it was sabotage. "He *can't* think I'd screw up on purpose?"

Howie was silent; the possibility had occurred to him.

"You know I wouldn't!"

"Janet? If he does want to stay inside? Could he be protecting himself?"

"From what? How much lower can you go than the county bedbug farm?"

"Six feet under?" Howie squinted at the window; *Mmmm Mmmm Koffee*, the billboard promised. "Someone tried to kill him. Perhaps he feels safer behind bars right now."

"Safer? Kiddo, prisoners are murdered in their cells every day of the—" I turned away, shaken. "Where the hell's my jacket?"

I got to the county jail half an hour before Jack's bail hearing. As the sheriff's deputy and I approached the short row of cells, I could hear someone retching, a drunk singing, voices speaking Spanish. I hoped Jack felt crowded enough to reconsider posting bail.

When I saw the other prisoners, I gripped the deputy's arm and pointed. "What are *they* doing here?"

The deputy brushed my hand off his arm. "Processed a few hours ago. Cocaine. Possession for sale."

For a moment I stared at the two handsome Latinos. The drunk stopped singing to leer at me. I scanned the remaining cells for Jack. He was lying prone in the cell between the drunk and the Latinos. His face was turned to the wall.

"Jesus! They've *killed* him!"

The deputy looked at me as if I were insane, especially after Jack rolled over and sat up.

I leaned back against the wall, one hand over my heart. "Listen, those two men knew Mary Sutter—they sold her drugs; they might have been blackmailing her sister!"

The young Latinos watched quizzically. The taller one murmured something in Spanish to the other.

Jack sputtered, "What the hell are you talking about?"

"The trouble is, you don't care if they kill you, do you, Jack? You won't give me the facts I need to acquit you, but you don't want to spend your life behind bars." Not the sort of thing a lawyer should say in public, but I couldn't stop. "Well, I'm not going to let you stay here and get murdered!"

The deputy stepped between me and the bars. "Nobody's getting murdered in my jail!"

"Nobody *else*, you mean?"

A month earlier a drug dealer had died in his cell on the eve of testifying against a codefendant. Neighboring prisoners hadn't "noticed" the dealer's head crack open on the bars between the cells. The sheriff had called it accidental death; a case of slip and fall.

I'd seen the body in a steel drawer. If the man slipped, he'd done it half a dozen times.

The deputy turned purple.

"Your Honor, not only is there no risk of flight in this case, but I believe the defendant is actually in physical, mortal danger if he remains in the county facility."

There were reporters behind me in the pewlike seats. I could hear excited whispers. I could feel the district attorney's fury, the judge's crotchety distaste for melodrama. But I didn't seem to have much choice. I explained about Jaime and Andy, handing the judge and the D.A. each a copy of the photograph I'd found in Jack's hutch. "These two men are now in the cell beside Mr. Krauder's, Your Honor. I believe they arranged their own arrest in order to kill my client before his trial."

The judge pounded his gavel to silence the spectators.

"Your Honor!" The district attorney sounded predictably skeptical. "We'll be challenging the admissibility—and the relevancy—of this photograph at another time, but I should state for the record that I have personal knowledge of the two men to whom counsel refers. Their names are Julio and Silvio Marcos. They were arrested for possession of narcotics on a tip from a reliable source!"

Reliable source—that's police code for any anonymous slimeball who phones them.

"At the very least"—I struggled to keep calm—"they should be placed in another facility until bail is posted!"

"I've never seen those men before!" Jack volunteered. "They're not Jaime and Andy!"

The judge, a sour old prune, glared at me. "Then I see little point in making special arrangements to separate these prisoners, do you, Miss Dale?"

I never thought I'd hear myself say it about my own client. "He's lying, Your Honor!"

The D.A. all but gasped.

"Approach the bench!" the judge barked. His tone said, Out to the woodshed with you, young lady!

I gripped the oak rim of the judge's bench and craned my neck to entreat him. "Please! I don't want to give away the details of my defense, Your Honor, but those two men are involved—"

The D.A. slapped the photograph I'd handed him. "These are different men! Even Krauder says—!"

"The sun's behind them! Look more closely! They're the same—"

"Janet!" The D.A. and I had faced each other in court too often to remain mere acquaintances. "I know you used to be married to the guy, but you're being paranoid here!"

Furious, I turned away from him. "Your Honor, it won't hurt to separate these men from—"

"Enough!" The judge thumped his blotter with a wizened hand. "This is not Los Angeles! You are well aware that we have only one facility here! And I am certainly not going to jeopardize the proceedings against these two men by busing them upstate, Miss Dale!"

I could see from his face that further comment was useless. I glanced at the D.A.; his air of concern was humiliating.

I stalked back to counsel's table. Jack's mouth twisted into a frosty sneer. He said loudly, "This woman isn't my lawyer! I don't want her representing me!"

The judge barked, "What? Miss Dale, did the defendant authorize you to state an appearance?"

I forced myself to look away from Jack. Idiot! "My associate, Howard Frost, is defendant's counsel of record, Your Honor. Mr. Frost couldn't be here this afternoon. He's in trial, and I'm filling in—"

"Then I don't want bail!" Jack's voice seethed with malice. "I'd rather stay where I am until—"

"Shut up, Jack!"

More commotion in the pews. The judge shouted with exasperation, "Miss Dale, why are you wasting this court's time with a bail hearing if your client—Mr. Frost's client!—does not wish—" He rapped the gavel several times. "Quiet! All of you! This is not a ball game, this is a court of law!"

There was very little doubt in my mind that with his next breath the judge would order Jack escorted back to his cell. I looked at Jack and hated him for what he was forcing me to do.

"I won't be a party to Mr. Krauder's indirect suicide, Your Honor!" I insisted. "That's what you're asking me to do!" I spoke louder, over the judge's fierce cry that I was in contempt of his court. "Jack knows he'll get killed in jail, and he doesn't care! He feels morally responsible— He wants to protect—" I gulped. I was losing control; I mustn't do that. "You'd have to know Jack to understand! Someone he cares about, someone he thinks he's wronged, is involved with drug dealers—with these two prisoners, Jaime and Andy! Don't you see, they're afraid Jack's going to implicate them . . ."

I looked around the courtroom: the judge's livid outrage; the D.A.'s shocked pity. Hysterical ex-wife, that's what they were thinking. And I was remembering last month's dead prisoner, with his broken, bloody forehead.

In a moment the proceeding would be declared over, and Jack would be whisked away. I played my trump card.

Jack's lips parted, then his jaw dropped. "Damn," he whispered, looking down the barrel of a revolver I'd just pulled from my briefcase.

I saw the district attorney motion to the bailiff, and I swung the gun toward him instinctively before deciding it was safer to keep it trained on one person. And because I was taking him with me, that person had to be Jack.

"Please," I begged the judge. "Try to understand why I'm doing this. If it turns out the prisoners aren't Jaime and Andy, okay. I'll bring Jack back. But I can't risk his going back in there and getting killed!"

There was a charged silence as the judge raised his arms. For a moment he was motionless, a robed scarecrow. Then he croaked, "Keep the aisles clear, please. I do not want the defendant endangered by any act of ours."

"I won't go," Jack growled. He lowered his head bullishly, eyes on the gun.

I extended my arms until the gun was inches from his face: Careful, *toro*. "I'm throwing my career down the toilet for you, Jack! My *career*! To save your miserable life! Cooperate with me for once, goddammit!"

The hand that held the gun was steady. I'd won trophies for marksmanship; I hoped Jack remembered them. After what seemed a span of years, he turned and led the way out of the courtroom.

Spectators stirred, a flash cube popped. My hand remained steady. No one got heroic.

The corridors were nearly empty; I'd asked for a late-afternoon hearing. The clerk of the court, a woman carrying a Danish, a lawyer slumped on a Naugahyde bench; they watched in pale alarm, making no move to interfere. We made it to my car, illegally parked beside the back entrance. I squealed out of the lot, checking for cruisers. Most of them were still across town, responding to a false alarm I'd phoned in before the hearing. I drove with one hand, bracing the muzzle of the gun against Jack's crotch.

"Don't try to grab it, Jack. If it goes off, you won't be dead, but you'll be awfully unhappy."

I glanced at him. He was as white as tapioca. His eyes were closed, as if in prayer.

It was imperative to ditch the car; the cops would soon have my license-plate number. I pulled into an underground parking garage. I was lucky; there was no one down there. I didn't have to worry about concealing the gun as I motioned Jack out of the car and into the elevator.

We got out at the top and found ourselves alone on a windy roof. Jack backed ten, fifteen, feet away from me before I raised the gun again. "Let's start over, Jackie. No more bullshit! Tell me what you know."

"This is only a four-story building. The fall might not kill me."

"The fall," I repeated.

"That's what you have in mind, isn't it? You'll say I confessed to the murder and jumped off in remorse. You'll say you tried to stop me, but I overpowered you. You'll cry about how much you loved me, and everyone will believe you because you were willing to be disbarred for me." His face twisted with contempt, and for the first time I felt my gun hand tremble. "Tell you what I know? I know you tricked me into marrying you and almost strangled me with your clinging and complaining. You were jealous of every woman I ever said hello to, and our divorce didn't change that one bit. You think I didn't see you spying on me and Mary? You and your damn telephoto lens! You took that picture of Stacy and her friends at our pool, didn't you? Thinking it was Mary."

The distance between us seemed to increase. "No."

"You say you found it at my house. If you did, you planted it there."

"Why would I do that?"

"So the police would believe you thought Jaime and Andy were in jail with me. You know damn well those two guys aren't Jaime and Andy! Hell, *you* probably got them busted. Your job puts you in contact with every drug dealer in town. All you had to do was choose two who looked a little like the picture and call the cops on them."

"Why should I—?"

"So you'd have a reason to do this: Get me out of jail and finish the job you started when you poisoned the coffee."

I looked at him across the sooty expanse of roof. Broad of chest, long-legged, black hair blowing; handsome damn bastard!

"You managed to sink some of my relationships, didn't you, Janet? I've often wondered what you said to my accountant to make her quit like that! But you could see that Mary and I—" He kneaded his chest as though it ached. "We were too much in love to let you come between us. And you couldn't stand it. You were going to kill both of us. But I skipped coffee that morning. And you know I'm not stupid. Sooner or later I was bound to see you'd done it; you're the only person I know who's crazy enough. I just wish to Christ I'd realized— I've had so much to deal with—" He slid both hands through his hair, gripping his head, rounding his shoulders. "I thought you were just being *you*. Until you pulled the gun, I didn't—"

"I love you, Jack!" If only he'd let me comfort him.

"Love!" The word vibrated with loathing. His arms snapped to his sides like a soldier's. "You'd have killed me when I got out on bail, wouldn't you? Who'd suspect my lawyer? And when I told you I didn't want to post bail, you had to arrange this little charade. Planting that photograph, getting those chicanos busted, the scene you played in front of the jailer so you could get his testimony later. And, of course, 'rescuing' me today. Maybe you'll get disbarred for it, but there's gonna be a lot of sympathy for you, too—even when they find out you were 'wrong' about those two guys in jail. You'll have a little breakdown, probably quite sincere, over my death. And your pal the D.A. will go easy on you. You might not even do any time—hell, if anyone knows all the angles, it's you!"

"You shouldn't have left me, Jack. Mary didn't love you like I do."

He spat at me.

"Fine, you *bastard*! Jump or be shot. Take your pick."

"What'll you tell them if you shoot me?"

"That you came at me to kill me."

"After confessing?"

I nodded.

"Well, it won't work, Janet. There's a witness." He pointed behind me.

And sure enough, there was Howie Frost, face crinkled in astonishment. "Janet?" He shook his head, not quite convinced it was happening. "My trial's in recess—I got their expert disqualified."

Well, well, he was learning. "I stepped outside and saw your car at the rear entrance. And knowing how you feel about Jacko . . . I thought I'd better pull my car up behind, keep an eye on it." Howie hugged himself. "Not that I really believed— Oh, Janet! You need help!"

I felt my lower lip quiver, my chin knot.

"Give me the gun, Janet, do! It'll be all right! We'll get you into therapy—get you all the help you need!"

" 'Help'!" Jack repeated. There was more than mere disgust in his voice; there was cold, concentrated hatred. "You think because you know every shrink and every judge in town, you're going to walk away from this, don't you, Janet? Beat the system like you do for the scum you represent!" He took a step toward me, raising a clenched fist. "Well, you're *not*! Not if I have to—"

"Oh, Howie—listen to him! He deserves to die! He's been mean to me all along, for *years*—cheating on me, lying to me. He's *got* to pay for it!"

"It's you I'm thinking of, Janet." Howie stepped between me and Jack, holding out his hand. He looked like a frightened deer. "For God's *sake*!" Howie, shrill? "For your own sake! Please! Give me the gun!"

I could see Jack moving stealthily closer, using Howie for cover. I took a sideways step, trying to get a clear shot, but Howie ducked sideways, too, blocking my path.

Damn Howie! He was *my* associate, *my* friend—and he'd sided with Jack! Everyone sided with Jack!

Howie reached for the gun, Jack three paces behind him. Another second and they'd have me. Unless—

I'd won a couple of insanity acquittals; I knew what the shrinks looked for. And I was a good actress; as a trial lawyer, I had to be. With luck I could pull it off.

Two shots was all it took.

*Susan Kelly says that her life ". . . becomes more like that of Liz Connors all the time." No wonder—both are tall, have red hair, are former college English professors, live in Cambridge, Massachusetts, and have a decidedly droll take on life. Susan has also written scholarly articles on medieval literature and taught report writing at the Cambridge Police Academy. Nominated in 1985 for an Anthony for Best First Novel for* The Gemini Man, *Susan brought Liz and her cop-boyfriend Jack Lingemann back in* The Summertime Soldiers *and* Trail of the Dragon.

*In "Blue Curaçao," Liz's offbeat humor helps—up to a point— when she steps into a situation that urban dwellers will recognize as one of their nightmare scenarios.*

# BLUE CURAÇAO

## by Susan Kelly

THEY SAY THAT drink is a terrible thing. I never believed them until the January night I walked into Godozik's Discount Liquors to buy a bottle of vodka and got taken hostage instead. It wasn't enough to make me swear off martinis, but close.

I'm being flip, and that's bad, because what happened in Godozik's wasn't funny, not at all. Somebody died, and maybe he shouldn't have. The cops would say he brought it on himself. I can appreciate their point of view. But still, I'll always wonder. Not whether the cops did the right thing, but if I did.

My name is Elizabeth Connors. I'm a free-lance writer living in Cambridge. I used to be a college English teacher—my specialty was English and Scottish literature of the fourteenth and fifteenth centuries. How's that for esoteric?

The fact that I once taught has some bearing on the rest of the story, which is the only reason I mention it here.

I like a peaceful life. Not only do I not go looking for trouble, I tend to go out of my way to avoid it. I guess sometimes I don't go far enough. Or maybe it's that what I write about now, for a living, is crime. Trouble and crime tend to go together.

Another relevant piece of information: For the past five and a half years I've been involved, seriously, with a detective-lieutenant in the Cambridge Police Department. That January night, he was out of town—in Chicago to visit his father, who'd had a mild stroke a few days earlier. Jack would be returning late Sunday afternoon, and I'd meet him at Logan Airport and bring him back to my place for dinner.

Actually, I wasn't going to Godozik's Liquors just to pick up some vodka. I also wanted a bottle of red wine to accompany the pot roast I'd serve on Sunday.

About five o'clock on January ninth, it began snowing. The flakes were large and fell in slow motion, like what you'd expect if a Normal Rockwell painting or a Currier and Ives print came to life. It made Cambridge Street in East Cambridge, not really the garden spot of the city, seem almost bucolic. Some of the shops and houses were still festooned with Christmas decorations, now looking a bit frayed and dispirited. But then, that was in keeping with the tone of East Cambridge in general—down-at-the-heels.

I went into Godozik's a little after six. The Saturday night booze patrol was out in full force, and it was a real cross section of society. A tall, lanky young man in a Tufts sweatshirt was picking up a keg of beer, no doubt for that evening's fraternity bash. A woman with straight, shoulder-length salt-and-pepper hair wearing a gathered wool paisley skirt, hiking boots, and down jacket was at the checkout counter paying for a jug of Gallo Hearty Burgundy. A young man in a Brooks Brothers gray suit was examining with great intensity the Pouilly-Fuissé selection. Several less obviously Cambridge types were browsing about, picking up this and that for whatever. I suppose I fit in with the crowd, a thirty-six-year-old, five-foot-ten-inch-tall redhead in Levi's and Fair Isle sweater and pile-lined windbreaker.

I got a bottle of vodka, tucked it under my right arm, and headed over to the wine racks. A skinny kid in a brown leather jacket and acid-washed jeans brushed past me, carrying a six-pack of Coors.

The wines were arranged according to country of origin. I started looking in France. I love poking around in liquor stores the way I do in bookstores and record stores and grocery stores. Clothing and jewelry stores, for some reason, don't excite me.

I would need a wine with body to stand up to the pot roast. I wished I knew more about wine. I wished I knew more about a lot of things. The older I got, the more I was amazed by the scope of my ignorance.

I squatted on the floor to study the bottles at the bottom of the rack.

The man in the gray suit found a Pouilly-Fuissé to his liking and took it to the register. Out of the corner of my eye I noticed the kid in the leather jacket get another six-pack from the cooler.

Still on my haunches, I shuffled crablike across the border from France into Italy. Some Bardolino might be okay with pot roast. On the other hand, so might a Burgundy. I edged back into France.

I heard a slight scuffling noise from, it seemed, the front of the store. Then the door banged open and shut, the bell above it tinkling brassily.

Fascinating as the wine displays might be, I couldn't spend all night here. I grabbed a bottle of Burgundy from the bin, rose, and started toward the checkout counter.

The kid in the leather jacket was behind the counter, beside the clerk. He had one hand twined tightly in her hair, yanking her head back, so that she was looking rigidly at the ceiling. His other hand was pressing the barrel of a gun into the soft flesh beneath her jaw.

My mind took it in—on one level, anyway—but my body didn't. Brain said, *This place is being robbed!* Body kept walking, somnambulist fashion, to the cash register.

The vodka bottle slid from beneath my arm and shattered on the floor. Liquor splashed up onto the left leg of my jeans and on my shoes.

The kid in the leather jacket stared at me. His face was sharply triangular and flat white. His eyes were wide and shiny-looking. There was a tremor in his gun hand.

I stood very still.

The clerk's mouth was open wide, her lips drawn tightly back over her teeth. With her head tilted and her face upraised, she looked as if she were screaming soundlessly at the ceiling.

Without relaxing his grip on the clerk's hair, the kid lowered the gun and pointed it at me, not steadily.

Oh, God, I thought. I'm going to die. And all because I couldn't make up my mind fast enough between Burgundy and Bardolino.

My legs felt like rubber snakes.

The door to Godozik's swung open, the bell above it tinkling cheerily. Reflexively I turned my head to the right. The kid snapped his to the left. What we saw, coming into the store, was a short, fat, balding man in an overcoat and wool muffler.

It took him, as it had taken me, a moment to absorb the scene before him. When he did, he stopped dead in his tracks, just a few feet over the threshold. For a moment he remained absolutely motionless. He looked over at me, his eyes wide. Then he looked at the kid.

The kid had gone back to watching me over the barrel of the gun.

The fat man put his hands on his head and began shuffling backward, toward the door. His movements were very tentative. The soles of his shoes made only the faintest of scraping sounds on the linoleum floor.

The tremor in the kid's gun hand grew more pronounced.

The fat man bumped up against the door. Very carefully he lowered his right arm, put it behind him, and fumbled for the handle. He pulled the door open, turned sideways, and sidled his bulk clumsily through the aperture. A swirl of snow blew in over the threshold.

The door thunked shut behind the fat man, and again the bell above it gave a merry little jangle.

Faintly, I heard sirens.

The kid heard them, too.

"You got a key for this place?" His voice was surprisingly deep and husky, for one so young. It had a frantic undertone.

He was speaking not to me, of course, but to the clerk. She didn't respond to the question. Probably it hadn't penetrated her shock.

The kid tightened his grip on her hair and gave her head a violent jerk. She let out a faint scream.

"I said, you got a fuckin' key to this place, bitch?"

She nodded furiously, her eyes huge now, not only with shock but with pain.

"Get it," the kid snapped. "Where is it?"

"Underneath the register," the clerk whimpered.

The kid shoved her down beneath the counter.

"You," he said. He gestured at me with the gun. "Over here."

My body felt loose and liquid, almost insubstantial.

"Move it!" the kid yelled.

I plodded toward him, feeling disconnected from my own corporeality.

The clerk rose slowly from behind the counter, a ring of keys dangling from her left hand. The kid snatched them and dropped them into his jacket pocket.

"You," he said to me. "Get back here."

He gave the clerk a hard shove, and she stumbled past me as I moved behind the counter. The gun was six inches away from my chest. I could feel the skin between my breasts tighten.

The clerk tripped over the base of a wire rack full of bags of potato chips and popcorn and fell heavily to the floor. The kid kicked her in the right thigh. "Go on, get out," he snapped.

The clerk heaved up on her hands and knees and began crawling toward the door. The kid backed after her, keeping the gun pointed at me.

At the door the clerk pushed herself to her feet. She stood with her head drooping and her arms hanging by her sides, moaning in a horrible kind of unceasing wail.

The kid reached behind him, as the fat man had done, and yanked open the door. Then he grabbed the clerk by her right shoulder, spun her around, and thrust her out onto the snowy sidewalk. I thought I saw her fall again.

The sirens were quite loud now.

The kid fumbled the keys from his jacket pocket and began jamming them serially into the door lock. On the third try he got it. A police cruiser screamed up in front of the store.

The kid ran back toward the checkout counter, vaulted it in one easy swing of the legs, and landed lightly beside me. I drew back slightly, pressing against the cash register.

He was marginally taller than I, perhaps about five-eleven. And not so much skinny, as I'd thought before, as wiry. And strong. It took strength and agility to leap as cleanly over the counter as he had.

The kid grinned at me. His teeth were small and white, with sharp canines. His eyes glittered like shards of green glass.

"Just you and me," he said. He waved the gun in a brief arc. "Sit down." He grinned again. "Gonna be a long night, maybe."

I sat down with my back to the shelves of bottles behind the counter. It was only then that I realized I was still holding the Burgundy. I set it on the floor beside me.

The kid looked at the bottle. "Big party tonight?"

I shook my head.

"You'da missed it, anyhow," the kid said, and laughed raucously.

I stared at him. Two minutes ago he'd been gripped by the kind of frenzy that could only be born of terror. Now, with God knew how many cops massing outside, he seemed . . . exhilarated.

Was he on drugs? If so, I was in even worse trouble than I thought.

I looked at the gun. It was a semiautomatic, that much I knew. Neither a Colt .45 nor a Luger, which were the only two types of pistols I could recognize. The kid's trigger finger stuck out stiff and straight. His other three fingers were curled tightly around the butt of the gun. I wondered if he'd practiced with it, or if this was his first go at an armed robbery.

The kid was bouncing back and forth on the balls of his feet, as if that were the only way he could vent some of the nervous energy boiling within him. He leaned forward across the counter, peering at the plate-glass windows that fronted the liquor store.

My legs were out straight before me, like a doll's or a little kid's. Not a comfortable position for a grown-up. I slid my feet toward me, drawing my knees up. The kid heard the slight scuffing noise my heels made on the floor and spun away from the counter, glaring at me.

"Kink in my leg," I blurted, feeling my internal organs freeze.

He stared at me for a moment longer. "Don't make no moves, I'm warning you," he said. "You don't make no moves unless I tell you, huh?"

"Sure." I didn't even nod. I noticed that his trigger finger was now hooked around the trigger guard of the gun.

The kid resumed his gentle side-to-side bouncing. I watched him, trying to be covert about it.

I thought he might be anywhere from eighteen to twenty-two. He had a high, broad forehead and high cheekbones that tapered to a small, pointed chin. His hair was medium brown and thick, with the gloss of health. His eyebrows were finely drawn and much darker than his hair. His eyes were large and heavy-lidded, the corners slightly downturned. The nose was thin and straight and the mouth well cut, with a full lower lip. There were slight traces of acne on his cheeks, but otherwise, he was a handsome boy.

The realization shook me. What he looked like was a college kid, like one of my own students. Dirtballs weren't supposed to look like Tufts or Harvard juniors. They were supposed to look like cruds. But put this kid on any campus anywhere and he'd have faded right into the dormitory woodwork. Until he opened his mouth.

His diction was what betrayed him. Not the language he used—all kids his age talked like longshoremen, male or female. It was his grammar and his accent—the coarse slur of the uneducated urban New Englander. Nobody ever thought Jack Kennedy sounded crude for dropping his final *r*'s. But then, Jack Kennedy hadn't hailed from East Cambridge.

I knew, by some instinct, that this kid was local. Very local.

Either I did a good job of pretending not to study the kid, or being appraised didn't bother him. He stopped dancing his little back-and-forth jig and turned to the cash register. It was the old-fashioned, noncomputerized kind. He looked at the keys for a moment, then pressed the no-sale button. The register drawer shot out. The kid peered into it.

"Hey, will you lookee here," he said. "Look at all the money." He glanced at me. "They keep the big bills under this"—he pointed at the tray—"don't they?"

I wasn't sure whether the question was rhetorical.

"Yeah," I said. "I think so."

The kid lifted the tray from the register and set it on the counter.

"Well, well," he said. He reached into the drawer and took from it a hundred-dollar bill. He waved it at me and then stuck it crumpled into the right hip pocket of his jeans. Then he picked up a wad of twenties in a paper band and shoved that into his jacket pocket.

While he rummaged through the register drawer I tried to collect my thoughts. More specifically, I tried to focus them on what I'd learned, from my reading on the subject and from talking to cops, about how hostages should act after they'd been taken hostage.

The currently popular theory was that the hostage try "to communicate and establish a relationship" with the hostage-taker. And above all, the hostage should stay calm. That was swell advice, of course, but I wondered if any of the people giving it had ever tried to act on it. How the hell was I supposed to establish a rapport with a kid almost young enough to be my own son, who moreover might or might not be drugged to the gills?

I had been a hostage once before this, several years ago. But this situation and that one had nothing in common.

The kid lifted the register tray from the counter and shoved it at me. I jumped slightly.

"Count what's in there," he said.

I took the tray and set it in my lap. I didn't like being given orders by twerps. On the other hand, I would like even less being shot by one of them if I disobeyed his order.

I pulled the twenty-dollar bills out of their compartment. The kid watched me carefully as I did so.

"Three hundred and forty-eight dollars," I announced after a few minutes.

"That's all?" There was outrage in his voice.

I hesitated a moment, then shrugged very slightly. "Places like this empty the registers three or four times a day."

"So what the fuck do they do with the money?"

"The owner or the manager deposits it in the bank." I didn't *know* that for sure, but it seemed logical.

"Shit." The kid drummed the fingers of his free hand on the countertop. "Gimme what's there."

I handed him a stack of bills. He rolled it into a cylinder and stuffed it into his jacket pocket. I set the empty register tray on the floor.

The kid pushed away from the counter and, in one fluid movement, dropped into a crouch beside me. He rested his arms on his knees. The gun in his right hand hung between his legs, pointing downward. I wondered if he was aware of the symbolism of the pose. In a way he probably was.

He gave me his sharp-toothed grin. "You ain't too bad-looking," he said. "For an old broad." His gaze dropped and traveled over my upper torso. "You got nice tits."

Oh, Christ, I thought.

He raised the gun and traced the end of the barrel very lightly down the side of my face. Then he shoved it, hard, into the side of my neck, just under the ear.

The phone on the counter rang. The sound cut through the thick silence like a chain saw through soft wood.

The kid pulled back from me. "What the fuck's that?"

I closed my eyes. "Answer it," I said. "It's probably for you."

The phone rang three more times. The kid rose, stepped over my legs, and grabbed the receiver. He brought it up to his face and said, "Yeah?"

I let myself inhale while the kid listened to whatever the cop on the other end of the line had to say.

Whatever it was, it didn't impress the kid. "Fuck you," he said into the mouthpiece, and slammed the receiver back into the phone cradle. He turned back to me, his face tense with fury. For a moment he stood over me, breathing hard enough for it to be audible. Then he bent down, grabbed the front of my sweater, and yanked.

"Get up," he said.

I did.

He let go of my sweater and gripped my upper right arm. The gun he pressed into my back. He pushed me forward, crowding against me with his body. His breath stirred my hair.

"Move," he said. "Over to the window. Go slowly."

I walked to the front of the store, feeling as if I were dragging an animate shackle. The kid hooked his arm around my neck so that the bend of his elbow was pressing against my throat. That, combined with the gun jamming into my spine, made my back arch. By the time we got to the window, I was almost on tiptoe.

The block of Cambridge Street in front of the liquor store had been cordoned off. There were at least seven police cruisers out there, and two ambulances. And, off to the right, the Channel 5 news truck.

The kid and I maintained our weird little pas de deux in the window for about fifteen seconds. Then he tugged at me and we stumbled backward toward the counter.

"On the floor," he said.

I sat down beneath the register, this time facing the shelves of liquor. All the bottles on them were nips, or half-pints, or pints, small items kept inaccessible so they couldn't be shoplifted. Directly in front of me was a row of liqueurs in rainbow colors.

"Cops wanted to make sure I wasn't in here by myself," the kid said.

I looked up at him.

"Also wanted to see if you was okay," he added.

I nodded.

"They ain't gonna do anything with you in here."

"No."

The kid squatted down, in his lithe way, beside me. Remembering what the phone ring had interrupted, I tensed, sure that his next move or utterance would be a sexual one.

I stared straight ahead of me, at the shelf of liqueurs. In a way it would be good if the kid tried to rape me. At some point he'd either drop the gun or set it aside. At which point I would grab the gun and blow the little son of a bitch's brains through the plate-glass window and clear across Cambridge Street.

When the kid spoke, what he said jolted me more than a hand tearing at my jeans or clamped on a breast would have.

"You hungry?"

"What?"

"You want something to eat?"

Without waiting for me to answer, he leaned across to the wire rack of packaged snacks and took from it a large bag of potato chips. He used his teeth to rip open the bag. Then he held it out to me. A dense smell of oil and ersatz sour cream flooded my nasal passages. My stomach heaved.

I shook my head. "No thanks."

He set the bag on the floor beside him and dug into it with his free hand. He crammed a fistful of chips into his mouth, crunching them noisily. A small shower of crumbs fell onto his jacket.

Before he'd swallowed the first mouthful, he was reaching for more.

The sight reminded me that he was just a kid.

So what? Some of the worst criminals were boys just like him, with the same soft, not quite formed faces. And voracious appetites for all sorts of things.

He finished most of the potato chips before he spoke again.

"Fuckin' things make me thirsty," he said. He glanced to his right, at the shelves of booze. Then he looked at me. "Any of that crap there any good to drink?"

He probably didn't know what Courvoisier and Grand Marnier and Rémy Martin were. They wouldn't have helped his problem, anyway.

"No," I said. "You'd be better off with a Coke or a beer."

Maybe I should have told him to slug down a bottle of Triple Sec. That on top of the chips would have made him so sick I could have gotten the gun away from him in no time.

Maybe.

He looked away from me and back at the shelves. His gaze seemed to fix on something.

"What the hell's that stuff?"

"What?"

He jerked his head at the row of liqueurs. "That blue shit."

"Blue . . ." I leaned forward slightly and squinted at the shelf. "Oh. I see." I glanced at the kid. "That's Blue Curaçao."

"So what the hell's that?"

"It's a—it's a liqueur. Like an after-dinner drink. Very thick. Very sweet."

"Oh, yeah?" He sounded interested. "It taste good?"

"Personally," I said, "I'd rather drink lighter fluid."

The kid laughed, this time with no trace of hysteria. "Hey, lady," he said. "You're a hot shit, you know?"

"Yeah. I know."

He laughed again, then reached over and picked up the bottle. He studied the label for a moment, his eyebrows furrowed. Then he looked up at me. "So how come they gave this shit such a dumb fuckin' name? Blue Cura . . ." His voice trailed off, and he peered down again at the bottle label.

"Cura-*sow*," I said.

"*Sow*," he repeated. "How the fuck you get *sow* out of" —he looked once more at the label—"out of C-A-O?"

"It's not English," I said. "Curaçao's a place, actually."

"Yeah?" He put the bottle back on the shelf. "Where's that?"

"It's an island in the Caribbean."

He gave me a puzzled look. I was used to that; some of my allegedly well-educated students had absolutely no grasp of even basic geography. The public schools stopped teaching it in 1957, I think. Long before this kid was out of diapers. Or perhaps even conceived.

"The sea between North America and South America," I explained.

"Oh." He thought for a moment. "Like where Puerto Rico is?"

Was I dreaming this conversation? "Well, sort of."

The phone rang. We both looked at it.

"Fuckin' cops again," the kid said. He made no move to answer the summons.

The phone kept ringing.

"Maybe you better see what they want," I said. "Otherwise they won't quit."

He made an exasperated noise. "Yeah." He rose and picked up the receiver. "Fuck off," he said into it. Then he laid the receiver down by the phone. He depressed the button in the cradle to break the connection, then turned to me. "I don't need to listen to their shit."

I gazed back at him, as steadily as I could. "You're going to have to, at some point."

His eyes narrowed. "I don't do nothing I don't want to, lady."

I wished we were still talking about the etymology of Blue Curaçao.

The kid resumed his crouch beside me. I listened to him inhale and exhale for a few seconds.

"Relax," I said softly. "They can't call you back now."

He looked over at me. I smiled, very faintly.

"What's your name?" he asked abruptly.

The unexpectedness of the question startled me into a brief silence. Then I said, "Liz."

He nodded.

"What's yours?"

He tilted his head and gave me a crooked half-smile. "Mickey."

"Oh. Well, hi."

"Hi."

I glanced unobtrusively at the gun. He had not stopped hanging on to it, very tightly.

"You still thirsty?" I asked.

"Nah." He shook his head. "I'm okay." Then he shot me a suspicious look. "Why you wanna know?"

I shrugged. "No reason."

"Well, I ain't gonna drink no fuckin' Blue Cura-shit."

I laughed. "I don't blame you."

He looked over again at the shelf of liqueurs. After a moment he reached out and took from it a bottle of rich-looking topaz liquid. He scowled at it for a moment, then dangled the bottle before my face.

"So what's this stuff?"

I looked at the label. "Lochan Ora," I said, giving the *ch* in *Lochan* an authentic Scottish glottal stop. I knew how to do that; I'd lived in Scotland for four years. Mickey would probably think I had catarrh.

If he did, he made no comment. "Lockin Ora," he repeated. "So what's that?"

"It's another liqueur," I explained. "It's made with a Scotch whiskey base, I think. It's a hell of a lot better than Blue Curaçao."

"Oh, yeah?" He looked at the bottle. "You want some?"

"Not right now."

Mickey hefted the bottle. Then he tossed it at me. It bounced into my lap.

"Open it," he commanded. "I want to try some."

I peeled the tax stamp off the stopper, unsealed it, and yanked out the plug. I handed the bottle back to Mickey. He raised it to his mouth and took an experimental slug. A peculiar expression crossed his face. Then he turned his head and spat on the floor.

"Fuck," he said. "It tastes like the dentist."

"Sorry. I guess it's one of those things that grows on you."

He shook his head disgustedly, then jerked it at the liqueur shelf. "Ain't there anything better there?"

I studied the shelf, running my eyes over its contents. If I suggested a kiwi-flavored drink to him, he'd probably try to shove the bottle down my throat after one sip. For which I wouldn't honestly be able to blame him. But he'd do the same after a slug of B and B. Nor did I think he'd truly appreciate a tot of Napoleon brandy.

I noticed a bottle of chocolate-mint liqueur. "Try that," I said, pointing at it. I thought the stuff would cause severe gastrointestinal dysfunction in a vulture, but a human Mickey's age might go for it. If not, I could always direct him to the cherry vodka.

I opened the bottle and handed it to him. He took a cautious sip. This time his expression was pleased rather than disgruntled.

"Not bad," he said. "Better than Blue Cura-shit."

"Almost anything is."

He took another swig of the liquid candy bar and then set the bottle beside him.

"You drink a lot?" he asked.

I was taken aback. "I try not to."

"So how come you know so much about booze?"

I shrugged. "I don't know, Mickey. I just picked it up, somewhere along the line. From reading, maybe."

He looked at me narrowly. "You know, you talk like a fuckin' teacher or somethin'."

I sighed. "Well, I was one. Once."

"No shit. What grade?"

I laughed uneasily. "College."

He stared. "You're shittin' me."

"No."

"Fuck." He turned his head to the right, his face twisted.

"What's wrong?" I said.

He looked back at me. "School sucks."

"I agree."

His eyes widened slightly.

"I hated school too," I said. "Elementary school and high school. The public schools, anyway. I went to a good pri . . . well, to a different school my junior and senior years. That was great. And I loved college and . . . graduate school." I realized I was babbling, and cut off the flow before I found myself telling Mickey that I'd actually enjoyed writing my doctoral dissertation. I was probably the only person in the known universe who had. I took a deep breath. "But before that," I continued, waving my right hand, "you're absolutely right. School sucked."

Still on his haunches, Mickey shuffled a bit closer to me. His face was vivid with disbelief. "You're shittin' me," he repeated.

"No."

He shook his head. "Teachers are supposed to love school." He gave his head another bewildered toss. "I mean, ain't they? They fuckin' act like they think it's great."

"College can be good, Mick. What comes before it sometimes isn't that hot."

"Yeah, tell me about it."

"I don't think I have to."

He picked up the bottle of chocolate-mint liqueur and took another sip of it. "Okay, so how come you hated school so much?"

"It started early."

"Like when?"

"When I realized I was smarter than my teachers."

He stared at me for a moment. Then he threw back his head and laughed. "Hot shit," he said. "Me too."

"Yeah?" I leaned toward him. "What happened to you?"

He picked up his liqueur and nipped at it. Then he wiped his mouth with the wrist of the hand that held the gun. "Oh, man," he said. "I don't want to talk about that shit."

I smiled. "Why not? What else is there to do?"

He grimaced. It made him look as if he were twelve. A deadly twelve.

"Go on," I said. "*I* told *you*."

"Yeah." He set the liqueur bottle down on the floor and rubbed the side of his head. "Okay." He was quiet for a moment. When he did speak, it seemed to be with some difficulty. Or at least reluctance.

"It was like . . . when I was a kid, I was like . . . I was, uh, kind of interested in dinosaurs, you know?" He looked a bit embarrassed by the disclosure, as if he'd just confessed to an obsession with child pornography.

"I was into dinosaurs myself," I said.

"Yeah?" His face cleared. "Oh, yeah. So, anyway, I had these like little plastic dinosaur models, you know? And I learned all the names of them."

"Triceratops," I said. "Diplodocus. Brontosaurus. Stegosaurus. Allosaurus."

"Yeah, yeah." His head bobbed up and down.

"Pterodactyl," I chanted. "And good old Tyrannosaurus rex."

"Right, right." He stopped speaking suddenly, and the light left his face.

"What's wrong?"

"Fuckin' teacher."

"What happened?"

"Ahh." His mouth quirked. "It wasn't no big deal."

Sure it was.

"We had like these art classes," Mickey said. "You could like do drawing or painting, or like make clay models and stuff, you know?"

I nodded.

"So I was gonna make some like clay dinosaur models, right?"

"Yes."

"Yeah, well, like I made one of a brontosaurus, okay?"

I nodded again.

"And I left it to dry. And then . . ." Mickey paused for a moment. "And then I went to art class the next time, right, and the fuckin' brontosaurus was all broken up, you know? Into all these little pieces."

"Yes."

"So I like asked the teacher, I mean, what the fuck happened, and"—Mickey took a deep breath—"he told me he broke it up."

"What the hell for?"

"Ah, he said the fuckin' thing was like, I don't know, like built wrong. Like it was just gonna fuckin' fall apart, anyway."

"Jesus," I said softly.

"So then he showed the pieces to the rest of the class and told them this was a good sample of how you wasn't supposed to make clay models."

"*Shit,*" I said.

Mickey looked at me funny.

I reached out, somewhat tremulously, and patted his knee. "Mick," I said, "the world is full of assholes. Unfortunately a lot of them are employed by the school system."

"Yeah."

"I've had experiences like—the one you had."

His face hardened. "So how come you ain't like me, then?"

I slumped backward against the counter shelves. His question was fair. And virtually unanswerable. What was I supposed to tell him? Having his brontosaurus statue pulverized by some birdbrained sadist wasn't the only event in his life that had brought him to this store, this night, with a gun.

Life wasn't wonderful for a lot of the kids in East Cambridge, even the ones who came from good solid families. The parents could try like hell to inculcate their children with all the traditional values— and East Cambridge probably had the most devoutly churchgoing population in the entire city—but the lure of the streets was always there. Kids like Mickey didn't grow up idolizing baseball players. They reserved their hero worship for the local hard cases—guys who'd done bad time in Walpole. In East Cambridge that was the mark of a *man*.

Who knew what Mickey's circumstances were? I wondered if any of his relatives had ever seen the inside of a state prison.

The kid was nipping at the chocolate-mint liqueur, his face sullen and brooding.

"Mickey," I said, "how old are you?"

He scowled at me. "What the fuck do you care?"

"I don't. I'm just curious, that's all."

He looked at the shelf of liqueurs. "Nineteen."

"Oh."

"You think I'm just some dumb-shit kid, huh?"

"No, actually the opposite."

He turned his stare to me. "What the hell's that mean?"

"It means I think you're probably too smart to be doing something as stupid as robbing a liquor store."

"Oh, yeah? Well, what the fuck do you know about me?"

"Enough to be pretty sure that this wasn't the way for you to go, Mick."

His breathing grew audible again. He took a quick pull from the bottle in his hand. Then he hurled it to his right, away from us. The bottle hit the side of the junk-food rack and shattered in a spray of viscous brown liquid. Some of it spattered on my clothing and on the side of my face.

I sat very still.

Mickey sprang to his feet and lunged at the counter. He swept his left arm along the surface, knocking a cardboard display stand of rolling papers to the floor. Then he snatched up the register tray and hurled it awkwardly but with considerable force at the window. It veered off-course and crashed against a stack of beer crates, scattering change all over the floor.

"Stop it!" I screamed. "For chrissake, what are you trying to do? Bring the cops in here shooting?"

He slammed his left fist hard enough on the countertop to make it vibrate.

"Mickey," I said in a much quieter, yet nonetheless emphatic, voice. *"Please."*

He kicked at the base of the counter. The toe of his shoe struck the bottom shelf, splintering the wood.

I was terrified the gun in his hand might go off accidentally. If the cops outside heard a shot, they might . . . I didn't know, really, what they'd do in that case. I didn't really want to find out.

Mickey bent over the counter, bracing himself on it with his left hand. His shoulders shook slightly.

It took me a slow moment to realize that he was crying. And as I watched him, hunched over in his silent anguish, something that hadn't been absolutely clear to me before was suddenly very obvious.

This furious, weeping child was a novice at violent crime. Tonight was his first time out, and he didn't know where the hell he was supposed to go from here.

Yes, and that was what made him dangerous, more so than any putative drug he could be on.

I was going to have to be very careful of what I did, or said, next. I was dealing here with something far more volatile than a junkie.

Gradually the kid's shoulders stopped shaking. I heard him make a soft noise, like a hiccup. He pushed himself away from the counter and stood up straight. He raised his left hand and made a swiping motion at his face.

I leaned forward and rested my forehead on my knees. If he turned around quickly, I didn't want him to catch me gawking at him. Much better to let us both pretend that I hadn't noticed him crying.

I don't know how many seconds, or minutes, I let pass before I lifted my head. When I did, Mickey was squatting with his back to the counter, again staring at the shelves filled with small bottles. In profile, his face had a flushed, congested look. His lower lip trembled slightly. God, what an infant he was, clutching so tightly to his talismanic gun. Trying so hard to be a man, by the local definition.

I reached out and plucked two nip-sized bottles from the shelf before me.

"Mickey," I said.

He flicked me a brief, sideways glance.

"I think I'm ready for a drink," I said. "You want one?"

Without waiting for his answer, I unscrewed the top from one of the little bottles and held it out to him.

He didn't take it. I set the bottle on the floor between us. Then I opened my own. Bourbon. Bourbon at room temperature wasn't my favorite drink, but vodka in that state was past loathsome. I swigged from the bottle. The shock of the undiluted lukewarm liquor on my palate made my eyes sting.

Mickey reached over with his left hand and picked up the chocolate liqueur I'd set out for him.

"Better than the stuff you had before," I said. "Try it."

He raised the nip to his mouth slowly and took a sip.

"Well?" I said.

He swallowed. "It's all right," he muttered.

I nodded.

We drank without further conversation, two strangers thrown into proximity at some surreal cocktail party. When I'd consumed about three quarters of its contents, I recapped the miniature. The bourbon hadn't been too terrific going down, but once it hit my stomach, it made a small, pleasant glow there.

Mickey finished his chocolate liqueur.

"Want another?" I asked.

He shook his head. A lot of the red had faded from his face. But he still wouldn't look at me.

I eyed him carefully. He *seemed* relatively calm. At this point. Would he stay that way after he heard what I was going to say to him next? No way to tell. Twenty minutes ago I'd made to him what I'd thought a perfectly innocuous remark. And he'd snapped like a length of rope pulled too tightly.

The risk was one I had to take.

"Mickey?"

A little silence. Then he said, "Yeah?"

"I think we ought to talk some more."

Another pause. "What about?" he mumbled in the direction of the shelves.

Now it was my turn to hesitate. The bourbon glow in my stomach had very quickly dissipated, leaving an acid chill in its place.

"About what we're going to do about the situation we're in," I said very delicately.

His shoulders went stiff.

Oh, God, I thought.

"Mickey," I said urgently. "Please. Listen to me."

It was like talking to a high-tension wire.

"Mickey, there's an army of cops outside that's not going to go away. They can wait you and me out. And they will. We have to deal with that, Mickey." I leaned toward him. "You can't take on all of them."

He bounced to his feet. "So you wanna go?" he spat down at me. He jerked his head at the door. "Then fuckin' go."

I looked up at him. "I can't. The door's locked, and you have the key."

He thrust his left hand into his jacket pocket, fumbled there, and yanked out the ring of keys. As he did so, the roll of bills he'd stashed in the pocket earlier tumbled to the floor. Apparently he didn't notice that it had. Or maybe he was past caring about the money.

He threw the key ring at me, into my lap. "Fuck off," he said. "Get lost."

"And if I do," I replied, "where does that leave you?"

"What the hell do you care?"

"I don't know exactly, Mickey," I said. "All I know is, it would be better if we went out together."

"Yeah? Better for who?"

I sighed. "You, Mickey. You know that as well as I do."

He took a step forward and dropped onto one knee, facing me. "Sure," he said. "It's gonna be fuckin' swell for me. I walk out there and I get fuckin' arrested. That's gonna be real fuckin' nice for me, lady."

"What do you think will happen to you if you *don't* go out there with me?"

He inhaled sharply, his face clenched.

"Mickey," I said, "I'm not going to kid you. Yes, if you and I leave here together, you're going to be arrested. And, yes, you're going to be charged with a very bad crime. But the longer you let this go on, the worse it's going to get. Even if you let me walk out. If you don't come with me, every minute you stay behind, the cops are going to come down on you that much harder."

I could feel myself growing frantic, and I fought to control it.

"Yeah," the kid said. "And like you give a shit what happens to me."

"I kind of do."

His features were informed with a sort of enraged disbelief. "Oh, right, sure."

I shook my head wearily. "Mickey, don't ask me to explain it. I—"

"Yeah, what?" he snapped.

"Oh, Christ, I don't know. It has something to do with the dinosaurs, I think." I closed my eyes and shook my head again. "I think. Oh, shit. I don't know."

"Dinosaurs?"

I looked up at him. The fury was gone from his face. In its stead was a burgeoning and vast bewilderment.

Maybe now I should launch into some flowery, do-gooder, humanitarian rap about how I thought he was a soul worth salvaging. And wouldn't he just love that?

I had no such rap to deliver.

"Mickey," I said, "I can't make promises. You're in big trouble you can't get out of." I paused, then added, "All I can say to you is . . . I'll tell the cops you didn't hurt me. I'll tell them we talked. I'll tell them that you were . . . you know, reasonable. And that will count with them." I drew a long breath. "But I'll only do that if you leave here with me, now."

He was silent, staring at the floor. I wished I could see inside his head. I could dimly imagine the turmoil there.

I wanted to grab him by the shoulders and shake him and shriek, "This isn't the way to be a man."

Which would be the worst mistake I could possibly make.

He mumbled something at the worn linoleum.

I leaned toward him. "What?"

He shook his head.

"Mickey?"

He looked at me. "I go outa here with you and I'm a pussy."

"No," I said. "Smart."

*Anyway, kid, you have no choice in the matter. Please realize that. Please.*

His face quivered and his eyes grew liquid.

"Mickey?"

He put his head on his knee. His shoulders heaved.

I made a fist of my right hand and pressed it hard against my mouth. I wanted to cry, then, too. But what did I have to feel bad about? I wasn't a nineteen-year-old kid looking down the road at fifteen years in the state prison.

And I wasn't a kid even more scared of not being a man.

Mickey gave a final snuffling gasp and then was quiet. He rubbed his face against his knee.

"Get it together," I said softly. "And then we'll go."

He took a long, shuddering breath.

I should have been feeling relieved. What I was feeling was lousy beyond description.

"Whenever you're ready," I said.

He moved his head just barely up and down. Was that a nod of acquiescence? I decided to interpret it as such. Very slowly and somewhat stiffly, I climbed to my feet, watching the kid steadily all the while.

For a few seconds longer, he remained in his crouch. When he did rise, it was with a heaviness to match my own. We stood separated by less than a yard, he with shoulders drooping and head lowered, gun hand hanging limply by his side.

"I better tell them we're coming out," I said. "All right?"

He gave me that tiny, volitionless nod again.

I replaced the telephone receiver in its cradle.

The phone rang almost immediately. I picked it up and said, "Hi."

The person on the other end of the line said, "You all right?"

I recognized the voice, that of the captain who was the night commander for the police department. He was a friend of my friend Jack. "I'm fine," I said. "We're coming out."

"Any problem?"

I glanced over at Mickey. "No," I said. "None whatever."

"Good."

"See you in a minute." I hung up the phone and cleared my throat. "Mickey?"

He raised his head and gave me an empty look.

"It's time to go."

"Yeah," he said, exhaling rather than speaking the word.

I held out my right hand. "May I have the gun?"

He hesitated a moment, then turned and set the pistol down on the counter very gently. I picked it up by the barrel, holding it away from me.

I gave Mickey a slight smile. "Okay?"

"Yeah."

We walked from behind the counter. I took his arm. That seemed, somehow, the right thing to do.

When we got to the door, I unhooked my arm from his and reached into my pocket for the keys. Doing it left-handed made the procedure very awkward, but I finally managed to get the dead bolt unlocked. I dropped the keys back into my pocket and put my arm back through Mickey's.

"I'm glad you're with me," I said.

He didn't reply.

I nudged the door open with my foot.

The snow was still falling. Perhaps three inches had accumulated on the sidewalk. I thought of winter wonderlands and silent nights. But not holy ones.

I pressed Mickey's arm. "Remember what I told you," I whispered.

Huddled together, we walked toward the waiting police. A fugitive gust of wind drew a veil of snow before my eyes. I shivered.

Mickey jerked his arm free of mine. He gave me a sudden, tremendously hard shove in the ribs, and then I was spinning in a half-circle, falling sideways and unable to stop. I snatched reflexively at the air with my empty left hand, and my feet slid out from under me.

As I hit the sidewalk I knew with an awful, bleak certainty what was going to happen.

"Mickey, no!" I screamed, rolling over onto my stomach.

I saw him take from his jacket pocket a gun much smaller than the one he'd surrendered to me. I saw him take one awkward, lunging step forward. I saw him fire the small gun into the police line. I heard somebody return the fire. And then I saw Mickey grow rigid, slump, and settle into a boneless descent to the sidewalk.

On hands and knees, I slithered over to him. He was lying on his side. I pulled him toward me. As he rolled onto his back I saw the red, ragged hole at the base of his throat.

"You stupid son of a bitch!" I screamed.

His eyes flickered up at me.

I clawed my fingers into his shoulder. "What the hell did you do that for?"

His mouth moved. It may have been a smile.

"I tolja," he murmured. "Ain't gonna be no pussy."

"You set me up for this."

The green eyes were growing opaque. A foamy, red bubble appeared in the corner of his mouth. I bent close to him.

"Wasn't nothin' else to do," he said.

His voice spiraled upward and away on the gentle wind. And around and above us, the snow continued to fall, enclosing just Mickey and me in a pure and unending white silence.

*Faye Kellerman's* The Ritual Bath *shared a Macavity award for Best First Novel of 1986. It introduced Rina Lazarus, a young widow trying to rebuild her life, and Los Angeles policeman Peter Decker, as it depicted the tensions and clashes that nearly thwart Decker and the LAPD when they try to get answers from an Orthodox Jewish community that is rocked by a brutal rape and murder. Rina and Peter returned for another chilling outing in* Sacred and Profane.

*In "Bonding," the teenage narrator starts out by complaining about her problems, her family, and her disaffection—but her shocking cure for boredom is only the start of her problems.*

# BONDING

## by Faye Kellerman

I BECAME A prostitute because I was bored. Let me tell you about it. My mother is a greedy, self-centered egotist and a pill-popper. I don't think we exchange more than a sentence worth of words a week. Our house is very big—one of these fake-o hacienda types on an acre of flat land in prime Gucciland Beverly Hills—so it's real easy to avoid each other. She doesn't know what I do and wouldn't care if she did know. My father doesn't hassle me cause he's never around. I mean, *never* around. He rarely sleeps at home anymore, and I don't know why my parents stay married. Just laziness, I guess. So when my friend came around one day and suggested we hustle for kicks, I said sure, why not.

Our first night was on a Saturday. I dressed up in a black mini with fishnet stockings, the garter lower than the hem of my dress. I painted my lips bright red, slapped on layers of makeup, and took a couple of downers. I looked the way I felt—like something brought up from the dead. We boogied on down to the Strip, my friend supplying the skins, and made a bet: who could earn the most in three hours. I won easily; I didn't even bother to screw any of the johns—just went down on them in a back alley or right in their cars. I hustled seven washed-out old guys at sixty bucks a pop. Can't say it was a bundle of yucks, but it was different. Jesus, anything's better than the boredom.

The following day, after school, me and my friend got buzzed and went shopping at the mall. I took my hustle money and bought this real neat blouse accented with white and blue rhinestones and sequins. I also saw this fabulous belt made of silver and turquoise, but it was over a hundred and fifty dollars and I didn't want to spend *that* much money on just a belt. So I lifted it. Even with the new electronic gizmos and the security guards, stealing isn't very hard, not much of a challenge.

Let me tell you a little about myself. I was born fifteen years ago, the "love child" of a biker and his teenage babe. I think my real mother was like twelve or thirteen at the time. I once asked my bitch of a mother about her, and she got *reaaallly* agitated. Her face got red and she began to talk in that hysterical way of hers. The whole thing was like too threatening for her to deal with. Anyway, I was adopted as an infant. And I never remember being happy. I remember crying at my sixth birthday party cause Billy Freed poked his fingers in my Cookie Monster cake. Mom went bonkers—we hadn't photographed the cake yet—and started screaming at Billy. Then he started crying. God, I was mad at Billy, but after Mom lit into him, I almost felt sorry for the kid. I mean, it was only a cake, you know.

Once, when I was around the same age, my mom picked me up and we looked in the mirror together. She put her cheek against mine as we stared at our reflections. I remember the feel of her skin—soft and warm, the sweet smell of her perfume. I didn't know what I'd done to deserve such attention, and that frustrated me. Whatever I did, I wanted to do it again so Mom would hold me like this. But of course, I didn't do anything. Mom just stared at us, then clucked her tongue and lowered me back onto my feet with an announcement: I'd never make it on my looks.

Well, what the hell did she expect? Beggars shouldn't be choosers. It's not like someone forced her to adopt me. The bitch. Always blaming me for things out of my control.

Did I tell you Mom is beautiful? Must have slipped my mind. We forget what we want to, right? Mom is a natural blonde with large blue eyes and perfect cheekbones. I've got ordinary brown hair—thin, at that—and dull green eyes. It's been a real bitch growing up as her daughter. Mom turned forty last year, and she treated herself to a face-lift—smoothing out imaginary wrinkles. Now her face is so goddamn tight, it looks wrapped in Saran. Her body is wonderful—long and sleek. I'm the original blimpo—the kind of woman that those old artists liked to paint. I'm not fat but just really developed. Big boobs, big round ass. My mother used to put me on all these diets, and none of them ever worked. I finally told her to fuck herself and gorged on Oreo cookies. Ate the whole package right in front of her, and boy, did that burn her ass.

She gave me this little smirk and said: "You're only hurting yourself, Kristie."

"I'm not hurting myself," I said. "In fact, I'm enjoying myself!"

Then she walked away with the same smirk on her face.

She once went to bed with this guy *I* was sleeping with. Can you believe that? Happened last summer at our beach house. I caught the two of them together. Mom got all red-faced, the guy was embarrassed, too, but I just laughed. Inside, though, I felt lousy. I felt lousy 'cause I knew that the guy really wanted to fuck her all along and was just using me as a stepping-stone.

You might ask where the hell was my dad when all this went down? I told you. He's never around.

My friend and co-hooker came down with strep throat today and asked if I could service her regular johns. I said sure. So I go to the room she rents. It's a typical sleazebucket of a place—broken-down bed, filthy floor, and a cracked mirror. Who should I see in it but my *father*? I turn my face away before he sees me. To tell you the truth, I barely recognize his face. Then I realize that he must have gotten a lift like Mom, 'cause his skin is also like stretched to the max.

I'm shaking—half with fear, half with disgust. That dirty son of a bitch. Doing it with teenage hookers. Then I remember a few years ago. How he eyed my friends when we sat around the pool. How he strutted out of the cabana wearing red bikini briefs and shot a half-gainer off the diving board. My friends were impressed. He popped through the water's surface, a strange expression on his face.

It was lust.

I sneak another glance in the mirror.

He holds the same look in his eyes now.

What the hell do I do?

I think about running away, but I know my friend will be real pissed. Jesus.

My dad.

I can't screw my dad!

Then I think to myself, My mom screwed *my* guy. . . .

But this is something different. He's my dad.

'Course, he's isn't my dad by blood. . . .

And it's been a long time since I've seen him. . . .

The thought starts to excite me. Yeah, I know it's real perverse, but my whole family is perverse.

And at least it isn't boring.

I take a quick hit of some snow from the vial I wear around my neck. Man, I need to be buzzed to pull this one off.

I'm real excited by now.

I drop my voice an octave—I can do that 'cause I have a great range—and tell him to can the lights. He starts bitching and moaning that he likes to do it with the lights on, and where the fuck is my friend. I tell him my friend has strep and it's hard to give head with your throat all red and raw, and if he doesn't want me, fine, he just won't get laid tonight.

He cans the lights. The only illumination in the room comes from a neon sign outside that highlights his semi. It's a good-looking one, and it turns me on even further. But I stay well hidden in the shadows of the room.

I wonder what he'll think of my body after laying Mom all these years. Maybe he'll think I'm too fat, but the minute he touches my boobs, his you-know-what becomes ramrod-straight. I let him bury his head in my chest, kiss my nipples. I give him a line of coke, then I take another snort. My face is always hidden.

I ask him what kinds of things he wants to do, and he says everything. I say it will cost him a hundred and fifty, and he gets suddenly outraged. A real bad acting job. I know what he makes, and he could buy all of Hollywood if he wanted to. Anyway, by now he's too excited to argue, and three fifty-dollar bills are slapped into my wet hand. I do whatever he wants as long as he can't see my face.

When it's over, I tell him I have a surprise for him. He's lying in bed now, smoking a joint. Still naked, I saunter over to the light switch, then suddenly flip it on. The cheesy room is flooded with bright yellow light. We both squint, then he sees me. It takes him a moment, then I see his tanned, tight face drain of all its color. His eyes pop out and he begins to pant. His skin takes on a greenish hue and he runs for the toilet. I hear him throw up.

Afterward he cries in my arms. But we both know it's not over.

* * *

Dad came home at eleven tonight. Mom and he start fighting. They always fight, did I tell you that? Probably why Dad started staying away. Anyway, it's the first time I ever remember Dad coming home in like twenty years or something. I'm no dummy. I know what the sucker has in mind, and that's okay by me. After all, I'm not really his daughter by blood, you know.

He comes into my room at around two o'clock. I make him pay, and no shit, he agrees. Man, I know you're gonna think I'm sick, but I gotta tell you. My dad's all right in the sack.

This goes on for the next month. If Mom suspects anything, she doesn't say a word. Then a strange thing happens. Life is weird— very weird. A real strange thing happens.

We fall in love.

Or something like it.

We consider all the options. The first is running away and giving me a new identity so that we can marry. The idea is discussed, then tossed in the circular file. Dad makes a couple a million buckeroos as a TV producer, and no way he could make that kind of money outside of L.A. Neither of us likes poverty.

We consider having Dad and Mom divorce and I'd live with Dad. That's out. California has stiff community-property laws, and the bitch would get half of *everything*!

There's only one option left.

First off, I gotta tell you that neither one of us really feel guilty about our decision cause: A, I'm not my dad's real daughter; and B, Mom has had this coming for a long time.

Way overdue.

We plan to do it next Saturday right after she comes home from one of her parties. She's usually pretty sauced and hyped and has to pop some downers to get to sleep. We figure we'll help her along.

She comes in at two A.M., surprised that I'm still up. I say I was having trouble sleeping and offer to make her some hot coffee. She nods and dismisses me with a wave of her hand. Like I'm a servant, instead of her daughter doing her a favor. I lace the java with Se-conal. Halfway through the drink, her lids begin to close. But she knows something is wrong. She tells me she's having trouble breathing and asks me to call the doctor. I act like I'm real worried and place the phony call. By the time I hang up, she's out.

Both Dad and I are worried. She only drank half a cup, and we wonder if it's enough dope to do her in. Dad feels her pulse. It's weak but steady. A half hour later her heartbeat is even stronger. Dad says, "What the hell do we do now?" I think and think and think, then come up with a really rad brainstorm.

I get ten tablets full of Seconal, crush them in water, and suck the mixture into my old syringe. Did I tell you I shoot up occasionally? When the boredom is just too much. I haven't done it for a while, but I keep the syringe—you know, just in case the mood hits me. I shoot the dope under her tongue. It's absorbed fast that way and doesn't leave any marks. A friend of mine told me that.

Dad feels her pulse for a third time. Squeezes her wrist hard. Nothing. *Nada!* We celebrate with a big hug and a wet kiss, then wash the cup and wipe the place clean of fingerprints.

A half hour later Dad places a panic call to the paramedics.

God, I'm a great actress, carrying on like Mom and I were like bosom buddies.

"Mommmmeeeee," I wail at the funeral.

Everyone feels sorry for me, but I don't accept their comfort.

My dad has his arm around me. He pulls me aside later on.

"You're overdoing it," he tells me.

"Hell, Paul." I call him Paul now. "I lost my fucking mother. I'm supposed to be upset."

"Just cool it a little, Kristie," Paul says. "Act withdrawn. Like someone took away your Black Sabbath records."

I sulk for a moment, then say what the hell. He's older. Maybe he knows best. I crawl into this shell and don't answer people when they talk to me. They give me pitying looks.

The detective shows up at our door unannounced. He's a big guy with black hair, old-fashioned sideburns, and acne scars. My heart begins to take off, and I say I don't answer any questions without my dad around.

"Why?" he asks.

"I don't know," I respond. Then I ask him if he has a warrant. He laughs and says no.

"I'm sorry," I say. "I can't help you."

"Aren't you supposed to be in school?" he asks.

"God, are you crazy?" I say. "I mean, with all that happened? I can't concentrate on school right now. I mean, I lost my *mother*!"

"You two were pretty close, then."

"Real close."

"You don't look much like her," he remarks.

I feel my face changing its expression and get mad at myself. I say, "I'm adopted."

"Oh," the detective says. His face is all red now. "That would explain it."

Then he says, "I'm sorry to get personal."

"That's okay," I say, real generous.

There's a pause. Then the detective says, "You know we got the official autopsy report back for your mother."

I feel short of breath. I try to keep the crack out of my voice. "What's it say?" I ask.

"Your mother died of acute toxicity," he says. "Drug OD."

"Figures," I say calmly. "She had lots of problems and was on and off all sorts of drugs."

He nods, then asks, "What kind of drugs did she take?"

Then all of a sudden I realize I'm talking too much. I tell him I don't know.

"I thought you two were close."

I feel my face go hot again.

"We were," I say. "I mean, I knew she took prescribed drugs to help her cope, but I don't know *which* drugs. Our relationship wasn't like that, you know."

"Why don't we just peek inside the medicine cabinet of your house?" he says.

I shake my head slowly, then say, "Come back tonight, when my dad is home. Around eight, okay?"

He agrees.

Paul has a shit-fit, but I assure him I handled it well. By the time the detective shows up, we're both pretty calm. I mean, all the drugs found in her stomach came from her own pills. And then there was the party she went to. I'm sure at least a half dozen people remember her guzzling a bottle or two of white wine. She loved white wine— Riesling or Chardonnay.

My mother was an alcoholic. Did I tell you that?

The detective has on a disgusting suit that smells of mothballs. It hangs on him. He scratches his nose and says a couple of bullshitty words to Paul about how sorry he is that he had to intrude on us like this. Paul has on his best hound-dog face and says it's okay. Now

I understand what he meant by not overdoing it. Man, is he good. *I* almost believe him.

"Sure," Paul says to the detective. "Take a look around the house."

I think about saying we've got nothing to hide, but don't. The detective goes over some details with Paul. My mom had gone to a party by herself. Paul didn't go 'cause he wasn't feeling well. At around three in the morning he got up to make himself a cup of milk. I was asleep, of course. He went downstairs and found my mother dead.

"Where'd you find your wife?" the detective asks.

"On that chair right there."

Paul points to the Chippendale.

The detective walks over to the chair but doesn't touch it. He asks, "What'd you do when you found her?"

Paul is confused. He says, "What do you mean? I called the paramedics of course."

"Yeah," the detective says. "I know that. Did you touch her at all?"

"Touch her?" Paul asks.

The detective says, "Yeah, feel if the skin was cold . . . see if she was breathing."

Paul shakes his head. "I don't know anything about CPR. I figured the smart thing to do was to leave her alone and wait for the paramedics."

"How'd you know she was dead?" the detective asks.

"I didn't *know* she was dead," Paul says back. His voice is getting loud. "I just saw her slumped in the chair and knew something was wrong."

"Maybe she was sleeping," suggested the detective.

"Her face was white . . . gray." Paul begins to pace. "I knew she wasn't sleeping."

"You didn't check her pulse, check to see if she was breathing?"

"He said no," I say, defending my dad. "Look . . ." I get tears in my eyes. "Why don't you leave us alone? Haven't we been through enough without you poking around?"

The detective nods solemnly. He says, "I'll be brief."

We don't answer him. We stay in the living room while he searches. A half hour later the detective comes back carrying all of Mom's pills in a plastic bag. He says, "Mind if I take these with me?"

Paul says go ahead. As soon as he leaves, I notice Paul is white. I take his hand and ask him what's wrong. He whispers, "Your fingerprints were on the bottle."

I smile and shake my head no. "I wiped everything clean."

Paul smiles and calls me beautiful. God, no one has ever called me beautiful. Want to know something weird? Paul's a much better lover than he is a father. We make it right there on the couch, knowing it's a stupid and dangerous thing to do, but we don't care. An hour later we go to bed.

The fucking asshole pig comes back a week later with all of his piglets. Paul is enraged, but the pig has all the papers in order—the search warrant, the this, the that.

Paul asks, "What is going on?"

"Complete investigation, Mr. James."

"Of *what*!"

"I don't believe your wife's death is an accidental overdose."

"Why not?" I ask.

Paul glares at me. The detective ignores me and I don't repeat the question.

"What do you think it is?" Paul asks.

"Intentional overdose."

"Suicide?" Paul says, "No note was found."

"There isn't always a note," the detective responds. "Besides, I didn't mean suicide, I meant homicide."

My body goes cold when he says the word. The pig asks us if we mind being printed or giving them samples of our hair. Paul nudges me in the ribs and answers, "Of course not," for the both of us.

Then he adds, "We have nothing to hide."

Now I'm thinking that was a real dumb thing to say.

They start to dust the Chippendale, spreading black powder over the fabric. Paul goes loony and screams how expensive the chair is. No one pays attention to him.

He stalks off to his bedroom. I follow.

"What are we gonna do?" I whisper.

"You wiped away all the prints?" he whispers back.

I nod.

"They've got nothing on us, babe." He inhales deeply. "We'll just have to wait it out. Now, get out of here before someone suspects something."

I obey.

All the pigs leave about four hours later. They've turned our home into a sty.

Paul is becoming a real problem. He's losing it, and that's bad news for me. When I confront him with what a shit he's being, he starts acting like a parent. Can you believe that? He fucks me—his daughter—then when he's losing it, he starts acting like a parent. Yesterday he didn't come home at night. That really pissed me off. I reminded him that we were in it together. That pissed *him* off, and he claimed the entire thing was *my* idea and that I was a witch and a whore. Man, what a battle we had. We're all made up now, but let me tell you something, we watch each other carefully.

Real carefully.

They arrested me this morning for the murder of my mother. They leave Paul alone for now. Apparently whatever they have is just on me and not him.

To tell you the truth, I'm kind of relieved.

The same detective asks me if I want to have a lawyer present. I say yeah, I'd better, knowing that Paul will get me the best mouth-piece in town. He has to, 'cause he knows that it's only a matter of time before his butt is on the line. I'm left waiting in this interview room for about an hour. Just me and the detective. Finally I say what I know I shouldn't say.

I say, "How'd you find out?"

"Find out what?" the detective answers.

"About my mom being murdered and all."

His eyebrows raise a tad.

"You mean, how'd I find out you murdered your mom?"

I know it's a trick, but what the fuck. I don't care anymore. I nod.

"Did you kill your mom, Kristine?"

He asks the question like real cool, but I can see the sweat under his arm pits.

"Yeah," I admit. "I offed her."

"How?" he asks.

"I laced her coffee with her own Seconal," I say. "When that didn't do the trick, I injected her with more. That finished her off."

"Where'd you inject her?" he asks.

"Under her tongue."

He nods. "Smart thinking," he says. "No marks." Then he pauses and adds, "So you're a hype, huh?"

I shake my head. "Recreational," I say.

"Ah."

"So how'd you find out?" I ask again.

"Two other things set an alarm off in me," the detective said. "The autopsy report showed bruises on the inside of your mom's right wrist. Like someone squeezed her."

"Maybe someone did," I say.

The detective says, "Yeah, like someone was feeling for a pulse. Yet your dad denied touching her."

I say, "Maybe she was playing a little game with one of her lovers."

"I thought of that," the detective says. "She went to a pretty wild party. But then the bruises would have been on both of her wrists."

I don't say anything right away. Then I say, "You said two things. What was the second?"

"Your mom had loads of Seconal in her body, along with booze and coke. She also had just a trace amount of heroin. Too little if she actually shot up a wad."

"My needle," I say. "I forgot to clean it."

"It's hard to remember everything, Kristie," the detective says. "I found it when I searched the house the first time, but I couldn't take it with me for physical evidence because I didn't have the proper papers. I waited a week until I had the search warrant in hand, then took it. We analyzed it, found traces of Seconal and heroin. People don't normally shoot Seconal. You should have dumped all your evidence."

"I never was too good at throwing things away. Mom used to yell at me for that. Called me a bag lady, always keeping everything."

I sigh.

The detective says, "Also, we powdered your mom's meds and found they had been wiped free of prints. If your mom had committed suicide, her prints would have been on the bottle."

"I should have thought about that," I admit.

"Well, you did okay for your first time out," the detective says. "The marks on the wrist were a giveaway. Started me thinking in the right direction. You—or your dad—shouldn't have squeezed her so hard. And you should have used a fresh needle. And gloves instead of wiping away the prints."

He leans in so we're almost nose-to-nose.

"Close but no cigar. You're in hot shit, babe. Want to tell me about it?"

"What do you want to know?"

"Why'd you do it, for starters," he asks.

" 'Cause I hated my mom."

"And why did your dad help you?"

"What makes you think my dad helped me?"

"The bruises on your mother's wrist were made by fingers bigger than yours, Kristie. It was your father who felt for the pulse, even though he emphatically denied touching her."

"You can't prove who made those bruises," I say.

The detective doesn't say anything. Then he sticks his hands in his pockets and says, "It's your neck. You could probably save it by turning state's evidence against your dad."

I don't say anything.

"Look," he says. "I understand why you offed your mom. She treated you like shit. And your dad offed her so he could marry his girlfriend—"

"What girlfriend?" I say, almost jumping out of my seat.

"The cute little blond chickie that was on his arm last night."

"You're lying," I say.

He looks genuinely puzzled. He says, "No, I'm not. What is it? Don't you get along with her?"

I feel tears in my eyes. I stammer out, "I . . . I don't even know her."

"Don't cotton to the idea of your dad making it with a young chick?" he asks.

"No," I say.

"Why's that?"

I blurt out, "Because *I'm* his girlfriend. We're *lovers*."

I hear the detective cough. I see him cover his mouth. Then he says, "You want to talk about what happens when you turn state's evidence?"

I shrug, but even as I try to be real cool, the tears come down my cheeks. I say, "Sure, why not?"


Old Paul is on death row, convicted of murder along with rape and sodomy of a minor.

Me? I'm in juvie hall and it ain't any picnic. The food is lousy, I'm with a couple of bull dykes, and everybody steals. So I can't make any headway in the money department. A couple of gals here say they were raped by their fathers, and they wanted to kill their mothers too. They talk like we have a lot in common. I tell them to leave me alone. Sometimes they do, sometimes they don't. But it's cool. I'm beyond caring what the hell happens to me. Just so long as I don't die from boredom.

All that attention. It was really exciting.

I've got to get out of here.

They assigned me a real sucker for a shrink. An older man about my dad's age who gives me the eye.

I mean, he really gives me the eye.

The other day he told me he was going to recommend my release to the assessment board. He says I have excellent insight and a fine prognosis.

The other day he also asked me why I became a hooker.

I mean, what's on *his* mind? I wonder.

Yeah, I have insight.

And I know what's on his mind. And I'll do what I have to in order to get out of here.

I need freedom.

At least juvie hall was a new experience for a while.

Just like killing my mom and fucking Paul.

I hate to be bored.

*Sue Grafton started her writing career by garnering awards for her teleplays and upheld the winning tradition with her novels. "A" Is for Alibi (1982) won the Mysterious Stranger Award from the Cloak and Clue Society; "B" Is for Burglar (1985) won a Shamus and an Anthony; "C" Is for Corpse (1986) won an Anthony. "D" Is for Deadbeat (1987) and "E" Is for Evidence (1988) continue the chronicles of Kinsey Millhone and Santa Teresa as Sue takes the venerable California private-eye tradition and puts her own literate, human, and supremely entertaining stamp on it.*

*In "Falling Off the Roof," Kinsey, in typically energetic Millhone fashion, pursues every lead and finds herself face-to-face with a cast of curious characters, including some that mystery fans will surely recognize.*

# FALLING OFF THE ROOF

## by Sue Grafton

IT WAS SIX A.M. and I was jogging on the bike path at the beach, trotting three miles in behalf of my sagging rear end. I'm thirty-two years old, five-six, weighing in at 118, so you wouldn't think I'd have to concern myself with such things, but I'm a private eye by trade, and I'm single on top of that. Sometimes I end up running for my life, so it will never do to get out of shape.

I had just hit my stride. My breathing was audible but not labored, my shoes chunking rhythmically as the asphalt sped away underneath my feet. What worried me was the sound of someone running behind me, and gaining too. I glanced back casually and felt adrenaline shoot through my heart, jolting it into a jackhammer pace. A man in a black sweat suit was closing ground. I picked up speed, quickly assessing the situation. There wasn't another soul in sight. No other joggers. None of the usual bums sleeping on the grass.

I veered off toward the street, figuring that with luck a car would pass.

"Hey!" the man said sharply.

219

I ran on, mentally rehearsing every self-defense move I'd ever been taught.

"Wait up," he called. "Aren't you Kinsey Millhone?"

I slowed my pace somewhat. "That's right. Who are you?"

His stride was longer than mine, and it didn't take long for him to catch up. "Harry Grissom," he said. "I need a private detective."

"Most people try me at the office first," I snapped. "You scared me half to death!"

"Sorry. The kid at the skate-rental shack told me I could find you out here. This seemed like a good place to talk."

I knew Gus from a case I'd worked, and I liked him a lot. I could feel myself become more charitable. "How do you know Gus?"

"I own some property on Granita. He rents a cottage."

"Why do you need me?"

"My brother, Don, was killed in a fall from his roof. The police said it was an accident, but I think he was pushed."

"Oh, really? By whom?"

"My sister-in-law."

By now we were jogging side by side at a healthy clip. He was a good-looking fellow, maybe thirty-five, with dark, bushy hair, dark mustache, and a runner's body, long and lean. He said he was a chiropractor by profession, with a passion for skiing and a modest talent as a painter. I think he told me all this to persuade me of his solid character and the sincerity of his concern about his brother's fatal accident.

"When was he killed?" I asked.

"Six months ago."

"How long had they been married?"

"Thirteen years, I guess. Don and Susie met at college, Don's junior year. They were wrong for each other, but you couldn't tell them that. They had a stormy two-year courtship. Finally they ran off and got married. It was all downhill from there."

"What was the problem?"

"For starters, they had nothing in common. Both of them were hotheaded, stubborn, immature."

"Any kids?" I asked.

"Amy, who's eight, and a little boy, Todd, who's five."

"Go on."

"Well, the two of them fought like cats and dogs, and then suddenly things smoothed out. Susie was a doll and everything seemed fine. Don and I talked about it a couple of times. He wasn't sure what was going on, but of course he was pleased. He thought their troubles were over."

"And you agreed?"

Harry shrugged. "Well, yeah. On the surface, everything seemed fine. I had my doubts. It wasn't like she got into therapy or was 'born again.' There was definitely a change, but it didn't seem attached to anything. I thought she might be having an affair, but I never said so to him. Nobody really wants to hear that stuff, and I didn't have any proof."

"What are you saying? That she took a lover and then arranged an 'accident' to get her husband out of the way?"

"Sure, why not?"

"Divorce isn't that hard to come by in California. Murder seems like a radical way to get rid of an unwanted spouse."

"Divorce doesn't pay benefits."

"He was well insured?"

"A hundred and twenty-five thousand in whole life, with a double-indemnity clause in case of accidental death. The lady netted herself a quarter million bucks. Plus she gets all that sympathy. Divorced, she'd have had a fight on her hands and probably come out a loser. Believe me, I'm single. Half the women I date are divorced, and they all tell the same tale. Divorce is the pits. Why should Susie go through the hassle when all she had to do was give him a push?"

"Had she been physically abusive to him over the years?"

"Well, no, but she did threaten him."

"Really," I said. "When was this?"

"Late June. July. Sometime in there, when the conflict was at its worst. I can't even remember now what they were arguing about, but she said she'd kill him. I was standing right there. Next thing I knew, sure enough, he was dead."

"Come on, Harry. Lots of people say things like that in the heat of an argument. It doesn't make them killers."

"In this case it does."

"I need more than your word for it, but tell me what you want."

The gaze he turned on me was cold, his tone dead. "Find a way to nail her. I'll pay you anything you ask."

I agreed to check into it—not for the money but for the look on his face. The man was in pain.

That afternoon he stopped by my office, signed a standard contract, and gave me a fifteen-hundred-dollar advance.

The next day I went to work.

He'd given me the few newspaper clippings about Don Grissom's death: SANTA TERESA RESIDENT DIES IN FALL FROM ROOF. According to the paper, Don had climbed up to inspect for leaks after a heavy rain had sent water pouring through the ceiling in the guest bathroom. The accompanying copy of the police report indicated that to all appearances, Mr. Grissom had lost his footing on the rain-slick red tile and had tumbled two stories in a fall that broke his neck. The coroner had determined that the death was accidental. Harry Grissom said the coroner was a fool.

I made a note of the Grissoms' address and presented myself at the doorstep with a clipboard in hand. While a cop is required by statute to identify herself (or himself) as a law-enforcement officer, a private investigator is free to impersonate anyone, which is what makes my job so much fun. I'm a law-abiding little bun in most instances, but I've been known to tell lies at the drop of a hat. The fib I cooked up for Susie Grissom wasn't far from the truth, and I sounded so sincere that I half believed it myself.

"Mrs. Grissom?" I said when she opened the door.

"Yes, that's right," she said cautiously. She was in her early thirties, with mild brown hair pulled up in a clip, brown eyes, freckles, no makeup, dressed in jeans and a T-shirt.

I held up the clipboard. "I'm from California Fidelity Insurance," I said. Now that much was true. I had worked for CFI once upon a time and did occasional investigations for them now in exchange for downtown office space.

"Yes?"

I could tell from the look on her face that *insurance* was the magic word. If what Harry said was true and she'd just collected two hundred and fifty thousand dollars, I could see how the subject might still fascinate. "Your husband had a policy with us," I said. "Our regional office just informed us that he's . . . uh, deceased."

Her face clouded properly. "That's right. He died September fourth in a fall from the roof. What sort of policy?"

"I don't have the details, but it was probably coverage he converted from a plan at work. Was he employed at some point for a large company?"

I could see a spark of recognition. Almost everybody has worked for a large company at some point.

"Well, he did work for Raytheon briefly in 1981, but I thought he let that policy drop."

"Apparently not," I said. "I'll need some data, if you don't object. Just so we can process the claim."

"Claim?"

"Automatic payment in the case of accidental death."

She invited me in.

Now, it's not like I'm psychic, but I have to say this: From the moment I set eyes on this lady, I knew she was guilty. I've seen enough widows and orphans in my day to know what real grief looks like, and this wasn't it. This was pseudo-grief, counterfeit grief, or some reasonable facsimile, but it wasn't real sorrow.

We sat in the living room and I quizzed her at length. Once I mentioned the face value of the policy—let's be generous, I thought, fifty grand—she was as cooperative as she could be. I sat and took notes and cooed and mewed. She played her part to perfection; tears in her eyes, nose all red.

"That must have been terrible," I murmured. "You were out that day and came home to find him dead?"

She nodded mutely, then blew her nose. "I'd been to a meeting of my mystery book club," she said. "I couldn't think what was going on at the house. Police cars out front. An ambulance and everything. Then I found out he was dead. . . ."

"Awful," I said. "What a shock for the kids. How are they taking this?"

"They don't really understand much. I've done the best I could."

I was wondering how I could corroborate her alibi. I assumed the cops had done that, but I wasn't sure. "I think this is all I need for now." I got up, and she walked me to the door. "Actually," I added, "I'm a mystery fan myself."

"Oh, really?" she said, her manner brightening some. "Which authors do you like?"

Oh, shoot. Faked out, I thought. "Oh, golly, so many. Uh, Smith, and White . . ."

"Teri? Oh, she's wonderful. As a matter of fact, we're doing women writers this month. Would you like to come?"

"I'd love it," I said. "What a treat."

Which is how I ended up at a meeting of the Santa Teresa Mystery Readers . . . STMR as they called themselves. I was wearing my all-purpose dress with low heels and panty hose, thinking that's what suburban housewives probably wore. For the first and only time in my life, I found myself overdressed, though everyone was very nice and pretended not to notice. We had tea and cookies and laughed and chatted about writers I'd never heard of. I kept saying things like, "Oh, the ending on that one scared me half to death!" or "I thought the plot line was a bit convoluted, didn't you?" I lied so well, I worried I'd be elected to office, but all that happened was that I was invited back the next month.

"I'll have Jenny give you the program for the year," Susie said. "In case you want to catch up."

The club secretary rustled up a copy of the calendar for me, listing dates and places of meetings and the books that had been discussed. We sat and sipped our tea while I tried a casual imitation of the women I could see. I'm not good at this stuff. I don't bake or do civic work. I don't know how to make small talk or sit with my legs crossed. I studied the program. As soon as Susie stepped away, I lowered my voice, leaning toward Jenny, who was probably fifty-five. She wore a matching tweedy skirt and sweater and a strand of real pearls. "This September meeting. Isn't that when Susie's husband was killed?"

She nodded. "We felt awful," the woman said. "She was in charge of refreshments that day."

"You were at the meeting?"

"Oh, yes. We had a guest speaker from the police department, and Susie had such a nice time talking to him. Afterward, of course, I worked with her in the kitchen while she was putting cookies out. All the time he was dead and she had no idea."

I shook my head. "God, I bet she fell apart. Were they very close?"

"Well, of course," she said, looking at me with interest. "How did you meet Susie? Have you known her long?"

"Well, no, but I feel I know her pretty well," I said modestly.

The woman sitting to my left had apparently been listening, and she broke in. "What sort of work do you do, Kinsey?"

"Insurance," I replied.

"Is that right? Well, the name just seems so familiar somehow. Did I see it in the news by any chance?"

"Oh, heavens. Not me," I said. I'd only been mentioned about six weeks before in connection with a homicide. "Is there a little-girls' room around here?"

I saw the two women exchange a look. Maybe I'd gotten the vocabulary wrong. "A powder room?" I amended.

"Of course. Right down the hall."

I lingered until I heard the group breaking up, and then I slipped away. The next day I canvassed Susie's neighbors.

The first was a woman in her forties; overweight, prematurely graying hair, a Mrs. Hill, according to the information I'd picked up from the city directory. "I'm from California Fidelity," I said. "We're checking into a claim for Mrs. Grissom next door. Could you answer some questions? She's authorized this." I held up a form with Susie's signature, which I'd recently faked.

"I suppose so," Mrs. Hill said reluctantly. "What exactly did you want?"

I went through a series of questions. How well did she know the Grissoms? Was she home on the day of his accident? She was singularly uninformative, the sort who answered each query without editorial comment. When it was clear she had nothing to offer, I thanked her and excused myself, moving on.

The house on the other side of the Grissoms' was dark.

I scanned the area, and on impulse tried the house directly behind the Grissoms', across an alleyway. The woman who answered the door was in her sixties and anxious for company.

"I'm from an insurance company here in town. I'm doing a report about your neighbors, the Grissoms. Your name is?"

"Mrs. Peterson. He crossed over, you know, in a fall from the roof. Not that she gives a hoot."

"Is that right," I said. Before I got my first question out, she was telling everything she knew.

"Well, you know, they quarreled so frightfully," she said, and rolled her eyes, hand against her cheek in a comic imitation of scandalized sensibilities.

"Nooo. I had no idea," I said in disbelief. "Did you happen to be home at the time he fell?"

"Oh, honey, I'm always home. I don't go anywhere now that Teddy's dead."

"Your husband?"

"My dog. I just seemed to lose heart once he passed away. At any rate, I was sitting in my little den upstairs, by the window where the light is good. I was doing cross-stitch, which can ruin your eyesight, even with glasses as good as these new bifocals of mine—" She took them off and held them to the light, then put them back on again.

"You have a view of the Grissoms' house from up there?" I cut in, trying to keep her on track.

"Oh, yes. The view is perfect. Come on upstairs and you can see for yourself."

I shrugged to myself and followed her dutifully, wondering if this was going to be another dead end. People who spend too much time alone will sometimes talk your ear off. She seemed all right, alert and well-oriented. For all I knew, though, she might be the neighborhood crackpot. We reached a small den at the rear of the house, and she showed me the window, which looked right out at the Grissoms' house at a distance of perhaps two hundred yards.

"Did you happen to notice him working on the roof?" I asked.

"Certainly. I watched him for an hour," she replied matter-of-factly.

I held my breath, almost afraid to prompt her.

She frowned. "I thought it was real odd he'd get up there in the rain," she remarked. "Why would anybody do that?"

"I heard there was a leak," I said.

"But that doesn't explain what that redheaded woman was doing up there too."

I could feel the hair rise on the back of my neck. "What redhead?"

"Well, I don't know who she was."

"But she was actually on the roof?"

"She crawled right out the attic window," she said comfortably.

"Mrs. Peterson, did you mention this to the police?"

"They never asked. I didn't want to cause trouble, so I kept my mouth shut. I thought if they were curious, they'd come around just like you. Now, you know, the whole thing's died down, and I don't think anybody even suspects."

"Suspects what?"

"That she pushed him off!"

"Mrs. Grissom did?"

"Not her. The redhead. She slipped around the far side of the chimney where he was removing the tile. She gave him a push, and off he tumbled. Never made a sound. Too surprised, I guess."

"And you saw all this?"

"As plain as day."

"Across both yards with the sky overcast?" I said skeptically.

"Yes, indeed. I had my little opera glasses trained on the roof."

"Opera glasses?" I felt like I was suffering from echolalia, but I was so astonished, I couldn't manage much else.

"I watch everybody with those," she said, as if I should have known. She showed me the binoculars and I had a peep myself. Wow, the chimney looked like it was two feet away.

"What happened then?"

"Well, the woman crawled back in the window and drove off. She had a little white Mercedes with a scratch down the side. She was parked in the alley right out back. That's the last I saw of her."

"Did you catch the license number?"

"Not from this angle. I'm up too high."

"Why didn't you call the police at the time?"

"Oh, no. Not me. No, ma'am. If that woman had any idea what I'd seen, I'd be next on the list. I may be old, but I'm not dumb! And don't think I'll repeat this story to the police, because I won't. They should have asked me all this when it happened. I'd have told 'em then. I'm not going to do it now that she's feeling safe and has her story down pat. Absolutely not."

At that point she decided she'd said enough, and I couldn't get another word out of her, coax as I might.

I went straight over to the police station and had a chat with Lieutenant Dolan in Homicide. He listened attentively, but his attitude was plain. He was not unwilling to reopen the matter, if I'd just bring him a shred of proof. The cops in Santa Teresa take a dim view of hearsay evidence, especially in a case where they've already decided no crime was committed. Proving murder, and then proving insurance was the motive, is exceedingly difficult. If I could give him corroborating evidence, he'd see what he could do. Otherwise all we had was Mrs. Peterson's word for what went on, and at this point she might well deny everything. It was frustrating, but there was nothing he could do.

I went back to the office.

As I stood in the corridor, searching through my handbag for my keys, I heard someone call my name. "Well, Kinsey! Isn't this a surprise!"

I looked up to see the secretary of the book club coming down the hall. She was really quite an elegant little woman, hair perfectly coiffed, nails freshly done. I wondered if she'd spot the KINSEY MILLHONE INVESTIGATIONS in big brass letters on my door. Automatically I eased myself toward the California Fidelity offices next door, hoping to redirect her attention. I hadn't exactly lied to the ladies, but I hadn't really told them the truth, either, and I didn't want Susie Grissom to find out what I was really up to.

"Hello, Jenny. What are you doing here?"

"I've just been to the dentist upstairs," she said, glancing at the California Fidelity logo. "Is this the company where you work? Well, isn't that nice. I'm just so pleased I ran into you. We've scheduled a special meeting tomorrow night, and we were hoping you could come, but nobody had your home phone. Here, I'll just make a quick note of the address and the time. It's at my house, and everybody's bringing cookies, so don't you forget." She jotted the information on a scrap of paper and handed it to me.

"What's the occasion?"

She lowered her voice. "We're having a speaker, and the subject is murder. Won't that be fun?"

Actually I thought it would.

What I pondered for the rest of the day was the notion of that redhead on the roof. Of course, the woman might have been Susie Grissom in a wig, despite everybody's swearing she was at the meeting of the mystery book club. It might have been somebody else, too, but in that case, how did the redhead know he'd be up there? How did she know the house would be empty and the setup so perfect? And how'd she get in? More importantly, what was her motive? On the surface, Susie Grissom had everything to gain, and until now, I'd been dead certain she'd done it. Now I wasn't sure what to think. Had she had an accomplice?

I called Harry Grissom at his office. "Did your brother have a girlfriend, by any chance? A redhead?"

"What?" he said, outraged. "Of course not! Who told you that?"

"Knock it off, Harry. Nobody said that. I'm on the track of something else."

"Well, what's the redhead got to do with it?"

"I'm not sure. I don't want to go into detail at the moment, but somebody's linked a redhead with the circumstances of your brother's death. I just wondered who it could have been. Did he ever mention anyone with red hair? A coworker? An old flame? Some friend of Susie's?"

Harry considered briefly. "I don't think so," he said. "At least, not that I ever heard about."

"Who else might have benefited?"

"No one. Believe me, I checked out every possible angle before I came to you. Why don't you tell me what's going on. Maybe I can help."

"Let me try one thing first, and then we'll have a chat."

After work the next day I stopped at the bakery and bought some cookies, which I arranged on a plate when I got home. I put a dab of jam in the center of each, lightly sifted on some powdered sugar, and covered the plate with plastic wrap. Looked homemade to me. At ten to seven I put on some clean blue jeans, a sweater, and my tennis shoes, grabbed the plate of cookies, my handbag, and Jenny's address. She lived close to the heart of town, not that far from my office.

There were so many cars in the area, I had to park a block away. Jenny's driveway was crammed, and I had to guess that most of the women had already assembled. I'd forgotten to ask who the speaker was. It might have been Lieutenant Dolan for all I knew. I rang the bell, standing on the porch while I waited for someone to let me in. The car parked right at the end of the walk was a little white Mercedes with a scratch down the side. I'd been staring at it idly for thirty seconds before the significance hit me. The front door opened right at that moment, and I gave a little jump, nearly dropping my plate. Jenny greeted me cheerfully and ushered me in.

"Nice little Mercedes," I said. "Whose is it?"

"Mine," a voice said behind me. I turned and found myself shaking hands with the redhead who was standing there.

"I'm Shannon," she said. "Ooo, cold hands."

I remembered then that we didn't have a dentist in our building, and I wondered what had really brought Jenny there the day before. In the living room I could see fifteen or twenty women all seated on folding chairs. Several turned to look at me, there faces blank and curious and dead. My stomach gave a sudden squeeze, and I knew I was in trouble. We were playing an elaborate game and I was "it."

"Uh, Jenny. Do you mind if I go to the potty real quick? I got a bladder the size of a walnut," I said.

"Surely. Right down here," Jenny murmured as she led the way. "Now you hurry back. I'm just putting out refreshments."

"I won't be a sec," I said. I eased the bathroom door shut behind me and flipped the lock. It was broken, of course . . . probably jammed. I tried the bathroom window, but it wouldn't budge. Call it precognition, intuition . . . anything you like. I knew as surely as I was standing there that the women of the Santa Teresa Mystery Readers had all pitched in. Susie Grissom had a problem, and they'd helped her out, providing her a surrogate killer and an alibi. I wondered how many other little domestic conflicts they'd resolved the same way. Meddlesome mothers-in-law, sassy stepkids. Tragic home accidents that everybody felt so bad about. Or maybe Don Grissom was the first, and they were waiting to see if they'd gotten away with it.

I was ice-cold, and under my sweater I could feel sweat trickle down my side. Heart pounding, I flushed the toilet and washed my hands, trying to maintain an outward semblance of calm. They had to know I was a private eye, and they probably guessed I was sniffing at the traces of Don Grissom's death. Did they realize that I'd already figured out what was going on? My only hope was to play dumb and wait for a chance to escape.

As I came out of the bathroom Jenny was just passing with a large cut-glass bowl of punch. How about right now? I thought.

"Careful," she sang.

"Oh, I will be," I sang back.

I shoved her so hard, the punch flew back in her face, the rim of the bowl banging into her mouth, ice flying everywhere. She yelped, going down, taking two other women with her, in a heap. The redhead grabbed me, but I kicked her in the shin, then decked her with a punch that caught her on the jaw. I pulled a side table over, took off toward the kitchen, and yanked open the back door. Behind me, I could hear shrieks and the clatter of heels. I leapt off the porch and tore around the side of the house. In two bounds I scrambled up the neighbor's fence and dropped into the next yard. I took two more fences in succession, heading through another yard and out to the street beyond.

It was fully dark by then, but the streetlights were on and I could see well enough. I glanced back in time to see two women drop over the fence behind me, toting baseball bats. They meant business! Even at a distance of half a block, I could hear several cars start up, and I knew they'd be bearing down on me soon. Headlights flashed around the corner toward me, and I doubled my speed, feet flying as I raced across the street.

I could hear someone coming up behind me, breathing hard, and I cranked up my pace again. Images clicked through my brain like still photographs. Dark houses. No foot traffic. No help. A car had pulled up ahead of me at the corner, four doors hanging open now as the occupants ran toward me. I didn't have breath to waste on calling for help, but if somebody didn't come to my assistance soon, I was one dead chick. They'd pound me unconscious and toss me off a bridge, load me on a boat and dump me in the sea, hack me up and keep me in their freezers until they figured out what to do next. The whole street seemed to thunder with the sound of running feet. I caught a glimpse of Susie Grissom coming up on my right. I straight-armed her like a quarterback and knocked her off-balance. With an "Ooomph!" she went down, but two more women took her place, and I sensed a third angling in from the rear.

My lungs were hot and I was gasping for air, but I was beginning to recognize the area and a plan was taking shape. I turned the corner, cutting left. I poured on the speed, heading for the lights I could see straight ahead. My brain felt disconnected, processing information at a leisurely rate while I ran for dear life. I was on Floresta now, a street I knew well. Just ahead, I could see four matching cars parked at the curb. Black-and-whites. Hot damn, I thought. The building behind them, which blazed now with lights, belonged to my beloved Santa Teresa Police. The members of the Santa Teresa Mystery Readers must have realized it, too, because I sensed that my pursuers were peeling away. By the time I reached the station house, there was no one left, and I flew up the front steps on winged feet, uncertain if I was laughing or crying when I finally burst through the doors.

*Mickey Friedman joined the ranks of full-time mystery writers after a stint as reporter/columnist for the San Francisco* Examiner. *Her 1983 debut,* Hurricane Season, *brought to vivid life the inhabitants and the atmosphere of a small Florida town.* Paper Phoenix, The Fault Tree, *and* Venetian Mask, *all critically acclaimed, followed. In 1988,* Magic Mirror *launched Mickey's first series and introduced Georgia Lee Maxwell, a freelance writer who makes Paris her home base.*

*In "Stormy Weather," Mickey's wonderful range—from elegance to grit, from sympathy to shrewdness—is apparent as we are treated to the most important performance a New York cabaret singer will ever give.*

# STORMY WEATHER

## by Mickey Friedman

I NOTICED THE man from California during "Stormy Weather."

It was the second set, midnight at least. I was wearing my white satin strapless, with sequins glittering deep in the tucks and folds. Casey, my accompanist, was stoned again, which meant he was playing like an angel. The notes surged as if they were pulsing through my bloodstream. I sang about how bad I felt that my man and I weren't together and looked out and saw the man from California.

Most of the people lounging at tables or leaning on the bar were in approximately the same condition as Casey, but the man from California looked alert. He had a drink, but I didn't see him touch it. He was focused on me, and I thought he was actually listening. I didn't know he was from California, but I knew he wasn't from New York. He didn't have the hunted look New Yorkers get, the palpable fear that they're going to get it done to them before they get a chance to do it to somebody else. At the same time there was nothing about him that said "tourist." He wasn't out for a good time, and he wasn't having one. He wouldn't weave up to me later and shove a twenty down the front of my dress and invite me to have a drink, but I thought I'd be hearing from him all the same.

It wasn't raining outside like in the song but the weather was damn cold, the wind bulldozing along the concrete, rolling untethered garbage can lids and crumpled newspapers and other urban tumbleweeds before it. When I'd come in earlier, the remains of the awning were shredding, but my photograph, in the glass display case on the wall by the door, was serene. It took more than a wind-chill factor of minus thirteen to wipe the smile off the face of song stylist Bambi Baker.

That night even Mo, who usually slept on the subway grating, was gone—either blown away in the gale or corralled and taken to a shelter. Mo hated the shelter. He once told me the men there smelled bad, which gave me a chuckle, and then he cried and said they'd stolen his shoes. The goofy old fart might have given them away and forgotten about it, but I handed him five and told him to get a new pair from the Salvation Army.

"You're a nice lady, Bambi," he said, sniveling, but who would've taken his word for anything?

I was brushing my hair, looking at my roots and wondering if I should switch shades from Copper Spitfire to Bella Rossa when the knock came. I share my dressing room, as we at the club laughingly refer to it, with cases of liquor, cardboard cartons of toilet paper, an array of chewed-looking mops. I hang my dresses from the hot-water pipes, but it's dicey because the pipes are always hot, and you can't touch the wire hangers without a pot holder. The room is suffocating, so I was sitting there in my bra and garter belt. I put on my robe, a ruffled pink one-hundred-percent polyester Charmeuse number given to me by an admirer in the wholesale lingerie business, and went to the door. It was the man from California.

"Hi. Come in," I said, stepping back.

He came in. He wasn't a handsome man in any way you'd remember, but he wasn't bad. He wore a sport jacket, an open-necked shirt, and a V-necked sweater vest. Over his arm was a raincoat I could only hope had a zip-in lining. His hair was brown, cut shorter than I usually prefer, and he was running slightly to jowls. The best way to describe him is what I already said—he looked alert. He was in his forties, probably. Old enough to have given up being a fool if he ever was going to. He said, "My name is Bill Turner, Miss Baker."

I motioned him toward my butt-sprung green armchair and sat

down again at the dressing table. "Pleased to meet you, Bill. Call me Bambi. How'd you like the show?" I applied a fresh layer of Brandied Cherries to my lips while he dug around in his pocket.

"Good. You're a good singer." He pulled out a calling card that said he was a lieutenant in the homicide division of the San Jose Police Department, then dug again and produced a plastic case with his official ID.

I gave them both a long look. When I handed them back, I said, "William D. Turner. Can I guess what the *D* stands for?"

He settled back, a man with time on his hands. "Sure."

"David?"

"No."

"Donald?"

"No."

"Um—Douglas?"

"No."

I fiddled with my earring. I'm crazy about earrings. This pair was made out of white feathers and hung almost to my shoulders. I rubbed my right lobe a second before laughing and saying, "This is tougher than I thought. How about Daniel?"

"No."

He was obviously prepared to sit there all night while I tried Dennis, Dominick, Dmitri, Darcy, and God knows what else. I put up my hands in the "don't-shoot" position. "I give up."

"Donovan."

"Donovan! No fair! That's a last name!"

He didn't crack a smile. "Not for me."

I was out of gambits. He let silence fall before he said, "Did you ever know a guy named Jimmy Henderson?"

Of course it would be about Jimmy. I gave my earlobe another massage and felt a feather brush my shoulder. "Jimmy. That was a long time ago."

"I'd like to ask you some questions, Bambi."

I spread out my arms, an open book. "Ask."

He still kept a straight face, letting me know charm wouldn't tug any human warmth out of him yet. But the warmth was there. I could feel it. He said, "You were in California a couple of weeks ago, weren't you?"

"That's right. I did some auditions."

"Thinking of moving out there?"

I shrugged. "Look at the weather, Bill. There's a song about liking New York in June, you know? But in January, forget it."

"While you were there, you visited a man named Woodrow Henderson. He was Jimmy Henderson's father."

I slipped my earrings off and put them on the dressing table, where they lay like the remains of some shot-down bird. "Well, I—"

"The neighbors saw you drive up to Woodrow Henderson's house. They were in their front hall, waiting for a friend to take them to the airport for two weeks in Hawaii."

"Two weeks in Hawaii! Some people have all the luck."

"They saw a redhead wearing shades in a red Camaro. We checked the rental agencies, and your name came up."

I let go of my earlobe. I said, "That's right. I was there."

"What for?"

"Looking for Jimmy."

He leaned on his elbow, Mr. Casual, as if it didn't much matter what I said, so I knew I'd better look out. "What happened?"

I bit my lip, then remembered the Brandied Cherries I'd applied and let up. I hate smeared teeth. "When I asked about Jimmy, the old man got mad, and I mean really abusive. He said he didn't know where Jimmy was, and he didn't care, and he didn't want me bothering him. He told me to get the hell out. I mean, I can take a hint. I got the hell out."

I could see the old man's face, ugly with hatred, his teeth gleaming slick and yellow when his lips pulled back. He was gray and humped over, wearing a shapeless golf cardigan and bedroom slippers. The living room smelled like stale cigarette smoke, dust, and pine air freshener. I could hear the roar of traffic on Highway 101, rocketing down from San Francisco.

Bill was saying, "Woodrow Henderson was beaten to death that day—broken ribs, contusions, ruptured spleen. He was a mess. He was still alive when the mailman found him. They were loading him on the cart when he whispered, 'My son Jimmy did it,' to one of the paramedics. He died on the way to the hospital."

I nodded. "I heard. It was on the car radio when I was driving to the airport that night."

"But you didn't get in touch with us."

"My flight left in an hour. I had a show to do here. Woodrow hadn't treated me too well. I thought, Let it ride. Somebody did the world a favor."

"But the neighbors came back and found out what had happened, and they remembered seeing you."

"Maybe I should hire them as press agents."

He ignored that one and let loose the big question. "Were you there with Jimmy, Bambi?"

"No."

"Where is he?"

"I don't know."

"Jimmy beat the old man up and killed him."

"So the old man said."

"Right. So the old man said."

"Bill, listen. That old dude hated Jimmy. He would've done anything to get him into trouble."

He laughed then. "So Woodrow Henderson battered himself to death so he could falsely accuse his son Jimmy of murder?"

I got giggly. It had been a long day. Tears started up in my eyes, and I blotted them with a tissue. "Oh, *I* don't know," I said.

He wasn't laughing anymore. He said, "Why don't you tell me the truth?"

"I'm telling you. I went there looking for Jimmy. Woodrow wasn't in touch with him. I left."

"Why were you looking?"

"You know that song 'Sentimental Journey,' don't you, Bill? Didn't you ever take a sentimental journey?"

He looked at me a long time. Attention is one of my weaknesses. I shook my hair back and met his gaze. "You know where he is," he said.

"Nope. Can't help you there."

He got up, shook my hand, thanked me for my time. I watched him go out the door, knowing I'd said good-bye to the one person in the world who cared as much about Jimmy as I did.

He'd said good-bye, but he didn't go away. The next day he talked to Marty, the owner of the club. When I came in, late that afternoon, Marty poured me a cup of coffee and said, "You got a new boyfriend, Bambi. Works for the San Jose P.D."

"I'm a popular girl."

Marty is a sweetheart. He's pouchy under the eyes, paunchy in the gut, eats and drinks and smokes too much. He gave me a job. He distributed a flyer that said the smoky contralto of song stylist Bambi Baker was gracing the elegant atmosphere of his club. Marty has no need of policemen, even if they're from San Jose. "He wanted to know if I'd ever seen you with a guy named Jimmy," Marty said.

"You haven't, have you?"

"No."

"Then tell him no."

Marty gave a grunt that meant he wasn't going to pursue it right now, but I needn't think he was going to forget it.

Bill Turner didn't forget, either. I'd see him around the neighborhood. He didn't have a hat, and his raincoat wasn't nearly heavy enough for a New York winter. The sidewalks were as cold as metal, the sky was dirty gray, and the weather was too mean to snow. The poor bastard was freezing his ass off, thinking I was going to lead him to Jimmy. I caught him hanging around my building one day, dodging the guys from the methadone clinic down the block, and took pity on him. "Come on up for coffee. Take a load off," I said, and without a word he followed me in.

My building is the traditional New York tenement structure, decorated with fire escapes and a row of garbage cans. Both pimps and methadone addicts lounge on the steps in warm weather, but you can tell which is which, because the pimps are better dressed. I share a studio apartment with a guy named Dan, who has a day job as manager of a health club. We only overlap a few hours a night, and we have twin beds with fitted covers to make them look like couches. The place is cluttered up with Dan's barbells and squash rackets and my sheet music and feather boas. It isn't perfect, but tell me something that is. Bill Turner walked in and looked around. I said, "Do you know your ears are *purple*? I never saw that before."

He walked to the window and looked down at the street below. "It was better before the clinic moved in," I said. I was on the kitchen side of the room, measuring coffee into the Chemex.

He surveyed the place. "Don't you get claustrophobic in here?"

"Claustrophobia isn't one of my problems."

He walked around studying everything while the water boiled. His ears turned back to their normal color. He stopped in front of a photo on the wall—me and a gentleman I used to know. "Who's that?" he asked.

"Guy who owned a club where I worked in Jersey."

He squinted at it closer and said, in a jokey way, "Mafia."

"God, you out-of-town cops."

The coffee was ready, so I put it and a couple of mugs on the dinette table. He sat down across from me. "Tell me about Jimmy," he said.

Bill Turner wasn't handsome. His eyes were dark brown, blood-shot from standing in the cold, and his hair had some gray in it but not too much. I sang, " 'Along came Bill, who's not the type at all,' " and he laughed.

"Sing me a song about Jimmy," he said.

Today I was wearing suede pants tucked into my boots and gold Gypsy hoops, huge ones. I fiddled with the right one and said, "What do you want to know?"

"Just . . . tell me about him."

I sipped my coffee. "When I knew him, he was a pretty unhappy character."

"Why?"

"His life wasn't right."

"Did he talk about his father?"

"Sure."

"What did he say?"

"They didn't get along."

"Yet you went to his father to ask where Jimmy was."

"A lot of time had passed. That can change things."

Neither of us spoke, and sounds from outside filled the room: rumbling traffic, a faraway siren, shouts from a dispute out on the pavement.

He stirred. "You're making trouble for yourself, Bambi."

"Believe me, it's one of my specialties."

"We're going to get him. If you turn out to be an accessory, you're in the shit."

I hummed a few bars of "Bill."

He said, "What the hell do you owe Jimmy, anyway?"

I didn't answer. We drank our coffee. When his mug was empty, he stood and picked up his coat. "Where are you going?" I asked.

"California," he said, and walked out the door.

I got my ears pierced a few years ago, at a hole-in-the-wall jewelry store in the Village. The customer ahead of me was a baby girl named Yasmeen. "She's six months old. It's time," Yasmeen's mother said. When Yasmeen was howling in her mother's arms, her tiny gold studs in place, the man beckoned to me. He was a skinny black guy, a nice, gentle man, and he had a hypodermic-style puncher instead of one of the fancy staple-gun types. As he looked at my right lobe, getting ready to do the deed, he said, "Hmm. Scar here, something."

"Yeah," I said. "Can you still do it?"

"Oh, sure." He swabbed it off with alcohol. "Funny place for a scar."

"Cigarette burn," I said.

He pulled back to look at me, and because he was a polite person, he didn't say anything at all.

I said, "I picked up the phone and forgot I had a cigarette in my hand."

"I see," he said gravely, and in a minute or two it was over, and I was drenched with sweat and feeling faint, and Yasmeen had stopped crying and was sucking on her pacifier.

Bill Turner came back a week later, walked in during "Cry Me a River," and took a place at the bar. Casey was straight, the piano plinking like a tone-deaf child was trying it out for the first time. Bill still didn't have a hat. He touched two fingers to his forehead and saluted me. I picked up energy from that and managed a good finish to the set.

Afterward, in my dressing room, he sat down in the butt-sprung chair and said, "Good show."

"Thanks."

The room was hot. The white satin dress I'd worn hung from the pipe, swaying like a ghost.

"So your father was right about who killed him," he said. He was looking straight at me.

*Along came Bill.* Not handsome, but one persistent son of a gun. "Sure, he was right. He was right about everything all his life. All you had to do was ask him."

"Why did you go there?"

"I told you. I was looking for Jimmy."

Rather than think it was pure masochism, rather than think I'd had to crawl back for one last drink from the poisoned well, I'd rather think I went because I was proud of Bambi. I was proud of Bambi, and I wanted him to be. Which of us hasn't wanted the impossible, at one time or another?

"What did he do?"

"He was himself. Just like always. And I couldn't stand it."

"He didn't want a daughter?"

"He never wanted a son, either. At least not one like me. He went to a lot of trouble to let me know it. He was one cruel bastard." My fingers touched my ear, where the feather earring hung in my scarred lobe.

I turned away from Bill and stared in the mirror. "How did you find out?"

"I located some of Jimmy's—of your—friends from the old days."

I shook my head. "They didn't know about the operation. That was a lot later, after I'd left San Jose."

It was in another country. I took the shots, the pills, and watched my body smooth out, soften, redistribute itself until I was ready to take the last step, to become. "Nobody knew," I said.

"They didn't know. I got a hunch and checked up on that later on."

"But if they didn't tell you about the operation, what—"

"One of them told me that when Jimmy Henderson gets nervous, he always plays with his right earlobe."

I started to laugh, explosive guffaws that bent me over the dressing table. Bill came up behind me, and I felt his hand on my shoulder. "I guess there are some things you can't change," he said.

*Susan Dunlap has a singular ability to put her finger on the murderous pulse of a community. In her Jill Smith series (Karma, As a Favor, Not Exactly a Brahmin, Too Close to the Edge, and A Dinner to Die For) it's Berkeley. For Vejay Haskell (An Equal Opportunity Death, The Bohemian Connection, and The Last Annual Slugfest) it's the Russian River area of California. And former forensic pathologist turned private eye Kiernan O'Shaugnessy uncovers shady dealings as she investigates the death of a young Catholic priest beneath the glaring Phoenix sun in Pious Deception.*

*In "No Safety," the exigencies of the real world are brought home to an idealistic San Francisco peacemaker in a most graphic and disturbing way.*

# NO SAFETY

## by Susan Dunlap

JEREMY COUGHLIN SHOULD have known. That was the one thing upon which everyone involved agreed.

When he was seven, Jeremy saw his father shot. An attempted holdup. Only momentarily did he think his father dead. He stared in horror, disbelief. And for the first time he felt a hollow sense of loss. Years later he would be able to describe it as feeling like all the air had been sucked out of his chest and his ribs were about to burst inward. But the seven-year-old just stared at the gun with hatred.

Determined to make the world more peaceful for any son he might have, Jeremy became a pacifist, one of the few who achieved legal status during the Vietnam War. He spent those years sweeping floors in Agnews State Hospital, walking softly on the violent wards, sitting softly with those patients whose depression robbed them of vitality and visitors, patients whose conversations wandered in sharp-cornered circles. He sat on the cold metal folding chairs, forcing himself to listen as the disjointed words tumbled out. When he could no longer give credence to the words, he could *appear* to listen, to provide the illusion of the bond the patients sought. He was good at it.

The early seventies came. A good time to be in San Francisco. A good time to marry, to rent the first floor of a Victorian in the Haight, half a block from the Panhandle of Golden Gate Park. In those days he and Anne sat on their garage-sale wicker sofa, their feet on the sill of the open bay window. They smoked a joint and watched as the ponytailed man in a tie-dyed T-shirt, the woman in an ankle-length Indian skirt, and the blond toddler with the star-shaped birthmark above his temple jumped down from their crimson-and-purple converted school bus across the street and meandered along the broad sidewalk toward the lazy twang of the guitars in the Panhandle. Sometimes after a second joint he and Anne followed them onto the green strip of the Panhandle. Jeremy sprawled against the thick trunk of a eucalyptus, letting the music flow through him like Pacific waves. The acrid smell of marijuana mixed with the tang of the eucalyptus. And in those moments he could believe that he belonged there in the narrow green land of the lotus-eaters.

Or almost believe. Ah, to climb on that crimson-and-purple bus and leap down wherever it stopped! To have no plans past the next song. To never have to sing a chorus!

He felt that familiar hollowness inside his rib cage. The freedom of the bus family cost more than he could afford. Jeremy ran the hose over the soapy top of his Volkswagen and watched the white water erase the muddy marks of their bare feet on the sidewalk. He never could be one of them. But he could talk to them, listen to them, and go with them when they battled the welfare or the health department or the police. He could make life more peaceful for them and their children. He could be their advocate. Yes, Advocates of Peace would stand with them.

With the years, the flowers wilted in their hair; mellow warped to manic. The San Francisco winters became grayer, colder, the rain more leaden. Those who would protect the innocents were replaced by the keepers of the purse. The posters from peace demonstrations frayed; Jeremy taped them back together. Once or twice a year the crimson-and-purple converted school bus turned up across the street from his house, its festive colors ever dingier. The soapy stream from the Volkswagen hood washed over bare feet that walked woodenly beneath drug-vacant eyes.

But Jeremy's dreams of peace and justice were not washed away with it. As the government moved to the right, he, in the name of Advocates of Peace, became stronger.

Demonstrations outside City Hall edged into violence; Jeremy Coughlin was called to mediate.

Representatives of fledgling groups asked his advice.

The chairman of the Mayor's Subcommittee on Individual Rights sold out, and was forced out. MSIR needed a man of integrity, a man of peace.

As Jeremy pulled a metal chair up to the long table, he scanned the committee members, the representatives of the street people, the homeless, the drug burnouts. In the audience he spotted the family from the crimson-and-purple bus. Gone were their bright clothes, their easy smiles, the buoyant freedom Jeremy had envied. They looked like ice sculptures slightly melted. The boy, eight or nine now, was no longer blond, but that star-shaped birthmark was still discernible. Only he responded to Jeremy's smile. Behind the table were the mayor's aide, a sheriff, a police sergeant. And between the groups, himself. How had *he* gotten here? he wondered. But as he looked out into the audience, at the family, as he called the meeting to order, that hollow feeling in his rib cage dissipated. By ten P.M., he had achieved a consensus. On a small point, admittedly, but a consensus nevertheless.

Amazed at his magical achievement—"a miracle of peaceful agreement," the mayor's aide called it—he shook hands with the city reps, pressed hands with the street-group reps. He looked for the family, suddenly anxious to share this moment with them, but they were gone. Back to their crimson-and-purple bus—parked on another street in the city, no doubt. Perhaps tomorrow it would be across from his own house again. He called good-bye to a priest from the Council of Churches. Then, still buoyant, he drove to the beach.

There were no stars in the January sky. Fog rested on the hills and caught on the tall bolls of the sequoias and the fronds of the date palms. Like a soaked goose-down comforter, it sagged onto the beach, creating a charcoal-gray unity of air, wet sand, and Pacific whitecaps. Only the most desperate of the homeless or the deranged huddled on the far reaches of the beach, against the thick cement wall. At night only the foolish walked alone, close enough to hear the breakers splat onto the sand.

No other time would Jeremy Coughlin have considered it. But tonight he felt as powerful as the breaking waves, the icy blanket of fog his protective shield. He skirted close to the water, letting the salty spray hit his ankles, stepping gently as if to avoid being jolted back to the reality of himself. He relived the events of the evening more with wonder than with pride.

Only when the fog had seeped into his clothes and penetrated his skin did he start back across the beach, moving quickly now, before that familiar hollowness inside his rib cage could catch him.

The gun was near the cement wall. The streetlight shone on its black barrel as it lay half concealed by sand. He glanced at the men and women huddled a hundred yards down along the wall. He couldn't leave that gun here for one of them to find. He picked it up.

Later he would agree that he should have known then.

He held the gun in the light, staring meditatively at the long, thin barrel, at the wooden stock with the crosshatch marks, at the *S and W* cut into the metal above the trigger. The gun looked surprisingly delicate, not like the fire-spitting handguns on the cop shows his daughter Meggie had become enamored of. He felt an odd attachment to *this* gun, as if it were a commemorative symbol of his evening's triumph. He held it closer, then laughed. What levels of fantasy! He would drop off his great commemorative symbol at the police station in the morning. For the night, it could stay in the garage. He wasn't so seduced by it that he'd take it in the house, not with Meggie there.

Pocketing it, he drove home and into the garage. He closed the door, turned on the light and opened an old empty toolbox. Then he pulled the gun out of his pocket. Sand still clung to one side. There was sand on his hands. Here in the light, the gun looked shorter, thicker, more powerful. Not the delicate impostor it had seemed before. He felt a shiver flow down his spine as he touched it, this manifestation of the violence he had fought against, and that shiver filled the hollow within him.

"You're late," Anne called as he walked in.

"The meeting time ran over, but it was worth it. We're onto a new kind of working here. We formed a consensus."

"You brought those guys together? Hey, kiddo," she said, flinging her arms around his neck, "you know, you really are something." Her kiss silenced his protest, and he let himself feel the warmth of her body against him, and the warmth of the illusion she believed, the fullness he still held.

After they were in bed, as he lay listening for that moment when her shallow breath sunk into the deep, husky exhalations of sleep, he remembered the gun and thought how odd it was that he had forgotten to mention it to her. Perhaps that was the moment when he should have known.

The weekend came before he realized he'd forgotten to take the gun to the police station. By then it was too late; he couldn't do it without answering a lot of questions he didn't have answers for. He closed the garage door, unlocked the toolbox, and lifted the gun out. The sand had dried. It flitted away at his touch. He checked the bullets. There were only three. Had the others been shot at a holdup victim like his father? Had they been pumped into the heart of an errant wife? Or had they been aimed at empty chili cans on a fence? What kind of person had owned this gun? He stared down at the gun, and at his sandy palm. But neither gave an answer. He put the gun back in the toolbox, locked it, and hung the key back under the workbench.

POLICE RAID ABANDONED BUILDING IN THE HAIGHT. THIRTY SQUATTERS EVICTED, the headlines proclaimed.

FREE NEEDLE CLINIC PICKETED.

DISABLED DEMONSTRATE FOR BUS ACCESS.

Advocates of Peace thrived. Jeremy found himself on call day and night. He rushed through the garage to the car, always almost late for an appearance before the Board of Supervisors, to give a workshop on peaceful disagreement, or chair a meeting between the University Hospital directors and the neighbors whose land they coveted. At one A.M. or two, more nights than not, he drove back in, too tired to worry whether the bond he created was real or another illusion, too tired to deal with the familiar hollow feeling. He patted the old toolbox as he passed. The intention of turning in the gun had faded. There was no reason for him not to have it. He wasn't going to shoot someone with it. No danger of that. He rarely had time to take it out of the box.

And yet it was there in his mind. He tried to imagine what his father's assailant had felt as he'd pointed his gun. Sometimes, when Jeremy stopped home between afternoon meetings, when Anne was out, he stood in the garage and held the gun. He flicked the safety on and twirled the revolver like an Old West gunfighter, all the time listening for footsteps, afraid his foolishness would be seen. But Anne never caught him. Only Meggie saw him. And she was delighted.

He found himself zeroing in on the handguns on Meggie's detective shows. Did Rockford, or Rick and A. J. Simon use a Smith and Wesson like his? He watched the detectives' moves, the way Rockford shot through the open window of his truck, or Cagney and Lacey braced their feet and held their guns out with a two-handed grip.

Meggie liked the company, and Anne was relieved that he hadn't refused the girl permission to watch her shows. "Who am I to imagine I can control a twelve-year-old mind?" he'd asked, laughing. "After all, I can't make her the one kid in the sixth grade to watch only *Masterpiece Theater*." And he had to admit, it was interesting to see how the private eyes viewed life. He found, to his surprise, that he could understand them. As an advocate, it was important for him to understand.

After a while he rarely looked at the gun. He rarely unlocked the toolbox at all. When he wandered down the stairs from the dining room into the garage, it was to get in the car, or more rarely to wash it.

The August fog was just beginning to roll in when he drove the old Volkswagen out onto the sidewalk and headed back into the garage for the hose and bucket.

He could have taken the car to a wash, or even hired someone. But there was a reassuring certainty to rubbing the soapy water over each section of faded metal. No magic here; half a cup of soap, two gallons of water, and forty-five minutes of soaping and hosing down invariably yielded dirt-free red paint and shining chrome.

He was soaping the hood when a hand hit his shoulder. "Hey, man, get your fucking car out of the way!" The guy wasn't big. Neither were the other two. He'd seen them ambling along Haight Street before. One time they'd been hanging angrily on the crimson-and-purple bus. Their eyes stared vacantly now, their fingers flitting as if they were working invisible cat's cradles.

Slowly Jeremy put down the bucket. "I'm almost done," he said in the peaceful tone that had become his trademark.

"*Almost!* Bullshit!"

"I just need to rinse the soap off the hood. Otherwise it'll be a sticky mess."

"Bullshit!" The speaker lurched toward him.

Behind him he heard Anne's panicked call. He grabbed the hose and aimed it at the three. "Beat it!" he yelled. They stared, looking more surprised than angered, as if the water had washed away the last few minutes. Shivering in the afternoon wind, they moved on.

Still holding the hose, Jeremy turned. Anne stood, arm around Meggie's shoulder. "Are you okay, Jeremy?"

"Yeah," he said. "Sure."

"You showed 'em, huh, Daddy?" Meggie pulled free.

"Yeah," he said, looking back at Anne. "Don't let them upset you, hon."

"It's not them," she said slowly. "I've never seen you react like that."

He nodded slowly. "Odd, isn't it? You know, I could have talked them down. That's my specialty. And these guys, they weren't hard cases. I could have done it. I just didn't. Of course, they didn't know my vaunted reputation. Alas, a prophet gets no honor on his own soapy sidewalk." He shrugged; glancing into the garage, he said, "On the other hand, I didn't wave a gun at them."

Meggie opened her mouth, then slammed it shut. But not soon enough.

He hesitated, then said, "Out of here, you two. I've got a soapy hood to deal with."

But he wasn't surprised to find Anne in the garage when he finished. And he wasn't surprised when she demanded, "What's this gun business?"

He hesitated only momentarily before getting the key from under the workbench and opening the toolbox. "I found it on the beach."

Silently she stared at it, waiting for the rest of the story. And when he had finished, she asked, "You are an Advocate of *Peace*. Why have you kept this *weapon*?"

"I don't know. I'll never use it. But there's something comforting about having it down here. It's like the ocean. We'll never swim in it, but it's good to know it's there."

"Jeremy, get that gun out of here!"

He put it back in the box and locked it.

Her voice was high and brittle. "If you don't get rid of it, I will. We have a child to consider."

"I *am* considering her. I want her to be safe. The neighborhood isn't what it used to be. Those guys weren't bused in here, you know. We've already had two robberies."

"Break-ins, you called them then," she insisted, her voice quivering. "They didn't take much. You said yourself it was probably kids."

"Still—"

"Still, what? You'd rather have shot them?"

His breath caught. For a moment he stood staring at her taut, pale face, and the fearful hunch of her thin shoulders. "I wouldn't shoot anyone. You know that. I've never considered using the gun. I don't even think of it as a weapon. It's more like a talisman."

"The police have no-questions-asked turn-in days."

He nodded. "Okay. You're right. You know," he said, looking

back at the sidewalk, "those guys, I could have talked them down. I just didn't bother."

Anne patted his shoulder.

He should have known then. Anyone would have. He should have gotten rid of the gun. Anyone would have.

The burglar didn't come till spring. Jeremy never knew how he got in. He was just there, in the back of the dining room when Jeremy brought Meggie home that Saturday night. The boy must have been so nervous, so drugged up, that he hadn't heard, or didn't compute, the garage door opening, the car pulling in, hadn't heard Jeremy's feet on the stairs, didn't notice the door sliding back into the wall. Jeremy was halfway through the door to the dining room when he spotted him.

"Hey!" he yelled. "What are you doing?"

The boy spun toward him. He was only a couple of years older than Meggie, maybe fifteen, but big, with long, wild hair. His eyes were pinpoints, his skin pimpled. He reached in his pocket and pulled out a knife.

Jeremy stepped through the door, shoved Meggie back, and slid the door shut. He took a slow step forward, his eyes never leaving the boy's face. He could see the boy fighting to concentrate; he could see the panic that the losing battle brought. Jeremy felt his body tense. He didn't have a hose this time. And the gun? No time to slide the door open, run downstairs, snatch the key, unlock the box, and get it.

He looked back at the boy, seeing not the street-tough facade but the adolescent fear beneath. And the hollowness when the facade hangs too loose.

The boy planted his feet, tightened his grip on the knife. "You got a kid. I can cut her."

Jeremy's breath caught. He didn't need the gun, he told himself. The boy's talk was bravado. The boy would be glad to have his decisions made for him. He was just a *boy*. Using the peaceful voice that had worked so well, so often, he said, "Nothing has happened yet. I'd like you to leave now. The door is past me, to your left. You'll need to turn the dead bolt first, then the knob."

Sweat covered the boy's face. His T-shirt clung to his chest. His fingers tightened on the knife.

Jeremy watched him, feeling that familiar sensation of hollowness. The boy took a step forward. "Give me your money, man."

Jeremy nodded. "My wallet is in my back pocket. I'm reaching for it." Slowly he extricated it and slid it across the floor.

The boy picked it up, yanked out the cash, and stuck it in his pocket. With a toss of the head he flung his hair out of his face. And Jeremy spotted the star-shaped birthmark.

Jeremy reached toward him.

"Hey, get back!"

"You used to live in the converted school bus. Your folks parked it right across the street a couple times a year for years. I've seen you around since you were a toddler, a little blond toddler going down to the Panhandle with your parents to listen to the guitars. Remember?"

The boy's hand tightened on the hilt of the knife. Panic was clear in his eyes. "You're making a mistake, man. You don't know me."

The words, the look, seemed to ricochet off the inside of Jeremy's rib cage. How could he have made such a dumb move? He had been distracted, thinking of the gun.

He thought he knew then. And the swirling fear within him scratched against his brittle facade. All these years? What had his work been for? *This* was the boy for whom he was going to make life better.

The boy looked around at the television, the VCR, the computer. But he made no move toward them.

Jeremy forced himself to concentrate. In his own hollowness he could read the boy, see his indecision. "A lot of trouble," he said, surprised at the calm in his voice, "when you can just walk past me and on out."

The boy hesitated. Then he turned toward the door. Jeremy sighed; he had won. He hadn't saved this boy, but he hadn't lost him, either. The boy would be okay. He could help him. The swirling slowed, and he felt solid.

The boy started forward, carefully keeping a distance between himself and Jeremy as he neared the doorway.

The shot resounded through the room. The boy grabbed his chest. The second shot was louder. And the third louder yet. The room smelled of burning. The boy's eyes opened wide. Then he dropped to the floor, on his side, the star-shaped birthmark lipstick-red against his bloodless skin.

Jeremy turned around slowly. Meggie stood on the step beneath him, feet braced apart, the gun held in both hands, in front of her.

The hollowness in his rib cage burst through his skin. It encompassed Meggie, and the boy, and the room.

And then he did know. But it no longer mattered.

*Dorothy Salisbury Davis, recipient in 1985 of the Mystery Writers of America Grandmaster Award for lifetime achievement, ranks among the ground breakers in presenting female sleuths who are independent, thoughtful, tough, and direct. Mrs. Annie Norris appeared in three books, including* Death of an Old Sinner; *Julie Hayes was introduced in 1975 with* A Death in the Life *and was featured most recently in* The Habit of Fear. *Dorothy's publication credits begin in 1949 with* The Judas Cat; *included among her twenty books is a short-story collection,* Tales for a Stormy Night.

*"Natural Causes," which first appeared in* Ellery Queen Mystery Magazine, *is a story of rebellion and acceptance, and of the extreme tests that confront a small-town nonconformist.*

# NATURAL CAUSES

## by Dorothy Salisbury Davis

WHEN CLARA McCRACKEN got out of state prison I was waiting to bring her home. We shook hands at the prison gate when she came through, and the first thing I was struck with was how her eyes had gone from china-blue to a gunmetal-grey. In fifteen years she'd come to look a lot like her late sister, Maud.

There'd been twenty years' difference in the ages of the Mc-Cracken sisters, and they were all that was left of a family that had come west with the building of the Erie Canal and settled in the Ragapoo Hills, most of them around Webbtown, a place that's no bigger now than it was then. Maudie ran the Red Lantern Inn, as McCrackens had before her, and she raised her younger sister by herself. She did her best to get Clara married to a decent man. It would have been better for everybody if she'd let her go wild the way Clara wanted and married or not married, as her own fancy took her.

Maudie was killed by accident, but there was no way I could prove young Reuben White fell into Maudie's well by accident. Not with

Clara saying she'd pushed him into it and then taking the jury up there to show them how. She got more time than I thought fair, and for a while I blamed myself, a backwoods lawyer, for taking her defense even though she wouldn't have anybody else. Looking back, I came to see that in Ragapoo County then, just after giving so many of our young men to a second World War, Reuben White was probably better thought of than he ought to have been. But that's another story and the page was turned on it when Clara went to prison. Another page was turned with her coming out.

She stood on the comfortable side of the prison gate and looked at my old Chevrolet as though she recognized it. She could have. It wasn't even new when she got sent up, as they used to say in those Big House movies. The farthest I've ever driven that car on a single journey was the twice I visited her, and this time to bring her home. Then she did something gentle, a characteristic no one I knew would've given to Clara—she put out her hand and patted the fender as though it was a horse's rump.

I opened the door for her and she climbed in head first and sorted herself out while I put her canvas suitcase in the back. There were greys in her bush of tawny hair and her face was the color of cheap toilet paper. Squint lines took off from around her eyes. I didn't think laughing had much to do with them. She sat tall and bony in her loose-hung purple dress and looked straight ahead most of the drive home.

About the first thing she said to me was, "Hank, anybody in Webbtown selling television sets?"

"Prouty's got a couple he calls demonstrators." Then I added, "Keeps them in the hardware shop."

Clara made a noise I guess you could call a laugh. Prouty also runs the only mortuary in the town.

"You'd be better sending away to Sears Rocbuck," I said. "You pay them extra and they provide the aerial and put it up. I wouldn't trust old Prouty on a ladder these days. I wouldn't trust myself on one."

I could feel her looking at me, but I wasn't taking my eyes off the road. "Still playing the fiddle, Hank?" she asked.

"Some. Most folks'd rather watch the television than hear me hoeing down. But I fiddle for myself. It's about what I can do for pleasure lately. They dried up the trout stream when they put the highway through. Now they're drilling for oil in the hills. That's something new. I thought coal maybe someday, or even natural gas. But it's oil and they got those dipsy-doodles going night and day."

"Making everybody rich as Indians," Clara said, and she sounded just like Maudie. That was something Maudie would have said in the same deadpan way.

What I came out with then was something I'd been afraid of all along. "Maudie," I said, "you're going to see a lot of changes."

"Clara," she corrected me.

"I'm sorry, Clara. I was thinking of your sister."

"No harm done. You'd have to say there was a family resemblance among the McCrackens."

"A mighty strong one."

"Only trouble, there's a terrible shortage of McCrackens." And with that she exploded such a blast of laughter I rolled down the window to let some of it out.

I felt sorry for Clara when we drove up to the Red Lantern. It was still boarded up and there was writing on the steps that made me think of that Lizzie Borden jingle, "Lizzie Borden took an axe . . ." Having power of attorney, I'd asked Clara if I should have the place cleaned out and a room fixed up for her to come home to, but she said no. It wasn't as though there wasn't any money in the bank. The state bought a chunk of McCracken land when they put through the highway.

While I was trying the keys in the front door, Clara stood by the veranda railing and looked up at the Interstate, maybe a half mile away. You can't get on or off it from Webbtown. The nearest inter-change is three miles. But one good thing that happened in the building of the road, they bulldozed Maudie's well and the old brew-house clear out of existence. Clara'd have been thinking of that while I diddled with the lock. I got the door open and she picked up her suitcase before I could do it for her.

The spider webs were thick as lace curtains and you could almost touch the smell in the place, mold and mice and the drain-deep runoff of maybe a million draws of beer. You couldn't see much with the windows boarded up, but when you got used to the twilight you could see enough to move around. A row of keys still hung under numbers one to eight behind the desk. As though any one of them wouldn't open any door in the house. But a key feels good when you're away from home, it's a safe companion.

The stairs went up to a landing and then turned out of sight. Past them on the ground floor was the way to the kitchen and across from that the dining room. To the right where the sliding doors were closed was the lounge. To the left was the barroom where, for over a hundred and fifty years, McCrackens had drawn their own brew. I knew the revenue agent who used to come through during Prohibition. He certified the beer as three-point-two percent alcohol, what we used to call near-beer. The McCracken foam had more kick than three point two.

Clara set her suitcase at the foot of the stairs and went into the barroom. From where I stood I could see her back and then her shape in the backbar mirror and a shadow behind her that kind of scared me until I realized it was myself.

"Hank?" she said.

"I'm here."

She pointed at the moosehead on the wall above the mirror. "That moose has got to go," she said. "That's where I plan to put the television."

I took that in and said, "You got to have a license, Clara, unless you're going to serve soda pop, and I don't think you can get one after being where you were."

I could see her eyes shining in the dark. "You can, Hank, and I'm appointing you my partner."

Clara had done a lot of planning in fifteen years. She'd learned carpentry in prison and enough about plumbing and electric wiring to get things working. I asked her how she'd managed it, being a woman, and she said that was how she'd managed it. Her first days home I brought her necessities up to her from the town. The only person I'd told about her coming out was Prouty, and he's close-mouthed. You couldn't say that for Mrs. Prouty. . . . It's funny how you call most people by their Christian names after you get to know them, and then there's some you wouldn't dare even when you've known them all your life. Even Prouty calls her Mrs. Prouty.

Anyway, she's our one female elder at the Community Church and she was probably the person who put Reverend Barnes onto the sermon he preached the Sunday after Clara's return—all about the scribes and the Pharisees and how no man among them was able to throw the first stone at the woman taken in adultery. Adultery wasn't the problem of either of the McCracken sisters. It was something on the opposite side of human nature, trying to keep upright as the church steeple. But Reverend Barnes is one of those old-time Calvinists who believe heaven is heaven and hell is hell and whichever one you're going to was decided long ago, so the name of the sin don't matter much.

I was hanging a clothesline out back for Clara Monday morning when maybe a dozen women came up the hill to the Red Lantern bearing gifts. I stayed out of sight but I saw afterwards they were things they'd given thought to—symbolic things like canned fish and flour, bread and grape juice, what you might call biblical things. When Clara first saw them coming she went out on the veranda. She crossed her arms and spread her feet and took up a defensive stand in front of the door. The women did a queer thing: they set down what they were carrying, one after the other, and started to applaud. I guess it was the only way they could think of on the spot to show her they meant no ill.

Clara relaxed and gave them a roundhouse wave to come on up. They filed into the inn and before the morning was over they'd decided among themselves who was going to make curtains, who knew how to get mildew out of the bed linens, who'd be best at patching moth holes, things like that. Anne Pendergast went home and got the twins. They were about fourteen, two hellions. She made them scrub out every word that was written on the steps.

During the week I went over to the county seat with Clara to see if she could get a driver's license. I let her drive the Chevy, though I nearly died of a heart attack. She had it kicking like an army mule, but we did get there, and she could say that she'd driven a car lately. I watched with a sick feeling while the clerk made out a temporary permit she could use until her license came. Then, without batting an eye at me, she asked the fellow if he could tell us who to see about applying for a liquor license. He came out into the hall and pointed to the office. Yes, sir. Clara had done a lot of planning in fifteen years.

It was on the way back to Webbtown that she said to me, "Some-body's stolen Pa's shotgun, Hank."

"I got it up at my place, Clara. You sure you want it back?" It was that gun going off that killed Maudie and I guess this is as good a time as any to tell you what happened back then.

Clara was a wild and pretty thing and Maudie was encouraging this middle-aged gent, a paint salesman by the name of Matt Sawyer, to propose to her. This day she took him out in the hills with the shotgun, aiming to have him scare off Reuben White, who was a lot more forward in his courting of Clara. It was Maudie flushed the young ones out of the sheepcote and then shouted at Matt to shoot. She kept shouting it and so upset him that he slammed the gun down. It went off and blew half of Maudie's head away.

I don't think I'm ever going to forget Matt coming into town dragging that gun along the ground and telling us what happened. And I'm absolutely not going to forget going up the hill with Matt and Constable Luke Weber—and Prouty with his wicker basket. Clara came flying to meet us, her gold hair streaming out in the wind like a visiting angel. She just plain threw herself at Matt, saying how she loved him. I told her she ought to behave herself and she told me to hush or I couldn't play fiddle at their wedding. Luke Weber kept asking her where Reuben was and all she'd say in that airy way of hers was, "Gone."

I couldn't look at Maudie without getting sick, so I went to the well and tried to draw water. The bucket kept getting stuck, which was how we came to discover Reuben, head down, feet up, in the well. When the constable asked Clara about it, she admitted right off that she'd pushed him.

Why? Luke wanted to know.

At that point she turned deep serious, those big eyes of hers like blue saucers. "Mr. Weber, you wouldn't believe me if I told you what Reuben White wanted me to do with him in the sheepcote this afternoon. And I just know Matt won't ever want me to do a thing like that." I pleaded her temporarily insane. I might have tried to get her off for defending her virtue—there was some in town who saw it that way—but by the time we came to trial I didn't think it would work with a ten-out-of-twelve male jury.

But to get back to what I was saying about Clara wanting the shotgun back, I advised her not to put it where it used to hang over the fireplace in the bar.

"Don't intend to. I got no place else for the moose head."

I took the gun up to her the next day and it wasn't long after that I learned from Prouty she'd bought a box of shells and some cleaning oil. Prouty wanted to know if there wasn't some law against her having a gun. I said I thought so and we both let it go at that. Clara bought her television from him. The first I heard of her using the gun—only in a manner of speaking—was after she'd bought a used car from a lot on the County Road. It was a Studebaker, a beauty on the outside, and the dealer convinced her it had a heart of gold. The battery fell out first, and after that it was the transmission. She wanted me to go up and talk to him. I did and he told me to read the warranty, which I also did. I told Clara she was stuck with a bad bargain.

"Think so, Hank?"

The next thing I heard, she got Anne Pendergast and the twins to tow the Studebaker and her back to the used-car lot. The two women sent the boys home and then sat in Clara's car until the dealer finally came out to them. "Like I told your lawyer, lady, it's too bad but . . ." He said something like that, according to Anne, and Clara stopped him right there. "I got me another lawyer," she said and jerked her thumb toward the back seat, where the old shotgun lay shining like it had just come off the hunters' rack in Prouty's. Anne asked him if he'd ever heard of Clara McCracken.

Seemed like he had, for when Clara drove up to where I was painting the Red Lantern sign she was behind the wheel of a red Chevy roadster with a motor that ran like a tomcat's purr.

"How much?" I wanted to know. Her funds were going down fast.

She opened the rumble seat and took out the shotgun. "One round of shot," she said. "That's about fifteen cents."

I didn't say anything in the town about the partnership I'd drawn up so that Clara could reopen the bar in the Red Lantern. For one thing, I wasn't sure when we'd get the license if we got it, even though Clara was moving full steam ahead. For another thing, I had to stop dropping in at Tuttle's Tavern in competition, even though it was a mighty limited partnership I had with Clara. I didn't want to be an innkeeper and it riled that McCracken pride of hers to have to go outside the family after a hundred and fifty years. We wound up agreeing I was to be a silent partner. I was to have all the beer I could drink free. That wasn't going to cost her much. Even in the days of Maudie's Own Brew, I never drank more than a couple of steins in one night's sitting.

The license came through midsummer along with instructions that it was to be prominently displayed on the premises at all times. Clara framed it and hung it where you'd have needed a pair of binoculars to see what it was. By then the rooms upstairs had been aired out, the curtains hung, and all the mattresses and pillows treated to a week in the sun. Downstairs, the lounge was open to anybody willing to share it with a horde of insects. Prouty had ordered her some of those fly-catching dangles you string up on the lightbulbs, but they hadn't come yet. What came with miraculous speed was a pretty fair order of whiskeys and half dozen kegs of beer with all the tapping equipment. I asked Clara how she decided on which brewery she was going to patronize.

She said the girls advised her.

And, sure enough, when I spoke to Prouty about it later he said, "So that's why Mrs. Prouty was asking what my favorite beer was. Didn't make sense till now. We ain't had a bottle of beer in the house since she got on the board of elders."

"Didn't you ask her what she wanted to know for?"

"Nope. I wanted to be surprised when the time came."

I suppose it was along about then I began to get a little niggling tinkle in my head about how friendly Clara and the women were. Most of those girls she spoke of were women ranging from thirty to eighty-five years old.

Going across the street and up the stairs to my office over Kincaid's Drugstore, I counted on my fingers this one and that of them I'd seen up there since Clara came home. I ran out of fingers and I'd have run out of toes as well if I'd included them.

Jesse Tuttle was sitting in my office waiting for me, his chair tilted back against the wall. I don't lock up in the daytime and the day I have to I'll take down my shingle. I felt funny, seeing Tuttle and feeling the way I did about competing with him, so as soon as we shook hands I brought things right out into the open. "I hope you don't take it personal, Jesse, that I'm helping Clara McCracken get a fresh start."

Jesse's a big, good-natured man with a belly that keeps him away from the bar, if you know what I mean. It don't seem to keep him away from Suzie. They got nine kids and a couple more on the hillside. "I know it's not personal, Hank, but it's not what you'd call friendly, either. I was wondering for a while if there was something personal between you and her, but the fellas talked me out of that idea."

I don't laugh out loud much, but I did then. "Jesse, I'm an old rooster," I said, "and I haven't noticed if a hen laid an egg in God knows how long."

"That's what we decided, but there's one thing you learn in my business: don't take anything a man says about himself for gospel.

Even if he's telling the truth, it might as well be a lie, for all you know listening to him. Same thing in your business, ain't that so?"

"Wouldn't need witnesses if it wasn't," I said.

I settled my backside on the edge of the desk and he straightened up the chair. I'd been waiting for it to collapse, all the weight on its hind legs. He folded his arms. "What's going on up there, Hank?"

"Well, from what she said the last time we talked, she plans to open officially when the threshing combine comes through." We do as much farming in Ragapoo County as anything else, just enough to get by on. But we grow our own grain, and the harvest is a pretty big occasion.

"She figures on putting the crew up, does she?"

"She's got those eight rooms all made up and waiting. She got to put somebody in them. I can't see her getting the cross-country traffic to drop off the Interstate."

Tuttle looked at me with a queer expression on his face. "You don't think she'd be figuring to run a house up there?"

"A bawdy house?"

Tuttle nodded.

I shook my head. "No, sir. I think that's the last thing Clara'd have in mind."

"I mean playing a joke on us, paying us back for her having to go to prison."

"I just don't see it, Jesse. Besides, look at all your womenfolk flocking up there to give her a hand."

"That's what I am looking at," he said.

Every step creaked as he lumbered down the stairs. I listened to how quiet it was with him gone. I couldn't believe Jesse was a mean man. He wouldn't start a rumor if he didn't think there was something to back it up with. Not just for business. We don't do things like that in Webbtown, I told myself. We're too close to one another for any such shenanigans. And I had to admit I wouldn't put it past a McCracken to play the town dirty if she thought the town had done it to her first. I certainly wouldn't have put it past Maudie. There was something that kind of bothered me about what was taking place in my own head: I kept mixing up the sisters. It was like Maudie was the one who had come back.

Clara drove eighty miles across two counties to intercept the threshing combine—ten men and some mighty fancy equipment that crisscross the state this time every year. She took Anne Pendergast and Mary Toomey with her. Mary's a first cousin of Prouty's. And on the other side of the family she was related to Reuben White, something Prouty called my attention to. Reuben's folks moved away after the trial. It wasn't so much grief as shame. I didn't like doing it, but it's a lawyer's job, and I painted the boy as pretty much a dang fool to have got himself killed that way.

The women came home late afternoon. I saw them driving along Main Street after collecting all the Pendergast kids into the rumble seat. Anne had farmed them out for the day. I headed for the Red Lantern to see what happened. Clara was pleased as jubilee: the combine crew had agreed to route themselves so as to spend Saturday night in Webbtown.

"And they'll check into the Red Lantern?" I said. Ordinarily they split up among the farmers they serviced and knocked off five percent for their keep.

"Every last man. Barbecue Saturday night, Hank."

"What if it rains?"

"I got Mrs. Prouty and Faith Barnes working on it—the minister's wife?"

"I know who Faith Barnes is," I said, sour as pickle brine. The only reassuring thing I felt about the whole situation was that Mrs. Prouty was still Mrs. Prouty.

I came around. The whole town did. Almost had to, the women taking the lead right off. Clara invited everybody, at two dollars a head for adults, fifty cents for kids under twelve. All you could eat and free beer, but you paid for hard liquor. I recruited young Tommy Kincaid and a couple of his chums to dig the barbecue pits with me. Prouty supervised. Mrs. Prouty supervised the loan and transfer of tables and benches from the parish house. They used the Number One Hook and Ladder to move them, and I never before knew a truck to go out of the firehouse on private business except at Christmastime when they take Jesse Tuttle up and down Main Street in his Santa Claus getup.

Saturday came as clear a day as when there were eagles in the Ragapoo Hills. Right after lunch the town youngsters hiked up to the first lookout on the Country Road. It reminded me of when I was a kid myself and a genuine circus would come round that bend and down through the town. I'd expected trouble from the teenage crowd, by the way, with Clara coming home. You know the way they like to scare themselves half out of their wits with stories of murder and haunted houses. The Red Lantern seemed like fair game for sure. Maybe the Pendergast twins took the curse off the place when they scrubbed the steps, I thought, and then I knew right off: it was their mothers who set down the law on how they'd behave toward Clara. In any case, it would have taken a lot of superstition to keep them from enjoying the harvest holiday.

Along about four o'clock the cry came echoing down the valley, "They're coming! They're coming!" And sure enough, like some prefabricated monster, the combine hove into view. Tractors and wagons followed, stopping to let the kids climb aboard. Behind them were the farmers' pleasure cars, women and children and some of the menfolk, dressed, you'd have thought, for the Fourth of July. The only ones left behind came as soon as the cows were let out after milking.

There was a new register on the desk and one man after another of the harvesters signed his name, picked up the key, and took his duffel bag upstairs. They came down to shower in the basement, and for a while there you couldn't get more than a trickle out of any other tap in the house. By the time they were washed up, half the town had arrived. I never saw our women looking prettier, and I kept saying to myself, gosh darn Tuttle for putting mischief in my mind. Even Clara, with color now in her cheeks, looked less like Maudie and more like the Clara I used to know.

The corn was roasting and the smell of barbecued chickens and ribs had the kids with their paper plates dancing in and out of line. There were mounds of Molly Kincaid's potato salad and crocks full of home-baked beans, great platters of sliced beefsteak tomatoes, fresh bread, and a five-pound jar of sweet butter Clara ordered from the Justin farm, delivered by Nellie Justin. Clara sent her to me to be paid her three dollars, but Nellie said to let it take care of her and Joe and the kids for the barbecue. Neither one of us was good at arithmetic. Peach and apple pies which any woman in town might have baked were aplenty and you can't believe what a peach pie's like baked with peaches so ripe you catch them dropping off the trees.

It was along about twilight with the men stretched out on the grass and the women sitting round on benches or on the veranda, dangling their feet over the side, when I tuned up my fiddle and sawed a few notes in front of the microphone. I never was amplified before and I don't expect to be again, but Dick Moran who teaches history, English, and music at the high school set up a system he'd been tinkering with all summer and brought along his own guitar. We made a lot of music, with everybody clapping and joining in. Real old-fashioned country. You might say people danced by the light of the moon—it was up there—but we had lantern light as well. I'd called round that morning and asked the farmers for the loan of the lanterns they use going out to chores on winter mornings. And when it finally came time for these same farmers to go home, they took their lanterns with them. One by one, the lights disappeared like fireflies, fading away until the only outdoor light was over the hotel entrance, and it was entertaining a crowd of moths and June bugs, gnats and mosquitoes.

Most people who lived in town weren't set on going home yet. Tuttle had closed up for the evening, not being a man to miss a good meal, but he said he thought he'd go down now and open up the tavern. Tuttle's Tavern never was a place the women folk liked to go, but now they said so right out loud.

Without even consulting me, Clara announced I'd fiddle in the lounge for a while. The women took to the idea straight off and set about arrangements. The old folks, who'd had about enough, gathered the kids and took them home. The teenagers went someplace with their amplifying history teacher and his guitar. The men, after hemming and hawing and beginning to feel out of joint, straggled down to Tuttle's. By this time the harvesters, with their bright-colored shirts and fancy boots, were drinking boilermakers in the bar. I didn't like it, but they were the only ones Clara was making money on, and she kept pouring. Prouty hung around for a while, helping move furniture. I asked him to stay, but he must have sneaked away while I was tuning up.

It gave me a funny feeling to see those women dancing all by themselves. I don't know why exactly. Kind of a waste, I suppose. But they sure didn't mind, flying and whirling one another and laughing in that high musical trill you don't often hear from women taught to hold themselves in. A funny feeling, I say, and yet something woke up in me that had been a long time sleeping.

Clara came across the hall from the taproom now and then, hauling one of the harvesters by the arm and kind of pitched him into the dance. His buddies would come to the door and whoop and holler and maybe get pulled in themselves. I kept thinking of my chums, sulking down at Tuttle's. I also thought Clara was wasting a lot of the good will she'd won with the barbecue. Man and wife were going to have to crawl into bed alongside each other sometime during the night.

Along about midnight Clara announced that it was closing time. Everybody gave a big cheer for Hank. It was going to take more than a big cheer to buoy me up by then. I could've wrung out my shirt and washed myself in my own sweat.

I couldn't swear that nothing bawdy happened the whole night. Those harvesters had been a long time from home and some of our women were feeling mighty free. But I just don't think it did, and I'll tell you why: Clara, when she pronounced it was closing time, was carrying a long birch switch, the kind that whistles when you slice the air with it, and the very kind Maudie had taken to Reuben White one night when he danced too intimate with Clara.

I was shivering when I went down to bed. I thought of stopping by Tuttle's, but the truth was I didn't even want to know if he was still open. I'd kept hoping some of the men would come back up to the Red Lantern, but nobody did. I did a lot of tossing and turning, and I couldn't have been long asleep when the fire siren sounded. I hadn't run with the engines for a long time, but I was out of the house and heading for the Red Lantern before the machines left the firehouse. I just knew if there was trouble that's where it was.

I didn't see any smoke or fire when I got to the drive, but Luke Weber, our same constable, waved me off the road. I parked and started hiking through the grass. The fire trucks were coming. I started to run. When I got almost to where we'd dug the barbecue pits, something caught my ankle and I fell flat to the ground. Somebody crawled up alongside me.

"It's Bill Pendergast, Hank. Just shut up and lie low."

I couldn't have laid much lower.

The fire trucks screamed up the drive, their searchlights playing over the building, where, by now, lights were going on in all the upstairs rooms.

Pendergast said, "Let's go," and switched on his flashlight.

A couple of minutes later I saw maybe a half dozen other flashes playing over the back and side doors to the inn. By the time I got around front, Clara was standing on the veranda with the fire chief. She was wearing a negligee you could've seen daylight through if there'd been daylight. The harvesters were coming downstairs in their underwear. A couple of the volunteer firemen rushed up the stairs, brandishing their hatchets and their torches.

By then I'd figured out what was happening, and it made me sick, no matter what Tuttle and them others thought they were going to flush out with the false alarm. Not a woman came down those stairs or any other stairs or out any window. They did come trooping down the County Road, about a dozen of them. Instead of going home when Clara closed, they'd climbed to where they could see the whole valley in the moonlight. The fire chief apologized for the invasion as though it had been his fault.

"I hope you come that fast," Clara said, "when there's more fire than smoke."

I was up at the Red Lantern again on Sunday afternoon when the harvesters moved on, heading for their next setup in the morning. Clara bought them a drink for the road. One of them, a strapping fellow I might have thrown a punch at otherwise, patted Clara's behind when she went to the door with them. She jumped and then stretched her mouth in something like a smile. I listened to them say how they'd be back this way in hunting season. They all laughed at that, and I felt I was missing something. When one of them tried to give me five bucks for the fiddling, I just walked away. But I watched to see if any extra money passed between them and Clara. That negligee was hanging in my mind.

A few nights later I stopped by Tuttle's. I figured that since I'd laid low with the fellows I might as well stand at the bar with them, at least for half my drinking time. I walked in on a huddle at the round table where there's a floating card game going on most times. But they weren't playing cards and they looked at me as though I'd come to collect the mortgage. I turned and started to go out again.

"Hey, Hank, come on back here," Pendergast called. "Only you got to take your oath along with the rest of us never to let on what we're talking about here tonight."

"What's the general subject?" I asked.

"You know as well as we do," Jesse Tuttle said.

"I reckon." I stuck my right hand in the air as though the Bible was in my left.

"We were going to draw straws," Pendergast said, "but Billy Baldwin here just volunteered."

I pulled up a chair, making the ninth or tenth man, and waited to hear what Baldwin had volunteered to do. I haven't mentioned him before because there wasn't reason, even though Nancy Baldwin was one of the women that came whooping down the road after the fire alarm. Billy wasn't the most popular man in town—kind of a braggart and boring as a magpie. Whenever anybody had an idea, Billy had a better one, and he hardly ever stopped talking. The bus route he was driving at the time ran up-county, starting from the Courthouse steps, so he had to take his own car to and from his job at different times of day and night. By now you've probably guessed what he'd volunteered for.

I made it a point to stay away from the Red Lantern the night he planned to stop there. I got to admit, though, I was as curious as the rest of the bunch to learn how he'd make out with Clara, so I hung around Tuttle's with them. The funny thing was, I was the last man in the place. Long before closing time, Pendergast, then Prouty, then Kincaid, all of them dropped out and went home to their own beds. Tuttle locked up behind me.

The next day Baldwin stopped by the tavern on the way to work and told Jesse that nothing happened, that he'd just sat at the bar with Clara, talking and working up to things. "The big shot's getting chicken," Pendergast said when Tuttle passed the word.

None of us said much. Counting chickens. I know I was.

Well, it was a week before Billy Baldwin came in with his verdict. As far as he could tell, Clara McCracken might still be a virgin, he said. He'd finally come right out and slipped a twenty-dollar bill on the bar the last night and asked her to wear the negligee she'd had on the night of the false alarm. At that point, Clara reached for the birch stick behind the bar and he took off, leaving the money where it was.

"You're lucky she didn't reach for the shotgun," Prouty said.

We all chipped in to make up the twenty dollars.

Things quieted down after that and I continued to split my drinking time between Tuttle's and the Red Lantern. Clara would get the occasional oiler coming through to check the pumps, and the duck- and deer-hunting seasons were good business, but she never did get much of the town custom, and the rumors about her and that negligee hung on. It wasn't the sort of gear you sent away to Sears Roebuck for, but the post office in Webbtown was run by a woman then and I don't think any of us ever did find out where that particular garment came from. Maybe she'd sent away for it while she was still in prison. Like I said early on, Clara had done a lot of planning in fifteen years.

Now I just said things quieted down. To tell the truth, it was like the quiet before a twister comes through. I know I kept waiting and watching Clara, and Clara watched me watching her. One day she asked me what they were saying about her in the town.

I tried to make a joke of it. "Nothing much. They're getting kind of used to you, Clara."

She looked at me with a cold eye. "You in on that Billy Baldwin trick?"

I thought about the oath I was supposed to have sworn. "What trick?" I asked.

"Hank," she said, "for a lawyer you ain't much of a liar."

"I ain't much of a lawyer, either," I said. Then, looking her straight in the face, sure as fate straighter than I looked at myself, I said, "Clara, how'd you like to marry me?"

She set back on her heels and smiled in that odd way of having to work at it. "Thank you kindly." She cast her eyes up toward the license, which I'd just about forgotten. "We got one partnership going and I think that ought to do us—but I do thank you, old Hank."

I've often wondered what I'd have done if she'd said yes.

But I've come around since to holding with the Reverend Barnes. Everything was set in its course long before it happened—including Clara's planning.

September passed, October, and in came the full, cold moon of November. You could hear wolves in the Ragapoo Hills and the loons—and which is lonesomer-sounding I wouldn't say. I've mentioned before how light a sleeper I am. I woke up this night to a kind of whispering sound, a sort of swish, a pause, and then another swish, a pause, and then another. When I realized it was outside my window, I got up and looked down on the street.

There, passing in the silvery moonlight—a few feet between them (I think now to keep from speaking to one another)—the women of the town were moving toward the Red Lantern. By the time I got within sight of them up there, they'd formed a half circle around the front of the inn which was in total darkness. One of the women climbed the steps and went inside. I knew the door had not been locked since I unlocked it when I brought Clara home.

I kept out of sight and edged round back to where I had been the night of the false alarm. I saw the car parked there and knew it belonged to Billy Baldwin. If I could have found a way in time, I'd have turned in a false alarm myself, but I was frozen in slow motion. I heard the scream and the clatter in the building, and the front door banging open. Billy Baldwin came running out stark naked. He had some of his clothes with him, but he hadn't waited to put them on. Behind him was his wife Nancy, sobbing and crying and beating at him until one of the women came up and took her away down toward the town.

Billy had stopped in his tracks, seeing the circle of women. He was pathetic, trying to hide himself first and then trying to put his pants on, and the moonlight throwing crazy shadows on the women. Then I saw Clara come out the door on my side of the building. She was wearing the negligee and sort of drifted like a specter around the veranda to the front.

The women began to move forward.

Billy, seeing them come, fell on his knees and held out his hands, begging. I started to pray myself. I saw that every woman was carrying a stone. They kept getting closer, but not a one raised her arm until Clara went down and picked up a stone from her own drive, which she flung at Billy.

He was still on his knees after that, but he fell almost at once beneath the barrage that followed. One of those stones killed him dead, though I didn't know it at the time.

Clara went back up the steps and picked her way through the stones. She kicked at what was left of poor, lying, cheating Billy as hard as she could. The women found more stones then, and threw them at her until she fled into the inn and closed the door.

Nobody's been arrested for Billy's murder. I don't think anyone ever will be. It ought to be Clara, if anyone, but I'd have to bear witness that the man was still alive after she'd thrown the stone. She's never forgiven the women for turning on her. She kept telling me how glad she was when they came to take Billy in adultery. And I wore myself out asking her what the heck she thought she was doing.

Along toward summer a baby boy was born to Clara. She had him christened Jeremiah McCracken after his grandfather. At the christening she said to me, "See, Hank. That's what I was doing." I'm going to tell you, I'm glad that when Jeremiah McCracken comes old enough to get a tavern license, I'll be in my grave by then. I hope of natural causes.

*Mary Shura Craig says that she ". . . loathes repetition and loves challenge." Prolific and always up to something, Mary is a whirl-wind. She's been a recipient of the award for Distinguished Contri-bution to Children's Literature, the Pine Tree Award, and the Carl Sandburg Award. Her list of mystery and suspense books, many of which were written for young readers, includes* Flash Point, The Third Blonde, The Sunday Doll, Don't Call Me Toad, *and* The Silent Witness. *Her pseudonyms (Mary Francis Shura, Meredith Hill, Emily Chase, M. F. Craig) cover more than fifty-seven books.*

*In "Caesar and Sleep" (definitely not a tale for the kiddies) a chill lurks in the background from the very start. As the threat deepens, the chill turns downright icy in this tale of love and death.*

# CAESAR AND SLEEP

## by Mary Shura Craig

THEY DECIDED THEY needed a dog the year the daughter, Mela-nie, turned seventeen. Melanie went out a lot the way high-school girls do, and the mother was afraid to go to sleep alone on that hill the way things were with the violence and all.

And, of course, the father traveled.

The three of them went together to select the animal. They were all self-conscious, not having joined in any single endeavor for a long time.

There were six pups in the litter, and the bitch was frantic with concern. The arch of her body hung with swollen teats like a young tree overburdened with fruit. The breeder restrained her while they examined the pups, but the shrill desperation of the bitch's complaint stained the mother's mind for a long time.

The breeder blathered on about which pups were pet stock and which ones had promise of show quality, but the mother's mind was made up from the first. She wanted Caesar. His name came to her just like that, when he staggered to her, nuzzling her nylons, and splaying his exaggerated feet against her legs, begging to be picked up.

The father had a different kind of dog in mind, something smaller maybe, he himself wasn't sure.

"If you insist on getting a Doberman," he warned her, "you'll have to have his ears fixed, his tail cropped."

"I know all that," she replied hotly, holding the warm folds of the puppy against her chest. She knew if she answered him in that tone, he would give in.

From the very first, Caesar was her own dog. Whenever she stopped her work, even for a minute, to catch a show on TV or sit down with the paper, Caesar was right there. He usually lay with his head on one of her shoes so that even if he fell asleep, he would know the moment she moved.

She never felt lonely after Caesar came, even though nothing else was really changed about their lives. She would still be working off alone while the other two, Melanie and her father, were laughing together or deep in some quiet, head-to-head conversation. But Caesar always stayed with her.

The mother signed up to take Caesar for obedience training and posted the class schedule on the kitchen bulletin board. The very first night she took him away, Melanie pulled what the mother called "one of those smart ones." The mother came home to find her house throbbing with rock music that spilled even out into the driveway. The living-room lights were turned off, but the room was filled with bare-legged girls and those hairy boys they liked. When she unlocked the door to come in, there was a lot of scrambling, but none of the disheveled young people seemed breathless from dancing.

Caesar had never shown the least sign of aggressiveness before. He braced his feet there in the foyer, lunging against the choke chain she had bought for obedience class. When he bared his teeth in a threatening puppy snarl, the mother was amused in spite of her annoyance at Melanie. Caesar felt the same way she did about the way those young people were behaving.

"My friends just dropped in," Melanie said, her eyes challenging on her mother's face. "Is there something wrong with friends just dropping in?"

The mother returned her stare and dragged the snarling puppy past them to the kitchen to feed the animal his evening meal. She didn't take Caesar back for any more training but stayed home where she could keep an eye on things.

Melanie's grades didn't qualify her for the university, but she did go away to college. The mother was glad. Suddenly she had long days with just herself and Caesar. Some nights she couldn't even remember where the hours had gone but only that she had been content.

Sometimes no human voice sounded in the house all day. She moved silently on her tennis shoes with Caesar padding along quietly behind her. The stridence of the outside spoke through the open windows, distant traffic sounds, the occasional wail of a siren, the complaint of a truck's motor toiling up that hill. The inside sounds were furtive, the hum of the refrigerator coming on, or the bumbling of a fly that spun in when the doors were open.

Caesar chased the flies until he trapped them against the glass of the sliding doors. She watched him paw them to a streak and wiped the blood away with a piece of paper toweling.

One of the few things she brought home from her mother's house after the funeral was the Waterford sherry decanter that her mother had always kept filled by her easy chair.

"I don't know what you want that thing for," her husband said, eyeing it with revulsion. "That's like saving the bullet that killed someone."

"What are you trying to say?" she asked, clutching the decanter in her lap with both hands.

"It's just that I can't imagine your wanting it around to remind you."

"Are you saying my mother was a lush?"

He shrugged and attempted lightness. "Let's just say that she stumbled a lot and didn't finish sentences."

Later she told herself that she would never have started keeping the decanter filled if he hadn't said that. But she did keep it filled and drank a glass now and then, sometimes in the morning before she took Caesar out on his chain. The wind blew cold on that hill, and the sherry glowed in her chest like an inner poultice. By the time they got to the crest of the hill, she would feel rosy and alive, enjoying everything, the way the trees clung to the rocks for life, the angle of a hawk playing its skill against the updraft.

\* \* \*

For some reason after Melanie went away to college, the father started giving things up. He quit drinking anything at home, not even having a beer with his sandwich when the day was hot. He quit smoking too.

"I read the papers," he explained. "Life is too good to send up in smoke."

She wondered what he found so good about life. He packed the same suitcase over and over and took airplanes away. He came home and ate stolidly before going to sleep in his chair in front of the TV. When she returned with Caesar from the late walk, he rose, scratched himself, and lurched into his bed to sleep like a stone.

He never turned to her anymore in that old, fumbling, jocular way. She wanted to ask him if he had given up sex, too, along with the booze and cigarettes, but when she framed the words in her mind, they sounded acid and mean. The loss of lovemaking was too painful to put into words, anyway. She lay beside him, trembling with longing and bitter anger that he could make her so miserable in his sleep, his eternal, rhythmic sleep.

The only good thing in *her* life was Caesar. She saw his beauty reflected in the eyes of strangers when she took him with her to the shopping centers. Because he wasn't friendly, no one ever tried to pet him, but she saw them admiring the chocolate-and-sable gleam of his coat, the slender, sensual grace of his body. And he always stayed so close to her that his warmth against her thigh made him an extension of herself.

She hated mirrors. She couldn't confront the unsmiling deterioration of her own face, the pulpy pallor of her overblown body. She never looked at mirrors at all, but pulled a brush through her hair or leaned way over to clean her teeth without raising her eyes. Caesar was beautiful for both of them.

And he was strong. She didn't realize how strong he was until he got away from her on an evening walk. The summer dusk had come slowly. She had drunk more sherry than she meant to before taking Caesar out. They left the road and cut through the woods to get the view to the west. She watched her step carefully, her head spinning a little from the extra wine.

She and Caesar were on the couple before they realized they were there. Just seeing the writhing whiteness of their twined bodies and smelling the licorice scent of the crushed weeds under them made her breath come short. Caesar lunged at them, almost tearing her arm from her body. She jerked the chain and strained against his weight, but it was too late. The woman was screaming and the man cursing wildly. Even in that dim light she saw the flesh of the man's thigh gushing blood all over both of them.

The man leapt to his feet, grabbed a stick, and flew at Caesar. Somehow she managed to pull the dog away and hold him back, even though Caesar was coughing and spitting foam from the pressure of the chain.

"Jesus," the man repeated over and over, as if he didn't believe his own blood that he was sopping at with his shirt. The girl or woman, or whatever she was, had covered her face with her dress and huddled there. crying monotonously.

"We won't press charges or anything," the man said, his voice raddled with shock. "But you better look after that damned dog. You just better look after him, I'm telling you."

The excitement and the sherry and her relief that the man wasn't going to press charges made her even giddier as they walked back home.

But indignant too. They had to be sinning up there on that hill or they would have pressed charges against Caesar. Why, she bet that girl had no more right to lie down with that man than she had herself. The thought made her flushed and restless all that night.

As she cleaned the blood from Caesar's jaws she tried to think of some way to tell her husband what had happened. She couldn't think of any way to phrase the story that didn't sound triumphant. In the end she bought a muzzle for Caesar to wear on their walks and never mentioned it to him at all.

Caesar didn't like the muzzle any better than he did the choke chain. She used them both, anyway. If anything took Caesar away from her, she had no reason to live herself.

Sometimes she wondered if the man had talked around privately. When she had Caesar in the shopping center or walked him along the village street, people acted warier than before. "That's fine with us," she told Caesar. "Let them keep their distance. We don't need anybody."

Sometimes she couldn't keep enough distance, anyway. Tradesmen were careless. Every once in a while a clerk making change brushed her hand with his. She always shuddered and felt a painful rush of blood to her head. It had been so long since a hand had touched her in tenderness that the very thought of two humans pressing warm, moist flesh together brought something acid and nauseous up into the back of her throat. She took to wearing leather gloves whenever she was out. People looked at her gloves curiously, except when she was with Caesar. Let them think she was protecting herself from the tug of that metal chain. It was none of their business, anyway.

There had been a time when the father called home during his travels. After Melanie left, they had so little to say to each other that he stopped that. Instead he left a yellow memo on the bulletin board. It showed where he could be reached and when she should expect him back. She didn't really care where he had gone, but she did check to see when to expect him home. If she had thought about it, she might have figured out that he kept Melanie informed of his whereabouts too.

When she heard the car in the drive that Thursday evening, she sat up in terror. The yellow sheet said he was due on Friday. Who would be coming into the drive like that on a Thursday evening? Caesar raged against the door as she pulled back the curtain to look out. Without a moon she couldn't be sure it was his car. She waited, breathless, for the bell to ring. When she heard the key in the lock, she slipped the choke chain on Caesar, her mind wild with questions. The dog had never threatened him, but she couldn't be sure, not the way he was carrying on.

Her husband stood in the doorway indecisively, as if he were not sure he was in the right place.

"You're home a day early." It came out sounding like an accusation, and she hadn't meant it that way at all.

"Fasten up that dog," he said. "I need to talk to you."

"He's not going to hurt you," she protested, still holding Caesar's chain because he was acting strange, his legs set wide and his eyes just slits watching the figure in the doorway.

"Fasten him up," he repeated. "I'm not alone."

When she returned to the living room, her husband was still standing, and Melanie was there beside him. She wanted to challenge the girl, to ask why she was here instead of off at college where she had been sent. The look on her husband's face held her words back.

"We could sit down," he suggested after a minute.

The mother pushed her coat off a chair and sat down. Melanie looked around helplessly before clearing a space for herself beside her father on the divan. The place looked a mess, but it was only clutter.

"Mother," Melanie spoke swiftly, staring down at her lap. Her face seemed to weave, getting indistinct and fuzzy. She looked much older than her mother could ever remember her looking.

The husband laid his hand on Melanie's bare knee, and the mother winced. "Maybe I should explain," he said. "Melanie has a problem."

"I'm pregnant," Melanie announced, her tone aggressive. "I'm caught with a baby."

The mother watched the room sway lazily, the way Melanie's face was swaying this. She was not hearing this. She was making it up in the skrimble-skramble of a bad dream.

"But we have it all worked out," the father went on.

"Worked out?" The mother stared at him, Not even in a dream would her mind do that! Melanie had been a baby with moist creases. She had smelled of powder and her arms had clung.

"The arrangements are all made. It's not dangerous the way it used to be. By the next day she won't feel a thing."

They weren't telling her the obvious things. Who was the father? What about the child? She didn't realize she had asked the last question aloud until her husband answered flatly, "There won't be a child."

"That's murder," the mother whispered.

"Nobody wants a child," Melanie said in a weary tone. "I don't. He doesn't. Daddy doesn't."

"But what about the child? What does it want?" The mother heard her own voice rising, but it didn't matter.

Melanie pushed her hair back from her face. "Peace," she said. "The blessed peace of sleep."

"I'll have no part of murder," the mother warned.

"We didn't come to ask you," the father said. "We came to tell you."

With Caesar fastened away, she was alone against them. They were a double set of eyes defying her, accusing her. Of what? She was pure. She was decent. Yet they accused her with their eyes. She spit her fury out in a foam of words. "Whore! Bitch! Nasty little strumpet!"

Her husband was swift across the room. His slap left her face blazing with pain. The touch of his flesh on hers made green horror gather behind her palate. She must have cried out because Caesar, behind the door, burst into a frenzy of barking and clawing. She rose and went to him, leaving the two of them standing there together as always.

She soothed the dog and lay on her bed with his long, fine head across her chest. He was still watching her eyes when she drifted off to sleep. Caesar awakened her, whining to go out. It was very dark and late, and he was desperate. When she staggered to her feet and opened the door, Melanie and her father were gone.

The flesh of her cheek was stiff and painful. The pain had leaked down to her neck, leaving it stiff. She didn't even dress, but bolted a glass of sherry for the pain and set off with Caesar across the road and into the woods he liked best.

As soon as the chill wind struck her, she remembered the choke chain and the muzzle back on the peg inside the door. Caesar was already across the road and running. She stumbled after him, trying to keep him in sight.

The boys had camped in a low, grassy place between two hillocks. She saw the dim outline of their tent and the coals of their fire. Two of the boys were wrestling, twisting together with all their strength, grunting in primitive combat, each trying to bring the other to his knees. The fire glowed on their flesh with a hellish, rosy luster. Behind them, two other boys watched eagerly, egging them on. Caesar lunged toward them, frantically barking.

"Caesar," she screamed, clutching at her robe. "Down, Caesar, down. Come back."

The tableau froze before her eyes. One boy was wearing something embroidered around his forehead, above a blunt nose and a sprinkle of freckles. His eyes were as blue as if the sky hung there inside his head. He stared at her, and then at Caesar. He would have turned and run, but Caesar was too swift. The child fell and twisted on the green as Caesar burrowed and gnashed at his throat.

She didn't even know where she grabbed the cudgel from. Its rough bark scraped the palm of her hand. She heard her own wail as she struck Caesar's head. She felt the sick cracking of his skull under her blow and moaned her loss. His dainty feet, as slender as fuchsia blossoms, curled a little as he crumpled in the grass. He jerked only once before lying still.

The other boys stood openmouthed, too horrified to move. They stared at her, waiting for her to be the adult, to do the things a grown-up would do about the freckled boy lying there in that untidy, silent way with his blood leaking onto the grass.

"The child wants peace," Melanie had said. "The peace of sleep."

She lifted Caesar into her arms. Staggering a little from his weight and the awkwardness of his long legs, she carried him back home, not looking back even once. The moment she turned, the boys began screaming, an offense in the air that vibrated around her until she closed her door on the night.

Her own house looked strange to her, as if she were seeing it through a lens battered from too much seeing. It was a cold house, an unkempt house. Her bed, half visible in the room beyond, was a rumpled mass of restless dreams. Caesar was cold in her arms. She thought of Melanie's child, hanging head down in a womb that rejected it.

With Caesar at peace near the foot of her bed where he always slept, she went to the kitchen and mixed a paste in the custard cup. Because it was too thick to swallow, she softened it with sherry and drank it standing over the sink, staring into the darkness beyond her window. She kept refilling her sherry glass and drinking it down quickly to cut the burning in her throat. She staggered against the walls, getting to the bedroom to lie down beside Caesar.

The police found her after they talked to the parents of the freckled boy. Of course it was too late. Even then it took two more days to find the husband, who had taken a short trip somewhere with their daughter.

Throughout all the questioning and the taking down of tedious details, the daughter just sat there, pale as a rag, letting people walk past her face without seeing them, as if she were sleeping with her eyes open.

The father answered their questions quietly enough, but he kept trying to twist the unspeakable into frames of reason. "We always kept that poison," he said. "Everybody does. You sign for it and paint it along the door sills to keep out ants."

As to the alcohol in her system, he took small umbrage at their questions. "She had a child of her own," he reminded them. "What did you expect after seeing that child with his flesh all torn and bleeding, her being a mother herself?"

When the questions were all answered, the father took the daughter, still staring straight ahead, back up the hill road to sleep.

*Although Dorothy Cannell was born in England, she has earned the right to be included as an American by virtue of living in that quint-essentially American town, Peoria, Illinois, for nearly twenty-five years. Dorothy's* The Thin Woman *delighted mystery fans in 1984. Ellie and Ben Haskell, now married, return in* The Widow's Club, *along with Hyacinth and Primrose Tramwell, who first appeared in* Down the Garden Path. *One of Dorothy's trademarks is her humor, at once gentle and deliciously wicked.*

*In "Come to Grandma," a young mother is haunted by family tensions that she wishes she could lay to rest.*

# COME TO GRANDMA

## by Dorothy Cannell

EMMA RICHWOODS HAD never adored her mother-in-law, but she would have proffered a polite welcome, had circumstances been different. At thirty-five, Emma had just given birth to her first child, and now comes the heart of the problem: mother-in-law Mildred had been dead almost six years.

Emma, a successful C.P.A., in partnership with her husband, Howard, was not subject to imagination. Her appearance—trim, tailored, dark hair brought up in a smooth knot, horn-rimmed glasses—bespoke her dislike of excess. Spiritualism was the stuff of which late-night horror movies were made, and the Richwoods always turned off the TV immediately following the ten-o'clock news in order to spend quality time with their portfolios. One of the oddest things about the situation was that rational Emma never considered the rational explanation—that her visitor was a manifestation of post-partum depression.

Mildred had made herself quite at home in the white-on-white apartment when the Richwoods returned from Community Hospital with baby Kathleen. She was camped in front of the TV watching a game show. Her hair—still done in spit curls—needed a tint, and her glasses—those vulgar checkerboard frames—were held together at one temple with masking tape. The only visible difference from her former self appeared to be that she wasn't breathing.

"Surprise! It's me, the late Mildred." She uncrossed her polyester legs, revealing that she had helped herself to a pair of Howard's designer socks. "And to think I was never late—not once in my whole damn life! Strange . . . !" She squinted around. "Seem to remember leaving you my grade-school and high-school perfect-attendance diplomas. Don't see them prominently displayed, Em. Guess they don't go with that picture of tire tracks!"

The artwork was *Rumination*, by a sound-investment artist.

Howard stared at the T.V. "This is appalling. Forgive me, dear! To leave the apartment without turning off the set! All I can say in my defense is that becoming a father so suddenly must have unsettled me more than I realized."

Transfixed, Emma felt him remove her coat. Seeing . . . hearing Mildred was like being given another spinal.

"Shucks, Howie, was it too much to hope that my only grand-child get named for me?" The . . . ghost began making goo-goo faces over the carry crib.

At that moment two aspects of the situation became clear to Emma. One, Howard could not see or hear his mother; his unobtrusive face, under the precision-cut auburn hair, did not change expression. Two, death had not improved Mildred.

"Some welcome this!" Mildred straightened up to her full four foot eleven. "Think it didn't take some wangling for me to get here? And I'd have been in the delivery room if old Pete had gotten dug out sooner from the paperwork." Sun, breaking through the wide windows, flashed on her breastplate of bowling "200" pins. A heave-less sigh. "Don't know why I thought things'd be any different on this happy occasion. But dumb bunny did. 'I'll be wanted,' says I to the gals in the choir. Begged to come and help out."

"Have you forgotten you are dead?" Emma moved close to the carry crib. Howard was off putting their coats away.

"And that makes me useless?"

"Unavailable."

"Don't give me that!" Mildred was bouncing the side of the carry crib so that it rocked like a boat in a storm. Odd, Kathleen didn't scream a protest. If anything, her tiny face seemed less scrunched up than usual. "You always did put your family first! Your mom and dad. Your sister! Aunts, uncles, and the rest of the stuffed '*shits*.' Know why the pill was invented, don't we?"

Mildred plugged a Winston between her lips, plopped down on one of the chairs that went with the smoked-glass dining table. Her eyes said, "Want to try making me sit out on the patio?"

"Your entire family is dead." Emma sounded as though she were evaluating a file. "No one left."

"Imprecise, Emma. I have you and Kathleen." Howard had come in soundlessly, and was turning the crib so that the baby was not in the sun's glare.

Emma slid down on a tubular steel chair, omitting to smooth her clerical gray skirt under her. A warm iron and a damp cloth would remove any wrinkles; but would anything remove Mildred?

"You are pale." Howard rested a hand briefly on Emma's shoulder before saying he would fetch her a glass of water.

Mildred dropped her cigarette into a vase containing roses sent by the rival grandparents. "Before we get down to picking up the pieces, Em—I'll get a few things off my chest. I wasn't thrilled with being cremated."

Emma fingered her black-and-white bow tie. "Mildred, it seemed best for all concerned."

"It seemed cheap."

"How long do you intend to stay?"

"That depends on . . . which way the wind blows." A gentle smile that made Emma wish to break the checkerboard glasses. What was happening to her—the woman who thought a raised voice on a par with blowing one's nose in public. If Mildred had manifested as a floating white sheet uttering mournful cries, could she have been blamed on hormones and dismissed with two Tylenol and an early night?

"Have you been talking to the baby, dear?"

Emma responded to Howard's popping up beside her by knocking the glass of water out of his hand. Upsetting. But the incident had its positive aspect. Emma realized she had been sliding out of control and put on the brakes. While Howard blotted up the wet spot in such a way as not to disturb the pile, she calculated her options and decided the soundest course would be to wait Mildred out. Shouldn't take her long to take the huff. Hadn't she divorced Howard's father (ten years before his death) because one night he had mentioned, conversationally, that the fried chicken was a little greasy? Incidentally, Mildred had not prepared that chicken. She had purchased it from Cluck Cluck's Carry-Out.

As of now she was back to making kitchi-coo over the carry crib. "A face only a grandma could love! Stuck with your nose, Em, but makes up for it with my red hair."

Emma's face remained smooth as ice.

"Naughty old Gran." Mildred went smack-smack to her own hand before lighting up another cigarette. Had she forgotten that smoking had killed her?

"Can't go saying I'm *breathing* germs over Kathleen." The bowling pins flashed along with Mildred's dentures—purchased, extravagantly, only weeks before her death.

"Emma, are you all right?"

"Perfect, Howard, thank you. I see clearly what must be done. We will think of her as a television set that won't turn off but can be tuned out." The words escaped before Emma could stop them.

Howard looked at her as though she were a balance sheet that . . . didn't.

Mildred wore her most motherly smile as she parked herself in a corner. "Woo me with rudeness, why don't you, Em?"

"I don't think I can agree to tuning Kathleen out, dear"—Howard brought his fingers together and assumed his pensive mein—"not until she is of an age when"—nervous laugh—"she begins to tune a guitar."

That night Emma went to bed before the ten-o'clock news, wishful, if not hopeful, of waking to a void—in the family circle. She sat up in her bed, called to account by Kathleen's demands for a night feeding and . . . other noises. Someone was clumping around the apartment. How could Howard continue to be deaf to his mother's invasion? Emma sent the other twin bed a displeased look and opened the door.

"For crying out loud, Em, you look like death warmed over. And me full of beans!"

This was going to be hell! Mildred kept getting between Emma and Kathleen during the diaper change—shaking talcum powder where it wasn't wanted and patting the small tummy. She wore a sweatshirt over a pair of men's long johns, and her head was a metal cap of bobby pins.

"What me, cause my boy to lose his beauty sleep? I hope I'm not that kind of mother! The excitement of having me back would cause Howie's blood pressure to skyrocket. I saw that soon enough and

kept the barriers up. Can't promise him that I'm here to stay."
Mildred looked upward. "Ours is a very uncertain world."

*What about my blood pressure?* Emma could feel her skin tight-
ening. *What about my sanity?* She knew she was not currently mentally impaired, but even lacking statistical data, she was prepared to
predict she would soon find she had crossed the line. She clung to
Kathleen's tiny hand and . . . that equally tiny hope. The visit
sounded temporary. Was Mildred subject to recall at a moment's
notice?

Mildred touched Kathleen's hair. "Ain't it a shame, red not being
a favorite color with accountants."

Why was this happening? Was the answer as simple as . . . spite?
Mildred had said frankly, when Howard first introduced the two
women, that she had no time for anyone who didn't know the bowling meaning of *strike*, looked down on Early American furniture,
and read books with appendices longer than their texts. For relaxation Mildred read romances set on lush tropical islands. For culture,
real-life accounts of the inner world of boxing.

Emma, about to pick Kathleen up from the changing table, found
her eyes fixed on her mother-in-law, outlined by the window frame.
A good-sized window . . . and open. Temptation did not come easily
to Emma. Every act was carefully premeasured. But how exhilarat-
ing, how therapeutic, to push Mildred out into the half-light. One
snag: It would have meant leaving Kathleen unattended on the table.

Morning fetched another idea. Emma telephoned a woman, Selina
Brown, a resident two floors down in Apartment 321, and asked if
she could stop by at—yes, ten-thirty would be fine. Almost out the
door, when . . . there was Mildred, adding her assurances to Howard's that the baby was in excellent hands.

Nerves shredded Emma's voice; she even lunged forward, hands
clawing. "You think I want to leave my baby with you?"

"*Our* baby, dear." Howard backed up, his face a wall of hurt.
The Richwoods had arranged on the night of conception that they
would both work at home for three weeks post-delivery.

"Forgive me, I was joking, Howard." How false the words
sounded. Emma never joked until after her seven P.M. cocktail.

Selina Brown was not a person Emma had ever wished to know,
other than as an elevator acquaintance. The woman had a face that
might have been tie-dyed. She wore cannonball earrings, lots of
fringe, and reeked of incense. Several of the residents had accused

her of moving furniture around in the middle of the night, her defense being that the occurrences were "involuntary."

Emma passed through the jangle of beads into a room of black draperies, gauzy fumes, and an atmosphere of peace. And somehow . . . she was in the midst of her account before she knew she had begun.

Selina leaned back in her woven grass chair, spread her Indian silk skirts across her mammoth lap, and wheezed. "Tell me, sugar, what's so hard in being a little giving, a little open? Think you've got a copyright on mother-in-law troubles? So she wants to make nice with her grandkid!"

"She is dead."

"So, Mrs. Richwoods, are most of my best friends." Selina lit up a thin black cigarette from a candle.

Emma pressed her feet and her hands together. "I try not to be emotional in my judgment, but Mildred was never my kind of person, never close. I disliked the way she ate, the way she spoke."

"Liked the way she made Howard, did you, sugar?" A wheezing laugh that caused the draperies to swirl.

"She swears, she smokes . . ." Emma repressed a blush as Selina tapped away ash. "She talks endlessly and unintelligently about her operations and the . . . constipation that followed."

"And now"—Selina held her smoking hand still, eyes closed—"you foresee listening to endless how-I-died stories. I begin to find it in my rocky heart to sympathize with you. The woman is a bore. Something a ghost should never be. See here"—another wheeze, and she flicked ash into the palm of her hand—"I have a friend; he's a parapsych prof at the junior college. I'll get in touch with him. Soon. He's off camping now with his kids. Tread water, Mrs. Richwoods, I'll get back to you."

Emma lifted her chin. "I am grateful. Thank you."

Her empty living room welcomed her back, and she saw nothing odd in ascribing it a personality—a day had made many changes. Howard must be in the nursery. As for Mildred . . . Emma determined not to get her hopes up. She sat on the nubby white sofa, drawing calm from the atmosphere of tubular steel and nude wood. She had not brought this unpleasantness on herself. Nothing here invited the . . . unusual.

Time to go to the nursery. Through the partially open door she could see Howard feeding the baby, the bottle held at the appropriate angle. The door to the guest room was also ajar. Hope seeped away.

Mildred was lying on the bed, reading a magazine that must have forced its way in there with her. *Male Marvels*. Depraved. A jar of generic cold cream was on the bedside table.

The telephone in the hallway shrilled, and Emma picked it up. Top marks for efficiency—if Selina had located her Authority.

"Emmie?" The voice coming through the receiver was Ruth's. Her sister. Those two had never been compatible. But time alters cases.

"How things going, Sis? Mind if I bring some of the kids along to see their new cousin?"

Emma removed the receiver an inch from her ear and smoothed her hair. "That would be nice, Ruth; however, I am getting somewhat housebound. I would prefer Howard and I to bring Kathleen over to you."

"Whatever. Sure you're up to the drive?"

"I hardly think," Emma snapped, a novelty with her, "that a fifteen-minute ride will exhaust me. We will come now, if that suits you."

She had barely hung up when there came the dreaded voice. "And if that ain't enough to make a pig shit! Taking my granddaughter away from me before we've gotten ourselves acquainted." Mildred had her arms akimbo. "Know what your problem is, Em? You head's too stuffed with schooling to have room for sense."

A soundless scream tore apart Emma's lips. "How often must I keep saying—your family is dead! Every one. Dead . . . dead . . . dead and buried." She drew a racking breath. Her throat hurt. My God, she rarely raised her voice. As for screaming . . . what must Howard think of her?

He stood rigid in the doorway, his face set in pacifying lines. "Relax, Emma." He sounded as frightened as that time when he found a decimal point in the wrong place. "You've been overdoing."

"Not on account of me, she hasn't." Mildred positioned herself inches from Emma. An ingratiating smile for the son who couldn't see her. "Never could understand, Em, why your mom and dad— the Bobsey Twins—rate so high above me. Not here doing their bit, are they? 'Course not! Off on some fancy-dancy cruise to the Para- keet Isles. How I do remember that first Christmas after you and Howie were married. Your mom gets a black silk nightdress. Me— I get an umbrella. And know what? It leaked the first time a bird pissed on it. Didn't matter. I already had three—still in their boxes."

Emma's eyes went wild. Worse, she hurled herself at Mildred. "You never would have worn a black silk nightgown."

"Certainly not, dear." Howard backed into the nursery. "Mind if I have a few moments quiet time with Kathleen?" He closed the door. There was a telephone in there. Was he about to phone Dr. Hubner, the gynecologist, requesting a referral to a psychiatrist?

Mildred adjusted her glasses. "Seems to me, hon, you and Howie aren't communicating like you should. Secrets hurt, not heal, a marriage—as you would know, Em, if you took time to watch the soaps. Best if I go to my room. Last thing on earth I want is to be a cause of friction."

Emma closed her eyes. When she opened them, she was alone. Entering the nursery, she found Howard holding the baby—not the phone. Kathleen was crying, which hopefully had kept him from turning in a report on his wife's unnerving behavior.

*Is that what she wants,* Emma questioned, *me out of the way in the psychiatric ward, and Howard and Kathleen all to herself? How I wish I had pushed her out the window* ... Her hands clenched as the futility struck her. Mildred couldn't be made to die twice.

"Howard." Emma opened the nursery door and crept up behind him, very much as Mildred had done to her. "Excuse my behavior out in the hallway—due, I believe, to some sort of waking nightmare." She grabbed at his arms.

"Careful!" He sidestepped her, his arms protecting the baby. Emma had lost sight of the fact that he was holding Kathleen. The baby's cries ripped through her.

"I will go and freshen up." Her smile, meant to be appeasing, appeared to frighten father and child. "I told Ruth we would go over for a little while."

"Emma"—Howard was frowning—"the baby is distressed."

"She'll be fine."

Escaping into the bathroom, Emma pondered what Howard would say to Ruth and her husband, Joe. Then all thought was drowned out by Mildred's singing—in a rusty voice, a ribald song about a monk and a cow. She was there—under the spurting shower, all lathered up and wearing a pink plastic cap.

"Shucks! Never a moment's privacy around here!" A snatched washcloth and the shower curtain swished shut.

Ruth's house became an oasis. Emma, while getting Kathleen wrapped up, fought the fear that her mother-in-law would decide to intrude along. Could Mildred ... manifest away from the apartment?

So far ... so good, they were out the door. Howard held on

to her arm as they crossed the car park. Hurry . . . ! And then she almost caused him to trip, along with the carrying crib, when she twisted around to look back up at the apartment window. There it was—the reproachful silhouette.

Howard frowned. "Emma, please—did you forget something?"

"I thought I might have . . . then remembered I hadn't."

Kathleen fussed during the short drive. A relief to pull into Ruth's toy-strewn driveway. Before Emma could get her door open, her nieces and nephews spilled out onto the porch, seven-year-old Sean yelling, "Aunt Emma, you won't believe who is here!"

She swayed against Howard. Logic should have told her that Mildred did not need a car for transportation. The children dragged Emma out of the car, and next she was in Ruth's burlap living room— where cereal bowls were stuck in among bookcases and jigsaw pieces made a broken mosaic on the floor.

"Who is here?" she managed.

Ruth was scooping up magazines and tossing them in a corner. "Uncle Mo and Aunt Vin; they called just after you and I spoke. The more the merrier, I said. Joe has them out back showing off his tomatoes. We're being taken over by them." She straightened up. "Jeez, Emma! You look wrung out! Here—take a load off." She dusted off a chair with a T-shirt. Always a slob, Ruth. Howard was afraid to eat in this house. So much for Mildred's accusations that she had been pushed out in favor of Emma's side.

"Hello, young Kath." Ruth took the carry crib from Howard. "You all want to stay for supper? Won't beat the socks off your gourmet fare, just a hot-dog casserole . . ."

"Are you making reference to the sort Mom used to make?" Emma squeezed the arms of her chair, ignoring Howard's pained expression.

"The same." Ruth gathered in Kathleen with practiced ease. "Want to bet there's not a hot dog on that cruise?"

The eyes of the sisters met, both seeing their mother squeezed into blue satin, prepared to eat a real live dog rather than admit she didn't understand the French menu. How would their father survive if they wouldn't let him have beer with his breakfast?

In came the children, followed by Joe, Uncle Mo, and Aunt Vin. And, totally unexpectedly, Emma wanted to be part of the warm muddle of this . . . her family. She wanted Kathleen to become the adored little cousin. She wanted Howard to stop looking as if he wished to reprogram everyone. What waited back at the apartment made this all seem . . . so structured. Emma knew she would have to regain control, with our without Selina Brown's help.

"Thank you, Ruth, we will stay for dinner," she said.

Back at the apartment, the air was stinky with cigarette smoke. How could Howard not notice? Hadn't he admitted once that his mother had controlled his childhood thoughts but that it had taken him years to untie the apron strings? Emma stood in the living room, holding onto the baby for strength. No clumping of feet. No sound at all; but Emma knew Mildred was in the guest room.

"Nice," she whispered against Kathleen's downy hair. "Granny may pout all she wishes if I can get through your night feeding without her help."

And, amazingly, things worked out that way. At two A.M. Emma found herself straining for any movement from her house ghost. A giggle escaped her. Embarrassing. And now an odd feeling came—a kind of . . . something verging on . . . pity for Mildred. Had she come back, hoping to repair their relationship? Emma stuck herself with a diaper pin, annoyance with herself welling up with the drop of blood. Mildred had come back to be a thorn in the flesh of the woman who had taken Howard away. And now she was using silence. But not for long . . .

Mildred did not appear at the smoked-glass breakfast table the following morning. Emma heard the shower going . . . and going. Howard was in excellent spirits, dancing a rattle over Kathleen. "Daddy's so proud of his little girl." He straightened up from the carry crib. "Emma, that visit to Ruth does seem to have put you back on the path to stabil—full strength. Mind if I go down to the office for an hour? Unless you object to being alone?"

"I will not be alone."

"No offense." He smiled ruefully at the baby.

Emma was glad when he left. She wished to assess her situation without wondering if he was still wondering about her state of mind. No sounds from the guest room. Emma tucked Kathleen back into her crib proper, and then . . . surrendered to the urge to open that door and look in on Mildred. She was lying on the bed, a washcloth wadded up on her forehead and a bottle of generic aspirin displayed alongside the pot of cold cream. Surely they could only be visual aids.

"Do you feel all right?" Emma asked.

Silence. A very negative silence.

Emma almost squeezed off the doorknob. How lovely and peaceful it would be to creep up and move that cloth down over Mildred's nose and press down . . . down. What would that make her—a murderess in name only?

She fell away from the door when the telephone rang.

"Greetings," came Selina Brown's voice. "My parapsych prof called, we picked at the bones of your situation, and he says he'll see you this afternoon."

"Not this morning?"

"Think you're the only one with problems, sugar?" A pause, and Selina's voice became a little less tepid. "So you say easy for him, right? How's 'bout if I come tell you the guts of what he said?"

"I would prefer that you did not," Emma whispered. "*She* might be listening."

"Then you hustle down here."

"I'm not sure. . . . Howard is at the office and the baby is sleeping. . . ."

"So?" Selina wheezed. "Who's to have you up for neglect with Grandma baby-sitting?"

"Very well, but I will not remain more than a couple of minutes." Emma hung up. If she went to take Kathleen, Mildred was bound to appear and demand to know where they were going. Emma squared her shoulders and smoothed her hair. She was being overprotective. For all her faults, Mildred wouldn't do anything to hurt Kathleen; the love of a real live grandma had been visible in those goo-goo faces.

"And so does Mommy love you." Emma felt self-conscious saying the words. Bending over the crib, she touched the fingers to the warm, round form under the quilt with its geometric shapes. Which matched those of the gently turning mobile.

The journey, down three floors in the elevator, was stifling. Selina was standing outside her own apartment door.

"Tell me," Emma said. Was she mad to believe in this woman wearing a purple turban and magician's robes?

"Sugar, you tell your mother-in-law to leave. You heard me. Subtlety isn't something she understands. She won't up and out until she's been sufficiently insulted. That way she can go tell her kindred spirits what a hellish time she's had of it."

Emma became her old self again. Each problem to its own solution, one need only look for the answer in the right column. How could she have been so slow-witted?

"Thank you, Selina. And do convey my appreciation to the professor. When she was alive, Mildred's visits always ended in her slamming out of the apartment. She would accuse us of kicking her out. And nothing else about her has changed. She still has a mouth like a sewer, is insatiably jealous of my family. Excuse me, I must hurry. . . ."

The elevator would not hurry. It stopped at each floor, then took its time opening its door. Emma hurried along the hallway, opened the apartment door, and then, slowing her pace and breathing, headed for the guest room. She was determined not to feel sorry for Mildred. This bon voyage must be final.

The guest room was empty. The bedspread neat and smooth. The pillow plumped up. The jar of cold cream and the bottle of aspirin gone from the nightstand . . . as was the pink shower cap from the hook behind the bathroom door. Emma stood in the hallway. This was perfect. She must telephone Selina with the good news. Mildred had already been sufficiently insulted.

Not a whiff of cigarette smoke. As for the whiff of . . . regret, Emma did ask herself: If she had known her mother-in-law's visit was to be so short, would she have been a little more welcoming?

Too late now, and if she did not hurry, she would be late for Kathleen's feeding.

She entered the nursery, her heart lifting at the sight of the geometric mobile spinning above the crib.

An empty crib. Pinned to the quilt was a note:

Dear Em,
   Guess I'm not cut to be a backseat driver. Never thought to ask me to go to Ruth's, did you? Well, two can play at that game. I'm taking my redheaded granddaughter, Mildred, Junior, to show off to my side of the family. Howie will know she's in excellent hands.

Mom

*Linda Barnes's* Blood Will Have Blood, Bitter Finish, Dead Heat, *and* Cities of the Dead *feature Michael Spraggue, who (like Linda) has an abiding interest in the theater.* A Trouble of Fools, *nominated for an Edgar for Best Novel of 1987, features Carlotta Carlyle, a tall, red-haired, cab-driving private eye who uses her inside knowledge of the Boston area and her deft touch with people to get the right answers.* The Snake Tattoo, *a continuation of Carlotta's capers, followed.*

*Carlotta was introduced in "Lucky Penny," which won an Anthony for Best Short Story of 1986 and was first published in* New Black Mask. *Says Linda, "Carlotta is not casually named. Carlotta cares. She's compassionate, committed, cool, competent, competitive—and she copes."*

# LUCKY PENNY

## by Linda Barnes

L T. MOONEY MADE me dish it all out for the record. He's a good cop, if such an animal exists. We used to work the same shift before I decided—wrongly—that there was room for a lady P.I. in this town. Who knows? With this case under my belt, maybe business'll take a 180-degree spin, and I can quit driving a hack.

See, I've already written the official report for Mooney and the cops, but the kind of stuff they wanted: date, place, and time, cold as ice and submitted in triplicate, doesn't even start to tell the tale. So I'm doing it over again, my way.

Don't worry, Mooney. I'm not gonna file this one.

The Thayler case was still splattered across the front page of the *Boston Globe*. I'd soaked it up with my midnight coffee and was puzzling it out—my cab on automatic pilot, my mind on crime—when the mad tea party began.

"Take your next right, sister. Then pull over, and douse the lights. Quick!"

I heard the bastard all right, but it must have taken me thirty

288

seconds or so to react. Something hard rapped on the cab's dividing shield. I didn't bother turning around. I hate staring down gun barrels.

I said, "Jimmy Cagney, right? No, your voice is too high. Let me guess, don't tell me—"

"Shut up!"

"*Kill* the lights, *turn off* the lights, okay. But *douse* the lights? You've been tuning in too many old gangster flicks."

"I hate a mouthy broad," the guy snarled. I kid you not.

"*Broad,*" I said. "Christ! *Broad?* You trying to grow hair on your balls?"

"Look, I mean it, lady!"

"Lady's better. Now you wanna vacate my cab and go rob a phone booth?" My heart was beating like a tin drum, but I didn't let my voice shake, and all the time I was gabbing at him, I kept trying to catch his face in the mirror. He must have been crouching way back on the passenger side. I couldn't see a damn thing.

"I want all your dough," he said.

Who can you trust? This guy was a spiffy dresser: charcoal gray three-piece suit and rep tie, no less. And picked up in front of the swank Copley Plaza. *I* looked like I needed the bucks more than he did, and I'm no charity case. A woman can make good tips driving a hack in Boston. Oh, she's gotta take precautions, all right. When you can't smell a disaster fare from thirty feet, it's time to quit. I pride myself on my judgment. I'm careful. I always know where the police checkpoints are, so I can roll my cab past and flash the old lights if a guy starts acting up. This dude fooled me cold.

I was ripped. Not only had I been conned, I had a considerable wad to give away. It was near the end of my shift, and like I said, I do all right. I've got a lot of regulars. Once you see me, you don't forget me—or my cab.

It's gorgeous. Part of my inheritance. A '59 Chevy, shiny as new, kept on blocks in a heated garage by the proverbial dotty old lady. It's the pits of the design world. Glossy blue with those giant chromium fins. Restrained decor: just the phone number and a few gilt curlicues on the door. I was afraid all my old pals at the police department would pull me over for minor traffic violations if I went whole hog and painted "CARLOTTA'S CAB" in ornate script on the hood. Some do it anyway.

So where the hell were all the cops now? Where are they when you need 'em?

He told me to shove the cash through that little hole they leave for the passenger to pass the fare forward. I told him he had it backwards. He didn't laugh. I shoved bills.

"Now the change," the guy said. Can you imagine the nerve?

I must have cast my eyes up to heaven. I do that a lot these days.

"I mean it." He rapped the plastic shield with the shiny barrel of his gun. I checked it out this time. Funny how big a little .22 looks when it's pointed just right.

I fished in my pockets for change, emptied them.

"Is that all?"

"You want the gold cap on my left front molar?" I said.

"Turn around," the guy barked. "Keep both hands on the steering wheel. High."

I heard jingling, then a quick intake of breath.

"Okay," the crook said, sounding happy as a clam, "I'm gonna take my leave—"

"Good. Don't call this cab again."

"Listen!" The gun tapped. "You cool it here for ten minutes. And I mean frozen. Don't twitch. Don't blow your nose. Then take off."

"Gee, thanks."

"Thank *you*," he said politely. The door slammed.

At times like that, you just feel ridiculous. You *know* the guy isn't going to hang around waiting to see whether you're big on insubordination. *But*, he might. And who wants to tangle with a .22 slug? I rate pretty high on insubordination. That's why I messed up as a cop. I figured I'd give him two minutes to get lost. Meantime I listened.

Not much traffic goes by those little streets on Beacon Hill at one o'clock on a Wednesday morn. Too residential. So I could hear the guy's footsteps tap along the pavement. About ten steps back, he stopped. Was he the one in a million who'd wait to see if I turned around? I heard a funny kind of whooshing noise. Not loud enough to make me jump, and anything much louder than the ticking of my watch would have put me through the roof. Then the footsteps patted on, straight back and out of hearing.

One minute more. The only saving grace of the situation was the location: District One. That's Mooney's district. Nice guy to talk to.

I took a deep breath, hoping it would have an encore, and pivoted quickly, keeping my head low. Makes you feel stupid when you do that and there's no one around.

I got out and strolled to the corner, stuck my head around a building kind of cautiously. Nothing, of course.

I backtracked. Ten steps, then whoosh. Along the sidewalk stood one of those new "Keep Beacon Hill Beautiful" trash cans, the kind with the swinging lid. I gave it a shove as I passed. I could just as easily have kicked it; I was in that kind of funk.

Whoosh, it said, just as pretty as could be.

Breaking into one of those trash cans is probably tougher than busting into your local bank vault. Since I didn't even have a dime left to fiddle the screws on the lid, I was forced to deface city property. I got the damn thing open and dumped the contents on somebody's front lawn, smack in the middle of a circle of light from one of those ritzy Beacon Hill gas street lamps.

Halfway through the whiskey bottles, wadded napkins, and beer cans, I made my discovery. I was being thorough. If you're going to stink like garbage anyway, why leave anything untouched, right? So I was opening all the brown bags—you know, the good old brown lunch-and-bottle bags—looking for a clue. My most valuable find so far had been the moldy rind of a bologna sandwich. Then I hit it big: one neatly creased brown bag stuffed full of cash.

To say I was stunned is to entirely underestimate how I felt as I crouched there, knee-deep in garbage, my jaw hanging wide. I don't know what I'd expected to find. Maybe the guy's gloves. Or his hat, if he'd wanted to get rid of it fast in order to melt back into anonymity. I pawed through the rest of the debris fast. My change was gone.

I was so befuddled I left the trash right on the front lawn. There's probably still a warrant out for my arrest.

District One headquarters is off the beaten path, over on New Sudbury Street. I would have called first, if I'd had a dime.

One of the few things I'd enjoyed about being a cop was gabbing with Mooney. I like driving a cab better, but face it, most of my fares aren't scintillating conversationalists. The Red Sox and the weather usually covers it. Talking to Mooney was so much fun, I wouldn't even consider dating him. Lots of guys are good at sex, but conversation—now there's an art form.

Mooney, all six-foot-four, two-hundred-and-forty linebacker pounds of him, gave me the glad eye when I waltzed in. He hasn't given up trying. Keeps telling me he talks even better in bed.

"Nice hat," was all he said, his big fingers pecking at the typewriter keys.

I took it off and shook out my hair. I wear an old slouch cap when I drive to keep people from saying the inevitable. One jerk even misquoted Yeats at me: "Only God, my dear, could love you for yourself alone and not your long red hair." Since I'm seated when I drive, he missed the chance to ask me how the weather is up here. I'm six-one in my stocking feet and skinny enough to make every inch count twice. I've got a wide forehead, green eyes, and a pointy chin. If you want to be nice about my nose, you say it's got character.

Thirty's still hovering in my future. It's part of Mooney's past.

I told him I had a robbery to report and his dark eyes steered me to a chair. He leaned back and took a puff of one of his low-tar cigarettes. He can't quite give 'em up, but he feels guilty as hell about 'em.

When I got to the part about the bag in the trash, Mooney lost his sense of humor. He crushed a half-smoked butt in a crowded ashtray.

"Know why you never made it as a cop?" he said.

"Didn't brown-nose enough."

"You got no sense of proportion! Always going after crackpot stuff!"

"Christ, Mooney, aren't you interested? Some guy heists a cab, at gunpoint, then tosses the money. Aren't you the least bit *intrigued*?"

"I'm a cop, Ms. Carlyle. I've got to be more than intrigued. I've got murders, bank robberies, assaults—"

"Well, excuse me. I'm just a poor citizen reporting a crime. Trying to help—"

"Want to help, Carlotta? Go away." He stared at the sheet of paper in the typewriter and lit another cigarette. "Or dig me up something on the Thayler case."

"You working that sucker?"

"Wish to hell I wasn't."

I could see his point. It's tough enough trying to solve any murder, but when your victim is *the* Jennifer (Mrs. Justin) Thayler, wife of the famed Harvard Law prof, and the society reporters are breathing down your neck along with the usual crime-beat scribblers, you got a special kind of problem.

"So who did it?" I asked.

Mooney put his size twelves up on his desk. "Colonel Mustard in the library with the candlestick! How the hell do I know? Some scumbag housebreaker. The lady of the house interrupted his haul.

Probably didn't mean to hit her that hard. He must have freaked when he saw all the blood, 'cause he left some of the ritziest stereo equipment this side of heaven, plus enough silverware to blind your average hophead. He snatched most of old man Thayler's goddamn idiot art works, collections, collectibles—whatever the hell you call 'em—which ought to set him up for the next few hundred years, if he's smart enough to get rid of them."

"Alarm system?"

"Yeah, they had one. Looks like Mrs. Thayler forgot to turn it on. According to the maid, she had a habit of forgetting just about anything after a martini or three."

"Think the maid's in on it?"

"Christ, Carlotta. There you go again. No witnesses. No finger-prints. Servants asleep. Husband asleep. We've got word out to all the fences here and in New York that we want this guy. The pawn-brokers know the stuff's hot. We're checking out known art thieves and shady museums—"

"Well, don't let me keep you from your serious business," I said, getting up to go. "I'll give you the collar when I find out who robbed my cab."

"Sure," he said. His fingers started playing with the typewriter again.

"Wanna bet on it?" Betting's an old custom with Mooney and me.

"I'm not gonna take the few piddling bucks you earn with that ridiculous car."

"Right you are, boy. I'm gonna take the money the city pays you to be unimaginative! Fifty bucks I nail him within the week."

Mooney hates to be called "boy." He hates to be called "un-imaginative." I hate to hear my car called ridiculous. We shook hands on the deal. Hard.

Chinatown's about the only chunk of Boston that's alive after midnight. I headed over to Yee Hong's for a bowl of won ton soup.

The service was the usual low-key, slow-motion routine. I used a newspaper as a shield; if you're really involved in the *Wall Street Journal*, the casual male may think twice before deciding he's the answer to your prayers. But I didn't read a single stock quote. I tugged at strands of my hair, a bad habit of mine. Why would somebody rob me and then toss the money away?

Solution Number One: he didn't. The trash bin was some mob

drop, and the money I'd found in the trash had absolutely nothing to do with the money filched from my cab. Except that it was the same amount—and that was too big a coincidence for me to swallow.

Two: the cash I'd found was counterfeit and this was a clever way of getting it into circulation. Nah. Too baroque, entirely. How the hell would the guy know I was the pawing-through-the-trash type? And if this stuff was counterfeit, the rest of the bills in my wallet were too.

Three: it was a training session. Some fool had used me to perfect his robbery technique. Couldn't he learn from TV like the rest of the crooks?

Four: it was a frat hazing. Robbing a hack at gunpoint isn't exactly in the same league as swallowing goldfish.

I closed my eyes.

My face came to a fortunate halt about an inch above a bowl of steaming broth. That's when I decided to pack it in and head for home. Won ton soup is lousy for the complexion.

I checked out the log I keep in the Chevy, totaled my fares. $4.82 missing, all in change. A very reasonable robbery.

By the time I got home, the sleepiness had passed. You know how it is: one moment you're yawning, the next your eyes won't close. Usually happens when my head hits the pillow; this time I didn't even make it that far. What woke me up was the idea that my robber hadn't meant to steal a thing. Maybe he'd left me something instead. You know, something hot, cleverly concealed. Something he could pick up in a few weeks, after things cooled off.

I went over that back seat with a vengeance, but I didn't find anything besides old Kleenex and bent paper clips. My brainstorm wasn't too clever after all. I mean, if the guy wanted to use my cab as a hiding place, why advertise by pulling a five-and-dime robbery?

I sat in the driver's seat, tugged my hair, and stewed. What did I have to go on? The memory of a nervous thief who talked like a B movie and stole only change. Maybe a mad tollbooth collector.

I live in a Cambridge dump. In any other city, I couldn't sell the damned thing if I wanted to. Here, I turn real-estate agents away daily. The key to my home's value is the fact that I can hoof it to Harvard Square in five minutes. It's a seller's market for tarpaper shacks within walking distance of the Square. Under a hundred thou only if the plumbing's outside.

It took me a while to get in the door. I've got about five locks on it. Neighborhood's popular with thieves as well as gentry. I'm neither. I inherited the house from my weird Aunt Bea, all paid for. I consider the property taxes my rent, and the rent's getting steeper all the time.

I slammed my log down on the dining room table. I've got rooms galore in that old house, rent a couple of them to Harvard students. I've got my own office on the second floor. But I do most of my work at the dining room table. I like the view of the refrigerator.

I started over from square one. I called Gloria. She's the late night dispatcher for the Independent Taxi Owners Association. I've never seen her, but her voice is as smooth as mink oil and I'll bet we get a lot of calls from guys who just want to hear her say she'll pick 'em up in five minutes.

"Gloria, it's Carlotta."

"Hi, babe. You been pretty popular today."

"Was I popular at one thirty-five this morning?"

"Huh?"

"I picked up a fare in front of the Copley Plaza at one thirty-five. Did you hand that one out to all comers or did you give it to me solo?"

"Just a sec." I could hear her charming the pants off some caller in the background. Then she got back to me.

"I just gave him to you, babe. He asked for the lady in the '59 Chevy. Not a lot of those on the road."

"Thanks, Gloria."

"Trouble?" she asked.

"Is mah middle name," I twanged. We both laughed and I hung up before she got a chance to cross-examine me.

So. The robber wanted my cab. I wished I'd concentrated on his face instead of his snazzy clothes. Maybe it was somebody I knew, some jokester in mid-prank. I killed that idea; I don't know anybody who'd pull a stunt like that, at gunpoint and all. I don't want to know anybody like that.

Why rob my cab, then toss the dough?

I pondered sudden religious conversion. Discarded it. Maybe my robber was some perpetual screw-up who'd ditched the cash by mistake.

Or. . . . Maybe he got exactly what he wanted. Maybe he desperately desired my change.

Why?

Because my change was special, valuable beyond its $4.82 replacement cost.

So how would somebody know my change was valuable?

Because he'd given it to me himself, earlier in the day.

"Not bad," I said out loud. "Not bad." It was the kind of reasoning they'd bounced me off the police force for, what my so-called "superiors" termed the "fevered product of an overimaginative mind." I leapt at it because it was the only explanation I could think of. I do like life to make some sort of sense.

I pored over my log. I keep pretty good notes: where I pick up a fare, where I drop him, whether he's a hailer or a radio call.

First, I ruled out all the women. That made the task slightly less impossible: sixteen suspects down from thirty-five. Then I yanked my hair and stared at the blank white porcelain of the refrigerator door. Got up and made myself a sandwich: ham, swiss cheese, salami, lettuce and tomato, on rye. Ate it. Stared at the porcelain some more until the suspects started coming into focus.

Five of the guys were just plain fat and one was decidedly on the hefty side; I'd felt like telling them all to walk. Might do them some good, might bring on a heart attack. I crossed them all out. Making a thin person look plump is hard enough; it's damn near impossible to make a fatty look thin.

Then I considered my regulars: Jonah Ashley, a tiny blond Southern gent; musclebound "just-call-me-Harold" at Longfellow Place; Dr. Homewood getting his daily ferry from Beth Israel to MGH; Marvin of the gay bars; and Professor Dickerman, Harvard's answer to Berkeley's sixties radicals.

I crossed them all off. I could see Dickerman holding up the First Filthy Capitalist Bank, or disobeying civilly at Seabrook, even blowing up an oil company or two. But my mind boggled at the thought of the great liberal Dickerman robbing some poor cabbie. It would be like Robin Hood joining the Sheriff of Nottingham on some particularly rotten peasant swindle. Then they'd both rape Maid Marian and go off pals together.

Dickerman *was* a lousy tipper. That ought to be a crime.

So what did I have? Eleven out of sixteen guys cleared without leaving my chair. Me and Sherlock Holmes, the famous armchair detectives.

I'm stubborn; that was one of my good cop traits. I stared at that log till my eyes bugged out. I remembered two of the five pretty easily; they were handsome and I'm far from blind. The first had one of those elegant bony faces and far-apart eyes. He was taller than my bandit. I'd ceased eyeballing him when I'd noticed the ring on his left hand; I never fuss with the married kind. The other one was built, a weight-lifter. Not an Arnold Schwarzenegger extremist, but built. I think I'd have noticed that bod on my bandit. Like I said, I'm not blind.

That left three.

Okay. I closed my eyes. Who had I picked up at the Hyatt on Memorial Drive? Yeah, that was the salesman guy, the one who looked so uncomfortable that I'd figured he'd been hoping to ask his cabbie for a few pointers concerning the best skirt-chasing areas in our fair city. Too low a voice. Too broad in the beam.

The log said I'd picked up a hailer in Kenmore Square when I'd let out the salesman. Ah yes, a talker. The weather, mostly. Don't you think it's dangerous for you to be driving a cab? Yeah, I remembered him, all right: a fatherly type, clasping a briefcase, heading to the financial district. Too old.

Down to one. I was exhausted but not the least bit sleepy. All I had to do was remember who I'd picked up on Beacon near Charles. A hailer. Before five o'clock which was fine by me because I wanted to be long gone before rush hour gridlocked the city. I'd gotten onto Storrow and taken him along the river into Newton Center. Dropped him off at the BayBank Middlesex, right before closing time. It was coming back. Little nervous guy. Pegged him as an accountant when I'd let him out at the bank. Measly, undernourished soul. Skinny as a rail, stooped, with pits left from teenage acne.

Shit. I let my head sink down onto the dining room table when I realized what I'd done. I'd ruled them all out, every one. So much for my brilliant deductive powers.

I retired to my bedroom, disgusted. Not only had I lost $4.82 in assorted alloy metals, I was going to lose fifty to Mooney. I stared at myself in the mirror, but what I was really seeing was the round hole at the end of a .22, held in a neat gloved hand.

Somehow, the gloves made me feel better. I'd remembered another detail about my piggybank robber. I consulted the mirror and kept the recall going. A hat. The guy wore a hat. Not like my cap, but like a hat out of a forties gangster flick. I had one of those: I'm a sucker for hats. I plunked it on my head, jamming my hair up underneath—and I drew in my breath sharply.

A shoulder-padded jacket, a slim build, a low slouched hat. Gloves. Boots with enough heel to click as he walked away. Voice? High. Breathy, almost whispered. Not unpleasant. Accentless. No Boston "R."

I had a man's jacket and a couple of ties in my closet. Don't ask. They may have dated from as far back as my ex-husband, but not necessarily so. I slipped into the jacket, knotted the tie, tilted the hat down over one eye.

I'd have trouble pulling it off. I'm skinny, but my build is decidedly female. Still, I wondered—enough to traipse back downstairs, pull a chicken leg out of the fridge, go back to the log, and review the feminine possibilities. Good thing I did.

Everything clicked. One lady fit the bill exactly: mannish walk and clothes, tall for a woman. And I was in luck. While I'd picked her up in Harvard Square, I'd dropped her at a real address, a house in Brookline. 782 Mason Terrace, at the top of Corey Hill.

JoJo's garage opens at seven. That gave me a big two hours to sleep.

I took my beloved car in for some repair work it really didn't need yet and sweet-talked JoJo into giving me a loaner. I needed a hack, but not mine. Only trouble with that Chevy is it's too damn conspicuous.

I figured I'd lose way more than fifty bucks staking out Mason Terrace. I also figured it would be worth it to see old Mooney's face.

She was regular as clockwork, a dream to tail. Eight-thirty-seven every morning, she got a ride to the Square with a next-door neighbor. Took a cab home at five-fifteen. A working woman. Well, she couldn't make much of a living from robbing hacks and dumping the loot in the garbage.

I was damn curious by now. I knew as soon as I looked her over that she was the one, but she seemed so blah, so *normal*. She must have been five seven or eight, but the way she stooped, she didn't look tall. Her hair was long and brown with a lot of blonde in it, the kind of hair that would have been terrific loose and wild, like a horse's mane. She tied it back with a scarf. A brown scarf. She wore suits. Brown suits. She had a tiny nose, brown eyes under pale eyebrows, a sharp chin. I never saw her smile. Maybe what she needed was a shrink, not a session with Mooney. Maybe she'd done it for the excitement. God knows if I had her routine, her job, I'd probably be dressing up like King Kong and assaulting skyscrapers.

See, I followed her to work. It wasn't even tricky. She trudged the same path, went in the same entrance to Harvard Yard, probably walked the same number of steps every morning. Her name was Marcia Heidegger and she was a secretary in the admissions office of the College of Fine Arts.

I got friendly with one of her co-workers.

There was this guy typing away like mad at the desk in her office. I could just see him from the side window. He had grad student written all over his face. Longish wispy hair. Gold-rimmed glasses. Serious. Given to deep sighs and bright velour V-necks. Probably writing his thesis on "Courtly Love and the Theories of Chrétien de Troyes."

I latched onto him at Bailey's the day after I'd tracked Lady Heidegger to her Harvard lair.

Too bad Roger was so short. Most short guys find it hard to believe that I'm really trying to pick them up. They look for ulterior motives. Not the Napoleon type of short guy; he assumes I've been waiting years for a chance to dance with a guy who doesn't have to bend to stare down my cleavage. But Roger was no Napoleon. So I had to engineer things a little.

I got into line ahead of him and ordered, after long deliberation, a BLT on toast. While the guy made it up and shoved it on a plate with three measly potato chips and a sliver of pickle you could barely see, I searched through my wallet, opened my change purse, counted out silver, got to $1.60 on the last five pennies. The counterman sang out: "That'll be a buck eighty five." I pawed through my pockets, found a nickel, two pennies. The line was growing restive. I concentrated on looking like a damsel in need of a knight, a tough task for a woman over six feet.

Roger (I didn't know he was Roger then) smiled ruefully and passed over a quarter. I was effusive in my thanks. I sat at a table for two, and when he'd gotten his tray (ham-and-cheese and a strawberry ice cream soda), I motioned him into my extra chair.

He was a sweetie. Sitting down, he forgot the difference in our height, and decided I might be someone he could talk to. I encouraged him. I hung shamelessly on his every word. A Harvard man, imagine that. We got around slowly, ever so slowly, to his work at the admissions office. He wanted to duck it and talk about more important issues, but I persisted. I'd been thinking about getting a job at Harvard, possibly in admissions. What kind of people did he work with? Where they congenial? What was the atmosphere like? Was it a big office? How many people? Men? Women? Any soulmates? Readers? Or just, you know, office people?

According to him, every soul he worked with was brain dead.

I had to be more obvious. I interrupted a stream of complaint with, "Gee, I know somebody who works for Harvard. I wonder if you know her."

"It's a big place," he said, hoping to avoid the whole endless business.

"I met her at a party. Always meant to look her up." I searched through my bag, found a scrap of paper and pretended to read Marcia Heidegger's name off it.

"Marcia? Geez, I work with Marcia. Same office."

"Do you think she likes her work? I mean I got some strange vibes from her," I said. I actually said "strange vibes" and he didn't laugh his head off. People in the Square say things like that and other people take them seriously.

His face got conspiratorial, of all things, and he leaned closer to me.

"You want it, I bet you could get Marcia's job."

"You mean it?" What a compliment—a place for me among the brain dead.

"She's gonna get fired if she doesn't snap out of it."

"Snap out of what?"

"It was bad enough working with her when she first came over. She's one of those crazy neat people, can't stand to see papers lying on a desktop, you know? She almost threw out the first chapter of my thesis!"

I made a suitable horrified noise and he went on.

"Well, you know, about Marcia, it's kind of tragic. She doesn't talk about it."

But he was dying to.

"Yes?" I said, as if he needed egging on.

He lowered his voice. "She used to work for Justin Thayler over at the law school, that guy in the news, whose wife got killed. You know, her work hasn't been worth shit since it happened. She's always on the phone, talking real soft, hanging up if anybody comes in the room. I mean, you'd think she was in love with the guy or something, the way she—"

I don't remember what I said. For all I know, I may have volunteered to type his thesis. But I got rid of him somehow and then I scooted around the corner of Church Street and found a pay phone and dialed Mooney.

"Don't tell me," he said. "Somebody mugged you, but they only took your trading stamps."

"I have just one question for you, Moon."

"I accept. A June wedding, but I'll have to break it to Mother gently."

"Tell me what kind of junk Justin Thayler collected."

I could hear him breathing into the phone.

"Just tell me," I said, "for curiosity's sake."

"You onto something, Carlotta?"

"I'm curious, Mooney. And you're not the only source of information in the world."

"Thayler collected Roman stuff. Antiques. And I mean old. Artifacts, statues—"

"Coins?"

"Whole mess of them."

"Thanks."

"Carlotta—"

I never did find out what he was about to say because I hung up. Rude, I know. But I had things to do. And it was better Mooney shouldn't know what they were, because they came under the heading of illegal activities.

When I knocked at the front door of the Mason Terrace house at ten A.M. the next day, I was dressed in dark slacks, a white blouse, and my old police department hat. I looked very much like the guy who reads your gas meter. I've never heard of anyone being arrested for impersonating the gas man. I've never heard of anyone really giving the gas man a second look. He fades into the background and that's exactly what I wanted to do.

I knew Marcia Heidegger wouldn't be home for hours. Old Reliable had left for the Square at her usual time, precise to the minute. But I wasn't one hundred percent sure Marcia lived alone. Hence the gas man. I could knock on the door and check it out.

Those Brookline neighborhoods kill me. Act sneaky and the neighbors call the cops in twenty seconds, but walk right up to the front door, knock, talk to yourself while you're sticking a shin in the crack of the door, let yourself in, and nobody does a thing. Boldness is all.

The place wasn't bad. Three rooms, kitchen and bath, light and airy. Marcia was incredibly organized, obsessively neat, which meant I had to keep track of where everything was and put it back just so. There was no clutter in the woman's life. The smell of coffee and toast lingered, but if she'd eaten breakfast she'd already washed, dried, and put away the dishes. The morning paper had been read and tossed in the trash. The mail was sorted in one of those plastic accordion files. I mean she folded her underwear like origami.

Now coins are hard to look for. They're small; you can hide 'em anywhere. So this search took me one hell of a long time. Nine out of ten women hide things that are dear to them in the bedroom. They keep their finest jewelry closest to the bed, sometimes in the nightstand, sometimes right under the mattress. That's where I started.

Marcia had a jewelry box on top of her dresser. I felt like hiding it for her. She had some nice stuff and a burglar could have made quite a haul with no effort.

The next favorite place for women to stash valuables is the kitchen. I sifted through her flour. I removed every Kellogg's Rice Krispie from the giant economy-sized box—and returned it. I went through her place like no burglar ever will. When I say thorough, I mean thorough.

I found four odd things. A neatly squared pile of clippings from the *Globe* and the *Herald*, all the articles about the Thayler killing. A manila envelope containing five different safe deposit box keys. A Tupperware container full of susperstitious junk, good luck charms mostly, the kind of stuff I'd never have associated with a straight-arrow like Marcia: rabbits' feet galore, a little leather bag on a string that looked like some kind of voodoo charm, a pendant in the shape of a cross surmounted by a hook, and, I swear to God, a pack of worn tarot cards. Oh yes, and a .22 automatic, looking a lot less threatening stuck in an ice cube tray. I took the bullets; the loaded gun threatened a defenseless box of Breyers' mint chocolate chip ice cream.

I left everything else just the way I'd found it and went home. And tugged my hair. And stewed. And brooded. And ate half the stuff in the refrigerator, I kid you not.

At about one in the morning, it all made blinding, crystal-clear sense.

The next afternoon, at five-fifteen, I made sure I was the cabbie who picked up Marcia Heidegger in Harvard Square. Now cab stands have the most rigid protocol since Queen Victoria; you do not grab a fare out of turn or your fellow cabbies are definitely not amused. There was nothing for it but bribing the ranks. This bet with Mooney was costing me plenty.

I got her. She swung open the door and gave the Mason Terrace number. I grunted, kept my face turned front, and took off.

Some people really watch where you're going in a cab, scared to death you'll take them a block out of their way and squeeze them for an extra nickel. Others just lean back and dream. She was a dreamer, thank God. I was almost at District One headquarters before she woke up.

"Excuse me," she said, polite as ever. "That's Mason Terrace in *Brookline*."

"Take the next right, pull over, and douse your lights," I said in a low Bogart voice. My imitation was not that good, but it got the point across. Her eyes widened and she made an instinctive grab for the door handle.

"Don't try it, lady," I Bogied on. "You think I'm dumb enough to take you in alone? There's a cop car behind us, just waiting for you to make a move."

Her hand froze. She was a sap for movie dialogue.

"Where's the cop?" was all she said on the way up to Mooney's office.

"What cop?"

"The one following us."

"You have touching faith in our law enforcement system," I said.

She tried a bolt, I kid you not. I've had experience with runners a lot trickier than Marcia. I grabbed her in approved cop hold number three and marched her into Mooney's office.

He actually stopped typing and raised an eyebrow, an expression of great shock for Mooney.

"Citizen's arrest," I said.

"Charges?"

"Petty theft. Commission of a felony using a firearm." I rattled off a few more charges, using the numbers I remembered from cop school.

"This woman is crazy," Marcia Heidegger said with all the dignity she could muster.

"Search her," I said. "Get a matron in here. I want my $4.82 back."

Mooney looked like he agreed with Marcia's opinion of my mental state. He said, "Wait up, Carlotta. You'd have to be able to identify that $4.82 as yours. Can you do that? Quarters are quarters. Dimes are dimes."

"One of the coins she took was quite unusual," I said. "I'm sure I'd be able to identify it."

"Do you have any objection to displaying the change in your

purse?" Mooney said to Marcia. He got me mad the way he said it, like he was humoring an idiot.

"Of course not," old Marcia said, cool as a frozen daiquiri.

"That's because she's stashed it somewhere else, Mooney," I said patiently. "She used to keep it in her purse, see. But then she goofed. She handed it over to a cabbie in her change. She should have just let it go, but she panicked because it was worth a pile and she was just babysitting it for someone else. So when she got it back, she hid it somewhere. Like in her shoe. Didn't you ever carry your lucky penny in your shoe?"

"No," Mooney said. "Now, Miss—"

"Heidegger," I said clearly. "Marcia Heidegger. She used to work at Harvard Law School." I wanted to see if Mooney picked up on it, but he didn't. He went on: "This can be taken care of with a minimum of fuss. If you'll agree to be searched by—"

"I want to see my lawyer," she said.

"For $4.82?" he said. "It'll cost you more than that to get your lawyer up here."

"Do I get my phone call or not?"

Mooney shrugged wearily and wrote up the charge sheet. Called a cop to take her to the phone.

He got JoAnn, which was good. Under cover of our old-friend-long-time-no-see greetings, I whispered in her ear.

"You'll find it fifty well spent," I said to Mooney when we were alone.

"I don't think you can make it stick."

"We'll see, won't we?"

JoAnn came back, shoving Marcia slightly ahead of her. She plunked her prisoner down in one of Mooney's hard wooden chairs and turned to me, grinning from ear to ear.

"Got it?" I said. "Good for you."

"What's going on?" Mooney said.

"She got real clumsy on the way to the pay phone," JoAnn said. "Practically fell on the floor. Got up with her right hand clenched tight. When we got to the phone, I offered to drop her dime for her. She wanted to do it herself. I insisted and she got clumsy again. Somehow this coin got kicked clear across the floor."

She held it up. The coin could have been a dime, except the color was off: warm, rosy gold instead of dead silver. How I missed it the first time around I'll never know.

"What the hell is that?" Mooney said.

"What kind of coins were in Justin Thayler's collection?" I asked. "Roman?"

Marcia jumped out of the chair, snapped her bag open and drew out her little .22. I kid you not. She was closest to Mooney and she just stepped up to him and rested it above his left ear. He swallowed, didn't say a word. I never realized how prominent his Adam's apple was. JoAnn froze, hand on her holster.

Good old reliable, methodical Marcia. Why, I said to myself, *why* pick today of all days to trot your gun out of the freezer? Did you read bad luck in your tarot cards? Then I had a truly rotten thought. What if she had two guns? What if the disarmed .22 was still staring down the mint chip ice cream?

"Give it back," Marcia said. She held out one hand, made an impatient waving motion.

"Hey, you don't need it, Marcia," I said. "You've got plenty more. In all those safe-deposit boxes."

"I'm going to count to five—" she began.

"Were you in on the murder from Day One? You know, from the planning stages?" I asked. I kept my voice low, but it echoed off the walls of Mooney's tiny office. The hum of everyday activity kept going in the main room. Nobody noticed the little gun in the well-dressed lady's hand. "Or did you just do your beau a favor and hide the loot after he iced his wife? In order to back up his burglary tale? I mean, if Justin Thayler really wanted to marry you, there is such a thing as divorce. Or was old Jennifer the one with the bucks?"

"I want that coin," she said softly. "Then I want the two of you"—she motioned to JoAnn and me—"to sit down facing that wall. If you yell, or do anything before I'm out of the building, I'll shoot this gentleman. He's coming with me."

"Come on, Marcia," I said, "put it down. I mean, look at you. A week ago you just wanted Thayler's coin back. You didn't want to rob my cab, right? You just didn't know how else to get your good luck charm back with no questions asked. You didn't do it for money, right? You did it for love. You were so straight you threw away the cash. Now here you are with a gun pointed at a cop—"

"Shut up!"

I took a deep breath and said, "You haven't got the style, Marcia. Your gun's not even loaded."

Mooney didn't relax a hair. Sometimes I think the guy hasn't ever believed a word I've said to him. But Marcia got shook. She pulled the barrel away from Mooney's skull and peered at it with a puzzled frown. JoAnn and I both tackled her before she got a chance to pull the trigger. I twisted the gun out of her hand. I was almost afraid to look inside. Mooney stared at me and I felt my mouth go dry and a trickle of sweat worm its way down my back.

I looked.

No bullets. My heart stopped fibrillating, and Mooney actually cracked a smile in my direction.

So that's all. I sure hope Mooney will spread the word around that I helped him nail Thayler. And I think he will; he's a fair kind of guy. Maybe it'll get me a case or two. Driving a cab is hard on the backside, you know?